Hop Pole Wedding

To Sue

with best wishes

Pete Arblaster

Also by Peter Arblaster

Blackcountrywoman
Locks and Keys

Hop Pole Wedding

Peter Arblaster

Hop Pole Wedding

Copyright © Peter Arblaster 2012

ISBN 978-0-9572275-5-2

First Published 2012 by
Direct-POD,
part of the Lonsdale Direct Solutions Ltd. group.
Denington Estate, Wellingborough, Northamptonshire NN8 2RA

Distributed by Peter Arblaster
petethefeet1@btinternet.com

Printed and typeset in Great Britain by

www.direct.pod.com

Acknowledgements

I thank my brother, Michael for his generous proof-reading and my wife, Hazel for her patience. Special thanks are due to The Bromyard and District Local History Society for their help with the dissemination, research and distribution of this book.

Front Cover

The clock is that of Saint Peter's Church at Bromyard. The Gypsies shown are from a collection of local pictures and were offered by the Bromyard Local History Society.

1. Tom, Rough Diamond

Tom could feel the excitement spreading through his limbs. He was excited! He stretched his arms, as if to make himself alive right to the ends of his fingertips. Today was the day. Today is the day!

The dawn, spreading slowly in shades of pink and grey across the Black Country sky, foretold a warm summer morning. The industrial cumulus of smoke was largely absent this Sunday. He had been waiting, forever it seemed, for this day.

Eighteen year old Tom Barr had been up and thinking about the near future, since four o'clock. There was still enough of the boy in him to get excited about going to work for long hours in dirty, filthy conditions, and sleeping in a barn, and then calling it a holiday.

Willenhall was certainly not booming but some firms had the promise of better times to come. 1923 had been happy so far, in some ways. There were plenty of orders coming in from the Empire for some of the more efficiently run lock-making firms. He was lucky to get the time off for the hop-picking

Tom stretched again, reaching toward the ceiling. Stretching seemed to both ease and extend his exhilaration. He moved to the table, put the fresh bread and cheese sandwiches into the large bag he was taking with him and lifted it onto his shoulder, feeling the weight with satisfaction. He had packed a spare shirt, and gloves to protect his hands from being scratched by the bines, as they had been in years past. His other necessities; tins of food, spare clothes, soap and towels were already at the station. He was ready to go, except for the goodbye. He was not looking forward to that. His mother's voice returned him to the moment.

'Come on Tom! You're dreaming again.' It was his mother, Elsie Barr. She often accused him of dreaming. 'You're going to miss the train if you don't get a move on!'

He started; feeling the moment. He would remember it for years. He turned and looked at his mother, seeing and sensing her as someone beautiful; the most important person in his life. This was two 'goodbyes'; goodbye in the conventional sense, that he was going away, but also goodbye to a phase in his life. He felt this, incapable yet of thinking in orderly thought. Sometimes it was better to just feel than to think. His mother was always telling him to think.

He answered her. 'All right, nagger; I'm as ready as I can be. Can you think of anything else I've got to do, our Mom?'

His eyes were still moving round as he spoke, taking it all in, and recording it as a scene in his memory, never to be erased. He took a last embracing look round the small, neat room where the whole family lived.

The wallpaper was patterned with pale pink roses set in pale green leaves, with a darker background. There was a scrubbed-white pine table in the centre of the room. He had been proud of that table; he had scrubbed it white when he was younger. Upon it there was a dark, almost black tablecloth, a small, plain white egg-cup half-full of salt, on a cork place-mat; a knife and fork, each with imitation ivory handles, already in position and ready for his father to come home to sit down for his dinner when he finished his shift at the lock factory. Tom, in his mind's eye, could see him sitting there, stern-faced, with his neat, concentric moustache, lifting a small amount of salt on his knife and tapping the blade gently to sprinkle it onto his meal.

On the wall facing the single sash window there was a dark framed painting; *Highland Cattle*. The picture was hung by a flat brass hook, onto the picture rail that ran all round the room. Tom had used the picture-rail to swing along when he had played at Tarzan, trying to get all the way round the room without touching the floor. He smiled at the memory.

There was a cast-iron fireplace with an oven to the left of it which sparkled from frequent polishing, and a shiny brass companion set which reflected the flames from the fire. There was a faint odour of tea from the teapot that stood on the top of the oven. On the floor in front of the fire there was an enamelled metal hearth plate with a blue and white tiled design, with an occasional blue flower set into the tiled pattern. Surrounding the hearth-plate was a polished oak wooden fender, to stop the hot coals from landing on the rag-rug made of cast-off pieces of different cloths interwoven through a rectangle of hessian, in front of the fender.

The rag rug was, Tom knew, a gathering of memories for his mother. The dark grey was from Dan's trousers, the dark red from her mother's best coat; the navy blue was from Tom's first pair of long trousers. There were three other rag rugs in the house, each made up of its own collection of memories. There was a container of spills, full of folded strips of newspaper. Ready-made spills were a rare luxury, for Christmas or some event of celebration.

Over the fireplace, the mantle-shelf was topped with a lace runner, with small crock and china ornaments arranged along it, with the pale yellow rent-book trapped between a china bluebird and the wall. Above that, a large oval mirror in a thick wooden frame, dark and polished, reflecting the mood of the room, deep and sad with edges of brightness this morning, like the two dark-stained and polished pine wooden kitchen chairs, at the corners of the table.

In the alcove to the right of the fireplace, to keep draughts out of the room was the heavy, brocade-curtained door, concealing the staircase that led up through the darkness to the two bedrooms. There was a dark, shiny piano on the wall opposite the fireplace with the music for *Londonderry Air* on the stand and beside it the door that led into the entry between their house and the next.

If he turned left out of that door he would walk into a yard, and at the back of the yard was a short entry with four small lavatories, each with a padlock to prevent use by other than by tenants. The front doors of four small back-to-back houses opened onto the yard. His thoughts returned to the house. He had grown up in this room; somehow he felt it would never seem the same again. He suddenly realised that it was all dark and bright at the same time, a glittering blackness of warmth that had nurtured him for as long as he could recall.

His mother, Elsie Barr, an attractive woman in her mid forties, her thick, slightly greying auburn hair piled high on her head, smiled up at him across the tiny room that served as a living room for four; she was looking at him strangely; was she thinking the same thoughts as himself?

'There's nothing else; just yourself. Come on now, Tom. I don't want to have to tell you again. Off you go to the train, or you'll miss it! Just remember to write to we. Here's a dollar to see you through.'

She pressed two half crown coins into his hand, ignoring his slightly false protest.

'Thanks Mom. I'll give it you back when I can.'

He quickly pocketed the half crowns. He knew she had dipped into her savings to find the five shillings and promised himself he would pay it back to her as soon as he arrived home. Somehow you always expected your Mom to have money. He had never questioned it before, but now he wondered, how did she manage it, when he could never find two halfpennies to rub together, no matter how much he earned? His mother was something of a mystery to him in many ways, but especially with regard to money.

'Yes, I know you will, you giddy kipper! Now be off with you.'

Her voice rose slightly with mock anger.

To change the way she was admonishing him he asked, smiling. 'Why do Wednesbury folk always say 'we' instead of 'us'?'

He always teased her about the way she spoke. He reached for her impulsively, kissed her cheek then, embarrassed, turned and walked out of the front door; it was time. He did not want to show his feelings, even in front of his mother; it was not manly. Strange thing, being manly; it made you choke.

Elsie Barr put her head out of the door, watching him walk along the street. She was going to miss him; he was growing up

4

now; five feet nine inches tall and broad shouldered from his work. The thick-soled leather boots he was wearing had cost her half a week's wages, but your eldest son wasn't eighteen every day, was he? She had loved the smell of the new leather.

The moleskin trousers were only just long enough, and the shirt he was wearing was just tight enough to show his muscular arms to the best advantage. He would be a man when he came back. She had seen it before; a boy went away and a man came back. He had the man-smell about him now; she had noticed that. She just hoped he would not get himself into trouble. He didn't have the experience yet, or sense, to walk away from a challenge or a dare - whichever it was. She turned; the little house was calling for her as it always did. It was her work and her comfort when she was feeling emotional; it provided her with a sense of continuity and permanence, always.

Tom walked along the street, hurrying, whistling; *'With someone like you, a pal, so good and true'*. He had always looked forward to the annual migration to the hop yards, but previously he had gone with the family, his mother and father, and his younger brother, Ted.

This year he would be going on his own, as a man. He would be deciding for himself what he would be doing with his wages. His mother had told him he should save half of his pay and do something worthwhile with it. He could not understand what she meant. She had some strange ideas. Sometimes he wondered what sort of life she had lived before he was born.

She seemed somehow different from the people who lived in Willenhall, even her hair style; curled up tight in a bun on top of her head. He had rarely seen her with her hair down. He knew she was respected in Willenhall, by the neighbours and the local trades-people but although he loved her, she still seemed slightly eccentric to him. Why should he save money when he could have a good time with it? People always looked at you with a bit of respect if you had coins to jingle, especially gold coins! He might not have the chance again to indulge himself, to throw his money about.

He was going to Bromyard, in Herefordshire, for the hop-picking, as the whole family had in years before, but his father and younger brother had steady employment now, and did not mean to jeopardise it this year, and his mother would not leave his father on his own. Tom had looked forward to it, right through the booking of his seat on the train, packing the hop box with the clothes and supplies and getting it to the station, the freedom from working in the factory, the travelling on the train and the hay wagon; getting settled in at the farm, renewing friendships with the lads and girls he had worked with before, and the feeling of wealth when he got paid.

He was eighteen this year; he would be able to go drinking with the blokes; order a round of drinks and pay for it himself. No one would question his age. He had told his mother how he felt and she had told him not to be so foolish. He should find something better to do with his money.

There was Selina, too. She would think more of him if he had money in his pocket to buy her a bit of bright jewellery and a drink in the pub. He'd winked at her in the street, the first time they had met on the way to the factory, and she'd winked back at him. That had started it. Now they were in each other's company whenever they got the chance. Whenever she looked at him, the look on her face was for him alone; her face and blossoming body filled his imagination in a way that made him feel wonderfully uncomfortable.

On the surface she looked like any of a hundred sixteen-year old girls, wearing a knee-length dark skirt in keeping with the fashion, with her unpretentious black leather shoes, and a simple white cotton blouse. It was the way she held herself; the way she carried her head, her hair up in a bun, with her back straight, but not rigid, that separated her, in Tom's eyes, from the other, more ordinary girls.

He had been looking out of the workshop window at the factory, the first time he had really noticed her; he had been leaning on his forearms when she had come up to him and touched him on the head, and, as he straightened up, rested her breast on his arm, almost accidentally, and looked straight into his eyes. He had noticed the perfume of her body, then. The odour seemed to go right into him and cause him to feel, not dizzy exactly, but slightly unsure of himself. He could identify her in the dark now; he knew he could. Her eyes were the deepest hazel he had ever seen, and they had smiled deep into him; she did not say anything, just carried on smiling then, with a toss of her head, she turned and walked away. He had never had a feeling like that!

Now they were together as much as they could be. He knew she liked him; she was travelling to Bromyard too, on the same train, so they would spend time, all their spare time together if he had anything to do with it!

Selina's family would not be coming to the hop yards. Her mother, Edie Brown, widowed last year, had taken up with a new man, Harry Bentley, a charge-hand at one of several small factories owned by William Corbett, a Dudley businessman. Bentley disapproved of the hop-picking; it was no place for decent people to be. Tom had heard him tell Selina that she should not be going. He had made it quite clear what he thought of hop-pickers, and factory workers and their families in general, and Tom in particular, having seen them out together.

He had pulled Selina away from Tom; told her to 'Get in the house!' Then he threatened Tom with his stick if he ever saw them together again. Later, Tom could not quite work out how Selina had managed to get permission from her mother to go hop-picking. She had said she needed a holiday and no one else was going to take her away, were they? She was going to have a break, whether Harry liked it or not. After all, he wasn't her father, was he? There had been no rebuttal to that.

Tom was working in a lock factory, Stones' Locks, still learning the trade, even if he was being paid full rate. Making locks was hard work, boring for a lot of the time; working at the bench, filing lock parts. Occasionally, he saw his father, Dan, at work as a locksmith and they sort of nodded to each other, man to man so to speak, but they did not have the same sort of relationship that he had with his mates. There were too many years of his father's absence in the Army; too many tellings-off, and incidents requiring discipline between them. His father had been a Sergeant Major in the South Staffordshire Regiment during the Great War; he was used to giving orders and having them obeyed without hesitation, and he expected his son to agree with everything he said.

Tom had grown up without him, and was used to being his own man. He had been forced to be, with his father away in the army for four years. Tom had barely recognised his father when he saw him in civilian clothes for the first time. They got along with each other now though, each recognising a little of themselves in the other. Tom still had memories of his father before he went away to fight. He had been fun, then.

Tom's younger brother Ted worked in the factory office, as a clerk. He would not have been able to cope with the physical activity that was required in the factory. He had been smaller and weaker than Tom since a childhood illness had struck him down. He had been a nuisance to Tom since he had been born, a constant source of things that had to be done. 'Tek the babby for a walk.' 'Look after the babby while I go up the road to the shop.' 'Change the babby!' The difference in age too, had always been a distance between them. Perhaps that would change, he thought.

Stephen Stone, the manager, had told Tom that it would be the last time he could give him permission to go hop-picking. Tom had a better relationship with him than with his father.

'You can't be a locksmith and an 'op-picker, my mon. You'll have to decide which side your bread's buttered.'

He had smiled as he spoke, but Tom knew he had meant it.

'Yes, all right Mister Stephen, you know I won't be going again. This is the last time. You know that.'

Tom had wanted to learn lock and key making since he was a child.; it was a good trade, with orders coming in to Stones' from all over the world, but he wanted to have one more year at Bromyard. He might never have another holiday, another period of relative freedom. He sensed that the manager knew that, and that was why he was giving way, just for this year.

What he did not realise was that the manager saw in him the qualities that were not present in many young men at that time; the desire to learn a trade, the living force of ambition that separated the few from the many. Tom had, unusually, been given the pay of a journeyman some time ago because of his skill. Numerous young men had been at the front, in the fighting in France, and they could not settle down to the humdrum life of working in a factory, standing on one spot all day, filing the intricate parts of locks. There was not enough excitement in it.

There were few other lads of his age going to the hop yards, unless they were out of work. Mostly it was women with their children, having a working holiday, and trying to earn enough to buy next years' school clothes, winter coat or some small luxury for their home. There would be some men of course; some of them worked in the hop yards all the year round, but often they were out of work drunks, vagrants and gypsies.

Tom liked the gypsies the best. They came in families, in their neatly painted horse-drawn caravans. The farmers they worked for respected them too, because they did a good day's work. They lived on the move, living romantic lives, with a different concept of honour and honesty to 'normal' people, always with an anecdote to recount round the campfire, of exciting escapes from wrathful fathers and irate husbands. There was intense rivalry between the gypsy families, and an almost feudal ranking system that was topped by a king. Not one of them seemed rich, but none of them were poor, either. Where did they get their money from?

Tom looked up; he was almost at the station. He hadn't noticed the passage of time, contained as he was within his own thoughts.

'Morning, Tom.'

'Morning, Arthur.'

There were others walking alongside him, acknowledging each other, in the morning mist, hurrying as they heard the distant engine whistling. It was as if the hidden engine was imparting a new spring in their step, like a lackey, anxious that its master might miss an important appointment.

The Railway station at Blowers Green, Dudley, was crowded with people waiting for the train to Bromyard. It was a 'special', laid on for the hop-pickers. It went straight through, without them having to change trains at Worcester. There were families, often without the father, if he had a job, or had been lost or wounded in the Great War. Sometime it was the only chance of a holiday that the Black Country folk would get.

Families often carried all they needed for the picking season in a tea chest. Tom's hop box had already been put on the train by arrangement with the porter. There were a few others, single men and women, standing in couples, talking or standing in waiting silence, holding the other's hand; one going, the other staying; others were looking up the line to see the first sign of their train. Tom could hear it in the distance.

It would not be long now. The scene seemed more confused than it actually was. As soon as the crowd heard the whistle of the approaching train, they made their way to their prearranged positions, and stood near the farmer's agents, who had bought their tickets for them. Suddenly the sun shone through the steam-clouds, and the train appeared, as if from some magician's hat. Tom strode over towards the tiny, rough looking woman, pinafore dressed, clogs on her feet, with a tally-board and pencil in her hands, surrounded by hands reaching for tickets.

'Got me ticket, Mrs Aldridge?'

She looked up from her board. 'Yes. Here you are, Tommy Barr! Don't get doing anything I wouldn't do'

'As if I would!'

They both laughed at the little joke.

He had known Granny Aldridge since he was a lad. She acted as agent to the farmers, finding labourers to work in the hop yards. It was said she found work for over a thousand pickers. She handed him his ticket and marked him off on her board. He went immediately to board the train to make sure of a window seat; he liked to look out of the window, facing the front, even if he did occasionally get a bit of clinker in his eye from the fire in the engine. As he made his way along the corridor of the train, he was looking in each carriage, to see if there was an empty compartment and whether Selina was already in one of them; the thought of being on his own with her was making him feel impatient.

He continued his search of the train without finding her. "I wonder if she got on after me?" he thought, and stepped back down from the train. He strode along the platform, looking in the carriages as he went, then saw her, leaning out of a window at the rear end of the train. She was waving and grinning at the same time unable to shout that she had acquired an empty compartment. It would have been too forward. He knew though and strode out towards the door that she was just disappearing from, ignoring the ribald shouts from some youths nearby. She was obviously playing a teasing game; he would show her!

He waved to the youths, some of whom he knew. The shouting they had been doing was just to show they were growing up and big enough to take the same place in the world as their fathers. Soon they would be working or looking for work. No one could take money for granted. As soon as they left school they had to get a job. There was no room for idlers.

2. Selina.

'You know why I'm going, Harry. I've got to get away from you. I like you but it ain't right, what we've been doing, and you know it.'

Selina stepped back, her unyielding expression bleakly showing her seriousness. Selina's potential stepfather felt the loosening of his arms around her and frowned with frustration. She had always attracted him, right from when he had first met her mother, Edith, the widow of one of his workers. Selina had been younger then but showing her first signs of blossoming womanhood.

It had been his duty to call round. Mr Corbett, the owner of the business, had asked him to take five pounds to help to pay the funeral expenses of her father, who had died in an accident at the works, the week before. The widow had been grateful; she had asked him in and let him know he would be welcome if he came back.

She had to survive, after all, and life wasn't easy without a man, and Harry was known as a respectable single man, just young enough to be still reputable. Both of Harry's parents were dead; he lived on his own in the house he had been brought up in. He was considered lucky to be in that situation. Nearly twelve per cent of the population were unemployed.

He had called back many times over the following months. Selina was the only child of the house, her older sister having married, and was very friendly when he called.

'She's working late at her shop,' she would say. 'Mom won't be long; you can come in and wait, if you like.'

She was completely matter-of-fact in the way she spoke and stepped out of the way for him to walk over the doorstep. He had walked in casually, but feeling the risk as something almost tangible in the air.

He had always liked young girls who were at their most attractive in their pre-pubescent years, just before they turned into women. He could never talk of his inclinations. No one would understand. He had heard people talking about other men who had similar feelings. "Animals, that's what they are!" That was the way one woman had described it. She wouldn't have understood him. Men never spoke about it; it was too close to the bone for comfort. They had to pretend that they felt about things the same way as women but after a pint or two, some would give themselves away. "If they're big enough, they are old enough," one of his mates had said, and Harry recognised what he meant but had not added a comment.

He and Selina had sat in front of the coal fire saying nothing for a few minutes, and then he had tried to start a conversation.

'I'd love a cup of tea if that's what you were going to ask, Selina.'

She had nodded but hadn't moved. He tried again, feeling that something was in the air but that he was missing it, somehow. He searched his mind for something to say.

'I suppose you'll be starting work, soon, Selina.' When she nodded, he went on. 'How old are you now?'

He paused feeling that trying to have a conversation with her was like talking to cotton wool.

'I'm nearly sixteen now, Harry.'

'What sort of work would you like to do? Have you thought about it at all?'

She nodded again and fell silent for a moment, and then she seemed to gather her thoughts. 'I think I'd like to work on locks. There's always the chance of making a new sort of lock and starting up on your own. You don't have to just do the same thing, day after day. It would send me crackers.'

Harry looked at her, amazed. He would never have thought she would have thoughts like that, at her age. Some people worked on locks all their lives without thinking innovative thoughts. Obviously she had. What else went through her mind?

There was a lot more to this young slip of a girl than was apparent. He was entranced by her in many ways. Her body was the greatest attraction and had been since he had first met her. He would try to hold her in the most intimate ways when her mother was not with them.

He felt that she enjoyed his touch as much as he but she would make no commitment. She enjoyed sitting on his lap, facing him, her legs wrapped around his waist, playing row, row, row the boat, rocking back and forth; each feeling the intimate contact to the high point of their feelings. On one occasion he had pushed her skirt up around her waist and buried his hands and head in her breasts as she had rocked faster and faster pulling him onto her until they both reached a mind-splitting climax. He never forgot it, and deluded himself into thinking that Selina felt the same way.

If the police caught him out, he would end up in prison; if he were caught out by one of Edie's relations, they would kill him. At the moment he was looked up to in the neighbour-hood because he was a lower member of management; he wanted to keep it that way. Selina was talking about going to Herefordshire with the hop-pickers. She had never been before but Edie was encouraging her to go, 'to help her to grow up.' She couldn't see Harry's objections to the trip. It was an opportunity for her to see more of him but not an opportunity for him.

The thought of losing Selina was painful to Harry but it was better than trying to move in with the two women. Selina had divulged that Edie had told her that she thought they were getting too thick. He had agreed that they should be more careful. She was more forceful; she had come to the end of what she wanted from Harry.

'Look,' she said, 'you know as well as I that we can't just play these games all the while. What would Mom say? You can hardly keep her going as it is! Listen to me. What do you think would happen if she walked through the door when we were, well, playing? She would go straight round to my Uncle Jim; he would sort you out! He'd kill you without blinking an eye.'

The risk hadn't really sunk in until then. Black Country people didn't always call in the police to solve a problem! Uncle Jim, as he was known, was well known for dealing out punishment where he thought it was due.

'Yes, you're right. Neither of us would want that, would we? All right then, I don't want to give you up but I suppose I'll have to.'

He sounded pathetic; she thought and made her intentions clear to him. 'Harry, I'm sorry; you've got to go now. Come back in about an hour so Mom don't know you've been here. I meant what I said. We can't play like that again. You'll have to marry Mom. You can have as much fun as you like with her, then. You like playing games; play; them with her!'

He did not answer; what could he say? What would he want to say? This was his way out, handed to him on a plate. She straightened her blouse and skirt, slipped her feet into her shoes and put a comb through her hair.

'I've got things to do now. I promised Mom I'd do the ironing while she was taking stock. I've got a train to catch in the morning, you know.'

He knew: she was going away for a month, to the hop picking. Although he had protested, he had been relieved in a way, knowing that he would no longer be exposed to the threat of the result of his sexual desires. He tidied himself carefully as he always did; he was a clothes conscious man; always tidy, in keeping with his position as a man with his foot on the first step of the management ladder, and looking to put it on the second. He felt elated with his position in relation to Selina; he had come out on top; the thought made him smile. He leaned towards her and put a kiss on the side of her face.

There was no one in the dark street when he slipped out of the door. He walked up the entry onto the street, knowing that if anyone saw him, he could have been coming from any one of six different houses. In a few minutes he was in his own house, a street away, still feeling the excitement, nervousness and guilt that he always felt at every encounter; not accepting that he would never have that pleasure again. There was another young girl in the next street who thought he was handsome; perhaps he would be able to arrange something there.

Selina sat on the sofa where she had just been playing with her mother's lover. She had felt forced to end it with him; it would have been madness to continue. Acknowledging that any decent young man could probably make her feel good, she decided that she would have to be more particular in her choices in the future. What they had almost done would not have been incest, but was close to it, in a way. Incest was quite common in the Black Country, probably due to the closeness that families had to live, in the tiny houses that often had to accommodate families of ten or more in one or two bedrooms.

She would have to look elsewhere for her pleasures now. She liked the look of Tom Barr. He had winked at her in the street and she had blushed, knowing he was interested in her. He made her feel like Harry made her feel, only more so. She had imagined what it would be like to make love to him, but did not want to be seen to be throwing herself at him. That was why she had felt so brazen when she had put her breast on his arm at work. She had not known what to do or say afterward so she had just flounced off, as if it had been a mistake. He had been waiting for her, outside the factory, that night and walked her home, pulling her into an entry and kissing her in the darkening gloom; without asking her permission too! It had been a shock but not so much a shock that she could not control things

Since then she had kept him on the end of a lead, not allowing him too much freedom with her body, always in control, 'nothing below the belt.' She did not know how long he would stand for that, not too long, she hoped. She wanted him, like she had wanted Harry, for the pleasure of the moment, but without the kind of risk that had been there, in her mother's house.

Tom seemed quite innocent in the way he spoke to her; a mixture of boldness and shyness that she liked. She would be able to twist him round her little finger. He seemed to think that she was virginally innocent, and she wanted to keep him thinking that way. That way, he would feel that everything that happened was his idea and his responsibility.

Her mother came in through the door looking tired. Selina had a pot of tea waiting for her on the oven top. She looked low, as if life was playing her a dirty trick.

'Didn't Harry come round? He told me he was going to call tonight.'

She drank the tea and made her way upstairs. She'd had enough. There hadn't been many walk into her little shop and that made her feel tired.

Selina looked up at the clock. It was time to go to bed. She had to be up early in the morning. The ironing was finished and folded neatly. Her bag containing a few clothes for working in lay on the chair. She picked it up, and then decided to leave it there. She mounted the stairs, slightly weary, but excited at the same time. Tomorrow was the first day of her new life picking hops and she intended to be as ready for it as possible. She knelt at the side of her bed and prayed that Tom would continue to like her as much as he obviously did now. That would make life worthwhile.

The red in the sky around her curtains met her eyes when she awoke the new morning making her feel as bright as a polished brass button, and wanting and needing activity. She wanted to be at the station before Tom, to surprise him. At seven o'clock she was on her way. She had already said her good bye to her mother.

Edith was not going to be able to see her off at the station. Her little rented general shop kept her away from the house for nine hours each day, and she checked the stock on Sundays. She was glad to be rid of her daughter, to have the freedom of time with her Harry. Even now, Selina thought, she was probably planning her wedding. She breathed a silent prayer of good luck to her mother. Then she had another thought. 'I've got Tom to look forward to.' The thought gave her a positive feeling about her future.

As she bent to pick up the bag, the moment of leaving home became significant when she realised that she had come to the end of this part of her life; she would return, if she returned, almost as a stranger. She walked out of the door, into the world of adulthood. Walking along the street, she daydreamed of the times she and Tom would spend together. They would find chances to be alone, and then she would cement their bond so that he would never want to leave her for anyone else. Maybe he would propose to her! She became excited at the thought of a wedding, vaguely aware that they had no money at the back of them to see them through the first few weeks of marriage, never mind a lifetime.

Love would find a way. It always did. She had read enough novels to know that the likely outcome would be happy. Probably Tom would come into some money from a rich relative or his mother had money tucked away for just such an occasion! Time would tell.

The station came into view and she quickened her stride, wanting to secure an apartment, just for the two of them, not that it would be theirs for long; soon it would fill with others but at least they would be able to spend a little time on their own. She already had her ticket; she only had to let Granny Aldridge know that she was there. The elderly agent was standing on a truck, her little form needing the height to look for her clients. Selina caught her eye and nodded, noting that Granny had put her pipe in her mouth while she crossed her name from the list, then hurried along the platform, jumped up the high step, onto the train, and made her way along the corridor, looking for an empty compartment. When she found one, she pulled down the blinds, effectively shutting the world out and creating a temporary private space for them.

She sat and got her breath back for a minute or two. This was what she wanted! The moment seemed to have a satisfaction all of its own like a culmination of her dreams.

The satisfaction of finding an empty apartment didn't last long. She wanted to share it with Tom! She left the compartment and stood in the corridor, looking for him. The time seemed to pass slowly and then she saw him, striding along the platform, obviously looking for her. Her sense of fun took hold of her and she called to him. Would he respond?

'Tom! Tom!'

Tom looked up at the sound and recognition of her voice. It attracted looks from some youths looking for places for themselves. She couldn't help knowing they would give anything to change places with him. He trotted briskly to the last door on the train, climbed up the step, and strode down the corridor to the compartment. She was smiling coquettishly, waiting for him as he had known she would be. He responded to the look with his own teasing words.

'What makes you think I'd want to travel with you?' He asked her the question mischievously, putting his arms around her and pulling her close.

'Well if you don't, Tom Barr, there's plenty as wouldn't mind changing places with you.'

She put her arms round his neck and pressed her body against his. He put his hand inside her coat, cupping her breast, feeling her breathing become faster and deeper, his fingers undoing the buttons on her blouse and sliding inside, to thrill to the feel and increasing size of her nipple. She pulled away with a gasp and she left him in no doubt what her thoughts were on the subject.

'We'll have none of that Tommy Barr! I don't know what my dad would have done to you if he could see you now.'

Tom blushed; there was no denying what she meant. He sat down, heavily, and then stood up again. He seemed to be submitting and fighting, all at the same time! Life was funny; it had so many twists that you could easily get mixed up, not knowing whether you were doing right or wrong.

Then there was the sound of the engine letting go of its breath and an added urgency in the sound of the people on the platform. The wheels seemed to try themselves out, squealing as they did so.

'There is no one here now to do anything or to say anything.

We are here, just with each other, with no one else and it's lovely.'

Tom was acting as if they could do anything at all just because there was no one to criticise them and it looked as if he wanted to go too far with her. That wouldn't do. She pushed him away again and he responded with a growl. It was a pretending growl that he used to tease her when he was making fun of her.

'Oh get away, you bear,' she said, taking his hand away. 'You want too much all at once. Just you wait; I'll show you a thing or two!'

She smiled to show that they were still lovers for evermore and sat herself back on the seat. They could hear noises from outside the carriage now. The whistle of the engine, the people's feet in their very practical shoes and boots as they strode up and down the platform. Most people wore the strongest boots they owned. Hop picking took it out of your footwear and whatever they had on, they'd got to last you at least a month. Very few had more than one pair of shoes and if they had, the best pair was kept for Sundays.

Tom sat down by Selina and tentatively put his arm around her shoulder and she leaned against him. There were still people looking for seats and they knew they could be interrupted any minute. Tom pulled the blind down on the door and hoped people would take the hint that they wished to be left on their own.

For some reason his mother came into his mind. He had been thinking that she was a mystery to him, always having money, never being skint like most people. She went round collecting rents in for old Mister Jenkins. He didn't own the houses; he just managed them, paying the rents into the owner's accounts and making sure the little houses were always in a decent state of repair.

Tom had never known her to be hard up. The rent collecting must pay well. She also worked at Stones' Locks occasionally and she was well thought of there. She had a pony and trap that she used to go to Wednesbury to collect rents from the houses and shops there. He also knew that she had a house reserved for her there in case she had to stay there overnight. This year, she was not going hop-picking. She was going to look after Dad. He didn't look as fit as he used to, probably because he was getting older. That meant Ted couldn't come, either. He had too many things in the office that he was interested in, especially Laura.

The Stones' girls were both quite beautiful unlike the girls and women who worked on the locks. They were better fed and better dressed than most and that probably made the difference. It seemed to be a good idea to look after the health of your children. He would remember that when they had any. How could he do that? He would have to ask Mom how she managed to always have money. Dad didn't know. Mom had suggested that he did the housekeeping and he had tried it for a week, then the idea had been discarded when he had borrowed cash to help him get through the week.

Tom smiled to himself. Mom always came out on top in any argument. She really was a dark horse. Not like Selina who was always open with him, as he was with her. What had she just said? He wanted too much? She would show him a thing or two? He might show her! He relented.

There was always the sense of a challenge in the air when they were together and it helped to build him to face it. There was nothing like a challenge or a dare to give you a thrill and the biggest challenge brought the greatest thrill. He knew that without the experience, just having the hope for the greatest thrill brought about the greatest challenge. It worked both ways!

3. The Journey.

It was as if he didn't know when he had the right to an opinion of his own! That was one of the hard parts of growing up.

'I'm sorry', he began, and then changed his mind, 'No, I'm not! I'll never be sorry for the way I feel. Why should I be? I feel marvellous. Don't you think it's marvellous? I wish I could feel like this all the time, don't you? There isn't a better way to feel than this, well, not much better.'

There was a pause as his words dropped into the air like a confession of guilt. He felt himself grow red again as he realised the implication of what he had just said. It was only when he was with Selina that he felt the freedom, although blushingly, to speak in this way. It was one of the pleasures of being with her. Who else would listen to him go on this way without reproaching him in some way? His parents never spoke to each other in that sort of way and he had never wanted to share his thoughts and feelings so freely with anyone else.

Selina was looking at him as if she knew all his thoughts. Perhaps she did. He often got the feeling that she tried mentally to get inside him, to know him better, perhaps comparing him with other men. That was not such a pleasant thought. He remembered thinking when he was younger, two years younger, that all women could read his thoughts. He smiled at himself.

Selina spoke, interrupting his thoughts; empathising with his views, being agreeable. 'I do feel like it, all the time you are near me, like that, Tom, but I don't want to get into trouble, and you don't want to get me into trouble, do you Tom? '

Tom knew he didn't want to get her into trouble but he also knew he wanted to hold her as tight as he could, as much as he could, for as long as he could but all he could do for now was to loose her, and sit opposite her in the carriage, and look out of the window and say silly, 'normal' sounding things like; 'Look, there's a cow.' or 'Is it starting to rain?'

He didn't know how to show how he felt; the feeling was one of wanting something he could not have. He was angry and excited, all at the same time. It was all to do with the rules and limitations that grown up society put on people. Why should he have to put up with it? He was grown up now, and should be able to do what he liked, providing he did not intentionally harm someone unfairly! The thought made him think. Perhaps he was right and everyone else was wrong. Perhaps there were others who agreed with his point of view. He put the thought to the back of his mind, to perhaps investigate later.

Other people were getting into the carriage now; a woman with two children, a boy of about ten years with a new rip in his short trousers, and a girl who looked about eight years old, but who tried to emulate grown up behaviour and would not stop talking; another young woman on her own who, they found, was meeting her young man at the farm when they got there, and a middle-aged man who told them he was going down to Leigh Sinton to visit his wife, who was already down at the hop-yards.

The carriage shelves were full of the abundant, assorted luggage of the travellers, and there was a pale blue-grey haze of tobacco smoke, hanging in the air alongside the talk and slightly pervading odour of the assorted occupants who were gradually sorting their positions and possessions out. It was if they were all bringing their own body odours along as part of their luggage, and mixing it with conversation to provide identities, and relationships, mixed though separate, a microcosm of the people who were travelling. They were a cluster of individuals, gathered for a time in a joint purpose and then parting, to go their different ways. There was a sense too, of a time of welcome relief from the rules they usually lived within.

After a short wait they heard the doors slamming as the guard made his way along the corridor. He was shouting the people onto the train and the children made their way up the steps and into the corridor to see the changing view through the windows. The whistle blew and they heard and felt the wheels moving, slowly at first, clattering raggedly, and then moving faster, the people on the platform, disappearing, as if a curtain had been pulled, and the train went through a dark cutting. Their journey had begun.

The train that was taking the hop-pickers ran on Sundays and Wednesdays throughout the picking season. Today was the first Sunday in September 1923. The annual migration from the Black Country to Worcestershire and Herefordshire started at the beginning of September when hundreds of families went to pick hops. Picking started, traditionally, on the first Monday in September.

The hops were mixed with barley to make beer, to give the brew its bitter taste. The hop-pickers spent a month to six weeks in the hop yards, living in barns, stables, even pigsties; cooking over an iron 'devil'; sleeping in the worst of conditions, often with the farm cattle underneath them, with small rodents scurrying past them during the night. They started work at seven o'clock in the morning and worked until darkness stopped them in the evening. If they had money, they would go to the local inn after a quickly prepared meal; if not, they would spend time round a camp-fire, spinning yarns, singing, discussing the events and people of the day amongst themselves then, gradually leaving the fire-light, to sleep or to become couples, finding darker places to do what couples do.

Today, the sun was shining, and the world was all right. The Great War had been over for nearly five years now and people were starting to return to what they thought of as a normal way of life. There were still a lot of single men, damaged by mustard gas and the effects of explosions and battle who would rarely come into public view because of the horrific nature of their wounds, mental and physical, and even more single women, many of whom would be loyal to the memory of a loved one lost in the war for the rest of their lives, but it was a period when mourning was just beginning to cease for most families had lost someone, but people were starting to live again. There was an atmosphere of increasing confidence, and people were becoming more adventurous, starting to travel more than before the war.

Tom had considered volunteering for the Army but had been too young; he had been fourteen when the war had ended in 1918 so there had been no opportunity for him at that time.

Tom and Selina were sharing bread and cheese and helping it down with a bottle of water. They seemed to be catching each other's eye all the time, giggling, as if they had a secret that they did not wish to share. Tom's eyes kept focussing upon Selina's body. She was aware of this, and wished that Tom had more sense. It seemed to give others the permission to do the same, and made her feel cheap. The older man opposite her was eying her surreptitiously, as if he would like to do things to her. She turned her gaze to the views they were passing through, ignoring him.

The young girl on the other side of the carriage was still talking, about the horses, sheep, cows, cuttings; it seemed to Selina that anything that caught the girl's eye caught her mouth. Her mother was lying back, relaxing in the corner of the carriage; obviously used to her daughter going on, and she seemed quite content to lean back on the seat and rest, to watch the passing scenery. Her son was dozing; he was nothing like his sister; he just sat still, his pale face immobile; Selina got the impression that he had been ill; maybe just recovering from some childhood illness. There had been diphtheria in Dudley last year.

The young woman sitting opposite Tom was eating an apple, cutting slices with a penknife and feeding them into her mouth, apparently quite unaware of the rest of the passengers. She had an anxious look about her. She had spoken to Selina at the start of the journey, explaining that she was expecting to be met at Leigh Sinton by Henry, her young man. They were going to work together, to put some money on one side for when they got married in the spring, about nine months away. Tom had the feeling that Henry would not be waiting. He could not explain why; it was just something about the anxiousness of her face. He whispered his thoughts to Selina, and she agreed with him. This searching alertness and intuitive insight into the make up of other people, was one of the sides to Selina's character that intrigued Tom. It sometimes seemed that she knew all about a stranger before they were introduced.

'We shan't be long now.' It was the middle-aged man, speaking for the first time. 'I'll be glad to see the missus. I bay' sin her for a fortnit.'

He smiled, and the smile seemed to take away the threat that Selina had felt from him. She wasn't always right in her perception of what other people were thinking and feeling, and she was glad to know she had been wrong this time.

'You'll know what I mean when you gets married, my lovely.'

Tom didn't know to whom the man was talking. He could have been speaking to any of them. He had not seemed as if he wished to cause offence, more as if he were speaking to himself. Tom felt Selina's elbow, gently probing his ribs, making him squirm. He turned to her; she was smiling at him with that special smile, making him want her close to him. She looked enquiringly at him. Sometimes he just could sit and enjoy the sensation of heat that he got from the thigh nearest to him. The feeling aroused him.

'How long before we get there, Tom? We seem to be going very fast, don't we?'

He had the feeling that she was referring to more than the journey, but was not sure, so he did not comment in the same vein but took control of his responding body as he answered.

'We should be there in about ten minutes. We'd better start getting our things ready for when we stop. We want to be among the first to get off. You might be able to get a seat on the wagon if you look sharp. If you don't, you'll have to walk all the way to the farm.'

She was glad that Tom cared enough to want the best for her, even if it was just a seat on a wagon, but he was slow, sometimes!

There was a sudden lurch and they could feel the train starting to slow down; they both stood and moved into the narrow corridor. Other people were also getting ready, and there was a great deal of good-natured pushing and shoving. The small boy was crying and his sister was telling him to shut up.

The train was stopping now; there were clouds of steam

everywhere; the platform was in sight. They gradually came to a stop and people started to get out of the train. Tom helped Selina down and then hurriedly moved through the exit of the station, and looked round for the hay-wagon that was to take them the rest of the way to the farm. There were a number of wagons and other vehicles outside the station. The smell of horse droppings was in the air, adding a further, slightly acid, dimension to the scene.

'Come on, Selina!' Tom suddenly shouted and pointed at the same time, 'I've got your things. Our wagon is over there.'

He broke into a trot; a bag in each hand and almost threw the bags onto the wagon and turned to look for Selina. She wasn't far behind him, giggling and attempting to run in her short black skirt and high heels, her hair blowing across her face so that she could hardly see where she was going, and her small bag, with her few spare clothes, dragging on the platform; pushing her way through the other passengers to arrive breathless alongside Tom at the side of the hay wagon.

'You went without me!' She complained, breathless in mock disapproval, 'I couldn't see where you went.'

She smiled at him to let him know that she did not mean it. He lifted her up by the elbows onto the hay-wagon and threw his bag alongside hers.

'Keep my place, Selina; I've got to get my hop box.'

He trotted across to the guard's van to recover his small metal chest, his hop box, in which he maintained a sense of privacy. It had a padlock, which he had made himself, to keep the contents available to himself only. The wagon was starting to move off as he heaved the chest onto the tail end of the wagon.

The farm where they were going to work was about three miles away and unless they were lucky, the pickers had to walk all the way. The wagon was almost full now of tea-chests, boxes and bags of different sizes and shapes, and people were scrambling for any remaining space. The drover, a ruddy-faced, pleasant looking man, consulted a list in his hand, called out their names, nodding to those, like Tom, who he knew, then climbed up onto the seat at the front of the wagon and picked up the reins to the two large shire horses. The last stage of their journey was beginning.

'Come on, walk on,' he drawled, 'Let's be having you.'

The huge shire horses started off, up the slight incline that led from the station waiting area, turned onto the main road and settled into a steady pace. They had been along this route many times and knew the way home well. They knew they would be fed when they got there. The sun was shining and the day was hot and abuzz with winged insects in the air as they moved through the Herefordshire countryside. There was just a low murmuring sound from the pickers, talking at the side of the wagon.

Not all of them had been able to find a seat and it was quite usual for many of the pickers to walk. The middle-aged man who had travelled on the train with them had gone striding in front. They noticed that he was not going the same way as them, but turned off shortly afterward, into a lane. Tom thought he must be in a hurry to get to the farm to see his wife. He had said how much he was missing her. He must know another route, or had made arrangements for someone to pick him up from Bromyard.

'I suppose I'd be like that. I wonder why he let her come down on her own.' he thought. He spoke his thoughts to Selina, adding, 'I wouldn't let you away from my side if we were wed.'

He stopped himself from going on as he realised what he had said.

'We ain't wed Tom, and if we had the same problems they've got, you might be glad to let me earn a shilling or two to help out.'

'How do you know what problems they've got, then?' He spoke sharply.

'Can't you see then?' Her answer came quickly. 'They are skint!'

He wondered how she had known what problems the couple had; sometimes she seemed to know things without being told. He felt that he would feel daft if he had to admit his own ignorance, somehow he felt he should be superior to a woman; he was too, in some ways; he could pick up twice as much weight as she!

He still wanted to know more though; he would have to learn to keep his eyes and ears open. His mother always told him to look and see, see what he was looking at. Sometimes it was difficult; seeing things, in the way his mother and Selina did. Tom felt his own ignorance at times. How could he know things he had never been taught? He had always felt impatient about the things he didn't know, as if he should have been born with knowledge of everything he encountered.

He lay back, relaxing in the warmth of the late summer afternoon, listening to the steady clip clop of the horse's hooves on the soft surface of the country road. They would be about another half an hour, he estimated. He had forgotten how it felt to feel this relaxed. There were country things to be seen that marked the distance they had travelled in more than miles. Just before they got there, some of the children would be sent running to get the best bedding down areas. Not that it made much difference; the farm to which they were travelling kept all the picker's quarters in good condition; white-washing them every year. They were even given Hessian sacking to hang as curtains and to give a small amount of privacy to the families who were billeted there.

His eyes were feeling heavy; it had been a long day and he felt like a part of the countryside, just allowing time to pass. He looked around the scene, forcing wakefulness upon himself, recognising familiar landmarks from other years, as they went along. The village church where his mother and father had taken him and his brother, on Sundays in years past; the pond in front of the manor house, where he had stolen a duck two years ago; his mother had strapped him, and then sat and feathered the duck, while he had sat and watched, mouth open at the hypocrisy until his mother had said,

'Well, I can't shop you, can I? So I might as well get the most out on it, and teach you a lesson at the same time.'

Typical Black Country philosophy, he thought. His brother

Ted had thought it most amusing. It was strange, how his brother came into his mind at times. A shout brought him back to the moment.

'Off you go, young Jim. Get us a good pitch.'

A man shouted to a lad sitting on the back of the wagon, and the lad jumped off, and started sprinting along the lane towards the farm buildings now coming into view. Tom jumped off himself, threw his bag over his shoulder and went sprinting up the lane, waving his bag in the air as if he were one of the young lads. His exuberance was infectious and Selina fell back, laughing at the sight of him, and the rest of the passengers on the wagon joined in. She watched him disappear through the gate into the farmyard and wondered where he had got to until, as they turned into the yard themselves, she caught sight of him, looking through a doorway, halfway up the side of the barn, trying to catch her eye. When he did so, he waved.

'Come on Selina! I've got us a place up here!' He shouted. 'Come up the steps at the end.' He was pointing animatedly towards the end of the barn.

Selina jumped from the now stationary wagon and made her way through the mud of the barnyard towards the steps. As she struggled, she realised that this arrival was what she had been looking forward to. They were here. This was where they would be, living together, for the next few weeks. All her hopes and desires were invested in this sharply delineated period of time. If Selina had her way, she and Tom would be bonded for life during that time. She had glimpsed the future, and meant to do everything necessary to bring it into reality.

Her mother and Harry were behind her now; she was determined to start arranging her own vision of life. This was her one chance to influence the course of events. After that, other things would control the way she lived. Work, health, the whim of more influential people, could affect her life later. She was determined to make the most of this one chance. Tom might be an innocent but she wasn't; she was going to wind him round her little finger!

4. Bromyard.

Selina looked around, taking in the scene. Except for the sound of the hop pickers getting their particulars into an organised condition it seemed almost silent. Then she noticed the birdsong. She had never heard as many birds at the same time. There were robins, blue tits, blackbirds, great tits, chaffinches and bullfinches. Along the road she could see the little wagtails strutting, their tails bobbing. In the trees she could hear the wood pigeons and collared doves cooing, with a different, more complicated note than that of the scrawny pigeons of Willenhall. As she cast her eyes further, she could see little red squirrels running along the branches of the great oaks, their tails like tail feathers, keeping them perfectly balanced as they jumped from branch to branch

Looking into the distance she could see a range of hills that she knew must be the Malverns. To the east there was nothing to interfere with the skyline. Later, she was told that the first thing in that direction that was the height of the Malverns was the Ural Mountains, further east than Moscow.

She felt she could see forever, the fluffy white clouds seeming to have no end. The sky itself was a wider panorama than she had ever seen before, giving her a sense of freedom to stretch out and grow as much as she wanted. The fields were greener than she could ever have imagined, with high hedges and trees dividing them into neat, but variably sized squares and rectangles. The contrast with the dirty, enclosing streets of Willenhall couldn't have been greater. It was like being in Heaven.

Nearer and lower, she could see fields, divided not by hedges but by tall poplars, to provide shelter from the winds. The fields were full of wooden poles about fifteen feet high, many thousands of them. All with a large green growth around them. A high wire seemed to connect the poles at the top. She supposed they were the hop poles she had heard about. Come to think of it, she could smell a strange perfume in the breeze; she couldn't make up her mind whether to call it a smell, an odour, or a fragrance. That would be the hops too, she decided.

It was better than the nearer smell of the cattle that were sheltered in the same building they were going to be sleeping in. The smell was very ripe; she had been warned about it and told she would get used to it, but at the moment she doubted it. She looked closer to hand; the other arrivals were moving up from the wagon on which they had travelled from the station. They were as mixed a group of people as she had ever seen. Men; women; young and old, some fit; some obviously unwell. Their voices were the voices of the Black Country, working folk, living just a small step above survival, using their wits and bodies to live just that little bit better, by the money they earned and the healthy environment they were in.

She was standing in the middle of the farmyard and she did not see how she was going to get across it, to the steps, without stepping in the cow-dung at some point. She looked across to the animals that were being led in.

The horses, four massive Shires, nearly a ton each and seventeen hands high, were being led into the stables for their evening meal. Selina couldn't get over the gentleness, dignity and beauty of the horses. The driver who was leading the horses seemed to regard them as his own personal friends, Selina thought. They too, seemed to have affection and respect for the man by the way they followed him into the stables and allowed themselves to be brushed down, as if he were their servant instead of the other way round.

Nearby, in the yard but under the cover of the overhanging roof of the barn, a fire was burning under a forged iron cooking-devil, and a smell of frying bacon was wafting through the air. Her mouth started to water. She suddenly realised that apart from the sandwich she'd had on the train, she hadn't eaten all day. The woman cooking looked up. She was wearing a red jumper, a dark blue pair of dungarees and a pair of Wellington boots. So much more practical than me, thought Selina.

'Fancy a sandwich, love?' The woman shouted, 'I've just about got two left.'

Selina nodded to her, smiling her thanks, then stood looking up the steps towards Tom, and was about to go up the stairs to him, to tell him about the sandwich offer, when she became aware of someone coming towards her from the farmhouse, someone quite large, a man. He was dressed in plain-woven clothes and large boots; everything about him seemed large. His tweed hat seemed large enough for her to shelter underneath, if it rained. The thought made her smile, and she looked at him with the smile still on her face. He was not smiling at all. He looked a very stern, angry man.

'And where do you think you're going, young lady?' He wasn't shouting but he had a loud voice. 'You can't climb up them there steps in those shoes; you'll break your neck. We had a girl fall down these very steps last year. Broke her leg, she did; couldn't get any work out of her at all, for weeks. Such a waste; she was a good picker as well. Wouldn't like to see the same thing happen to a pretty young thing like you, would we, Jenny?'

He turned and looked at a slim little blonde-haired woman who Selina hadn't been able to see before. She was dressed in a long black skirt topped by a bright red jumper. Her feet were in sturdy country boots. In spite of this, she was one of the most petite women that Selina had ever seen. The man had been standing in front of her, hiding her from view. The woman glanced up at the tall man and smiled at Selina.

'Don't you take any notice of him, my dear. He tries to frighten all the young girls. He wouldn't harm a fly really. I'm sure you have some more suitable footwear, my dear.'

The smile seemed to light up her face as she walked round the man, but she still wore the question in her eyes, and Selina found herself nodding in deference to the authority she wore with little apparent effort.

'Yes, I've brought some boots with me. I just haven't put them on yet.'

The little woman spoke again, introducing herself, not that she needed to. It was obvious from her demeanour that she was the highest authority here.

'I'm Jenny Walker and this is my husband, Albert. This is our farm and we like to see to everyone when they arrive. We know Tom. He has stayed here before, with his mother, but I don't know you, my dear.' There was a question written on her face again as she looked at Selina. 'Are you together?'

She was not accusing, just enquiring. Selina was not used to such a neutral attitude. Tom stepped forward; accepting what he felt was his responsibility. He meant to start as he meant to go on.

'Yes Mrs Walker. Selina and me are together. We're getting married when we get back to Dudley.'

He stood back awaiting a response. Mrs Walker turned to her husband.

'There we are Albert; another wedding for the Parson to perform. He'll be pleased to hear that; I know he will.'

She looked at Selina as if they had a shared secret, and Selina did not know how to respond. She turned to the tall man, Albert Walker, but he just scowled and turned away, his face red, his lips moving, as if he were cursing to himself. Jenny Walker spoke up, a twinkle in her eyes.

'You mustn't take too much notice of him, my dear. He doesn't like some of our old country ways. He thinks everything has to be done by the Church of England prayer book and it don't.'

She smiled again, her face lighting up with a smile.

'She always seems to be smiling', Tom thought, trying to probe the character of the little woman. 'I wonder what she meant by that remark about the Church of England.' He realised he was beginning to look, listen and see, like his mother had told him. Mrs Walker was talking to him.

'Come on now then, Tom, Selina. Get yourselves settled in. It'll be time for dinner soon. You'll find some cooking devils in the barn. Pick yourself one out. There's hay for the hop-pockets as well, and some blankets. I suppose it will save a lot of trouble if we treat you like ordinary married people. Anything else would be a waste of time, I suppose! Well I've got a lot of other folk to attend to. I'll see you later, I expect'

They listened to her voice retreating down the steps, looked at each other and then burst out laughing. Selina remembered why she had been running up the steps and pulled his arm, excitedly.

'Come on Tom,' she pointed excitedly, 'That lady down there just offered us a bacon sandwich and I'm starving; how about you?'

She took his hand and tripped down the few steps she had climbed up, and went under the overhang of the barn to where the young woman was cooking bacon and mushrooms on the devil.

Tom looked down to where she had pointed. The woman, who looked about twenty or so, was still standing there, by the cooking devil. She was holding out sandwiches, two thick slices of bread, with bacon in between. He could smell the wonderful aroma from where he was.

'Well, do yo' want it, or not?' she asked in a rich Black Country accent, her hand on her waist, 'It'll soon goo if yo' don't want it.'

Tom ran down the steps, took Selina by the hand and pulled her towards the steps.

'Of course we want it. Thank you. We've been travelling all day. It's about time we ate.'

He smiled gratefully down at the woman, wondering where he had met her before; her face seemed familiar to him, then they ran down the steps to where she was waiting, a sandwich in each hand; it made them feel like a pair of children, being called in from play by their mother.

'Hello,' she said, 'Here you are. I've got no plates. If you want some sauce on, help yourself. It's at the side of the devil. My name's Kate Myatt. I'm from Tipton in the Black Country. I've come here every year for the last five years. I've seen you before, ain't I?' She looked at Tom. 'Yes, I know you, but you look bigger this year. You came last year with your Mom and Dad, didn't you? How is she? She used to have pains in her hips, last year. I got on all right with 'er, and your Dad. Your Mom told me he wouldn't be coming this year. His Gaffer won't let him. He's got too much work on. He must be one o' these key workers. That's a joke. He's a kay mekker, ain' 'e? He's in the lock business, ain' 'e? When are you two getting married? I heard the missus talking to you. Are yo' goin' to 'ave an 'op pole wedding? That's what she was on about when she was talking about the Parson. Have you never heard of an 'op pole wedding? How do you like the sandwich? I got the bacon from the bloke who brings the groceries round. He comes round every Saturday and Wednesday. This is from Saturday's delivery so don't worry it's from Wednesday's. It's quite alright, you know. What did you say your name is, love?'

She stopped talking. Tom and Selina looked at each other, and then Selina started to laugh, gently at first, then opened her mouth and let the laughter out as if it had been imprisoned. She was gasping for breath, but still managed to speak. The laughter was infectious. They all started to laugh, big, belly chortles that let all the tensions of the day out.

'I'm sorry,' Selina spluttered, 'I didn't mean to rub you up the wrong way but I thought you was never going to stop for breath, then.'

She looked at Kate, her eyes still laughing, and Kate started to laugh too. When they had calmed down, Kate looked at them, her eyes seeming to be trying to gather other things than the look of them inferred.

'I suppose I do go on a bit, don't I? That's what comes of being on your own for too long. When you do get the chance to talk, it all comes out at once. D'you know what I mean?' She stopped. 'I'm doing it again ain't I? Now it's your turn. Why are you here? Where do you come from, love?' She was addressing Selina, who was standing, looking at her appraisingly. 'You're from the Black Country, as well ain't you?

Selina was wondering why Kate was being so friendly. She wasn't used to virtual strangers offering the hand of friendship so quickly. Kate seemed friendlier than anyone she had ever known. It seemed strange that she and Tom had been chosen as potential friends. Perhaps Kate had taken a liking to Tom. She recalled the question that she had asked, 'Do yo' want it, or not?' Had she been referring to the sandwiches, or to something else? She had also let them know that she was on her own. Why? Selina admonished herself sharply. Why be cynical? All the woman had done was to offer a sandwich and a friendly word. Why read something else into it?

She should be grateful that there was someone she could turn to if she wanted to know anything about the place they were working at. She suddenly felt released from a tension that she did not know that she had been suffering.

'I'm Selina Brown; I'm from New Invention, in Willenhall and so is Tom,' she said, 'Tom's learning the lock-making trade, as you know. He's finished his training.' She spoke proudly, and Tom felt himself expand slightly as she spoke. 'I work at the same place as Tom; Stones' Locks Company. Do you know it? They've been there for years. Tom's Dad works there as well. He's a locksmith as well.'

She spoke forcefully; she didn't know why; she felt she was in friendly competition with the strange girl. She wasn't really strange; she was just new to Selina. It was part of meeting people.

'She's found her voice ain't she Tom?' Kate spoke again and Tom noticed that she spoke as if he and she were talking about Selina, 'I know Willenhall well. Humpshire they call it, don't they?'

Tom smiled; it was an old story of the locksmiths and key-smiths who nearly all lived and worked in that area, and spent all their lives, working at the bench, filing the wards and keys for the locks. Their posture suffered from the physical position in which they spent all their working days. They gradually developed a hump on their back. The story was that they built their houses with a deep cavity at the side of the

39

fireplaces, to accommodate their hump. It was a story that was told about 'Humpshire' to strangers, for a laugh. He laughed and replied,

'I haven't been there long enough to get an 'ump. I suppose if I stop there long enough, I'll get one, but I don't intend to spend the rest of my life filing locks.'

Kate spoke again. 'I was brought up in Willenhall as I told you. I usually stay at home with me Mom and look after the house but she told me I should get out and see more of the world. She always brought me down here with her but she wanted to spend some time on her own and she thought I was old enough now, to come down on my own.'

She fell silent. They all seemed to relax. The sandwiches had gone down well, and the boredom of travelling had been relieved by the new and strange people and places they had encountered. They had settled in, made friends, and were looking forward to the work that the following day would bring them.

There were other people from the Black Country, other people they had met before, even if they weren't close friends. Selina spoke to Agnes Hollerenshaw, from Willenhall and they exchanged views of the farm. Agnes was glad to get away from her part-time job in the lock trade. Her daughter was looking after her house. Selina wondered why she couldn't have brought the daughter with her but perhaps she didn't live in a place where you felt safe all the time.

They wandered around, meeting other Black Country people who had travelled that day. Tom knew some of them from previous years, and there were raucous comments from some of the lads who had seen him get on the train with Selina. All of it was taken in good humour and Tom was still aware that he was undergoing a learning process, but thought little of it. He was used to learning. He seemed to have been learning for as long as he could remember.

The rest of the day was occupied with unpacking their few

clothes and tidying the small area that they had been allocated for their own personal and private use. They also wandered round the buildings, becoming familiar with the layout of the farm. Tom had been there before and he knew where he was going, as they walked around the farm. There was an orchard in the field nearest the farm and he told Selina about the time when he had made himself sick, eating the apples.

He took Selina round the farm, showing her where she could buy eggs, milk and butter, at the back door of the farmhouse. The Walkers had no children of their own at home so Emily, a young, Bromyard woman in her early twenties who worked at the farm, served them.

'Just you come and see me, and I'll give you anything you might need.'

She smiled as she told Tom, and once again he got the feeling he was being offered more than eggs or butter. He looked at her more closely. She was shorter than him, and fuller in build than Selina, though she wore longer skirts, and a warm-looking jacket on top of the tightly stretched knitted jumper. She had a certain perfume, an odour that hung around her and demanded attention. She gave him more information.

'I'm here from five 'til six every night, for the pickers needs, but Mrs Walker does it on Thursdays 'cos it's my day off. If you want me on Thursdays, you'll have to catch me where you can find me. I'm usually at the picture house. I live in Bromyard and I walk it to work every morning. It takes me about half an hour, and the same to get home, at seven o'clock.'

'Well, it's nice to know how you spend your time; looks as if you lead a busy life!' Selina replied to all the information that was coming from Emily. 'I am sure I shall find it useful if I want to know where I can catch hold of you.'

She spoke over-effusively and Tom caught the undertone of sarcasm in her voice as she spoke to the girl, and decided to ask her what was the matter, when they had left the farmhouse.

'What was all that about, Selina? Why were you so, against,

no, that's not the word, anti, hostile, antagonistic to the girl? What's she done to you?'

He looked at Selina for a reply.

'Well, she was a bit obvious, wasn't she? All she wanted to do was to lay herself out on a plate, for you to pick up. You are a bit green, Tom. Don't you know when a girl's making a pass at you?'

Then Selina wished she hadn't said anything about the girl; Tom might get ideas that he wouldn't have got if she hadn't opened her mouth!

Emily was just pleased to have got so much attention. She watched the young couple walk away and decided that even if Selina did explain to Tom what was happening, the effect would still be the same. Tom was now aware of Emily in a way that he hadn't been, before, and that was what she'd wanted, wasn't it? She smiled to herself and put the butter away. The hop-picking season was suddenly more promising. Perhaps that Tom would be round, requesting something she could supply. The thought gave her a little shiver.

She was an orphan; her father had been killed in the war, just one of the nearly three quarters of a million British servicemen who had lost their lives in the conflict, and she had not known the type of discipline that many had endured. She had been left by her mother to find her own way. Her mother had been hard put to find her own way, Emily thought, what with trying to keep their heads above water and trying to keep away from ill-intentioned men. Emily knew what she wanted, a man; as simple as that, and she intended to have one, whether it was to be honoured or dishonoured she didn't care. She just wanted to answer the call of nature.

Tom would do as well as anyone but if not him, then anyone. There were gypsies coming down later and maybe they would steal her away. She could end up as the favourite of an Arabian sheik! She was fed up of dreaming and trying to induce the kind of feelings that she thought would be hers if she got a man of her own. She had seen the Hollywood actresses on the screen and thought it unfair that they had all the romance while she was just… waiting. She would not tolerate waiting any longer.

She would go out and capture one of her own! The thought raised her spirits and her energy level. Tom didn't know what he was letting himself in for. By the time she had finished with him, he would know! The thought gave her a strange feeling but not unpleasant. It was nice to plan and dream but it would be better when it finally happened! There were plenty of men from the Black Country and if not them, the Taffies. They were always singing. They even sounded as if they were singing when they were just speaking. One of them had offered to take her up the mountain last year. Perhaps she wouldn't mind this year.

5. The Gaffers.

Albert Walker was angry. Why did it happen every year? He turned on Jenny.

'I wish you wouldn't go on about the Parson every time we get a courting couple down here, to work, Jenny.'

Every time Jenny met a new pair of lovers, she wanted a hop pole wedding. One of their itinerant Romany workers, expected in the next few days, was known as the Parson. For years the gypsy had carried out completely illegal 'weddings' among the Black Country and Welsh people who came to Herefordshire. The 'marriage' lasted until the end of the picking season, when the couples went their own separate ways. Sometimes nature intervened, and the marriage had to be extended by a more formal arrangement to ensure that the final outcome had legitimacy.

Whatever the result, Jenny always loved it, to the chagrin of Albert. It was against all the teachings of the Church. Mostly, the hop pole wedding was a practice that, although frowned upon by the establishment, was not actually considered to be a threat to the official ceremony, and was therefore allowed to continue. It was also a good excuse for a party, to relieve the monotony of the hop picking activity. Jenny considered that the hop pole wedding was derived from jumping the broomstick, a pagan ceremony when the couple jumped over a birch broom. The couple were then 'hand-fasted', betrothed for a year and a day.

Albert Walker was a farmer as had been his father and grandfather. Hops were grown as a cash crop, alongside other crops, sometimes giving a nice profit at the end of the picking season. Rhubarb was also grown 'to add flavour' to the farm. He was also a dairy and beef farmer, breeding his own Herefordshire cattle, so his was a mixed responsibility. Sometimes he felt that he ought to specialise to gain the benefits of larger purchases and economies of scale; at others he was certain that mixed farming helped to reduce the risks that a farmer had to face. If his farm ever became victim to foot-and-mouth disease he would be bankrupt. Either way was a compromise and a risk, whatever he decided to do. All farmers knew the risks, and lived with them anyway.

He was conscious of his position in local society and felt responsible for the pickers who spent a month each year, working in his fields. Although he did not have much respect for the pickers as they were, in his eyes, just itinerant workers and far below his social standing, he still felt a sense of duty for their well-being.

He had been brought up to accept responsibilities, unlike his wife who had been brought in a more gentile and educated way. He could not understand why Jenny got so much pleasure in these old country customs. They had mostly died out, now, anyway. Considering her family's religious background he was always surprised. He certainly did not intend to encourage such goings on. Deplorable! He could imagine what his father would have said. The vicar would be scandalised if he knew. What on earth would happen if this new girl got herself pregnant? Would her father blame him? Would it be his fault? Her parents should not allow her to stay in company like this.

They couldn't expect the farmer of Herefordshire to take on the responsibility of parents from up in the Black Country. The Black Country folk had a different idea of society, with different sets of rules and silly-sounding jokes, although he'd had to laugh sometimes when he had heard them. The expectation that he would look after his workers as if they were family was too much for him. It was not fair. He would not take it on. Whatever they did, it was their own fault if any thing happened. He looked sternly at Jenny, across the kitchen table.

'Have you got young Emily prepared for what she has got to do, Jenny? There doesn't seem to be a lot of stock by the back door.'

He looked at her quizzically but she answered him in her usual, straightforward way. 'Don't you worry, Albert, I've got everything I need. Jim gave me a hand the other day, to move the apples near the front of the little out-house, so Emily could get to them when she needed to. There are some tinned goods and flour and dry goods. It's like a little grocery shop in there, but I've told her to just bring enough to see her through the hour that she spends working there. We don't want everything laid out like an ordinary shop. It makes it too easy to steal the goods. We don't take all that trouble just to let some bright Black Country sparks help them selves. Don't you be concerned about my side of the business, just look after your own side, and I'll make sure that young Emily minds her ways. I know what she's like; she's the same as all young girls, trying to get her self in trouble as quickly as she can!'

Jenny had seen Emily through the window, talking to Tom and Selina, and she meant to keep an eye on her. She turned her attention back to Albert. Whenever he was angry with Jenny, her eyes seemed to sparkle. He could never quite decide whether she was trying to stop smiling or crying.

Whichever it was, he always seemed to have this lump of emotion that welled up inside him, and embarrassed him if he was in company. He knew that he would never want to make her cry. The pain would be too much for him to bear, right or wrong. She was his one weak spot, and she was smiling at him now. He felt, as he always did, a great lump of emotion for her. He had a deep sense of gratitude for her very existence and often wondered what he had done to deserve her. Her smile was the key to his feelings.

'Oh, Albert, my dear, you do make me laugh! You pretend you don't care about these young people, but you do! You want to be father to all of them, and you can't. They're all grown up and will make their own minds up about what they want to do, won't they?'

His answer came fast. 'It's all right for you to say that but we both know what can happen. You shouldn't encourage them, or that charlatan who calls himself a Parson. He's no more a Parson than I am! I've heard he's got something to do with them silly women who dance around on the Downs, in the middle of the night.'

He paused, embarrassed again. He knew he shouldn't bring up local gossip. Jenny always knew more about local affairs than he did. How she did it beat him; whenever he brought up a matter of local interest, she was able to discuss it with him as if she had been at the event in question. She was able to do it about the event in question, and soon gave her opinion.

'Oh, you mean the coven. You shouldn't believe everything you hear, Albert. They're just a group of silly women, trying to get a bit of excitement into their lives. I was talking to Mrs Pudge the other day. She said the vicar was most concerned. He was going to call on them, one at a time, and read them the Riot Act; something to do with what it says in the Bible about worshipping one God only. It's just a nine-day's wonder and we should just ignore it. You really are too much at times, Albert, taking all these things so seriously! People have to experiment with life. They always have, and they always will. I remember you wanting to experiment with life, in the back of a haystack! You can't expect young people to want different things to you, can you, Albert?'

He looked at her again. She was right, as usual. Jenny shouldn't bring up things from the past. He well recalled the day he had been in the hayrick with her, and the excitement it had given them both. They were lucky they hadn't been caught, or they would have been married six months sooner!

If some silly wenches wanted to cavort around in the moonlight, in the nude, that was up to them, nothing to do with him, or Jenny, as long as she didn't take part! His imagination filled his head with mental images of Jenny, naked, moving to flute music, on the top of the hill, with the Parson having his way with her, and he did not know whether to be amused or angry.

He turned his attention to the hot meal that was in front of him, and relaxed. His collar was tight round his neck so he decided that he would not wear it for the rest of the day. He reached to the collar studs and sharply removed them. They lay in his hand, but he could not decide what to do with them. Jenny reached out hers, and sheepishly he dropped them in. There was no doubt who was the leader, and who was the led, he thought. He worshipped her and would deny her nothing.

He tried to pick up the conversation they had been having, to save further embarrassment.

'Do you know how many pickers have turned up today, Jen? Sixty-four! We'll soon have the farm full at this rate. The hops feel and smell ready as well. It looks like being a good year, if the weather holds.'

He was on safe ground now, and could talk all day about hops, crops, pickers, weather and business. Jenny went along with him to keep the peace.

'Yes, it will be nice to have a few pounds we can spend on ourselves for a change. If we do well, we could paint the house out. 'She changed the subject again, just to confuse him. Two could change the subject! 'What do you think of that Tommy Barr then, Albert?'

She glanced up at him over her large cup of tea. She would get him going again!

'What do you mean, what do I think of him?' He was a little off course now. 'He was a good worker last year and he's taller and he looks stronger this year. Not that muscle makes a good picker; it's what you do with the muscle that counts. Is that what you mean?'

She had the disconcerting habit of asking one question, and expecting the answer to an entirely different one.

'No, what I meant was, do you think he'll fit in as an adult? Last year he was a big boy, doing a big boy's job, and getting into mischief all the time, which was to be expected, but at least we knew that we could complain to his parents. I know that Elsie Barr would soon put him in his place. The silly young men's sort of behaviour wouldn't do now, would it?'

She looked at him questioningly and his face showed agreement. 'No, I couldn't allow that, but we'll have to see how he goes on. Most young chaps manage to grow up you know. I think I'll give him a job he can use his muscles on, this year;

poling, or something like that. To tell the truth I am more concerned about the young woman he's got with him. What's her name, Selina isn't it? She looks as if she'll get a bit of attention from the pickers, don't she?'

He immediately realised the trap he had talked himself into and bit his lip.

'Well I just hope she don't get more than her fair share of attention from you, Albert Walker. There'll be trouble if she does.'

She peered over the teacup again with mock seriousness, and he felt himself blushing, as he did when she admonished him. They had been married for nearly twenty years, he was forty-two years old and he still felt like a callow young man when she spoke to him this way. Still, there was something in what she said. That Selina was a bit of all right and he wouldn't mind an hour in the hay with her! The chance was not likely to come his way although, over the years, some of the pickers had given him looks that had told him he would be welcome in the hay with them. He had taken advantage a few times but he had never allowed himself to form a liaison. That way led to disaster.

There was no sense in pursuing the subject so he finished his meal in silence and then, nodding to Jenny, strode out of the kitchen door. He was glad of his own company at times, and this was one of them. There was a lot to sort out, the pickers were coming in thick and fast and he had to make sure they were all getting along in the accommodation they had had prepared for them.

Earlier in the year he'd had the barn and the old cowshed painted white to conform to the regulations for living conditions for hop-pickers. What would it be like, for this chap, Baldwin, who had the whole country to run? It was a shame Lloyd George had been obliged to go but a new mind was needed now. The problems of peace weren't the same as the problems of war. He had given his support to the Welsh Wizard, as the then Prime Minister had been called, during the war, but now was the time for a change. He brought his mind back to the task in hand.

Some of the families would have brought their children with

them, a fining offence; five shillings for taking time off from school, but they just ignored the regulations in order to get the bit of extra income that the child's work would bring them. He always felt guilty about taking them in but they were an extra source of labour, cheap too, and that was his main concern, making a profit. The quicker and sooner the crop was picked, the better. What the pickers did about their children's schooling was up to them. His responsibility didn't extend that far.

In each sleeping area he had allowed sacking curtains between the beds, so that there would be a little privacy for each family group, and there were also old 'hop pockets', the long, sack like bags, which would be filled with straw, to act as mattresses. Each family would fetch their own hay, to fill the pockets. He had to make sure there was enough hay to go round and he was glad he had Jim to help him to sort out these little details. He had a last look round then decided he would ask Jenny to check who was sleeping with whom so that he would know how many pockets for each curtained space. She seemed to be better at that sort of job than he was.

In the farmhouse kitchen, Jenny filled the sink with the crocks they had just eaten from and poured hot water onto them. They were not dirty, really, they just needed a swill. She too, had a lot to do today, even though it was a Sunday. She wanted to do a bit of washing; Albert wouldn't approve although he was glad to have a clean shirt every morning. She wouldn't hang it on the line, today. She had a small line at the back of her rambling roses where they could have a blow. Bert, the drover had gone back to the station to await the next trainload of pickers and she wanted to have a look at them. That should be the last. They would arrive in the dark. She would have to make sure there was fire, to give a bit of light round the barn.

Tomorrow the picking would start. It would be hard going for the next four to six weeks, but if the weather held fine, and if they didn't have a strike, touch wood, they would get a nice bit of cash profit at the end of it. She thought back to Selina, the new girl. If her first opinion of her was right, she was very healthy and all her glands were working away. She could be trouble. Still, she had faced other problem girls, and solved them easily enough. She had been a problem girl, herself. To her, that just meant having an open mind and being able and willing to absorb new ideas.

The washing up finished; she made herself a cup of weak tea, which she took outside, sitting on the rough wooden bench by the window, surrounded by her roses, her favourite spot in the summer months. Her cottage garden was her own special space, with snowdrops and crocuses at the start of the year, followed by daffodils and wild primroses and then hollyhocks, foxgloves in the summer, along with her beloved roses. This was a place where she grew herbs for her healing skills; lavender and rosemary; mint and thyme, fennel and barley-grass, mixing their culinary uses with other, more esoteric applications.

She was very happy with her relationship with Albert. She always felt she had the upper hand, if it came to the crunch. Although he had logic and expertise on his side, she was a better arguer, and often, when she wanted something that he was unwilling to concede a point on, she was able to convince him to change his mind, simply by repeating what she wanted until he found a way of giving in without losing face. Then, he often thought the about-turn was his idea.

She was a leading member of local society, if you could call it society. There was the Women's Guild and the Girl Guides; all very worthwhile but a lot of work. A number of local women had got together to find ways of making their lives more interesting. It had started during the Great War, when they only really had the company of other women to sustain them through the loneliness of being parted from their men folk, who might not come home.

In a way, the war had opened new doors in her life. Her very Church of England farmer parents had brought her up strictly, but although her marriage to Albert had been a match designed by both sets of parents, it had suited Albert and Jenny, too. They had fallen in love at eighteen and he had inherited the family farm three years before the war began. His mother had lived with them for a few months, until she had followed her husband.

Albert had volunteered for the Worcester's soon after the war started, as had many of the local farming community. The women had been left to carry on as best as they could.

The collective interests they had spent their time on had opened the door to new interests. Some of them had taken an interest in healing and witchcraft to help with their aches and pains, not getting anywhere through the services of the few available local doctors. Many of the remedies had been handed down the female side of their families for generations, and had a good basis for use, in the experience of many. The Parson, also, had an expertise in natural cures. She was always glad to see him, the rogue, always trying it on with her, making her feel younger and she played along with him, leaving him with the impression that if he tried a little harder, he might have his way with her. He might, too!

The cream he had given her for the skin condition on her arm had been efficacious, the eczema clearing up in a month. She wondered if it would have cleared up anyway. He had his own way of gently stroking the cream into her skin that felt like a caress. Some of the remedies were a little far fetched. Mary Pudge had consulted him about the wart on her young son's hand. The Parson had taken a drawing pin, stuck it into the wart, held young Fred's hand and they had walked around their rowan tree widdershins, that was, anti-clockwise. As they had walked, the Parson had chanted 'Rowan tree, Rowan tree, won't thou take this wart from me?' Then he had stuck the pin into the tree and told the boy that the wart would be gone in a month. True to his word, a month later the wart was gone. Jenny could never decide how his cures worked. She knew that Rowan trees had protective properties. Often they were planted on the four corners surrounding a house, to keep evil spirits away. Perhaps it was all in the mind! Mary had been glad to pay the Parson what he asked though Jenny never did find out what his consultation fee was! It was all very suspicious according to Albert. If you weren't careful, you could die from some of these old wives' cures. She looked up at the sky; the sun was starting to move down toward the horizon now.

The sounds of the pickers could still be heard, bringing life to the farmyard that was usually almost silent except for the clucking of her hens. The pickers added a feeling of excitement mingled with a bit of nervous fear. Some of the men who came down were strangers and she always felt unsure of herself with strange men, although she tried to maintain an air of dominance. They were such a mixture; tramps, gypsies, out of work drunks; all sorts. Albert was her husband and she loved him but he was such a stick-in-the-mud at times! She threw the dregs of her tea onto the little rose patch and standing, stretched herself. It was no good sitting around all day. She had things to do. Washing and ironing to start with! In the morning, she thought, that'll do.

Albert had been brought to a defensive position when she had brought up the subject of Selina. He hadn't even thought that she might have an interest in young Tom. He would be shocked if he knew her thoughts and feelings! Jenny considered herself a modern, educated woman even if others just thought she was a rural bumpkin. She had a wide range of knowledge that included her expertise in healing and medicine. Her friend Millicent Brookes had introduced her into what the local women called the coven and she had started a training course in their esoteric mysteries that was second to none. There was no question of anything being likened to the Churches way of looking at things. As far as the members were concerned, everything had to earn its place; nothing was taken for granted or given importance simply as a result of where it came from.

6. The Hops.

Hops have been grown in Herefordshire and Worcestershire since a time so far back that no one now remembers. The pickers, mostly from the Black Country and Birmingham, some Welsh from the Valleys, gypsies, and local people known as 'the neighbours', were employed for four to six weeks, dependent on the weather and the quality of the yield in that particular year. The diverse groups did not always mix well, and often went to different farms, in different parts of the county, to avoid meeting.

Earlier in the year, the accommodation for pickers had been prepared by whitewashing the barns, barracks, cowsheds, or even, on occasion, pigsties. The areas had been divided up to give a degree of privacy to the families who would be billeted there. By late August the crop was usually almost ready for picking and the agents who recruit the pickers had been instructed to make their conscripting arrangements.

Wood for the pickers use had been stacked in the farmyard; the 'devils', large iron braziers, have been inspected; cribs or, more commonly, bins, long cradles for the pickers to put the picked hops into, had been checked and repaired as necessary. These bins were about ten feet long, one for each family or small group, working together. They were made of chestnut poles nailed or lashed together, with sacking nailed to the sides to form a sort of cradle into which the picked hops would be dropped.

The hops grown at the Walker's farm were of the type known as Fuggles after their introduction by Richard Fuggles. The Latin name for hops, Humulus Lupulus, means 'wolf of the willow'. Hops have been used medicinally for hundreds of years. Nicholas Culpepper, a Seventeenth Century physician, recommended them as a cure for 'venereal disease, scabs, itch, and other breakings out of the body'. He said that hops, 'kills worms in the body, brings down women's courses, and expels urine.' Worcester and Hereford hop growers have been consistently successful while always looking for a new hop that would give better resistance to the hop-wilt.

After an early start, the busheller would come round to check the amount that had been picked. He would use a large basket for this purpose, and sometimes he would press the hops down in the crib to ensure the farmer was getting a full measure. Some bushellers pressed down more than others and were known as hard bushellers. The busheller did his checking twice a day. Everyone in a family helped the group; even small children were encouraged to contribute their labour, picking loose hopheads into an umbrella placed upside down on the ground.

Pickers were paid by the bushel, the price varying from year to year and from farm to farm. A good picker could pick five 'houses' of hops, a house being a stretch of hops which was picked clean before the pickers moved on to the next.

Tom, Selina and Kate decided to work together temporarily as a group; they had been told that they would be under the orders of Jim Miller, a busheller. They had been out to see where they would be working and had picked out a 'drift', a working area, to start on.

Jim Miller, the busheller, introduced himself and accompanied them. He and Tom took the two girls round the farm to familiarise themselves with the whereabouts of everything, and showed them how the picking was done. Selina found the smells overpowering at first, then gradually got used to the heady mixture of the odour of hops, cows and pigs. The result was so different to the smells of town. Tom found himself cast in the role of expert, although he had been but a youth the last time he came. He took Selina on a walk through the hop yard and it was a revelation to her urban eyes.

She found herself walking between the immense curtains of the hop bines, sixteen feet high, hiding the sun, and giving an intimacy and warmth to the atmosphere that made it feel like a theatre that was about to open to a new production. The sounds of the surrounding area were muffled by the myriad pole-climbing bines, increasing the sense of intimate closeness.

As they walked, their hands kept playing with each other, and then with other attractive parts of each other until they could tolerate it no longer and they turned and clung to each other, feeling that their closeness would last forever. This was a new familiarity that seemed to signal the start of a fresh phase in their relationship, bringing about the bonding that 'paired' them. It was, they knew, only a matter of time before their final submission to each other.

Gradually, like the ripening of the hops, their bodies warmed to the increasing sensitivity of each other's closeness. They moved through their senses; sight being the first sense to be called into play. Tom noticed that women's breasts seemed to attract his sight more than when he was younger, not just Selina's. His last thoughts at night were of breasts, Kate's, Jenny Walker's, Emily's, but especially Selina's. He badly wanted to move from looking to touching. His body ached from desire, making his dreams more productive. The feel of Selina's breasts raised his feelings until he could barely contain himself. She had sympathised, and had taken him in hand, bringing about a wonderful release that had been matched by hers.

His arms seemed to attract Selina; she was constantly imagining them around her body. The pressure of his aroused body against hers seemed to bring about an unfinished rhapsody that was occasionally relieved as she relieved his. The company of Kate seemed to create not an intrusion but a shared intimacy, as if she were part of their 'pair'.

On this first Sunday they walked along the aisles of hop plants, Tom with an arm around each of them, trying to reach as far round as he could to the rise of a breast, sometimes being allowed the pleasure of feeling a small rise, and at other times being gently fended off. The warmth of the sun warmed their bodies, drawing from them the body odours that identified them as separate from the hundreds of others working on the bines. The scent made them able to identify each other, even in the dark. It was as if they were three pairs, Tom and Selina, Tom and Kate and Kate and Selina, all bound up in a wonderful trio of friends, each linked by their shared intimacies.

Tom had great respect for the busheller's knowledge of the hop industry and wanted to know more. In past years he had spent hours discussing the different types of hop.

'There are many other varieties of hops apart from Fuggles that were in favour at different times and in different parts of the country', Jim told Tom as he walked round with them.

'Fuggles and Goldings grow to about thirty feet, Tom, but they are usually topped, that means pinched out, at about fifteen to eighteen feet. They are dioecious. Its flowers are restricted to separate male and female plants. That's what dioecious is defined as, see? They take about three years to get sufficiently mature to carry hops but then they can be active for another ten to twenty years. Herefordshire and Worcestershire together are the smaller part of the hop-growing areas. Kent grows two thirds the acreage with Herefordshire and Worcestershire growing the other third.'

Tom was surprised at the knowledge that the busheller had, and listened to him with rapt attention. He always felt as if he were in the middle of a learning experience, and sometimes he wondered if he would ever know enough to feel confident about his own knowledge.

In the nineteen twenties, hops were picked by hand, although there was talk of a machine being designed that would do the job without a need for pickers. Many hundred of men, women and children were employed at the time, reducing the number of the unemployed. Tom stopped what he was doing, listening to what Jim was saying,

'There are special skills to hop growing and picking, Tom. The hops have to be grown with the male plants to the windward side, and this allows the wind to blow towards the female plants and helps to bring about their fertilisation. The burr, the female hop cone, of the female plant is the part that's used to make beer bitterer. This part, see?'

He took the outer petals off, and held the burr for Tom to see. To Tom it was just a funny looking flower but he tried to respond to Jim's enthusiasm, continuing to listen.

'When they're ready in September, the bines are cut back by hand to a height of about three feet before picking, then when the fields are cleared, they're cut back to the ground and left until the new shoots start to grow, the following April. The shoots are grown up the supporting strings until they are at their best height, about eighteen feet, in the middle of June. If new plants are needed they are created from cuttings taken from aerial shoots or where underground stems have grown above the rootstock.

Jim Miller sucked on his pipe again; it seemed to Kate that he used the pipe as a way of giving himself time to think of what he was going to say next. She tried to think of a question that would show him she was interested.

'What happens after they are picked, Mister Miller?'

She asked the question, linking her arm into his; gently, blushing as he glanced at her arm in his. He gathered his thoughts, trying to give her the information she wanted in an easy way to assimilate. He was enjoying the feel of her arm and body close to his.

'Well, after the hops are picked, they're separated from the leaves and the bines and then removed to the hop kiln; that's what we call it. In Kent, a similar building is known as an oasthouse. This is where the hops are dried out in a constant draught until most o' the moisture's gone. Then they're packed into large sacks called hop pockets, weighing about a hundredweight and a half. They have to have the name of the yard printed on it, with the weight and a number.'

He reached into his waistcoat pocket for his pipe and lit it, imbibing the delicate grey smoke that curled upward.

'Anything else you want to know, young lady?'

'No thanks, Mister Miller. I reckon I know all about it, now, don't you? There can't be much left, after you've told a body.'

She looked at Miller out of the corner of her eye. He started to say something then realised that Kate was ribbing him. He laughed and then turned to Tom, taking on the demeanour of a lecturer

'Well, as a matter of fact, Tom there is just a little bit more than you can learn in a ten minute tea break, but I don't expect you'll have much time for listening, what with all these young women you seem to attract. Maybe they'll be able to teach you something!'

Tom did have time for listening; he seemed to enjoy the absorption of new facts and bits of knowledge. He came to realise that all knowledge was just an accumulation in the mind, or brain, of tiny bits of information that you didn't know you knew until you needed that tiny bit. That was the way he saw it. As for, 'the young women you seem to attract', he hadn't thought about it much. He was more concerned about the way they seemed to attract him.

The hop-yard, although populated by hundreds of pickers, seemed to have opportunities for intimacy. A hand, touching another hand, a thigh, accidentally touching another, the closeness of mixed body odours, all seemed to have the effect of heightening his perceptions, making him want to make these small intimacies last just a little longer. The girls he was working with seemed to Tom to have no perception of the way he was feeling and he was aroused to the point of wanting to grab one of them, it didn't seem to matter which one, and just hold her tight.

They both seemed to be teasing him; Selina would touch his cheek as she went past and allow her breast to brush past him. Kate was different; she seemed to want to appeal to his sight, occasionally stretching her body upward, her breasts being silhouetted against whatever the background was. She smiled at him when she saw him watching her.

'What you looking at, Tom? Do you like what you see?'

She didn't make those comments when Selina was looking. She was different then. She seemed to be more interested in Selina. Tom couldn't work out why.

The picking would soon roughen up their hands, Tom thought, and he advised the girls to soak them at night, to ease the pain. He had always tied string around his trousers to help to protect his legs against the scratching of the bines, though it didn't seem to make much difference; it was a matter of dressing up for the job. They came back to the barn just as Albert Walker was walking round the farmyard. He stopped and looked at them appraisingly.

'Hello, Tom. Have you been learning the ropes with the girls?' He turned to the young women. 'Take notice of anything he tells you. He knows more than you could imagine. Hello, Selina. I'm glad to see you've a decent pair of shoes. They'll serve you better than those tiny things you were wearing the other day. Have you got any Wellingtons? If you haven't, Jenny usually has half a dozen pairs to spare. If I were you, I'd come and try some. The ground might seem to be firm at the moment but it's a different story when it's been raining.'

Selina blushed. Mr Walker always had that effect on her. She didn't know why. She thought it might be that he was so big, and superior, not in a nasty way, but as if he was naturally like an old time squire, with the power of life and death over his minions. Perhaps it was his bigness compared to Mrs Walker; she was so small.

Kate had no problem with him, being more self-confident. Selina felt that Kate could hold her own in any company. She had noticed that Kate seemed to pose whenever Tom was around, or, for that matter, whenever there was a man around that she liked the look of. She supposed that she should be jealous, but of which one should she be jealous? Although Tom was her man-friend, she also found herself feeling as if Kate was her girl-friend, not in a sexual way, she thought, but as a personal friend. It was a strange feeling. There were all sorts of things at work here, and she was used to being able to get things worked out. Perhaps it was all due to the effect of the hops; they had a strange compelling odour and it was as if they were intoxicating, but there was no alcohol in the hops.

The main thing, she thought, was that there was no one around to tell them what to do. Mr and Mrs Walker sort of kept an eye on things, but there was no Mom and Dad to wield the stick if anyone stepped out of line. They were out on their own. They had to learn or create their own rules, and implement them if anyone transgressed.

Tom was the most naïve. He had been to the hop-yards before but not as his own man; in a way he wasn't a man, not yet; he still had to make that final, irrevocable move that separated him from the boys. Jim Miller was the more mature. He had seen more of life than any of them, in France, and the Army. Even so, there was still an unbending, not quite dogmatic, but certainly less flexible manner about him, as if he had his own set of standards to which he adhered, and from which he would not be moved.

Kate was a closed book at the moment, waiting to be opened, Selina thought. One minute she was all over the men, posing for attention and getting it. The next she seemed to be all coy, a young girl saving for her bottom drawer. One day she would break out and show all of them; perhaps she would have an outlook that differed from all of them. Selina tried to figure it out. Sometimes she was able to work out what a person was like, and sometimes she couldn't.

What am I like, she asked herself? What if somebody is trying to work me out? What affect will the hops have on me? I came down here, a young girl who thought she knew all of it; now I am still asking questions. Just because Harry was able to seduce me, doesn't mean that I am some sort of fast woman. I was just a young fruit, ready for the picking, and I enjoyed being picked; now I want something more than just being picked.

What will Tom be like, when I pick him? There's a thought. Perhaps it won't be me that picks him. Perhaps it will be Kate, posing in front of him all the time. The thought didn't please her at all, and she swiftly dismissed it. Later, she thought about it again and stood, posing for herself, in the mirror in Mrs Walker's kitchen, thinking, 'I look all right anyway. I could pose as good as Kate. I will have to try it.'

Kate was going to the farmhouse after they had finished picking, to select something for the evening meal. As she started out, Selina called to her.

'Kate, I'm coming with you.'

She trotted the few feet until she caught up with Kate, who looked at her quizzically.

'What's your hurry then, Selina? You don't usually bother to have anything to do with the grub. You usually leave it to me.'

She continued walking as she was speaking. Selina decided to tell her the truth.

'To tell the truth, Kate, I just wondered what I looked like in that big mirror in the kitchen. I haven't seen myself in a glass since we left home. For all I know, I look like something the cat's dragged in!'

Kate turned, looked at Selina and burst into laughter.

'Something the cat's dragged in? Are you serious? There's nothing more beautiful this side of the Malverns!'

She turned her face away swiftly, blushing, and then she carried on walking, almost ignoring Selina. Selina looked at her, trying to see what was wrong, why she was acting so strangely. What was all this fuss about? All she had said was she thought she might look like something the cat had dragged in. Another thought crept into her mind. Was Kate one of those queer women? Was she a lesbian?

Selina decided to ignore what had been going on during the last few minutes; if there were anything waiting to be revealed, it would show itself sooner or later. Until then, she would just act normally.

Mrs Walker was in the kitchen, talking to Emily, the girl from the town who helped in the little shop that was run by Mrs Walker.

'Come on, my girl. It's time the shop was open. Here are your first customers and you've nothing ready yet.'

Emily scurried into the small room that was used as a shop, lifting the hatch and turning as she lowered it behind her.

'Yes, is there anything I can help you with, ladies?'

She swirled round, as if to open a theatrical curtain, Selina thought, and her eye caught Kate's and they smiled at each other, as if they had both had the same thought. Kate was the first to speak.

'I'd like five pounds of potatoes, please, Emily, and a pound of carrots, and if you have any other root vegetables I'll have two pounds of mixed, please.'

She waited until Emily had bagged the vegetables then continued with her order.

'A quarter of Typhoo tea, a pound of sugar and a pint of milk, please, and one of those lovely cakes; did Mrs Walker bake them, herself? Just pop one into a bag for me. How much is that, please?' She held out a ten-shilling note and waited while Emily added it up and passed her change. 'Thank you, Emily. We shall certainly shop here again, shan't we, Selina?'

The two of them turned and walked smartly out of the room, back into the kitchen. Mrs Walker was still there. Selina placed her hand on Kate's arm.

'Wait a moment, Kate. I just want to see if I'm still the most beautiful thing this side of the Malverns!' She stopped in front of the mirror and posed, her hand elegantly reaching as if she were smoking a cigarette. 'Yes, I'll do. What do you think, my dear?' She made a caricature out of herself, turning her body into what she thought a fashion model must arrange her body, a strange, contorted shape. 'Never mind; as long as I'm satisfied, it doesn't really matter what anyone else thinks. Come along.'

She smiled sweetly at Jenny Walker and stepped out of the kitchen door. Jenny looked, and then smiled. The young ones had to have their fun. Emily hadn't seemed to have gathered what was going on, but she had. It was all part of learning more about the hops! There was more to it than met the eye!

Selina had confirmed Jenny's opinion of her. She was a young woman with all the needs that that implied. It wouldn't be long now, before it showed.

Jenny turned back to the potatoes she was scraping. She had plenty to do without forecasting the behaviour of young women. She couldn't always forecast her own!

7. The Start.

The light of the sun, peering over the Malverns, caught his eye and made him start; awakening his senses. He listened; he could hear someone banging a bucket outside. Tom pulled aside the square of sacking that acted as a curtain between the beds, and looked at Selina. She was lying awake, her hand pulling the other curtain back so that she could see the sun too.

The light seemed to have a different quality here, as if it was bigger, brighter and cleaner. The sun behind her silhouetted the outline of her breast and Tom felt his hand, as if it had a life of its own, reach out to touch her. She gasped and her hand tightened on his. She moved over closer to him, pressing back against his body, each wanting the final intimacy that they had not yet enjoyed, knowing that they could not prevent it for much longer, but aware that now was not the time. She smiled to herself and anticipated how it would feel, her body telling her in advance. His cool hand tightened on her breast, causing her to gasp and giggle at the same time. She took back control.

'What time is it, Tom? The sun seems to be bigger here, as if it's late, already.'

Tom had noticed it before, when he had come down with his mother. It was almost as if it was a different sun from the one they were accustomed to. You could nearly tell the time from the look and position of the sun.

He pulled out his birthday fob watch, and wound it as he answered. 'It's about six o'clock; we can have a few minutes more, if you like.'

He let his hand move across her breast, caressing her nipple and she moved her back against him, moving her buttocks. The stimulus was almost more than he could bear and he pulled her against his body, his manhood searching for her womanhood. A cock crowed, his challenge sounding above the others. Selina turned and looked at Tom.

'What a cock! He must be a champion!' She said, still moving herself in time.

She suddenly realised the import of her own unintentional double meaning phrase and smiled at him.

'Please, Tom, our time will come. I don't want to be caught like this.'

He let her go, reluctantly relinquishing his hold of her, still retaining the feeling, the passion, the power, the emotion of the moment before. She was leaning on her elbow, looking at the view; changing the direction of the conversation.

'It's lovely, isn't it, Tom? I've never seen it like this before. Is it always like this?'

He looked at her and smiled. 'Course it isn't. Sometimes it rains and rains for days on end, and you think you are never going to see the sun again. You have to make up for it, when it does shine. Come on, lazy bones! You'll have to hurry if you want a wash before breakfast. Put the frying pan on and we'll have a piece o' dip and a couple of eggs before we know it.'

Selina smiled to herself with the knowledge that she had once more successfully resisted his impulses. He swung his legs round and stood up, pulling his trousers on at the same time. This was the best time of day for him. The thought of actually performing hard physical work was a pleasure. Striving and straining always seemed like running in a race and he always wanted to be the first and fastest past the line. He had an expectation of competition with others, no matter what he did, and the thought thrilled him. He had a need to try to be the best, fastest, highest and first at whatever he did.

He could hear the sounds of people outside. A large number of people had arrived after them, the day before, some whom he knew and some that he did not. They were like a large stew, with all sorts of people in it. Within a few hours they would all 'muck in', get to know each other and start to work in the fields. Selina had gone downstairs already. He looked through the window. She was outside, talking as she cooked their bacon. Not every one had bacon; some just had slices of bread, which they were dipping into the melted lard in the pans. Selina was talking to Kate, whom they had met yesterday. He noticed vaguely that they were both extremely good-looking young women, Selina with an appearance of innocence but blossoming, and Kate with a more mature type of shape, a full-blown woman, he thought. She seemed to sense him looking at her, and smiled up at him, her arms akimbo, emphasising the curve of her waist. His body responded to the look of her, and to the smile that welcomed him. He might try his luck there. There was stimulus everywhere! Which was the most attractive, the most irresistible?

The air was crisp, with a feeling of frost in it, but the sun was still shining, making the scene pleasant to behold, and be part of. Tom skipped down the steps, stepped outside and strode over to the large bucket, threw the dirty water out and refilled it, pumping the water vigorously, then dipped his hands into the cold water and threw it over his face and neck. It was cold, colder than he had expected. He looked for soap, rubbed it on his hands to create lather, reached for a towel, rubbed his face and dried himself. The whole wash had taken him about half a minute. He spluttered and looked up.

A man he hadn't seen before was watching him, smiling.

'It's cold, aye it, mate?'

It was Jim Miller, the Black Country busheller, but he looked more like one of the neighbours, as the local people were called.

Tom was appraising the man. He seemed to have an air of authority about him, as if he were used to telling people what to do. Tom had seen it before. Somehow it was like his father; he possessed it, too. He wondered how people got it, whether people could develop it within themselves. The man seemed to be appraising him, too. It was part of meeting strangers; each wondered things about the other. Tom wondered why he hadn't met the man before, in other years.

'Sometimes I'm one o' the pole pullers, Jim said, 'Sometimes I'm a busheller. It all depends on what the gaffer wants me to do on the day. Today I'm counting how many pickers we've got. It's been looking as if we'd be shorthanded, the last few days. We've been trying to get the cribs out, ready for the pickers, but there ain't been enough hours in the day. Do you fancy giving we an 'and? You'll get a bit extra in your pay and it'll gi'e you a bit o' schooling. Something else you'll be able to do, if you get my meaning. The sun'll be out soon and then it'll get warmer.'

Tom thought quickly. 'Giving we an 'and?' He had to be from Wednesbury! Selina seemed to be getting on all right with Kate. She'll be able to work with her for today.

'Yes, I'd like that. I'll just tell the Missus.'

He felt self-conscious about the name, but wanted to establish that Selina was with him. He stepped over to where the two women were talking. Selina turned and saw him and offered him a large bacon sandwich.

'What's up, Tom? What's Jim want?'

She seemed to know, as usual.

'It's nothing really,' said Tom, 'He's our busheller, or gaffer, I don't know which. I've just been offered a bit more money for helping Harry get the cribs out to the drifts, ready for the picking. Will you be all right, working with Kate?'

He looked at both of the women, quizzically and it was Kate, who replied,

'O' course she will, won't you, Selina?' She turned to Tom, 'You should take every chance to get on, Tom. You never know where it might lead to, you know. You might get to be a gaffer yourself, one day'

Tom smiled, 'I might fly if I had wings, as well.'

Kate looked at him, seriously. 'Don't you mock me, Tommy Barr! You should think more of yourself. Gaffers ain't born with a collar and tie on, you know. Same as your dad wasn't born with a sergeant's stripes on his arm. He had to earn 'em in the Staffies; and risk his life doing it. Did you ever think o' that?'

Tom stopped smiling; the thought had never crossed his mind. How did Kate know that his father had served with the

Staffordshire Regiment? She had worked with his mother before, he recalled. She would have told Kate about his father's time in the Army. A gaffer was just someone who gave out orders. He had never thought that there was anybody who would give him a job that he knew nothing about? He supposed that all gaffers knew everything about the job, whichever job it was. He would have to give some more thought to the subject when he got time. In the meantime he'd better catch up with Jim, who was now nearing the end of the field.

He broke into a trot, chewing on his bacon sandwich as he ran. Jim was not going towards the hop field. He was going towards the pole-yard, an area at the back of the farmhouse. Tom caught up with him just as he swung open the long, five-barred gate.

'How long have you been working at this farm, Jim?' He asked, slightly out of breath, 'You sound like a Black Countryman but you dress and act like a local.'

Jim turned to look at him and looked as if he was thinking something about Tom.

'Well spotted, Tom. I've been here about three years now, usually up at the other farm. I came out of the Staffies and tried a bit of this and a bit of that but couldn't settle to anything 'til I came here. Albert Walker is an old mate o' mine. We went through half the war together and he said he'd help me if I needed it. There was no work in Wednesbury after the war so I wrote to him for a job and he offered me a chance. His family have farmed here for hundreds of years. I couldn't face going back into a factory, never seeing the sky, always looking down at what you're doing at the bench. Albert Walker's all right in my book. I'll always remember what he did for me.'

He stopped, obviously embarrassed. Tom was surprised. Gaffers were usually disliked - because they were gaffers. No other reason was considered necessary. Gaffers had the power to take you on, or sack you if your face didn't fit. Tom had never thought that they might have feelings like other men. The thought intrigued him. He had the feeling that he was going to learn a lot at the hop fields, this year. They passed through the gate, into the pole yard. He noticed that there were two other men, stripping the bark from the long chestnut poles. There were long, curly shavings everywhere. He stood watching for a moment or two, waiting for Miller to speak.

'What d'you want me to do, Jim?'

The scene was so completely rural; it was as if it had been pulled out of a painting and hung in front of him. Hens were clucking around, a dog barked and birds were flying in and out of the farm buildings. Two ducks waddled over to him and looked up expectantly. He smiled at their antics. The two men were carrying on with what they were doing as if they were on their own.

'Just watch Bill and Harry for a little while, and then you have a go yourself.' Jim turned to the older of the two men. 'Bill, this is Tom; he's going to give you an 'and. Just put him right, will you?'

Without waiting for an answer, he strode away; he obviously had something else on his mind.

'Right oh gaffer.' Bill spoke to Jim's back. 'I'll do that. I'll put him right. Don't 'ee worry about him. Come over here young Tom. Just you watch Harry and me. You'll soon get the hang on it. I've been at it twenty-five years, so you'll soon be an old hand.'

Tom stood watching for a few minutes, enthralled as the curly shavings of chestnut appeared, as if by magic, from the large spoke-shave.

'Just bring us a few o' they poles over, Tom.' Harry was looking at Tom, pointing to a pile of hop poles lying in a corner of the yard. 'Not too many, or we'll never get a blow.'

They were removing the bark from the long hop poles, making them smoother and easier to work with. The spoke-shave was not hard to use and after a while Harry passed it to Tom.

'Here, you have a go, Tom. See 'ow you get on. It ain't hard if you just try.'

Tom picked up the tool and examined it. He had seen one before, but had never actually used one. Tentatively he slid it along the pole, as far as he could reach and the spoke-shave lifted a curl of wood that was just as good as Harry's. The two men put down the last of the poles they were working on, and lit up, Harry his pipe and Bill a cigarette, handing one to Tom.

Harry was the first to speak. 'Do a bit an' leave a bit, Tom. That's the way. You'm always doin' something then, an no-one can say you'm a skivin'. Ain't that right, Bill?'

'You don't want to take any notice of him, Tom. He's just a natural born layabout.'

Bill was smiling as he spoke and Tom realised that they were ribbing him gently.

'Well, Where I come from, they say yo' cor' do too much for a good gaffer.' he said, his eyes twinkling, and belying his words. 'There ain't many good gaffers, though.'

'Hmph! In my experience, yo' cor do enough for any on 'em.'

A voice broke in on them, 'That'll be the day, Billy, when you do enough for me.' The voice came from Jim Miller, who had returned and was standing, leaning on the gate. Billy spluttered,

'I was only saying to Tom…'he started.

'Don't bother to explain Billy. I know you couldn't talk your way out of a paper bag.'

Jim Miller was smiling. He had heard it all before, many times. He knew Billy would give him a decent day's work.

'How are you making out, Tom? Have you learned anything?'

Tom thought, and then spoke.

'Well, yes. I've learned that if you listen long enough, the end of the day'll come, an' it'll be time to knock off an' you'll have a day's pay without 'aving to do anything for it. Apart from that I've learned that chestnut is the best wood for hop poles, 'cos its long and straight an they're heavy if you try to pick up too many at a time, an' I've learned that you can have a good laugh while you work an' the day goes quicker an' you get more done if you do.'

He stopped. Jim Miller was staring at him, wondering if he was mocking him. Bill started to laugh, and then Harry and Jim joined in. 'He'll do, you know,' said Jim, 'but pole stripping ain't really what I've brought Tom down here for. We've not got enough cribs ready yet, and it'll be no good starting the picking without the cribs, will it? Bill, you hitch up the cart while Harry and Tom load it with cribs. Tom, you can start putting them out on the drifts. We'll have them at the top end o' the North Field, to start 'em off. The walk'll do 'em good first thing in the morning.'

Tom knew what a drift was; the pickers worked in rows, close together, between the hops and these working areas were known as drifts. He walked over to where the cribs were piled against the barn wall and started to load them onto the cart.

'Check them over to be sure they don't fall apart as they're being used. Bill will mend them while you and Harry take the first load over to the field.'

He walked away and Bill turned to Tom,

'That's a good gaffer. Trusts you to get on with it; don't stand over you all day. Give us an 'and to put these cribs for mending, by the bench; then you can go with Harry.'

When the first load was ready, Harry and Tom perched on the driving seat of the cart and started towards the North Field while Bill started to repair the cribs. It did not take long. They were lashed together with coarse string and were soon re-lashed if they had worked loose. Bill had been working at the farm for many years and he seemed to repair the cribs in a matter of a few minutes. The cribs usually lasted for a season or two, with minor repairs. The sun came up over the hills and Tom started to feel the heat on his neck.

'That feels nice,' he said appreciatively. 'Feels like summer again.'

The weather had been cool of late and today was pleasant by comparison. Harry turned and looked at Tom.

'Can you drive a cart? If you can, I'll have a pipe as we go along.'

Tom took the long reins, and Harry lit his clay pipe. The big shire mare had no difficulty with the cartload of cribs and within a few minutes they were at the gate of the field. Harry jumped down to open the gate and Tom turned the cart into the field, and then waited for Harry to jump up. Everything seemed to get done in slow motion.

'This is really exciting, ain't it Harry? Don't anything ever happen round here?'

He looked at Harry, quizzically, waiting for him to settle down with his pipe. The countryman spoke after a short pause to reflect on what he was about to say.

'Now what do you want something to happen for, Tom? Just you be content. You won't get any more money if anything exciting happens. All you have to do is, do as you're told, keep your nose clean and pick up your pay at the end of the week, or when you go home at the end of the picking. That's the best o' course, and then you've got something to show for the trip, if you know what I mean.'

'You sound like my Mom, Harry. She's always going on about saving money.'

'Sounds to me as if your Mom's got her head screwed on right, Tom. I bet she's got a few bob tucked away in case of emergency, like. What would you do if you suddenly needed some money, eh?'

Tom thought on the question. He's right. If I needed some money, I'd go to Mom. I always expect her to have money, even though she hasn't got a proper job just collecting a few rents. Why should I expect her to have money? Where does she get her money? I should have money of my own, in case I need it. How can I hope to get married if I haven't got any money to buy furniture, or pay the rent on somewhere to live? But how much should I save? How much should I spend? Who should I ask? He turned to Harry.

'It's all right for you, and my Mom, to tell me I should save, but how much should I save? I don't always earn the same amount, so I can't always save the same amount. When is it all right to have a good night out and when isn't it?' He looked quizzically at Harry and then spoke again. 'Why aren't you well off, Harry? You stand there, telling me what I should do but you don't seem any better off than me. Why aren't you living in a big posh house if you are so clever? My Mom isn't any better off, for all her knowing what I should do with the money that I earn, so what's the point? I might as well have a good time with what I pick up at the end of the week.'

He fell silent, angry that these 'clever' people could act so superior, and yet were no better off for it. If he could see the reason for saving, he would be willing to take advice, and act upon it.

Harry was looking at him now, as if he was trying to give him the answers to his questions. He seemed to change his mind.

'Jump up, Tom. We've got to put these cribs at the far end of the field.'

They skirted the edge of the field, between the first row of hop-laden poles and the hedge, picking their way to avoid the ruts, and make it easier for the horse. This row was a little wider than the others, to allow access for the cart. There was a slight slope to the field so Harry applied the long brake to prevent the cart from rolling back, then turned and stepped over the seat, onto the flat back of the cart.

Tom jumped down from the seat and took the crib that Harry was handing down to him, then asked, 'Where shall I put them Harry?'

'Lay them out down this row, about ten or twelve feet apart. There should be enough for this row. When you've put four out, jump back on the cart and we'll move on a bit.'

They worked on, in silence, until they had put out all the cribs they had with them, and then started back for the pole yard, Tom with the reins in his hands, and Harry puffing his pipe. Tom was struck by the silence. In the industrial environment that he was used to, there were very few times when it was silent, even during the night, but here, unless you actually spoke or made a noise, it was eerily hushed, and almost oppressive in the lack of sound. All that came to your ears was the sound of birds and animals and even those sounds were partially muted by the growing hops.

Harry seemed to be quite content, just leaning back against the seat of the cart. Tom felt irritated. There should be something to do. Even the horse did not require any control, just picking a way through the few puddles, knowing the route through and through. He picked up his previous train of thought. He was used to the philosophy that if he did more, he got paid more, and here there was nothing he could do to increase his pay by increased effort. He became aware that Harry was looking at him.

They had almost arrived at the farmyard, now. The sky was covered in clouds and large blue pools of naked space. The sun was lower, making longer shadows at the foot of the trees as they rolled past them.

'What's it like, working in a factory, Tom? I suppose it seems busier than this, don't it?'

Tom thought; how could he tell the countryman what it was like in Willenhall? There were no similarities at all. A different set of skills altogether was needed in the Black Country, and a knowledge that only living there could give. How could he explain a different way of life?

8. After Work.

Tom smiled; trying to think how he could describe the excitement he felt when he went to work each morning. It was so different from Bromyard! There were about forty people working at the lock factory, and they all started work at the same time. Each worker had a personal number and this was stamped onto a brass disc, which was hung onto a large board at the gatehouse. As they entered the works, they moved their disc from the board to a hook on another board. When the hooter signalling the start of the shift was sounded, the gateman closed the doors and locked the board. Anyone arriving after that time had to seek permission from his own foreman to start work. Often a latecomer was told, 'Come back tomorrow.' If the employee was late too often, they would be dismissed and 'given the sack', to carry their tools away in.

'Harry, it's nothing like this. Even though the work itself can be boring, you've always got something to do. Even if you know you've finished one order, there's always another. It's always noisy; there's always your mates taking a rise out o' somebody, having a joke or 'avin' a bit o' fun with the girls. I'd like to move into engineering, if I could get a job at a bigger place, and learn more about turning or milling, shaping or planing, and machine tool-fitting; there's a lot to it, you know, even the scraping of flat surfaces for machine slides. They even finish them off by feathering them with a scraper. You make your own scrapers out of old files, to put a pattern of curly feathers across the slide, so that the oil can find a way all over the slide.

'But I like it where I work now. I like to do something where you have to think a bit before you can do it, if you know what I mean. There's a lot o' girls work there, and you can have a bit of fun with them, as well. That's where I met Selina. We are getting married one day, when I've got enough money. She don't like the factory as much as I do. She'd like to open a shop, like her mother, only bigger, although I know it takes a lot of money to do that.

That's another thing I like about working in a factory; the feeling on a Friday, when you pick up your wages. It happens as regular as clockwork and you know what you've got to spend, and what you're going to spend it on.'

He stopped talking to get his thoughts into order. It was difficult, trying to explain another way of life to the countryman. Harry interrupted his thoughts.

'You don't have to wait for 'one day', if you have a hop-pole wedding, you know Tom. It doesn't cost anything except a few drinks for your friends. There is no lifetime liability either. The Parson'll fix it up for you. You'll be meeting him in the next few days, I expect. Nor you don't have to wait forever for the chance to open a shop. You just have to save a part of what you earn, and put it on one side and then you buy your stock with it and rent a shop. You're a lot luckier than you think, Tom.'

He leaned back again, moving in rhythm with the movement of the cart, completely relaxed, but ready for any unusual movement. His eyes seemed to almost close. Although he seemed quite passive, he had put the possibility of action to Tom's thoughts; shown him that his dreams were a practicable possibility and told him in a few sentences what he should do. Tom hadn't thought about what he should do, he had just seen his dreams as dreams, without a real prospect of making them come true. Once again Tom felt he was learning and what he learned could be kept to be used when the time came. He came back to the present.

'What do you mean, luckier than I think, Harry?'

'This is what I mean, young Tom. If you lived in Germany, you would be getting paid twice a day, and go and spend it as quick as you could, 'cos by teatime it would only be worth half as much. It's called inflation, and if it ever happened here, we would all be skint twice a day instead of once a week!'

More knowledge! What next? There was always something. Another thought came to him.

'Who is the Parson, Harry? I heard Mr Walker and his wife

talking about him. Is he the local vicar?'

Harry smiled softly; this one was naïve, but he wouldn't be for long, if he kept asking questions like this. At least he'd got the sense to ask questions.

'No, Tom. He's a gypsy who comes around at the picking season and helps out with whatever needs doing. Him and his family have been coming here for years. He can turn his hand to almost anything that needs doing on a farm. His family are quite high up, among the gypsies. One of his kin is the king o' the gypsies. The Parson holds hop pole weddings for them that might be interested.'

He stopped for a moment and while he did, Tom thought of a question to ask him.

'What exactly is a hop pole wedding, Harry? What does it entail? What's the difference between a hop pole wedding and an ordinary wedding, in a church?'

Harry looked at him and sighed.

'The trouble with you, young Tom is you're all questions. Any answer I give you is followed by twenty more questions. There's no end to your supply of questions. You never seem to run out of them. I've run out of answers for now, but I'll tell you this. A hop pole wedding is a wedding between two young people. They swear to be faithful to each other until the end o' the pickin', and they usually are, although it's just a bit o' fun, really, and if one of them fancies someone else, there's no law against it, if you know what I mean.

'Often, they have the wedding at the end of the season so they don't use up valuable picking time. Then it's just a bit o' fun, with no rules to say how long it's to last. We all know we have to be honourable, do the right thing by our women, but it's only because we have been brought up that way. If you watch the gaffers and their social superiors, they don't live that way at all. Some of them make up their own rules as they go along, and their equals go along with it. If one of us did what they did they would be punished for it, one way or another, by their uppers – and by their own mates and neighbours and relatives.'

He went quiet, and puffed again on his pipe. The pipe seemed to be part of his character, like the waistcoat he wore. Tom responded to what he was saying.

'You don't 'alf give a bloke something to think about when you start, Harry. I thought when I came down here I was just going to stand on a drift and pick hops all day, same as I did last year and the year before. Now I've had to start thinking about money, inflation, gaffers, and how they are made, class rules, 'cos that's what you mean, ain't it, Harry?' He did not wait for a reply, 'I've had to think about hop-pole weddings and the way they affect your life. Nothing seems as simple as I thought it was going to be. And you complain 'cos I ask questions! What do you expect?'

They both sat quietly for some time, mulling over what they had both been saying. Then Harry broke the silence.

'Well, it's a bit like going off to University, Tom, like the gaffers do. They go off to learn all about life. Well, that's what you are doing; learning a bit about life. There's no examinations to see if you're good enough and sometimes the approval of your mates don't really satisfy you. Sometimes you have to strike out on your own, make up your own mind about what's right or wrong for you, and that's what sets you apart and makes you your own man. People don't always like you for what you do, but they respect you - and that's worth more. At the moment you're what some people call a rough diamond, that's a diamond that has not yet been cut.' He paused again, sucking at his pipe as if his ideas would flow in rhythm with his breathing.

'You're just getting experience, and each experience takes a bit of the rough edge from you. In a year or two, you will be mostly cut diamond, with your real value shining through. Then you'll be your own man, valuing yourself, not caring too much for what other people think of you. People will talk about you, but it won't worry you. The time to worry is when no one talks about you. If that happens, you are a 'nothing' and I can't see that happening to you.'

Tom thought on what Harry had been saying as they arrived back at the pole yard. He was right! It was like getting an education. Every day he seemed to be having fresh ideas thrust upon him. Linking them to the expectations that he already had was a complicated series of mental steps. Fitting them into his ideas of right and wrong was even worse. Right and wrong seemed to alter, day by day. For instance, he wanted to act honourably and 'right' to Selina; to do the right thing; to be faithful and true.

Yet he could feel like jumping into bed or a hayrick, with any number of girls. Sometimes he went through the day counting the girls off, who he could 'do it' with. His best was seventy-three, on a hot summer's day last year when all the girls had seemed to come out of their houses, shops, offices and factories like butterflies out of their cocoons. He had spent most of the day in a physical state of readiness for an event that never occurred until he was alone in bed that night. There was no link then between 'rightness' and 'wrongness'. It just happened.

Perhaps that was how life was. You had ideas of how to act and, when the time came, you just seemed to scratch an itch; you acted nothing like you thought you would before, so to speak. He smiled to himself at the way his thoughts were going. Most of his thoughts were about girls. He did not dare to think about 'sex'. That was too obvious. He just reacted, physically, to the stimulus of the moment. He thought back to how Kate had looked up at him, the day before, with her breasts pressing against her dungarees; almost like an invitation. Perhaps it had been. Should he have rushed down the stairs to put his hands on her? That was what he had felt like doing. Did she, did girls, feel the same way? Sometimes he felt that girls could divine his thoughts and feelings, and it embarrassed him, especially if his feelings showed in his trousers! The thought made him feel that way again; it was getting to be a nuisance.

They were just turning into the pole yard. Bill was standing by the pile of chestnut poles, smoking.

'Where have you two been? I've had to do all these poles by myself. How do you think young Tom is going to learn all he's got to learn, if he is looking after you all the time, Harry? I bet you've had him lighting your pipe as well as driving the cart while you just sat there, smoking.'

'Stop moaning, Bill. You know there are plenty of poles for Tom to learn on. I'm sure you are looking forward to standing over him, watching him doing as you say.' He turned to Tom, 'You can work with Bill for an hour or so, see if you can pick up the skills it has taken him a lifetime to accumulate. That should be easy enough!'

'You cheeky old bastard; I've stripped more poles than you've had 'ot dinners, young fellow me lad. You just go and suck your pipe; that's what you're best at.'

They are like a couple of retired sparring partners, Tom thought, smiling to himself. He walked, with Bill, to the stack of poles and picking up the first one, started to use the great spoke-shave as he had seen Bill use it. The next two hours saw him sweating as, under the eyes of Bill, his skill gradually increased, and the rest of the working day seemed to pass in a few moments.

Later, Tom walked over to the steps leading up to the little space that he and Selina had made their own. Harry had filled his head with impossible thoughts. All that talk about rough diamonds and Universities had made sense when he listened but he couldn't see how it was going to benefit him, how he should use the philosophy. He could not tear his mind away from the possibility that he might finally make love to Selina. Although she had given him the idea that they were a couple, she had never let him make love to her, beyond kissing and petting. His hands ached to feel her breasts and she would allow this occasionally, but 'nothing below the waist.'

He wondered how she felt; did she have these urges that were practically violent? Was it different for girls? Did they feel things differently? Did she feel the need for his body, like he felt the need for hers? Sometimes when their bodies were close together, he was sure that she felt the same as he did, but she would not let him touch her intimately.

He walked up the steps, looking for her. She had been going to get their clothes ready for the picking, tomorrow. As he stepped up the last of the stairs he could see the silhouette of her body, behind the sacking screen. She was washing herself, kneeling down, splashing water from a small bowl onto her face; she was naked to her waist. He could not resist; he knelt behind her and reached to cup her breasts in his hands. He felt and heard her gasp and she turned.

'Tom! I didn't know who that was!'

They each had a flurry of emotion; divided between want and wait. The impulse was too strong for Tom, who tightened his grasp.

'Well you do now!'

She was responding to his kiss, pressing herself against him. He moved his head down from her lips to her breast, gently sucking, feeling the nipple increase in size. Her hand was exploring his body too. He lifted her skirt and noted, almost in passing, that she had no clothes beneath her skirt, and felt her folds. Her hands pulled his trousers over his hips and their bodies touched, caressed, and met, moving as if they had a will of their own. He had never been this close to a woman before, had no expertise and would have pre-empted their coupling if Selina had not helped him. She also had never felt, in this intensity, the feelings that were coursing through her. She wanted it to last forever and wanted to help Tom to learn how to make love. She slid her hand under the small sack between his legs and lifted it, lifting his manhood at the same time. He felt that she was just about to take him in when she heard footsteps, coming up the stairs.

'Someone's coming!'

She whispered to Tom, and swiftly righting her clothes, started sorting the food for their evening meal.

'Cooee,'

A voice called. Looking round they could see it was Kate, the girl they had been talking to earlier. Tom pulled back the sacking curtain and nodded to her as he saw her head appear above the floor.

'Hello Kate. We're just sorting out something for dinner; we're going to have sausage and eggs; do you fancy some?'

Why the hell did she have to appear then?

'Why yes, Tom. That'd be lovely. I've got some black pudding. That'll go down nice with the sausage and egg.'

She smiled at him and retreated down the stairs, and they heard her walk across the farmyard to the other barn, where she slept. Selina looked at Tom, a look of curiosity.

'I wonder what she wanted. She didn't really have any reason to come up here. Do you think she was looking for something to steal, Tom?'

'No, she isn't the stealing kind, Selina. She was probably looking for somebody. We ought to keep an eye open though, just in case. I don't think she would take from her own kind, do you, Selina?'

'No, you're probably right, Tom. I wonder who she was looking for, though. It makes you think.'

Just then, the figure of Jenny Walker, the farmer's wife appeared in the farmyard, saw Kate go into the opposite barn, and followed her. That looked as if the problem had been solved. Kate must have been searching for Jenny. A few minutes later they both came out and Kate had a bag in her hand. She walked over to the devil, which was burning hot, and slicing the black pudding, put it on to fry. She looked up to the window, from which Tom and Selina were watching her and shouted,

'Come on, you two! Your dinner's on. It'll be burnt if you don't hurry up. Where's the eggs?'

Selina picked up the eggs that Jenny Walker had sold her earlier, and scrambled down the steps. The steps were very steep, and she almost fell on the last step, which was loose. She gave a little shriek but righted herself.

'That needs mending, Tom. Can you do it?'

Tom reached into the tool-bag that he always kept near him, and took out a claw hammer and a bag of nails, all different lengths, and knocked two, four-inch nails through the board that made up the step. He looked up as he heard footsteps approaching.

'What's all the noise, Tom? Oh, I see, you've mended the step.' It was Albert Walker. 'I like to see someone who can use his head, instead of waiting to be told that a job needs doing. Mind you, I did tell that young lady of yours that she should be careful on those steps, in those shoes, isn't that so, Selina?'

Selina blushed at being spoken to, then realised that he was not really criticising her, just giving her a friendly warning.

'Yes, Mr Walker. I'm sorry Mr Walker. I'll put my other shoes on right away.'

She looked at him and saw that his eyes were exploring her body and this made her blush even more. She didn't want anyone but Tom looking at her like that! She turned and went up the steps to get her other shoes, feeling his eyes on her as she went. Albert Walker turned to Tom, who was apprehensive at first about what the gaffer might say to him.

'How did you get on with Harry, this morning, Tom? I hope he didn't work you too hard on your first day.'

Tom wondered how he knew what he had been doing. It must have been Jim Miller who told him, he thought, and then realised that it had all been arranged between Mr Walker and Jim, and wondered why. That's what gaffers do, he thought, they arrange your life for you, to suit them.

'I enjoyed it, Mr Walker. I enjoyed it very much.'

It was the truth, whether it had been arranged or not.

'Good, Tom. I like to see someone who is willing to have a go at something different. I can't stand these people who can only do one sort of job. I don't know how I would go on if I could only do one job. You can knock off, now. You've done enough for your first day. I don't want you exhausted already, do I?'

He turned on his heel and walked away leaving Tom puzzled. He had already knocked off, but had an expectation that he could be told to perform some task, at any time. He had never been told to stop work before; he had always worked until the hooter sounded and then, had run for the factory gate as if he were escaping. Life was different here, he thought. Not bad at all. If this was work, he could stand it, he had taken in the fact that the speed of work seemed slower here than in Willenhall, but between them, this afternoon, they had accomplished a great deal. There was more than one way of getting work done!

There was a lot to learn about work that he had never considered while working in the lock factory. Stones' just wanted as much as he could get, out of every worker, out of every hour, out of every machine, out of every square foot of factory space. In the country, there were acres of space for everyone who worked there. The things of nature; the light, the season and the weather decided the hours and type of work.

He wondered if it would be possible to apply the same sort of principles to working in the town. Probably not, the men and women of the Black Country wouldn't be able to make the adjustment, he thought. It would be interesting to try, though. He let his mind wander, his mind's eye seeing workers coming to work just before light, to save electricity, and going home just as it got dark. He laughed to himself. Your mind could get carried away if you weren't careful! That was one thing about the country though; you had time to think without wondering if the gaffer was peering round some corner to see if you were working your eyeballs off.

He let his mind move back to sexual things. That Emily had fancied him! Selina had let him know by the way she had spoken to the girl that he must have some sort of attraction to girls. It was an exciting thought. He made up his mind to flirt with Emily, the next opportunity that arose. There was that Kate as well. He felt sure she had been offering herself to him, as she posed with the bacon sandwich. The image of her body shape came into his mind and he responded to the feeling. It was a pleasant thought and a pleasant sensation.

'Well, I see you know a body when you see one, Tommy Barr. What do you think of it then? Would you like to hold me like you hold Selina? I bet you would, on the quiet! I bet you'd like a quick feel!' She took his hand and slid it across her breast, just for a moment, almost as if it was an accident. 'Here! We'll have none o' that! What sort of girl do you think I am?'

She shook herself free and gave him a playful push. What sort of girl was she? He couldn't believe she had done that. It had been nice, though. He knew he would like to do it again. He looked at her. Her face was red, but smiling, as if she had liked it too, but wanted to keep it a secret. He reached for her, to hold her again, and just managed to touch her shoulder when she moved away.

'Eh! That's enough. Off you go to your little beauty. That's enough, for now!'

Her hand touched his, and then she gave him a push. 'Sleep well, tonight, Tommy.'

'Goodnight, Kate.'

He leaned forward, conscious of his boldness and kissed her lightly on her cheek. Then he moved out into the sunshine, the last of the day. Selina was waiting for him. That was the most important thing, the thing he had been hurrying for when Kate stopped him.

There were too many girls! There was always one of them to think and feel about. Still, it was nice. It hadn't used to be like this when he was a boy. Then, he had been shy of girls to the point of actively disliking them

Was the way he felt any better? How could he answer that question? It was more exciting now, that was for sure!

9. Secret Betrothal.

Selina was on her own, working. She had never picked a hop in her life until yesterday. She still ached from the efforts she had made yesterday, to keep up with everyone. Why they called it a holiday she would never be able to work out.

She was standing in the shadow of the bines. They were a full eighteen-foot high, now; stretching into the distance; long green curtains with a dark green hue that left her feeling slightly breathless and dizzy.

Tom had gone off with Jim Miller, the busheller and Kate had gone off to work on her own, leaving Selina with no one to work with, no one to ask advice from and no one to talk to. She could see Kate talking to Jim, further along the row; somehow it didn't seem fair that she should be left on her own. She turned her attention to the hops in front of her, pulling the bine close to her, so that she could strip it easily. The skin on her hands was raw and fast becoming a dark yellowy black with the stain of the hop leaves. The colour wouldn't seem to wash out, although she had been told by others workers that it would come out, eventually!

She grabbed at the bottom of the bine and pulled it down to where she could work on it more easily. Her unaccustomed movements made her feel clumsy and she caught herself on a part of the growth, pulling a small slice of flesh from the back of her hand. She gave a cry of pain and lifted her hand to her lips, sucking on the sore spot. She cursed softly to herself. What a life!

There wasn't even anywhere for her to sit down to have a rest. This was not what she had had in mind when they had travelled down. It was not like the dreams she'd had before they started out. She had imagined a romantic arboreal scene, with the sunlight just warm enough for comfort and herself in the middle of a group of young people, all with romantic hopes, like herself. She turned her mind back to the small abrasion on the back of her hand, a low sob showing her self-indulgent mood at that moment.

'What's the matter, love?'

It was Kate. She had decided that working on your own wasn't as much fun as she'd hoped. Jim Miller had come and gone. She wouldn't get anything else out of him, today. She looked at Selina's hand, took it in hers and examined it closely, and then she spat on the back of it and rubbed it vigorously, then took hold of it more tightly. There was a small cleaner patch on the back of Selina's hand where the spittle had removed the surface dirt. She smiled at Selina.

'There you are my beauty. It'll soon get better now. It's no good making a fuss about every little scratch you get.' She didn't let go of Selina's hand. She just stood there, holding it. Then she bent her face to the scratch and kissed it.

'Doesn't that feel better, already? A bit o' spit and a kiss works wonders, my Mom used to tell me. You've got lovely hands; so soft for a factory girl. I bet you look after them. I bet Tom tells you all the time, don't he? There now, my little babby. Don't cry any more.'

She was emulating the 'baby talk' of mothers talking to children, but Selina could sense that there was an undercurrent to her talk. She was very tender, Selina thought, the way she was continuing to hold her hand but it didn't really seem at all motherly!

'Here, you are, love; here's another kiss to make you feel better all over. Don't you feel better all over?'

Selina did feel better but this time the kiss was not on her hand, it was on her cheek, a teasing sort of kiss that seemed to trail from her cheek to her lips, just for a split second, then travelled and teased across to the side of her neck, bringing strange sensations. A touch and move on; a touch and move on. She closed her eyes and allowed herself the pleasure of the feeling. A hand seemed to insinuate itself from round her waist, to her breast, it made her jump, then felt rather than heard reassurance from Kate. She felt a tension rise inside; she wanted more of this! Selina was fully aware of sex, and the effect that Harry and Tom had on her but she'd had no experience of sexual advances from another woman. Although the caresses were outside her experience she found them pleasant enough to not want them to stop. She found herself responding and her lips met Kate's, who moved her attention from her lips, back to her breast. She moved Selina's blouse, exposing her nipple, then Selina felt soft lips searching her nipple. It was too much. The feeling was too intense. She pulled away. Kate was looking at her strangely; a look she had never seen before. It frightened her.

'No! I've never done anything like that before. You shouldn't do that!'

Selina knew she should be horrified but she wasn't. She was just shocked. She just hadn't thought Kate was that way.

'No, I know I shouldn't do that.' Kate said, softly, 'It's just that a feeling came over me. I've never done anything like that, either. I just think you are so beautiful; you make me feel, I don't know, broody I suppose. You didn't seem to mind too much, either. Do you think we are a couple of, I don't know what they call them, women who like women? I've never thought so. Perhaps you can like men and women. I don't see what's wrong about it, do you? You hear of men who prefer men, don't you? Why shouldn't women like women?'

Kate put her hand on Selina's, tenderly. Selina didn't move it; just held Kate's hand, gently and thought out her reply. Kate continued. 'I don't suppose it's anything to worry about. It won't stop me liking Jim but it's nice to have a secret sort of love; someone you can turn to if you need someone to talk to. It's time we got something done, now! Something else, I mean!'

She turned to start picking again but Selina took her arm. 'Wait a minute, Kate. I was just getting used to that. It was nice. I wouldn't mind carrying on a bit longer.'

She slid her hand along Kate's arm and insinuated it inside the large baggy sleeve until she was touching the edge of Kate's breast, then she moved round to the back of her. This enabled Selina to slip her hand onto the nipple that was growing in response to her touch. Time stood still in the shadows in the hop yard as Selina touched her lips gently to the side of Kate's neck. They stayed standing, almost without movement; just the slightest move bringing about another electric thrill, taking them higher and higher emotionally. Selina allowed her hands to roam and search as if they had a mind of their own, finding places and encouragement from Kate, to the extent that she completely lost herself in the mystery, powerful passion and possession that she was experiencing.

The sun was starting to go down on the day and the bines were casting long shadows in the space between them. There was a sort of romantic atmosphere, and they both felt, in a way, that they had started a commitment that might last well into the foreseeable future. It was an unspoken commitment but just as real as if one of them had gone down on a knee and proposed. A look passed between them, a look that carried the scent of body and bine, shadow and shine. Now and forever, not to be confused with the feeling they had for the men in their lives. The moment came to an end, not a real end but a gap until the next occasion.

A shout caught their attention. It was Jim Miller. 'Come on you two! Get that last crib filled. It's time to weigh in. You won't earn much more, now.' He strode the last few paces and joining in, filled his bushel basket alongside them then emptying it into their crib. 'That's it. That's the lot for today. You've done well for a couple of beginners.'

Kate had picked hops before, but she didn't see why she should remind him. She glanced at Selina and touched her hand. It was like a secret betrothal, what they had done. That was what it was, a secret betrothal!

'I suppose we have done well. We must have earned a few bob, today. I suppose couples do this, don't they, Jim? Do you get many couples working together, Jim? Do you ever get secret betrothals among the pickers?'

She took another quick glance at Selina. The message had been received!

'Yes, o' course we do. That sort of thing goes on everywhere.

We even get queer blokes, sometimes. I don't take any notice, myself. Live an' let live, eh?'

They had arrived at the barns, now. Tom was standing looking out of the loading bay window, waving. He had been helping Harry again and had managed to impress him with the amount of work he had enabled them to get done, so Harry had told him to, 'Knock off.'

The weather continued the same for the next few days. They all had to go out and earn their money. It was the reason they were there, although the reason seemed to grow further from their minds. Sometimes they were together as a foursome; sometimes they were all alone, depending on the way the work had been allocated.

Today, the rain was pouring down Kate's neck. Her arms were aching. Her clothes were sticking to her body. Her feet were covered with mud. She had forgotten to bring a hat. The change in the weather had caught them all by surprise. She could see, looking along the drift, that others, too, were soaking wet. The busheller had just pressed her hops down in the crib and there weren't as many as she had thought. '

'There ain't enough in there, yet, young lady.'

Jim had said it smilingly but with but courtesy, and she wasn't at all pleased by it. Bloody yokel locals'd work in any conditions!

'I suppose you want blood as well, for your money,'

She gave him the tart reply. She knew he didn't benefit from the amount of hops she picked, but she was just feeling ill tempered. He didn't respond; just walked away, smiling.

Everything seemed to make her feel more determined to fill her crib as quickly as possible, to get as much pay as she could to pick up at the end of the season. She adjusted the rim of the large hat so that she could see better, and carried on picking.

She was angry with life for making it necessary for her to work like this, but she felt compelled to carry on, knowing that it was the only way she could achieve her ambition, to fill her bottom drawer with nice things to bring to her marriage, not that she had been asked; she just felt it was her duty to bring as much as she could to the union, when she was asked. One day, she thought, I will walk down the aisle of some posh church and all my friends will be envious, but she would have earned the right to the day of celebration.

Kate Myatt was twenty-two, unmarried, unattached, no immediate prospects but had an ever optimistic outlook. She knew, as surely as if it had been etched in copper, that she would meet a nice looking young man, fall in love and live happily ever after, just like all the heroines in the books did.

There were one or two young men here who would fill her list of requirements. Albert wouldn't do, of course; he was already married and he was too old. There was that chap Tom, who was with Selina. She wouldn't mind him playing games with her, the same as he played with Selina, and the same as she had played with him. She had shocked him! Come to think of it, she hadn't minded Selina playing games with her! What a mixture they all were!

She brought her attention back to the hops. Her crib was filling up nicely now. She seemed to do better when she let her mind wander. Her mind seemed to wander through sex filled fields and she allowed herself the pleasures of the thoughts and feelings that accompanied them. She smiled to herself, and as she did so, noticed Jim Miller, the busheller, looking at her again. She blushed, as she always did when a man looked at her.

For all her dreams of a grand wedding to some man she had never met, she was ill at ease in the company of men, feeling that they had the power to make her do things that she might, or might not, want to do. She had some suspicions of the things they might want her to do, but no idea what she might want them to do. Selina seemed to be more experienced in the company of men. The thought made her wonder; had Selina ever, done it? When she thought about it her hands seemed to want to caress her own body, like they did now. The busheller was still looking at her, smiling and, to try to take the tension out of the moment, she spoke, 'How is my crib now, Mr Miller?'

She felt stupid, asking the plain little question. She knew her crib was full, ready for the tally. Her overall was soaking wet and she was conscious of the way it revealed the shape of her body. She was one of the few women who picked on their own. Most women were part of a family group, picking together, as she had at first, with Selina, but then found that she preferred sometimes to be independent sometimes and count her own bushels. It was as if she were banking her own money! Anyway, Selina could be too much of a distraction!

'Your crib is fine, Catherine. I must be a poet, and don't know it.' He saw the look on her face and spoke again, more kindly, 'I mean it. You work harder than most so really, you should have the most; it's only fair you know, and I don't mean to be mocking your name. I just like saying it; it sounds like music to me. Which way do you say it? I like it better if you say it so that it rhymes with bine instead of bean, Catherine, Catherine, Catherine.'

He looked at her enquiringly, obviously sincere in his questioning. She had always been called Cathereen as if it rhymed with bean; the thought made her smile to herself, and he smiled with her. She wouldn't tell him.

'If you don't mind, I shall call you Catherine; that rhymes with fine and bine and shine.'

She was quite pleased really, that a man might notice her. She was used to being self-effacing, almost making herself invisible. The sun came out and shone on both their faces, making it seem a very significant moment. They seemed to be closer together without moving at all and their closeness did not seem to be an encroachment on each other's personal space. It was a pleasant closeness, she thought. He was holding her hands, looking at the way the picking was beginning to form callous on them, gently stroking, as if to try to make them go away.

'You should wear gloves. Nice hands, like yours shouldn't get like this you know. You should look after yourself, or I shall have to do it for you.'

He became silent; as if he were slightly embarrassed by the way he was talking. They had never spoken much, and then only about the details of their daily work, as required by their working relationship. She did not know what to say; she did not wish to reject him, to spurn him, as she romantically felt it would be, but she did not know whether to encourage him or not.

He was about ten years older than she was; she had heard that he had been in the Army with the Gaffer, in the Great War and had rendered him some great service, and been offered a job for life on the farm. He was, she realised, a 'catch'. She had never seen him in that way but now that she thought about it she wouldn't mind exploring the possibility.

She imagined herself walking down the aisle with him and the prospect seemed pleasant. Apart from that, he was quite good-looking, tall, broad-shouldered, with an air about him, she had never heard him raise his voice but people seemed to do what he told them to do. She knew he had been in the Army with Mr Walker, during the War. He must, she felt, have been of some importance. Mr Walker had been an officer she knew. Perhaps Jim had, too! He looked as if he wanted to say something but didn't know how to say it. He was still holding her hand.

She realised that it was up to her to respond but just stood there, blushing, then found that blushing was just the right thing to do. He held her hand more firmly and looked her in the eyes, and she saw that his eyes were as blue as cornflowers. She moved closer to him hesitantly, and answered him.

'I wouldn't mind if I had someone to look after me. I think it would be grand if someone cared enough, just to want to look after me.'

She couldn't believe she had said the words. How could she be so forward? She didn't know whether to snatch her hand away or let the heavenly pleasantness of the moment continue. She had lowered her eyes in embarrassment but found the courage to look at him. It was obvious that she had said the right thing. He was smiling.

'That'll be my job in future then, looking after you, my Catherine.'

She was flustered now. He was taking too much on himself, the cheek! Just because she had said she would like some one to look after her, he thought the job was his; and now speaking so possessively!

'I'm not your Catherine if you please, and I would be grateful if you wouldn't act as if I were.' He immediately looked contrite and lost the smile on his face. She listened to her own words and tempered them, trying to make amends for the sharpness with which she had spoken. 'It'd be manners if you asked; jumping in as if I was a bit o' spare washing, hanging on a washing-line; waiting for someone to take me in!'

Now his contriteness had a smile to it, as if he knew she had not meant to sound harsh.

'I'm sorry Catherine. I know I shouldn't have been so familiar but you did say it would be nice to have someone to look after you. All I wanted to do was apply for the job. You see, Catherine, it'd be nice to have someone on my arm, and with your lovely hazel eyes and your pretty smile you would look just right, there. Would you like to go for a walk after supper and we could talk about it some more?'

She was delighted! She had rarely been 'asked out' before. It made her feel good about herself. She thought carefully, and then answered him.

'Well Mr Miller, if all you want to do is go for a walk, I don't mind, and you won't mind if I bring a friend, will you?' She did not wait for his reply. 'I'll bring my friends, Selina and Tom, if they have nothing better to do, and I'll see you about eight o'clock. In the meantime, I've got a living to earn!'

She turned back to the bine that she was stripping of hops, leaving him standing there. He patted down the hops in the crib, almost as if it were a caress, testing for solidity, then spoke softly to her.

'You've done enough now, Catherine; more than enough.'

He walked away smiling, his face lit by the sudden Hereford sunshine. When he looked back, she was smiling too, and the sun came out from where it had been hiding behind the rain-cloud, and lit up her face. Why was it that, at times, the simplest of words and actions could make you feel so good?

She looked at the retreating figure of the countryman and a tearful, almost choking sensation came to her, crumbling her face with the intensity of the emotion. It was as if life was suddenly perfect, almost too good to last, and yet she felt somehow, that it would. She often thought of her life as a rag rug, with people and events all making a place for themselves on the dull, hessian backing material of her life. Jim and this day would be represented by a small jewel on a cutting from a rich coat and would shine out from the rest of the darker cuttings.

She stood trying to visualise the rag rug in her mind and the way that this summer had altered the pattern that was building up on it. There were a lot of fresh parts to it, this year! Jim Miller was a completely unknown person at the moment. She had not spoken to him in years past. She had just seen him as a figure who told the pickers when to start and when to stop work.

She wondered what he had done for Albert Walker, to make him so grateful that he had offered him a job for life. She imagined the conflict, and a tiny part of it, with two heroic figures, one carrying the other over a shoulder. Perhaps that was what had happened! She turned and started back on the long walk to the group of farm buildings. Perhaps she would never know; it was enough that he was taking an interest in her. Her pulse seemed to pick up speed; that was two men who had shown an interest! What would happen next?

The day had turned out nice. The rain had stopped now and there was steam rising from the bines and the promise of an exciting time tonight. She found she was hurrying without a real need. She wanted to see Selina again. She was missing her already. It had been really awful, working in the rain but it had been nice before when they were getting intimate with each other. His hand wandered without impulse, moving over her body. It was wonderful to know she had someone just of her own.

She moved her thoughts to Jim. It had been nice when he had

held her hand and called her Catherine. Not that they were betrothed like she and Selina were. That was special; really special.

10. Betrothal.

Selina was carrying the large bucket across the yard when she heard the shrill cry. Putting the bucket down gave her the chance to get her breath back and as she straightened up, and looked round, saw the source of the call. She let out her breath.

'Hallo Kate, what are you looking so excited about? You look as if you've just found a sovereign. Your face is all pink. Mind; it suits you.'

Kate was walking briskly across the farmyard to Selina, looking animated, her face red. When she spoke, she sounded out of breath.

'Jim Miller, you know, the busheller, has asked me to go for a walk with him. He held my hand, and said he wants to look after me. I told him I wouldn't go with him unless you and Tom came along as well, so please say you will come. We needn't go far. I don't want him getting ideas above his place in life! He's ever so nice, Selina, but I can't go with him on my own, not yet, anyway. Will Tom mind? You must ask him. I cannot and will not go without a chaperone!'

She looked so distraught about the situation that Selina could not help laughing to herself, but she did not want to mock Kate for fear that she hurt her feelings. She had reservations about the way Kate was acting. On the one hand she seemed to be completely naïve, seeking support from Selina; while at other times she appeared to very much the woman of the world. Either way, Selina liked her.

Her answer was quick and to the point. 'Don't you worry, Kate. Tom and I will come with you, and see fair play! Jim Miller, eh? You could do a lot worse. We'll make up a foursome tonight, shall we? We could walk down to that public house in the town. They serve hop-pickers don't they? Some pubs don't, I know. Perhaps Jim and Tom will buy us a drink. I like a glass of lemonade on a hot night, how about you? I'll go and sort it out with Tom when I've got this bucket of water heating. See you later then; just don't forget we are betrothed!'

She smiled mischievously at Kate, touching her on the arm. She picked up the heavy bucket and made her way across the farmyard. You would think Kate would have given me a hand she thought; then dismissed it. Kate's thoughts were elsewhere at the moment. Tom would like the change from monotonous routine, she knew. It would be the first time they had been away from the farm and she was looking forward to it for the difference in activity.

There are warm, moonlit nights on a Herefordshire late summer that are perfect for a walk and this was one of them. Tom had, of course, agreed to a walk to the village. The thought of acting as chaperone to Kate amused him. He had the idea that she could look after herself quite well. Jim Miller had appealed to him as good company so he welcomed the opportunity to get to know him better. Tom felt better in the company of someone who had power, even if only a small way. Somehow, he felt more at home, as if that was where he belonged.

The walk to the town occupied about half an hour and then the four of them sat round a table outside the inn. Their talk varied from opinions of the beer, the weather and the quality of the crop. Jim was explaining that the type of hops that were in favour at the moment were Fuggles. They had been introduced by a Mr Fuggle in the last century. The time went easily, becoming more comfortable as they gradually developed an easier way of being and talking with each other and succumbed to the drink.

'Hello, Jim, how are you?' It was a deep gentle voice that spoke from the shadows. They all looked round and saw a dark, gypsy like figure standing. He had on a white shirt, open to the waist, and a handkerchief on his head but that did not seem to make him easier to see. Jim Miller was the first one to speak.

'Evening Parson, I'm very well. How are you? What are you doing, creeping up on folk? Come and have a drink with us.'

Jim motioned to the table in a welcoming way. The figure moved and sat at the end of the table. He was nothing like any

Parson they had ever met; yet he had a certain air about him, an exotic air of mystery. He soon fitted in, after the introductions. He was entertaining, full of stories about this and that, about the weather in 1918 and the influenza epidemic that came with it, the drought in 1916, foot and mouth outbreaks, the way things should be done and not done. He told them about the weddings he had officiated at and the people he had 'married'. That was why he was called the Parson.

'Good folks, they are. I've known some as never bothered with a church wedding; just accepted that they were married, and that was good enough for them. Proper weddings, they were. Hop pole weddings are something like a celebration, with everyone joining in.

'Nothing like they church weddings! Oh no! You have the happy couple, or sometimes, couples if there was more than one wedding taking place. Bridesmaids, pageboys, matrons of honour, all dressed up with hop wreaths round their necks. All drinking as if their lives depended on it; with some of it bought by the Gaffer and the Missus. She always loves a hop-pole wedding, Jenny Walker does. Even Mr Walker has always come, when he's been invited. You can't beat a proper gypsy, hop pole wedding, with all the trimmings.'

Tom's imagination filled with the idea of Albert Walker dancing round a bonfire, and he smiled to himself. The Parson continued.

'When everyone is nice and merry I bring them all to attention, so to speak, and remind them of the seriousness of what they are there for. I have two bridesmaids, each holding the opposite ends of a decorated hop pole. Two pageboys hold another pole, one at each end. Then comes the ceremony, and I tell everybody present of the solemn nature of the proceedings, and the importance of the vows that are made by the participants.'

He paused, reached for his glass, went to take a draught then seemed to realise it was empty. 'Excuse me folks; I've got to get a refill.'

He went to turn but Tom stopped him, 'I'll see to that Parson. Just you sit comfortable. Does everyone want a drink?'

He picked up the glasses from the table, put them onto a tray and disappeared into the taproom. He felt good. This was the feeling that he had tried to explain to his mother, the feeling of benevolent power. The Parson was talking about him; Tom could hear him in the background of conversation.

'Nice young man, that. Not like some you get, with airs and graces. Which of you lovely young ladies gets to keep him? I bet you've got him hung, drawn, quartered and shared out between you. Let me see; I bet he belongs to you!'

He turned and pointed at Selina, who gasped in excitement and bewilderment.

'How did you know that, Parson?'

He stood there, curling the ends of his moustache, looking nonchalant, as if he had second sight to aid him in his judgement, not replying to her query. She suddenly remembered that he had been stood in the shadows before he had joined their company. She decided to let him have his moment, knowing that she had the secret to his second sight.

'You must have a gift in the shadows, if you can tell things like that, Parson.'

She spoke sincerely, but with a twinkle in her eye. The Parson looked at her and realised that he had been caught, but not delivered, and so he became her co-conspirator, to play the game with Kath.

'Aye lass, it's a gift right enough, but it has to be paid for in other ways. Many a time I've had to give a girl the bad news about the sort of young man she is carrying on with; take this one for instance.'

He turned to Jim, who had been silent for some time and was about to say something when Jim interrupted.

'Don't you dare! I'll tell them all of the time you convinced old Stallybrass that he had leprosy, you old fraud! And then you had the nerve to sell him a cure!'

His smile bespoke his serious tone of voice and they all started laughing. Then Tom was returning, with a tray full of drinks and sandwiches. The tray was quite a weight to carry across the turf, with five drinks, all with foam floating on the top. When the drinks had been shared out, the Parson returned to his theme.

'Well, it worked didn't it?' He changed the subject slightly. 'Mrs Walker, Jenny I calls her, loves a hop pole wedding; gives her a chance for a bit of romance, not that she would be unfaithful mind, but it puts her in the mood, if you know what I mean. I'm not saying I would turn my back on her if she were offered on a plate, if you know what I mean. To tell the truth, I don't know what I mean, if you know what I mean!' He seemed to pull himself together, as if he were trying to get his story straight as he told it.

'Albert Walker is the other way, always concerned what other folk might say about him. He wants to be seen as the upright citizen, but he's got feelings, just like anybody else. I've seen him looking at the young pickers. His eyes give him away, just like anybody else's eyes do. You can't hide the way you feel, can you? I bet you've seen the look in his eye, ain't you, young lady?' He took a drink of his ale and winked at Selina, when she blushed.

'He says he doesn't approve, but he's always there, just to keep an eye on things, he says, so nobody comes to any harm. To give him his due, he usually buys his share of the ale, but he won't stand for a wedding this early in the season, so if you four are thinking of it, wait for a few weeks, 'til the hops is gathered in, then you'll really celebrate!'

Kate and Selina looked at each other and laughed. No one had suggested the idea of a wedding! Jim and Tom looked at the Parson then Tom spoke.

'Nobody asked you to arrange anything. If you want a wedding, get married yourself. Me and Selina are getting married when we are ready, when we go home, at the end of the season – if I ask her, and if she wants me!'

He looked at the Parson who was bent over, laughing. He stood up and slapped Tom on the arm.

'If you could have seen your face then, young Tom! I really caught you on the hop then, didn't I? I know as well as you that you wouldn't be interested in a wedding. I was just playing. Don't take me too seriously, Tom. I'm always playing around.'

Tom caught the look that Selina was giving him. She seemed to be suggesting, with just a lift of her eyebrows, that he should give serious thought to the idea of a hop pole wedding. He wasn't used to being told what to think, especially just by the raising of eyebrows; he didn't know if he liked it, but when he thought about it, the thought of the wedding and the implications of what would follow seemed very attractive. He didn't know which way to jump, if he went one way, the Parson had caught him, if he went the other way, Selina had. The drink had filled him with excitement and enthusiasm. He came to a decision.

'Who said I wouldn't be interested in a wedding, Parson? Sounds like it might be a good idea, eh Selina? How does it work? What actually happens then?'

He looked round the group of drinkers. They, like himself, had been drinking and were all in a gay mood; ready for any challenge that might come their way. The Parson too, glanced at each of their faces and read the possibilities for having his palm crossed with a bit of silver from these wanters. He started to tell them again, of the way the ceremony was carried out; in his own imaginative way, of course. There was not a proper or correct way because the whole ritual was outside the law and lacking in legal recognition. He decided to enhance the proceedings and introduce some complications. His face was serious as he spoke.

'Every body is brought together in an organised way, with the bride and groom all decked out for the occasion, then, when everybody has been told of the awful consequences of breaking the solemn vows they are about to agree to, the music starts and everyone begins to dance. Not quicksteps or foxtrots, mind you; the old dances that come from just the listening to the music, so you just want to move, slowly at first, then faster and faster, and then it stops, and the most important bit of the wedding takes place.'

'What's that, Parson? What's the most important bit?'

It was Kate, and when everyone looked at her, she blushed, bright crimson, as if realising her unintentional double entendre.

'The most important part is when the couple jump over the pole, o' course. What did you think it was, eh?' The Parson winked at her again, making her feel like a young maid, then continued. 'The jump shows that that they have moved, in an instant, in what they call a symbolic way, from their single world, to their double world. On one side of the pole they is free, and have no responsibilities. After they have agreed to the vows and jumped the pole, they is never the same again; they have someone to look after and someone to be looked after by. Never again can they look at other men or women. They have to be content with the one they took the vows with.'

He paused to let his words sink in, and the crowd were silent.

'Sounds all right to me! I wouldn't mind doing that, with the right girl of course, if I could find a nice girl'. It was Jim speaking, in a cajoling way, 'My old granny says you can't find a nice girl nowadays. What do you think, Tom?'

Tom dodged as Kate's handbag flew through the air towards him.

'I think you're right, Jim. It's dangerous, even being in the same company as some of them. You could get seriously hurt if you spoke out of place, never mind if you offered to try to make honest women of them!'

Selina stood up, arms akimbo, a challenge in her eyes. 'Well Tommy Barr, if you don't think I'm the sort of girl you want to mix with, you knows what you can do!'

She put on the countenance of mock seriousness that matched her words, but beneath the play, Tom could detect an unspoken challenge and he responded immediately.

'How could I fail to recognise the girl of my dreams? Anytime you want, we'll jump the pole together, and find eternal happiness.' The decision made, he went down on one knee and looked up at her imploringly, then took her hand. 'Selina, will you have me to jump the pole with, 'til we're too old to jump?' He reached up and pulled her down to sit on his knee then in serious face he asked her again. 'Come on old girl, it'll be a bit of fun at the end of the season. A chance for a party, a drink and a dance, and I bet the gaffer's missus will lay on a bit o' grub for us.'

She looked at him deeply, and nodded, smiling. There was a clapping and they turned to see that all the occupants of the public house had turned out to witness their betrothal, for that was what it meant. The mood of the night seemed to bring everyone together, Jim Miller let out a roar,

'Hurrah! They've gone and done it! Tom and Selina are getting wed! Eh, wait a minute. You can't do this on your own! We'll make it a double! What do you say, Kate; are you game? Will you jump the pole with me? I told you that all I wanted was to look after you. Will you let me?' He picked up her hand and held it to his lips as he lowered his voice and repeated his question, 'Catherine, will you let me look after you, for life?'

Everyone waited for her answer, and when she whispered, 'Yes', the roar went up again from the crowd.

The rest of the night was just a blur. The ale flowed, the songs were louder and longer, the words easier to sing. The intimacies between lovers, supposedly unseen by others, were seen and ignored in the custom of the time. Plans for the wedding and the life thereafter were made, changed, settled upon and changed again.

They all wanted to be involved in the arrangements for the wedding, but no one seemed to want to make decisions. Both of the girls getting married wanted white weddings but neither of them had much money tucked away to provide them. The men would just have white shirts, open in gypsy fashion.

The discussion about the arrangements continued all the way home, sometimes agreeing in a delightful way, it seemed to them, and sometimes arguing, to create a sort of hierarchy of importance, to see whose opinion counted for the most. The journey took them over an hour, singing and dancing, and holding each other. Finally, Tom and Selina collapsed into their beds, exhausted in spite of their youth. In a few moments they were both fast asleep. Outside, Kate stayed with Jim a little longer, in the shadow of the barn, making plans as lovers do. They gradually became closer in the shadows as they allowed each other more freedom with their bodies.

The next day went quickly, all of them suffering the effects of the drinking, the night before. Later in the day, Selina and Kate approached Jenny Walker as she was cooking her evening meal.

'Mrs Walker, er, Jenny. Kate and I have some plans. We wondered if you would help us with them.'

Selina fell silent. Jenny Walker looked at them both sharply then invited them into the farmhouse kitchen.

'Perhaps you'd better tell me all about them, then, starting at the beginning.'

Selina, hesitant at the start, suddenly blurted it all out. 'We are getting married, well, not married; we're having a hop pole wedding. Both of us; Kate and me. Tom and me and Kate and Jim Miller. Not now; at the end of the picking so we don't interfere with the picking. We don't have wedding dresses or anything. We wondered if you knew anywhere we could borrow the things we need.'

She stopped, but Kate carried on her theme. 'I've got some money laid by for my bottom drawer but it isn't very much, so if you know a second-hand shop in Bromyard that might have dresses for us to wear?'

Kate had always had to pay for everything herself, had to earn the money, then pay for it. She was genuinely scared to ask for anything at all. She had been refused so many times that she had now come to think that it was no good asking for anything. She stood by as Selina spoke quietly and persuasively to Mrs Walker.

Jenny Walker had noticed the look in Kate's eyes and recognised what it meant. She too had been in a similar position when she had thought that she had no right to ask for anything. She had come past that situation now, and was determined to help the young woman. She thought hard about how to help them then thought about all the clothes she had got, hidden away in wardrobes and old chests. Either of these young women would enhance her old things! It would do Albert good, too. He was getting too much of an old stick in the mud; she would soon put him right!

Jenny looked at the young girls, their faces revealing half-innocent, half-knowing young women. She seemed stern to them, as if she could command them to do anything, without argument. Then she swept them both into her arms.

'How lovely, my lovelies! How lovely! How lovely! How lovely!'

They thought she would never stop saying the phrase. Her face seemed to light up with the anticipation of the ceremony, and all its implications. They did not know that she had been in a hop pole wedding ceremony herself, as a young girl. She, more than anyone, would be able to tell both of them how to prepare.

'Just you come with me, my young beauties, and we'll see what we can find.'

She led them up the stairs, past the first floor, into the attic in the roof. It was dark and shadowy and seemed a little creepy to the girls.

'Come here; I'll open the curtains so we can see a bit better.'

She turned to them, still smiling; she seemed to be wearing her smile as if it were Sunday, thought Selina. She smiled to herself then realised that she was doing the same thing. She looked at her companions again. Each of them had happy looks imprinted. Why not, she thought, why not?

She could not remember ever having been so happy. She had Tom, and she had Kate! Most girls were still mourning men lost in the war. She had lost an uncle, a brother of her mother's, but she had not felt the grief that most other girls were feeling in this September of 1923. She had known other young men from

Willenhall who had never returned; boys and schoolmasters; shopkeepers and their assistants; distant relatives, but she had never felt the deep agony that many endured. Her thoughts returned to the present. How was Jenny going to help them?

Jenny was handing Kate a most beautiful dress and Kate was handing it to her. This was a creation, a work of art. She turned her back, let her own blouse and skirt drop onto the dusty floor and allowed Kate to put the dress over her head. It fitted. She knew instinctively that the dress was Jenny's wedding dress. They were of a similar height, Jenny being a little shorter and although Jenny had put weight on since she had worn the dress, you could see that the dress had been made for her. Selina felt that her additional height, making the dress look slightly shorter would make the dress look more fashionable, now.

The white dress had a full skirt that was longer at the back than at the front, so that the bridesmaids had something to catch hold of. The sleeves were slightly puffy without being bulbous. They were finished in bows of silk in shiny silver white. The waist was caught with a large bow at the back that became a plain belt for the front. Selina looked round for the shoes that she felt certain would be with the dress, and saw them in the bottom of the wardrobe, still in the box in which they had been bought, dainty silvery white with a small matching bow at the front. She slipped her feet into them and lifted the dress so that she could see them. Her eyes lifted to the mirror; she looked beautiful! She gave a twirl and as she turned, noticed a tear in Jenny's eye.

'It's lovely, Jenny. I have never worn anything so beautiful. You are not going to let me wear it, are you? You are, aren't you?'

She moved over to where a large dressing mirror stood, near the window. She tried to see herself but the mirror was covered with dust, impeding her view. Kate moved forward, dusted the mirror gently and turned it on its hinges, allowing Selina a full frontal view of herself. She took in a deep breath. The girl in the mirror was beautiful; old fashioned perhaps but still beautiful. Jenny and Kate were staring. Selina had never had anyone stare at her, before. Kate broke the silence.

'I've never seen you look like that, Selina. I could fall for you myself!'

She whispered the last sentence as if it were a secret, thought Selina. Jenny was standing transfixed, as if she were trying to turn the clock back and Selina felt strangely as if she were privy to the thoughts of the other two and was pleased with what she now knew. The sun seemed to go behind a cloud, darkening the long attic room and the effect was to bring the three women back to normality.

'I don't think I shall have to make any alterations to that one, do you, my dear?'

Jenny turned to Kate for confirmation of her own thoughts as she stood looking at Selina.

'No, no Mrs Walker. I think it looks absolutely gorgeous as it is. Oh, Mrs Walker, it's wonderful'

She gave a little shriek to cover up the tiniest feeling of envy that she had felt upon seeing her friend in the sumptuous outfit. She picked up the other pair of shoes that lay on the floor. Anything rather than admit to these terrible feelings! The trying on of the shoes allowed the three of them to collect their feelings and thoughts and within a few seconds they all looked quite normal.

Then it was Kate's turn. Mrs Walker pulled out an ivory dress that, like the wedding dress, seemed to fit first time. Kate looked into the wardrobe to see if there was anything else that she could see that might suit her, but came to the conclusion that Mrs Walker knew what she was doing when it came to choosing dresses. The ivory dress was a wedding dress, but looked as if it had never been used. She slipped out of her top clothes and allowed the dress to be poured over her shoulders. Then she walked over to the mirror and let her eyes wander over her reflection.

What she saw satisfied her. The top didn't expose her bust line exactly but seemed to accentuate it. The dress bunched up at the upper arms slightly, concealing them, to her approval, because she had always felt that her arms were too chubby. The ivory tint enhanced her natural colouring, giving an exotic Mediterranean look to her appearance. Her dark hair lay on her shoulders with just a gentle wave as it lay. She turned to the others, seeking their judgement; getting wholehearted approval.

'Oh Kate, it's just right for you!'

Selina was thrilled by her friend's appearance and her sincerity came through in a transparent way. Kate felt a sob of happiness and turned to Jenny Walker for confirmation of what she was thinking about herself. To her surprise, Jenny was crying.

'Why, what on earth is the matter, Mrs Walker? The dress is lovely; don't you think so?'

Mrs Walker tried to explain. 'Our son Robin was going to get married when the war was over, but he died in one of the last aerial engagements of the war, and his fiancé died of influenza in 1918. That's the dress that she was going to wear for their wedding.' She started crying again and then seemed to get a hold of her feelings. 'At least I know what she would have looked like. She was very like you, you know.'

Kate didn't know how to respond to Jenny's outpouring of grief at first. Would it upset Jenny if she were to wear the dress? She looked at Jenny again. She was silent, now. Anybody would be, she thought.

'It's a lovely dress, Mrs Walker, and I would be honoured to wear it, but if it would upset you, I wouldn't dream of getting married in it.'

She stepped back, trying to avoid attention being drawn to herself. Mrs Walker smiled.

'Of course you shall wear it, my dear. You will look absolutely a dream in it.'

They all seemed to accept the idea that the dresses that Mrs Walker had shown them would be suitable. Kate was the one to realise that the young men would have nothing to wear.

Jenny put her mind at rest. 'That's no problem at all. You will find that there are all sorts of men's clothes in the large wardrobe at the other end of the attic. All they have to do is come up and choose something. You might find that they don't want anything too flashy. It might make the ceremony too real for their taste, when it's only a bit of fun.'

She didn't show them what was available for the men but led them back down the stairs. Albert Walker was just entering the house. He looked at them quizzically but didn't comment on their being there, just nodded and passed into the kitchen of the large farmhouse. Jenny led the girls to the front door.

She lowered her voice as if what she was saying was a secret. 'I'm so glad we were able to find something to suit you both. I've got to see to Albert's dinner, now. I'll see you tomorrow.'

She gave them a quick, meaningful look, closed the door on them and went back into the kitchen. She didn't want them to know how she was grieving for her son and his fiancé. Albert knew the reality of her pain but she could share it with no one else; when would the pain ever leave her?

11. Preparations for the Wedding.

'Well! She's a strange one at times.'

Kate voiced their feelings. Jenny Walker was like a disconnected person at times. She was never hostile, but she seemed to change her character. What could be the explanation? There was no sense brooding on it, Selina thought. The answer would unfold; she felt sure it would. Kate brought her into the present time.

'Shall we tell Tom and Jim?'

Why had Kate said Tom and Jim? If Jim were the most important one in Kate's mind, she would have said Jim and Tom! Why do I always try to discover a different meaning from the words that people use? Selina felt that she was always analysing what people said.

'No, definitely not; not yet anyway.' Kate answered. 'If we do that, they will get all excited and want to go up into the attic or they might not like us making such a drama of it, and cancel the whole thing. Tom can be funny at times, like Jenny I suppose.'

In the kitchen Jenny Walker was still brooding about the dresses. How fashions had changed since she was a young girl! What a difference money makes to the style of dress that could be utilised? She recalled the wedding of Lady Elizabeth Bowes-Lyon, earlier in the year.

She had worn a Nottingham machine-made lace copy of a classical Malines pattern of the lace of the late Eighteenth Century incorporated in the dress, which had been designed by Madame Handley-Seymour. It was made of ivory chiffon mousmé, a new material of watered, satin-faced georgette. In a break from tradition, the sleeves had been 'baby' sleeves and the bodice had been embroidered with silver and pearls. A veil of Brussels lace that had been lent to her by the Queen topped the whole ensemble and a wreath of bog-myrtle along with bunches of orange-blossom and white roses completed the picture. The eight bridesmaids made the whole affair look like something out of a fairy story.

Jenny sighed to herself; what wouldn't she give to have another wedding? She had always been a hopeless romantic, and the slightest romantic happening made her become obsessed with the event. One thing she knew, she preferred her girl's shapes. The fashionable boyish look was detrimental to the female form and she would never have worn anything like that. A woman should look like a woman!

She knew that Lady Bowes-Lyon had had a four-tier wedding cake, made by the biscuit company, McVitie and Price and that the knife to cut it had been eighteen inches in length. Tom and Selina would have to be happy with whatever she could find for them.

Her hands flew among the ingredients for the wedding cake. She was going to make something special; nothing as grand as the Duke and Duchess of York's of course, but you couldn't expect to be able to compete with them. Their cake had weighed in at over seven hundredweight and had been nine feet tall. She stood back from the kitchen table and tried to envisage it. It wouldn't have had room to stand up in this kitchen, even if you had placed it on the floor.

They had received all sorts of presents too, a dozen cigarette cases and four snuffboxes, along with nineteen clocks and two pianos, never mind all the other gifts. Sometimes it didn't seem fair.

There was a sound from the living room. It was Albert. In her deeply absorbed state of mind she hadn't noticed him go out! His head appeared in the doorway.

'What are you doing, Jen? Any chance of a cup of tea? You making the Christmas cake? I thought you'd done that, earlier in the year. Thanks, love.'

As she handed him the large teacup, she placed a few biscuits on a plate at the corner of the table. Albert stood uncertainly, silently. He had walked out on Jenny, yesterday and they hadn't made the quarrel up yet. Not that it had been a proper quarrel. He had just been placed in a defensive position about the possibility of his thoughts regarding Selina and the other young female hop-pickers. She had picked on thoughts that he had thought were known only to him.

'Nice cup o' tea, Jen.'

This was his olive branch, murmuring a few words of approval. He wondered what the cake was for. She was silent but her arm seemed to move with more vigour as she stirred the cake mix. This cake would just have one layer, with a decoration of some sort crowning it. She looked up; he was still there, trying to repair the damage he had done yesterday. Silly old fool! As if she would ever fall out with him. Albert sighed and decided to drop his attempt at reconciliation. Least said, soonest mended. The yard was awaiting his attention. If Jenny couldn't give him a decent word, well, that was up to her.

'See you later, Jen.'

He stood and walked out. He was feeling frustrated lately. It had been some time since he and Jenny had made love. He walked round to the front of the house to get a drink of milk from the little room they called the 'farm shop'.

'Hello, Mr Walker, come to buy something?'

It was Emily, cracking one of her little jokes. She always made him feel that she had two meaning when she spoke. She was sitting on a bale of hay, leaning back against another as if she were about to have her picture painted. She was a little temptress, she was, and it would serve her right if someone took her up on the other meaning in her words. The thought translated into words.

'What are you offering then, Emily? Any bargains going today?' He walked over and touched her. 'This looks like a nice bit of arm. How much do you want for it, eh?' He stroked her arm and she made no attempt to move it. He went on. 'This looks like a nice length of leg as well, but I never buy until I have seen the whole of the animal.'

He put his hand on her skirt and lifted it over her knee, exposing her thigh. She stood and lifted her skirt so that both legs were open to his view.

'Why buy one when you can have both, Mr Walker. I say, with legs, two always looks better than one, don't you? You might get a discount for quantity as well.'

She lifted them further until he could see the top of her thighs. She took his hand and placed it on her leg. He could see that the young girl was getting excited.

'Does that feel like a bit of good meat, then, Mr Walker? Would you like to make an offer?' She was laughing at him but she wasn't moving away; she was moving closer. 'Are there any other cuts you would like to see? How about a nice bit o' topside, then?'

She pushed out her buttocks. It was too near the bone for Albert. He removed his hand from what suddenly seemed to be a very hot thigh and turned on his heel, not willing to test his suddenly aroused body with the young girl. The possible consequences would not be worth the risk. He picked up the measuring jug and poured himself a mug full of the cool liquid.

'You can't beat a drop o' the good stuff.' He smiled at the young woman. 'Oh well, I had better check on the pickers. The gypsies should be arriving soon. I just hope we don't have a strike this year. If we do, I'll just send them packing. I shan't stand them again! The Parson and his family came last week, but I am expecting the Smith's family to arrive. I suppose there'll be sparks flying then. See you later, Emily.'

He strode out of the room, forgetting her as he went out of the door. Other things were encroaching on his mind. He had discerned the purpose for the presence of the two young women in the kitchen. Jenny was baking a wedding cake! They had obviously been to see about a wedding; it must be a hop pole wedding! Jenny must know that he would find out sooner or later, but he had found out without being told. All he had to do now was to be patient and the news would be given to him. He could pretend to be shocked, then. He smiled to himself. There'd be a party at the end of the season.

It was just a pity that Emily wasn't getting married; that was what she needed, before she was tempted away by the other attractions available during the picking season. It had been a tempting but dangerous situation that he had walked away from. He would have to see what he could arrange for her. There were a number of men among the locals who might be attracted by Emily. It was a nice problem. If Kate hadn't come to work, he might have encouraged Jim to have a look at Emily but as it was, he was far too old for her.

Emily stood staring after him for a moment, and then smiled ruefully. He had been roused; that was what she had noticed, then he had walked from her! When was someone going to notice her! She had all these strange feelings but no one seemed interested. She had seen the bull being led to a cow and it had made her feel the strangest sensations, as if she wished, in a way, that she could change places with the cow! What a terrible thought! It was a good job she didn't have to make a confession like them Catholics; she wouldn't know how to put it! She giggled in vicarious excitement and smoothed her long black skirt back down over her legs. What would she have to do to get the same excitement from a man?

She had an idea what men did with women but she had never seen it done. Come to think, when would she be likely to see it? She didn't really like the long skirt that her mother made her wear. It made her feel that she was hiding her body, and she didn't want to do that. She wanted to dance and shout and tell everyone that Emily was grown up and what were they going to do about it?

She would go to the gypsy and have her fortune told, when they arrived. She knew they were close. Perhaps she would be able to tell her something, or give her a charm. She had heard that gypsies had charms for almost anything; to get rid of warts, to find out who you were going to fall in love with, to attract a lover. She always wanted the thing immediately, whenever she thought of it. Her mother had told her not to be silly. Some things were better when you had waited a while. Mother must know. She had waited for father when he had been away in the war.

In the distance she could hear the traces of wagons. She could hear the greeting of the great shire horses. Horses were friendly to their own kind; always whinnying out a welcome before they were in sight. It made her excited. She looked through the window and she could see, in the distance, the bowed tops of three Romany caravans. Two of them were yellow and the other was red so they must have got their yellow paint at a discount. She set about making herself neat and tidy. They would want fresh milk and bread. They didn't make their own when they were on the move. She looked through the window again and saw them draw into a triangle in the corner of the nearest meadow, close to the hop fields. Two small children and a youth dropped off the back of the last caravan and started walking towards the house. Emily was nervous; she had never had much to do with gypsies. They walked into the room, separating immediately, the eldest coming over to her.

'Hello, my lovely. How long have you been working here, then? I haven't seen you before. I would have remembered a pretty girl like you.'

Emily was on her guard. People didn't usually speak to her in that nice, flattering way. She looked round to see what the younger children were doing. They were fiddling with the stock.

'Oy!' she shouted, 'What do you think you are doing? If you want anything, come and pay for it.'

The youth ignored the children. He was looking at Emily. 'I think I'm falling in love. I've never done that before, have you?

Emily stopped and gave him an appraising look. She hadn't really taken much notice of him. He was dressed in an open-necked white shirt, embroidered on the front. His boots were long, covering his calves. He was darkly handsome, a proper gypsy. He was looking at her, paying her attention. He moved closer to her, making the moment more intimate. Emily had her attention on the young boy. She noticed that the young gypsy smelled as if he had just walked out of a stable.

'Did you hear what I said? If you want it, you have to pay for it.'

She was talking to the young boy who had his hands all over the chocolate bars. He walked over to her.

'Yes, can I have a bar?'

He looked at Emily, not at the youth. Emily didn't know what to say. She felt that he was trying to trick her in some way, but all he was doing was asking if he could have one. Of course he could have one, if he paid for it! She opened her mouth.

'Yes, of course you can have one, if you pay for it.'

The small boy picked up two bars and threw one to the girl, who seemed as if she were his sister. He undid the bar and put it in his mouth.

'Pay the lady, Ike.' The small boy said, and walked out of the room. Emily didn't know what to do. She didn't want to leave the others in the room while she chased the boy. She stood her ground.

'That'll be sixpence please.' Her heart banging in her breast she faced the youth. She felt sure he was with the two young children.

'It's nothing to do with me. I don't know them.' He looked her right in the eyes. 'I heard you say they could have the bars if they paid for them, and then he ran off. I never said I would pay for them!' He stood there, stony-faced for a minute, it seemed, and then his face broke into a smile. 'I will, though. I will pay for them, just this once. Do you see how easy it is to trick people? That was my brother Jack and my sister Karen; either of them could rob a bank without blinking.'

His face broke into a grin. He seemed very good looking. Emily returned his look. Suddenly, things had turned out brighter than she had thought, today. Perhaps she would be able to dance at this hop pole wedding they were all going on about!

'What's your name?' She asked, on impulse. She wanted suddenly to know more about the young man. Perhaps there was a potential for the future. She had to reach out, somehow, to find out.

'Ike; well, Isaac, I am named for a Bible character. Nobody mentions the character, and they have shortened my name to Ike. That's good enough for me. Short, sharp and to the point. I know your name. It's Emily. You live in Bromyard. I know 'cos I always get Jack to find out what he can about a place, before we stop. My Dad is a high-class gypsy. I could be king of the gypsies, one day. We are moving in today, for the hop picking; we shall be here for about a month, I expect. We are always on the move, you know. It's the way we live, not tied down to one spot like you lot.'

He closed his mouth and picked up a straw, seeming to get great benefit from sucking the golden tube.

'Why do you do that?' She asked suddenly, wondering why he kept picking up the straws.

'Because I want to, well, it's because I haven't got a cigarette and anything is better than nothing.'

Emily reached into her overall pocket and pulling out a packet of five Woodbines, offered them to him. 'Here you are, then. Have one of mine until you've got some. You can always give me one of yours, then, can't you?'

The young man took the proffered cigarette and slid it into his mouth. It was obvious that he was gasping for it.

'Why haven't you got some, then, Ike? Can't you afford them? I can't afford them either, but I started smoking last year. My Dad'd kill me if he knew I smoked.'

Emily suddenly felt powerful, as if she had the power to give or deny what Ike wanted. She slid a cigarette from the packet for herself and put her lips forward, anticipating that Ike would light it for her.

Instead, she felt his arm around her shoulder, pulling her towards him. She allowed herself to be moved, and then felt his other hand on her waist, and her whole body seemed to be pressed against his. She could feel every lump of him and it gave her strange feelings. She suddenly felt insecure, unsafe, but still liking, no, thrilled by the closeness of one to the other.

She closed her eyes; that was what the film stars did. His lips touched her. They were not what she expected. She had taken out the cigarette and pursed her lips as a preparation for the kiss but she was surprised when she felt his lips on her neck. They brought a strange tingling to her. He moved his lips to a different part of her neck and she felt herself go weak around her legs. She held onto him to prevent herself falling, and his hand made its way to her breast. The feeling was incredible. She felt that she didn't want him to stop, ever. He moved away from her and she opened her eyes. He was standing, just looking at her.

'You are lovely, Emily, just like a picture. I shall have to go, before I get tempted by you. You could get me to do anything, right or wrong, you know.'

He moved away a bit further and she felt he might run out of the door. In the small moment that she stood appraising him, she realised that his words were meant to bring about some agreement from her, about something, she didn't know what. Perhaps he wanted her to say the same as he had just said, then she would be putty in his hands, ready to do anything he asked! She brought herself back to the moment.

'Well, all I want you to do is to pay for that chocolate that your brother and sister took. If you don't, I shall ask Mr Walker to get the money from you!'

She had a feeling now, of how she might have been manipulated. He had already had a cigarette from her. If she went along with his clever suggestions, she might give him half of the stock – and lose her job. She stood her ground, her hand held out. She felt that she had done something clever. He held his hand out with a shilling in it.

She took it and smiled. 'Thank you. It was nice to meet you. If there's nothing else, I am closing the shop now.' She took his arm and steered him out of the door. 'The shop is open again at five o'clock tomorrow, for an hour. See you again.'

She spoke in a businesslike way as she moved him out, and

locked the door behind her. She turned and he was standing beside her. She felt her legs tremble again. Why should an ignorant stranger make her feel like this? She moved away silently, still feeling anxious as she entered the farmhouse kitchen to hand in the keys. She knew without looking that he was still staring after her.

12. The Hop Pole Wedding.

The news of the impending hop pole wedding went round the farm workers like a forest blaze. There were no formal invitations; everyone knew they would be welcome and that a small gift would be expected. It was arranged, after consultation with Albert and Jenny Walker, that it would be the last Saturday in September, the day before they went home. The picking would be finished by then and there would be little time left before they all made their way back home to Birmingham and the Black Country.

Kate and Jim were seen together as often as work allowed, and Selina and Tom were always in each other's company. It was the first time that a double ceremony had been carried out on the farm so there was a good deal of excitement.

Selina and Tom, although they were often with each other, were shy, less impetuous with the closeness and intimacy of each other's body space. There was a sense of saving themselves for after the ceremony. This was especially true for Selina for, although she was more experienced than Tom, she wanted their first real intimacy to be as if it were her first, too.

Tom willingly went along with this unspoken concept of virginity; he was proud to think that he was going to be the first man that she had known. He had little idea of how he was supposed to behave; simply relying on what he thought would be natural body responses. They never spoke upon the subject, each hoping for the best.

Jim and Kate were also treating each other in an 'honourable' way, avoiding too much closeness, each not wanting to be the one to initiate an intimacy that led via frustration to the final familiarity of intercourse. Jim was the experienced one in their relationship, having been in the Army, in France, during the Great War, and having met many young women during that time. Although he wanted Kate in an honourable way, Jim was very aware of Selina as a desirable woman. He felt that she was more experienced than she was letting on, and she kept coming into his thoughts. Selina was a sensuous woman who had sexually physical needs, and although her body wanted Tom, it was also aware of Jim, and it was as if they had decided to keep apart for that very reason. They were never in each other's company unless the other one's partner was there too.

Both couples were preparing for the ceremony in their own way. Tom asked Albert Walker if he could do more work, to try to build up his small supply of money, to buy drinks for their guests. He would then 'sub' his wage on the day of the wedding. Selina continued saving for her 'bottom drawer', although being aware that the ritual that they might go through was illegal and might be regarded as just a bit of fun. She had no real lasting confidence that it might be the precursor to a lifelong relationship, although that likelihood seemed a wonderful dream.

Jim and Kate had a tin box in which they put a few coins as often as they thought about it. Kate had not informed Jim of her own private savings. She kept that separate and secret, not feeling sufficiently trusting towards any man to tell about it. The time sped; the days were long, with little leisure time, but the four of them usually managed to walk down to the village pub on Saturday nights for a singsong, when the Parson would bring the wedding to their attention.

'What ho, Jim,' he would say, 'I hope you got a bit o' silver tucked away now. You're going to need it, come the end o' the picking.'

He was the prime factor in the drive towards the wedding ceremony, and he kept the half-serious plan alive in their minds. There was the potential for a profit and he didn't want to lose it.

The novelty of the event was beginning to wear off now, for all four of them, although they had not actually cancelled the event. They all knew that it had no lasting significance and that even if it had; there was no place for them to set up some sort of home. The problem started to encroach on their normally easygoing relationships, with quarrels flaring up over trivial reasons and as quickly being made up. Any advance by Tom was seen by Selina as trying to take advantage of her in the situation, whilst any lack of loving attention was seen as proof that he did not care for her.

Matters were at their worst at break of day, when they first awoke, often in each other's arms, wanting each other but being unwilling or unable, to make the first concession. At least, when the day's work was done, and they had been in each other's company, they could relax a little. Matters came to a head on the Friday evening before the day of the wedding. They were both frustrated by the way things were working out.

*

Tom walked across the farmyard toward the barn. His feet were aching. His boots, suitable for walking round a factory floor were not ideal for country living. It was the end of September. Nearly all the bines had been stripped and the yards were looking empty. He was hungry. He had fallen out with Selina and did not know how to mend the rift that had come between them. The last two days had seen them almost silent with each other, and this morning he had been quite surly. He started up the rough steps towards the upper floor that was their living quarters, as it was for the other families. A pleasant smell of stew wafted across his nose. It was coming from the large pot that Selina used to cook with.

She was standing by it, a smile on her face. 'Come on, Grumpy,' she said, 'Perhaps you'll be a bit more sociable if you get some home-made stew inside you.'

She stepped across the floor and kissed him on the cheek, and suddenly he felt foolish for having fallen out with her. At least she had had the pluck to make the first move!

'Come here then.'

He reflected on the way they had separated only this morning, and was relieved at her response and contrite for his part in it. He held his arms open to her.

'I love you, you know, and I'm sorry that we ended up the way we did this morning, but you know why, don't you?'

He looked her in the eye, a question in his. She was quick to reply.

'Tom, I love you as well. You know I do. It's just, well, how we get you, you know, all worked up with nowhere to go, if you know what I mean.'

She was trying to explain her frustration in words and terms that he would understand, without appearing unladylike. She was not a virgin, like Tom; she knew the pleasures of sex in ways that Tom had not yet learned, although he was pressing her acceptance of his needs. The very act of refusing his advances was difficult and she did not want to refuse him much longer. The thought brought her into his arms, into a closeness that belied all their refusals. He held her in a tightening embrace, his lips on her neck and his hands playing with her senses. They heard the sound of feet on the steps and separated. It was Kate. Sometimes it seemed that she was always there when they were enjoying their time alone together. She smiled at them.

'Hello, you two. Jim and me are going for a walk later on. Do you want to come with us? It's a lovely warm evening and we could have a shandy at the Lamb and Sceptre.'

She looked askance at them, seeing their emotions still written upon their faces.

'Shall I come back a little later, when you have had your dinner and you have cooled off from your day's work?'

The words seemed to convey double meanings. She has a talent for it, thought Tom; she's always talking so that her words could be taken in more than one way.

'There's no need to come back later, Kate. We'll see you in about half an hour; when we have eaten this bit of stew. That's alright isn't it Tom?' Selina glanced at him for an answer. 'Yes, that's alright by us, Kate. We'll see you as soon as we're ready.' He sat down and started eating. 'This is nice stew Selina; come on, don't let it go cold.'

Kate disappeared down the steps and Selina sat, close to Tom, her hips touching his thighs. He could feel the heat from her body, and when he turned to look at her he could see that she was not really interested in the meal. He turned closer and put his arm round her.

'I think we'll have our meal after.' He whispered the words, sliding his hand up to the back of her neck and leaning over, kissed her, just below her ear. He had learned that she liked that.

'What do you mean, after; after what? There isn't any after.'

She stopped eating and turned to face him, moving closer so that her breast touched his chest. 'I mean after we have had enough of the first course, and maybe a little of the second course. I've missed getting our first courses, just because we fell out over nothing.'

His mouth moved round her cheeks until it met on hers, and his tongue slid gently but forcefully into her mouth and met hers with a little jolting climax of emotion. They clung tighter to each other, feeling almost desperate for the ultimate closeness that they both desired, and their caresses simulated.

He stood up and turned Selina so that her back was against the wall and slid his hands up the back of her legs until he was pulling her against him. She was breathing hard now, pressing her body against his, in response to his embrace. They were drowning in the heat of the moment; leaving their individuality behind to become a single body. The world, slowly disappearing, suddenly encroached upon them once more. A shout from below interrupted their fervour with a painful insertion of noise.

'Tom! Selina! Are you coming?' It was Jim, the busheller, 'It's taking you a long time to eat that bit o' dinner. If you've got something better to do, that's all right. We'll just carry on, and see you when we see you.'

They separated and peered over the edge of the floor to Jim, who was standing in the middle of the farmyard, looking up to their place. He was smiling, as if he knew what they were doing. Selina was blushing, a brilliant red. She was angry too, Tom noticed. He was embarrassed too, but not angry, when he noticed Kate looking out of the door where she kept her belongings. She has arranged for Jim to shout up, like that, he thought. That's why Selina is mad with her. She knows that Kate deliberately arranged that interruption. There was more going on here than he had thought. He put it to the back of his mind and straightened his clothes, as Selina was doing, and together they started down the steps, each putting on a brave face.

The two couples slowly walked along the lane; Bromyard Downs lay spread before them, they would arrive in the town in thirty minutes or so. It was a quiet walk, as if each of them were immersed in their own thoughts. Jim knew that his time with these younger people was nearing an end. He would stay on, in the cottage that Albert and Jenny Walker had given to him as a tied home until he was too old to work. It seemed almost medieval in concept, that a man could be cast off when he could no longer provide labour of sufficiently good quality to satisfy an employer. With luck it would be many years before that fate came to him. In the meantime he could find himself a wife to tend to his needs, as he would attend to hers. He thought of Kate and their increasing intimacy with pleasure. Could she be the one? They each got pleasure from the company of the other, but they had not yet consummated the relationship, although they took pleasure in the closeness of the touching and kissing that they gave to each other. The thought gave him pleasure again and reaching for her hand, was accepted with a smile. Kate was also feeling slightly frustrated. Although she was a virgin, she had been made aware by Jim of the pleasures of sex, and had been as close as she could, to losing her virginity. Selina was the most aware sexually, despite being younger than Jim, and more experienced then either Kate or Tom. At the moment she wasn't feeling too bad; they were out for the night and she had plans of her own for livening up the evening. She mused on these as they strolled along.

The Crown and Sceptre came into view, as did the Railway Station. There was a crowd of people, standing and sitting around the grounds of the public house. She knew most of them. Some were of the town itself, the neighbours, as they were known, working for the duration of the hop picking season and then finding other work.

Others were women up from the Valleys of Wales; they never really got on with the Black Country people. It was strange really because both groups managed to have a good time with the Herefordshire folk; it was as if there was competition for the work that was available, but the dispute did not include the neighbours; they had rights by living there. The areas of disputed control of the Herefordshire countryside seemed to divide at Bishop's Frome, pronounced Frume by the locals. Then, the areas to the north were temporarily populated by the Black Country people and, to the South West; it was the Welsh who held sway.

They were at the public house now; Tom was pushing a pint of mild ale into Jim's hand. Tom was always generous, generous to a fault, thought Jim as he picked up the other glasses, a mixture of beer and lemonade, shandies, for Kate and Selina. He looked round for them. They were sitting at a table in the grounds of the public house. Sometimes he had caught Kate looking at young Tom with that certain look in her eye, that certain expression on her face. Women were funny that way. Sometimes they would be with one man, whilst desiring another. Mind you, he thought, I'm the same; Selina had a body that was made for the enjoyment of a man.

The thought brought him back to his surroundings. The four of them had a good time when they were out together. They usually had a bit of a singsong towards the end of the evening, when they had lubricated their throats. This evening was no exception and it was eleven o'clock before they were almost forcibly evicted from the grounds of the public house, walking first of all with one of the girls and then the other. The atmosphere was silent when they stopped singing, and, at times like this, the contrast between country and urban living was at it's most obvious, with the still darkness like a liquid through which they were momentarily passing. Their way led them through fields and they had to pass through stiles, from one field into another.

The darkness was all-surrounding as they moved like shadows through the Herefordshire countryside, enclosing them in a pocket of group intimacy. When the moon came out from the back of the large clouds it was as if they were being starkly revealed on a theatre stage; four players in an enduring lifelong drama.

There was a pleasure in friendship, Selina thought. They were lucky to find such good friends so quickly. Kate had started it with her offer of bacon sandwiches on the day of their arrival, and Jim had added to it with his offer to take Kate for a walk. It was surprising how they had all merged, almost like a large extended family. Her relationship to Kate was still evolving; she had never had feelings like that, alongside her feelings for Tom. Jim was a more dour personality, although it could be seen that he was really attached to Kate. It seemed entirely possible that the four of them would be lifelong friends.

In the Black Country she had never known such a relationship. Everything seemed to have been engineered to conform to the needs of the bosses. Perhaps there were other pairs of couples who had been able to find the contentment that she was finding now. She thought again of her imaginary rag rug. She had mentally added three cuttings to it in the last month, and the colour of it was lightening up. The idea of having a relationship with a woman was still strange to her. She did not think that sex came into it; they were just very good friends.

Jim was thinking of the future. A true countryman now, he was wondering if he and Kate would have enough sons to perhaps improve their position in the Hereford ranks. It was his ambition to improve his stock, starting with himself. Kate was a fit looking person who made friends easily. These were valuable traits for a farmer's wife. If he could get on the right side of Kate's mother, a real wedding could take place. The thought filled him with pleasure and he pulled her close to him. He did wonder what would happen to Kate's mother if she became ill. That was something to be considered in the future. His pleasure with Kate burst out of him.

'Oh, Kate, you do give me some joy when I am with you, I must confess.'

He turned and saw that the three of them were looking at him.

It had not occurred to him that he was speaking so loudly, and he was red-faced with embarrassment. Kate spoke with amazement on her tongue

'Jim, I've never heard you speak like that before! I get pleasure from you as well, but you sound like a poet when you talk to me like that.'

The group carried on after the small outburst, and in a few minutes were over the top of the rise, making their way down to the farm where they had their temporary sleeping quarters. It was there that the tension increased by the simple act of wishing their friends goodnight.

The two men kissed their partners and then turned by instinct to kiss the other's companion. Tom held onto Kate and she responded with a passion that he was not expecting. The sensation of feeling her ripe body against his aroused him and he was reluctant to let her go. Jim too, was caught up in the enthusiasm that Tom showed, and as he took hold of Selina he found her willing to continue a little longer than seemed necessary, just to say goodnight to a friend. He pulled her against him, their bodies enjoying each other.

The pairs merged in the darkness of the barn, the substitution of the other's partner seeming to give an added excitement to the night. Selina found that Jim's hands were giving her that feeling again and she allowed him to touch her in ways she had not been touched since she had lived with her mother and had been seduced by Harry. Eventually the couples parted from each other and slid further into the shadows, their hands and bodies finding things to do to stimulate the other. Time passed and a little later they all seemed to realise what they were doing and moved apart again, returning to the partner they had started the evening with and saying their goodbyes again.

'Goodnight, Tom.' Kate was the first to break off, and Selina followed her lead, although reluctantly.

'Goodnight, Jim' She pulled away, unwillingly it seemed to Jim, but pull away she did, her breathing laboured by the passion she was feeling. What, she thought, were the limits to the breadth and depth of her feelings?

Kate was still trembling from the supposed friendly goodnight kiss from Tom; she had been dreading the prospect that she would be expected to kiss Selina goodnight, and she didn't know if she could carry it off. In the event, there was no problem. Selina merely touched her hand. That was enough! What could follow from that?

Selina had been entranced and engulfed by the feelings that had swept over her as she had kissed and touched Jim goodnight. She recalled the sensations that his hands had aroused as he touched her just more intimately than ever before. The feelings she had made her excited, shivery and guilty all at the same time. She had now had strange feelings for each of her three companions! Was she destined to feel like this after every small social encounter with a man?

Jim was less bothered by the encounter with Selina; he had learned to just enjoy the pleasure of a woman, without expecting a long term relationship to follow. He smiled to himself as he observed the others saying goodnight. They all had a lot to learn, he thought, and then gradually understood that he was learning too. He had thought that he had learned all the lessons of love when he was younger but it seemed he had been mistaken. There was plenty more to be learned and it would be exciting, he could see.

How would Tom respond to his friend making love to his potential wife? He would just take it in his stride, he hoped. They had all pushed back the boundaries of friendship and he was in no position to criticise. He too, had made advances to Kate – and enjoyed it.

13. The Wedding.

When Selina awoke, it was raining. She could not make out what day it was. Oh yes, it was Saturday 29th of September 1923, the day of her hop pole wedding. She had a moment of panic, seeing the weather. She had been told to expect rain, but improving later. The hops were all gathered in. Mr and Mrs Walker would be pleased and relieved about that. Apparently it had been a good year, with few hold ups in the form of strikes, illnesses or hop wilt.

With a bit of luck, Jenny Walker would be quite helpful, and Albert would buy them a round of drinks to celebrate his good fortune, as well as to wish them theirs. She had all day to get ready. Turning over, she reached for Tom but he was not there. She looked over the yard and saw him talking to Jim, the busheller. They were probably reminiscing about last night. She waved, and Jim saw her and waved back. He had enjoyed himself last night. They all had; there were no recriminations to come.

Tonight's ceremony would crown the whole month's experience. She had grown up, she knew, in the last four weeks. So had Tom; he was years more adult than when he had arrived, a month ago. Tomorrow they would be catching the 'special', home, back to Willenhall. How would things be, there? Would her mother and Harry have cemented their relationship?

She jumped up. There was a lot to do! It was eight o'clock already and she and Kate had each other's hair to do, ready for the big event. She had decided to wear the white dress, with baby sleeves, that Jenny Walker had found for her. Tom had not seen the dress, yet. He was expecting her to arrive in her Sunday best. He would be wearing a new white shirt, and would unknowingly complement her appearance. They would be a handsome couple! She looked out, again.

At the end of the farmyard, by the gate into the North Field, a clean area had been made. It was roped off to stop the Herefords from straying, when they came in for the milking. This had already been carried out, and the cattle had been led into Monk's Leasow, the lowest field, for the day. The way was clear now for the ceremony to be carried out in the barn if the rain persisted or outside if it became fine.

Tom, too, was thinking about the night before. He had not known how to act with Jim this morning but all Jim had said was, "what a night eh, Tom?" then walked off, to work. Kate had made him feel; he did not know how, wonderful, but more than that, more of a man. Her body kept coming into his mind. He had very little work to do, today. He decided to look for Kate, and strode across the yard, nearly walking into Selina. She stopped and blushed, as she looked at him.

'Good morning, Tom. How are you? Have you sobered up, yet?'

He did not know whether she was admonishing him, mocking him or just simply wishing him the time of day. She smiled and, as always, his world came together.

'Hello my lovely. I'm fine. How about you? That was quite a night, last night, wasn't it? Tonight will be different, I think. There'll be just the two of us. I'm looking forward to that, eh?'

He was trying to bridge the gap; she could see that, holding out a hand of reconciliation. She leaned across and kissed him.

'Yes, I can't wait for us to be just on our own, but I'm looking forward to the wedding itself, as well. That's something else we've never done, as well, isn't it, Tom? I'm looking for Kate; have you seen her? If you do see her, remind her that she's going to a wedding today!'

She flounced off, across the yard, towards where their sleeping quarters were.

Tom entered the shed where Kate stayed. She was lying on the hay, looking as if she were fast asleep. He tiptoed across and bending down, kissed her. She opened her eyes, grabbed hold of him and looked him straight in the eye, a smile on her face.

'That's a lovely way to be woken up, Tommy Barr, and me almost a married woman! Still, I think we all learned a lot, last night, don't you?'

She pulled him down to her, her lips teasing his, and then pulled away. No accusations from Kate, either. The world hadn't come to an end, then. What lessons he had learned! He wouldn't mind another! He blushed slightly as he answered.

'Well, I did, and you were the teacher; any chance of another lesson?'

He moved as if to take away the blanket in which she was wrapped.

'Just you keep your hands to yourself, Tommy Barr. I can still feel them from last night. That's the last time we behave like that. Jim is not as young and open minded as the rest of us; he will want me just for himself. The same as you will want Selina just for yourself, if I know you. You'll have to get your lessons from her, now.'

It was true. The idea of someone else being intimate with Selina filled him with horror and anger. People were strange, he thought; on the one hand, he was aroused by Kate and would jump into the hay with her at the smallest encouraging sign, but he wouldn't like it if Jim felt the same way about Selina. Old Harry was right. It was like going to University. There was something new to be learned, every day. Could he accept that others had the same feelings and thoughts that he had? He knew he had to come to terms with that idea. He felt that he had passed out, graduated.

There was just the graduation ceremony to come, tonight. That was going to be an event! How would the two couples end up? They couldn't really give a repeat performance of last night's scenes. That would be too much to tolerate.

Kate felt that everything was going well. Jim had been in a loving mood with her this morning, first thing. No word of any accusation about last night; just a short comment.

'From now on, it's just you and me, eh, Kate? Last night was an experience, but we'll have no more of them sort o' nights.'

He had buried his head in her breast and breathed her in. That was the way she had felt about what he was doing, breathing her in. Then he had kissed her lightly on the forehead and went off to work. She thought back to the previous evening. That Selina was a dark horse. She must have been working off all her frustrations, last night. Kate had deliberately led Tom on, last night, just to see how Selina and Jim would react to being close together. Well, she had found out, hadn't she? She couldn't really complain now, could she?

Perhaps Tom too was frustrated, wanting, needing the sexual activity, but held in check by custom; the desire to do the right thing. Come to think of it, she hadn't resisted the chance herself. What was worse, she had enjoyed the closeness of Selina. She shouldn't be thinking, feeling things like this; people would think she was one of those queer women who dressed like men. Selina hadn't drawn back in horror either, had she? Perhaps it was just a phase that they were going through, and wouldn't be repeated. On the other hand, perhaps it was natural. Who knows what's natural and what isn't? The memory was pleasant enough, anyway. Tom was still standing, looking at her with his lamb's eyes.

'Come on, Tom. Its time we were at work. Oh, I just realised! There is no work today. We are doing something else, aren't we?'

She moved over, under the blanket, and Tom was tempted to lie down by her side. She caught the look in his eye.

'Away you go Tom Barr, before you go too far!' She smiled, threw the blanket off and sprang to her feet. 'Selina and me have got to go and see Mrs Walker straight after breakfast. She wants to tell us what we have got to do at the ceremony. She's been to a few so she knows all about what happens.'

She was walking as she was talking over her shoulder, walking quickly through the barn door, unwilling to allow her feelings to emerge. She was glad she hadn't told Tom about the wedding dresses.

Later that day, they all got together. Because of the closeness within which they were all living, it was not possible for them to avoid seeing each other to conform to normal tradition. The ceremony was to take place at seven o'clock. They were going to take a chance on the Herefordshire weather and hold it outside. A trestle had been put up, and it would be filled with sandwiches and tasty cakes at the last minute to avoid the attention of the ever-present flies. The ceremonial hop poles, all decorated with hop bines and roses, were ready, leaning against the barn.

The day soon passed; they were kept busy with the preparations. Tom had bought a new white shirt for the ceremony, as had Jim and they had to be ironed and starched, ready to receive a tie for the half an hour of the rites. The ties would then be taken off for the rest of the evening.

At five o'clock, the two girls made their excuses and made their way into the farm house where Jenny was waiting for her. She had brought the dresses down from the attic and was as excited as the two brides. Her friend from the coven, Millicent Brookes was there too, looking very serious but with a smiling face, all at the same time. She helped Jenny to prepare a small meal of sandwiches, telling the girls that they must keep their strength up for the ordeal of the evening and night!

Then it was time to dress. They had both had their hair styled and the dresses fitted ready for the occasion. It was just a matter of putting them on and the two older women were both crying at the sight of the young ones. Millicent moved round them, clearing the air of any evil spirits and making them pure for what was to come.

The Parson turned up at six o'clock. He appeared to have started his celebrations early. He had two other families of gypsies with him, all dressed for the occasion and they occupied the centre of the yard, performing limber dances in time with strange melodies and rhythms, with the Parson acting as master of ceremonies. The whole congregation soon joined in, mixing traditional, gypsy and the latest popular tunes. Jenny and Albert Walker had invited some, especially chosen friends, too, from local society. Millicent Brookes, seemed to be on very good terms with the Parson, and helped him with the arrangements. Jenny had confided to Selina that she was reputed to be a witch, and would offer a blessing to the couple. There seemed to be a natural break at seven o'clock, the congregation going quiet when the Parson stepped out into the middle of the Yard, holding his arms above his head dramatically and shouting to make himself heard.

The farm workers were gathered in the farmyard, all attired in their Sunday best. Selina and Kate had kept out of sight until the ceremony was about to start. They were beckoned from the farmhouse where they had kept themselves hidden, by Jenny Walker. There was a gasp from the crowd as they walked in. Kate was wearing the ivory wedding dress that Jenny had found for her, and Selina looked radiant in her elegantly styled white wedding dress.

Two young girls, daughters of a Black Country family, had been given creamy white dresses to wear as bridesmaids. Albert Walker had supplied a barrel of local ale, fortified with his own hops. He had been gruff about it, but they realised that it was just his way.

Jenny Walker seemed to be everywhere. She had pulled Tom down to her ample breasts and told him, in a secret whisper, that she wouldn't mind swapping with Selina, if he felt like it. Tom, as usual, was amazed that women, who he had never considered as a possible partner, regarded him as a figure of desire.

'Please, can I have your attention?' The Parson was attracting their attention again. 'On behalf of the gypsy families, who have been invited, and the hop-pickers and workers, I would like to thank the generosity of Mr and Mrs Walker, in providing such big-hearted help with these proceedings. This is to be the wedding of two lovely young couples, within the eyesight of all you witnesses. This is the first time a double wedding has been carried out at Hope Farm and we hope that the hope is for life-long happiness. To proceed, can I have the pleasure of the company of Miss Selina Brown and Miss Katherine Myatt, spinsters of this parish, and Misters James Miller and Thomas Barr, bachelors of this parish, please? Come along now. Just stand in front of me, in a line in front of your peers.' He stood silent while they complied. 'Now, will the Head Bridesmaids come forward, please?' He waited again. 'Thank you. You stand, one at each end of the hop pole, ready to pick it up when I tell you. Not too high, just enough so that all these good people can jump over it without too much trouble and effort. We wouldn't want them to break an ankle on the night of their wedding!'

Emily stood holding the end of the pole and a gypsy girl held the other end. The audience tittered as he held them with the force of his charismatic gypsy persona. They waited to hear whatever they could hear from him, and they were not disappointed.

'Let it be known that this event, this binding of these young people, is being attended by very important people. Let the representatives of my own people step forward. First of all; Joseph and Mariana Smith! The true King and Queen of the gypsies, they have agreed to grace this occasion with the splendour of their attendance!'

The audience clapped and applauded the two, who, stepping gracefully into the firelight, were dressed for the occasion in traditional gypsy costume. Both wore white embroidered blouse tops; Mariana wore a brilliant flaring red skirt, while Joseph wore tight red trousers. They seemed almost Spanish in their entrance, turning and spinning to a roll of the gypsy drum. They certainly had a regal effect upon the gathered crowd. The Parson spoke again.

'Now, we have a representative of local society, who will offer a blessing upon this auspicious occasion; I give you – Miss Millicent Brookes!'

Again there was a round of applause for the middle aged, attractive woman who stepped forward. She stood there waiting for the quietness to gather round the group; then she spoke, in a calm but clear Hereford voice.

'Thank you, Parson Smith. Before you perform the binding ceremony that holds these pure and innocent folk together, I wish to bring and present the gifts and blessings from my own group.'

At this, a line of women stepped forward, each with a wreath of flowers, which, with a dramatic flourish, were placed over the heads of the four main attendees. Millicent stepped into the centre again and spoke the witches' creed.

'An it harm none, do what thou wilt. Be happy. Be full of life, bring forth life; live your lives!'

She stepped to each of them and wand-touched each participant on the forehead with great ritualistic significance. Then she handed the ceremony back to the Parson with a flourish.

'May the making of these individuals, bachelors and spinsters, into married persons be carried out with the dignity it deserves!'

She retired from the centre of the scene, curtseying and allowing the Parson to resume. He beckoned the bridesmaids to pick up the hop pole to about six inches above the ground, and then quietened them all with a pass of his hands. Then, as he spoke, the gypsy drum seemed to add importance, with a beat at each word, spoken to each of them individually.

'Do you,' he spoke each name, 'promise to keep to only your chosen partner, to discard previous loves and fancies, for as long as you may live? If you agree, say I do!'

Each of them uttered the magic words, as they do in all weddings; then the Parson motioned the two young girls to lift the hop poles.

'As you jump the pole, you will move from the single stage of life into the married stage. May you all be happy tonight and have many years of happiness!'

Each of them, helped by their chosen partner, jumped over the pole, to the roar of approval from the gathered congregation. The gypsy violin and drum started to play, and the gathering started to clap and shout. The Parson finally took up control again.

'Ladies and Gentlemen: Brides and Grooms! Your attention please! This is the moment in the ceremony when you become couples.' He took a length of white ribbon from his pocket and, putting Tom and Selina's hands together, tied them. Then he performed the same significant act with Jim and Kate.

He stood back from them and showed the tied hands to the congregation. 'It is my privilege and pleasure to announce to all the witnesses here present, that you are now married men and women! You may kiss your brides and grooms.' He paused while his instructions were carried out, and then raised his voice again. 'Let the night be long and merry! May your strength last you all until the dawn!'

'Dance: Dance!'

He pronounced the command and the two couples started to move to a rehearsed movement around the farmyard and as they did, the guests all started to join in, the drum and violin picking up the beat from the movement of the performers. Each of the dancers separated from their partners and invited another to dance. In this way, all of the congregation were soon gathered into the dance. The music was easy to dance to at first, and then became faster and more complicated in rhythm and steps. The rest of the evening went in a kaleidoscope of colour and movement that bedazzled them all, and left them exhausted in the early hours.

The stimulus of the evening had other effects too. Many couples remembered their wedding nights, and the memory re-stimulated their desires. Albert and Jenny Walker had been twenty-one when they were joined at the local church and neither had forgotten the event. The Parson and Millicent Brookes shared similar beliefs and had led interwoven lives, coming together occasionally at times dictated by the seasons and the coincidences of their way of life. The King and Queen of the gypsies brought the excitement of their lifestyle, tempered by the toughness required to live in their way. They all thought of each other and of the young couples joined that night.

Tom became weary of the dancing and decided to sit out for a while and watch the others moving in time to the violins and drums. He had never really taken a lot of notice of the gypsies. They had just been there. He sat observing the violinist and drummer, in turn.

There was real skill in the way they formed the changing patterns of melody and harmony merging with the voices of the other gypsies, singing. The Parson was nowhere to be seen, a surprise to Tom, who was expecting to see him dancing with Millicent. Where was she? A movement in the dark of the barn door had caught his eye earlier and he walked over to investigate. As he got nearer he could see that it was the Parson and Millicent in the shadows, entwined in each other's arms. He abruptly turned and walked away, unwilling to pry on their behaviour. He had his own life to live. Where was Selina? He sat down on the edge of the dancing circle. She was in the middle of the floor, dancing with a gypsy, and obviously enjoying herself. Tom made to get up then decided not to interfere. It was her last chance to live loosely, he thought. Let her enjoy it!

Jenny Walker had her time dancing with many of the guests, while Albert had a few, in between drinking with his men. As he danced with Jenny, he recalled how, in his youth, he used to try it on with the locals, Millicent included. He had never told Jenny about her!

Selina left the floor red-faced and breathless, but happy to join Tom in the shadows, feeling tender now that the ceremony was all over. She sat at his side and his arm went around her shoulders. They were now separate from any other group. They became closer to each other and they came to the slow realisation that they should not be there.

At last the night came to an end and the two couples left the fire-lit circle to find their own private hiding places, away from the ribald remarks of the Black Countrymen who had teased them earlier. They had never thought, a month ago, that their lives would have changed so much, in such a short time. Even Selina, who had planned in her mind that something permanent between her and Tom would come about, had not thought to be a white-clad bride so soon.

Tom felt that he had just been swept along on a wave of love, lust and enthusiastic learning, taking every new experience in, with no thought for the future. It was another phase in his education, another test that he was about to try for himself.

Jim felt strange about the whole affair. He had had sex many times; in the Army and in France during and after the War. This was going to be different. He had never had anyone that he felt he had to be loyal to, before. He had sometimes felt that he should put down roots, but he had never felt sufficiently strong about it, to take the final step. Now he had committed himself to being half of a couple. There was no turning back; or was there?

It was not an official ceremony nor was there any recognition of the promises made. That was true of the official ceremony; no one could force you to keep the vows you made. There were no penalties for unfaithfulness; it was strange; you could be imprisoned for marrying two women at once but not for being unfaithful. Still, you had to answer to yourself and your own ideas about life. How was he going to respond to the call?

He had grown into the Herefordshire way of thinking and feeling, running his own life as he would a stud farm, looking for the most suitable partner, with a family in mind. Kate, to him, seemed just the sort of woman who would enhance his family. She had wide hips, making it easier for her to have children and she was beautiful as well.

The four of them left the others still thinking of bodies they weren't supposed to be thinking of. The feeling soon left them as they merged with the partner of their choice, memories of other lovers soon leaving them as they became submerged in their own private torrent of love and lust.

14. Stones' Locks.

Stones' Locks, at Willenhall, in Staffordshire is an old family lock manufacturing business that runs alongside other small enterprises of the family members. In the front of the Victorian-fronted building, Mabel Stones' and her two daughters, Laura and Jean run a small but busy children's and ladies fashion and clothing shop, whilst her husband, Stephen, his brother Bert and his son, Stanley, run the lock and key-making factory at the back of the property. Old Albert, Stephen's father, still works as many hours as he can spare but often takes a day off. He is more interested in the girls than the work.

Mabel runs her shop with enthusiasm and expertise but not much method. Deliveries of clothes, from liberty bodices to grown up dresses, not sold within a month or two, are consigned to a pile of clothes in a corner of the floor at the back of the shop, so that the latest styles are always in front of the customers. The piled up mound of clothes, consequently, becomes higher and higher. It is rumoured that some of the clothes, on the bottom of the pile, are fifty years old but, as the shop is only forty years old this is not given much credence.

Mabel is a believer in the Victorian adage that 'do not a lender or a borrower be', so consequently no credit is given and the low prices reflect this. Most small businesses give a few days grace to their customers to settle their bills, and charge extra for the credit and the risk taken. Mabel has never given credit and consequently is able to offer slightly reduced terms. Her better off customers have accused her of being prejudiced against them, but they continue to favour her with their custom, knowing that they get a better bargain from her. The local, self-made trades-people respect the qualities in others that have contributed to their own success and reward her methods. Samuel Smiles' self-help philosophy is a popular conviction and support for its adherents is a natural by-product.

Mabel is aware too, of her responsibilities to her two daughters. They are not encouraged to indulge in any sort of social contact with the 'hands' who work on the manufacturing side of the business. The daughters are encouraged to move in a 'trade' circle of friends. They also have to conform to a Wesleyan way of life. The factory hands are put off as much as possible, and told to stay in the factory, away from the shop. Naturally, this is seen as a challenge to the young men of the factory, and also to Mabels' daughters whose eyes often look towards the eyes looking from the factory.

There, nearly two score of men, youths and young women working on the many types of locks produced, for export to all parts of the British Empire. Stones' specialise in special purpose padlocks, which have arms of various lengths. The firm is busy. Although Stones' are lucky and they have more orders than they can handle, they do not want the orders to be taken away from them, to be given to their competitors.

They often work overtime, hours beyond the normal working week, in order to complete a special order by the promised date. Bert, Stephen Stones' younger brother, is encouraged to be responsible for the work produced during overtime, in order to help him to acquire some expertise in the trade. He always jumps at the chance because there is a less disciplined atmosphere during overtime working and he can mix with the men and women without having to preserve his 'management' appearance.

The fact is that he does not feel like management. He makes too many mistakes, due to lack of proper training and his want of confidence in his own ability. He has often wished Dan Barr could be his father, showing him the mysteries of the trade. Dan has always seemed to have infinite patience. His own father, Old Albert, makes him feel inferior and this makes matters worse. The work-hands pick up on his evaluation and reflect the manager's attitude to Bert.

Stanley Stone, Stephen's youngest, is bright, enthusiastic and efficient. Although he is the junior, his work in the factory is far superior to that of his uncle while his extrovert social skills ensure that he is a favourite of the hands, who are always willing to give him tips of the trade. Although he is only seventeen years old, his father seeks him out when a fresh mind is needed to solve a problem. Stanley does not always come up with the answer to the problem instantly but he can always seek advice from the more experienced hands. He is a favourite of the girls in the factory, too, often being consulted on how to perform a particular task. He is sufficiently mature to take advantage of these enquiries without allowing himself to be drawn into long lasting relationships.

Bert often sits in the office, watching the locksmiths working at their benches through the glass window. He sometimes sits there for an hour, waiting for a hand to leave his position. Then he will let his father know and watch the ensuing disciplinary interview with pleasure. This pattern of habit is known to most of the work hands and adds to the lack of respect that they have for him. Nevertheless, they all know that they have to watch out for his eye. If he is about, the hands will point to their own eyes and nod with their head to indicate where Bert is to be found.

Today, Dan Barr, the charge-hand, is in the office. Stone is complaining about the delay of partly finished lock components moving from one department to another. There is a bottleneck in production, with hundreds of padlock parts awaiting a piercing operation before they can be assembled and painted. Bert can hear their voices, slightly raised as each makes their points. His father is speaking.

'And if that isn't enough, young Tom is away for six weeks, or more. We can't keep up with orders now; how are we supposed to manage without him? I should never have given permission for him to go wandering off to Herefordshire, or wherever he's gone.'

Stephen Stone looks over his glasses at Dan, accusingly. Dan smiles to himself. He knows that Stones' Locks would not come to a stop, simply because Tom is down in Herefordshire for a few weeks. Stone has been consulted at every step of the way. Something else must be sticking in his throat. It will come to the surface when he is ready.

Stone clears his throat and Dan knows that Stone always does that when he is about to raise a subject that he doesn't feel confident to talk about. He looks up, playing the attentive employee. Stone speaks as if their stations were reversed, an unusual exchange of status.

'Dan, do you think your Elsie would do us a few hours a week, just for a couple of weeks? We would make it worth her while.'

He colours as if he does not like asking favours of an employee. Dan gives it some thought. Elsie has helped Stones' out before. She is an experienced hand, having worked in the haberdashery and the lock-making side of the business. She would probably jump at the chance to tuck a few more shillings away. She is always tucking a few shillings away. She wouldn't thank him for speaking on her behalf, though. Stone is waiting for an answer.

'I don't know, Gaffer. She usually will, as you know. She likes to get a few quid in the bank- or wherever she puts it. I'll ask her tonight and she'll tell you in the morning. She's got a mind of her own about such things, as you know. As for the lock-jam, I'll go and see what I can do about that, myself.'

He moves away, wondering what is getting on the Gaffer's nerves. He does seem a bit edgy. Probably it's his son, Bert. He is always making daft mistakes in the business, and no one has sufficient respect or liking for him, to put him right. Only last week they had been obliged to chase an order halfway to the dock because of the silly inclusion of some German padlocks in the consignment that was intended for Brazil. It wouldn't have mattered much, thought Dan. The rate of inflation in Germany means that they are obliged to pay with goods; Marks have little or no value. God knows what would happen if the same conditions occurred here.

Dan often wonders if he will be offered the chance to take over the management of the lock making side of the business. He knows damn well that he can do the job better than that idiot, Bert, or even young Stanley, for that matter.

His route takes him back through the yard, to the japanning shop, where the locks are painted black by a special process to prevent them rusting. There is a lot of work waiting to be done here. The large hand press is in the workshop next door. His own normal work could wait for a bit while he helps to move the locks through this part of the production process, to even the flow of work.

He takes hold of the swing handle of the press. The press has a large iron ball loosely fastened to the top of the swing handle. It is there to give extra weight to the press as the top tool is lowered into the bottom tool, piercing the blank. There is a full work pan of blanks waiting to have holes pierced in them, for the key-holes and small rivets that hold the lock together. His left hand reaches down into the pan, picks up a handful of blanks, places them within easy reach on the top of the worktable, and places one of them in the bottom tool of the press. His right arm reaches for the handle and, grasping it, pulls it in an easy, continuous movement, the tool descending into the blank, cleanly piercing the small apertures.

He examines it for faults automatically and reaches for the next blank. Then his body becomes part of the production process, programmed to place the blank, swing the arm, time after time, blank after blank falling into the work-pan containing the finished lock components. His mind wanders from the work, as he becomes an automaton. The sweat springs from his forehead and is ignored, as the pile of finished components piles higher in the work pan.

He will work a little later tonight. With a bit of luck this order would be finished by the middle of tomorrow. That should keep the Gaffer sweet, and might make Stone see him in a better light. It was about time Stephen Stone gave him a bit of appreciation for the trouble he took, to get things running right. An office of his own; this was his ambition. At the moment he had to keep himself organised with a small mound of paperwork in a large bulldog clip on a nail fastened to a little corner of his workbench to save it being blown away by a draught. Everything he did had to be done in a restricted area, and that added to the frustration he felt at seeing his own talents used, while the owner's son had no talent, but was better thought of. He let go of his thoughts and allowed his mind to wander again, in a fresh direction.

He might take Elsie out tonight. The thought came tripping, unbidden into his mind. Perhaps things would be all right, tonight. He had always felt inferior about his impotence, always hoping that the problem would not recur, and occasionally he was able to make love fully. Things hadn't really been right since France.

He'd been all right then! His thoughts led him back to the shell-blasted café where he and his friends had been wont to meet during the few times they were given a brief day or two of leave from front line duty. The contrast between the front line, with all its signs of death, and the small café, was striking. The young women there had seemed like something out of heaven. Not angels, because that was the last thing they were, but very friendly, and that was enough. Every day, every hour, every second had seemed larger then, not knowing whether they would ever see another sunrise. They had taken advantage of every opportunity to indulge themselves with the few young girls who still stayed in the area.

Many of their comrades had come home diseased. Dan had been lucky. It was a chargeable offence to get poxed up; 'behaviour detrimental to good order and discipline'. It had never occurred to him that he might not have been as lucky as he thought; that his experiences with the pubescent and easily pleased young girls had made it difficult for him to respond to the needs of a more mature woman. He had never had to consider the needs of the partner of the night, whoever it happened to be. He had just satisfied himself, paid his money and gone back to his unit.

His thoughts returned to the present. It would be pleasant to go out. They hadn't bothered for some weeks. They hadn't really felt sufficiently happy with each other's company to want to make the effort. Sometimes it was like that; finding the thought of spending time in the company of the other one disturbing, especially if the 'other one' got inviting looks from strangers.

He turned his mind back to the batch of work he was working on, fifty dozen padlocks for France. It was a good order, considering that France had its own lock-makers. Stones' had outdone the French lock and safe-makers at their own game. How had Stones' got this order? He knew they had representatives all over the world, not employees as such, but agents, on commission, perhaps Stones' paid more commission than the French firms. It might be exciting, to go out into the world, to fight for orders against all comers, for this small firm in the Midland town. He wouldn't mind going back to France, to see what it looked like, now.

This batch of locks had long 'U' arms, to enable them to fasten the special bolts that are used on a certain type of industrial door. Stones' Locks are the only firm producing this particular item. It is a difficult task to make the 'U' arms in such a way that they will slide easily, when the key was turned.

They also make safe locks, a specialised branch of the trade, for the French, German and Belgian trade. One of their representatives has been asked if they can produce these items and luckily an employee has worked at Chubb's', one of the major producers of locks and keys. The employee had advised Stones' on the best way to manufacture the locks, giving them an advantage. The result had been a good order and an increase in prestige. They have continuous orders now, from the recommendations that have followed.

Back in the office, Bert moved from his seat. He was getting bored. It was five minutes away from the works finishing time. He had recently been given the task of ensuring that no one goes early. He had to stand at the gate, watching for people trying to sneak out. He didn't like or want the job. It made him less popular with the factory hands, who didn't have a lot of respect for him, anyway. He strode the few paces to the gateway and stood there, feeling the stares of the youths who braved the rules and assembled, ready to run at the slightest indication from him that it was all right to do so.

Sometimes, he felt that they were mocking him and the feeling made him want to run and let them all go. He countered this by opening his little pocket book and writing the name of whoever was nearest the gate. The name that comes up the most often is drawn to the attention of his father, who usually gave it to Dan Barr to handle. Dan sometimes has the work-hand in the works office to admonish him; it is always a youth, never one of the young women. Dan had tried to explain to Bert that young men always responded to rules by trying to break them: it was a natural part of growing up.

'Girls don't need to show how brave they are. They are more used to being looked after. Boys turning into men always want to show how much of a man they are. It makes them feel bigger. You do the same sort of thing yourself, but in a less direct way.'

Bert reflected on what Dan had told him. Dan was always explaining things to him. His father never seemed to have the time. Perhaps, when a little more time has passed, he would acquire the skills that Dan was trying to teach him. Perhaps he will see himself as more attractive to the girls. He has the feeling that they mock him, too. When they walked out of the gate at night, he had caught one or more of them talking behind their hands, a smile written on their faces.

He had dreams about some of the girls. He did not have a favourite; they all looked attractive to him, in their figure-moulding overalls and dirty, sexy faces. It was strange, really, that a dirty face attracted him more than a scrubbed clean look. Perhaps it was because Mother always makes sure that his sisters are all squeaky clean. Occasionally he has dirty thoughts about one of his sisters, but nothing like those he has about the factory girls.

Rarely, one of them has made a flirtatious advance to him, lifting a skirt just a little higher than she should, or allowing her overall to open at the top to reveal the outline of a breast. When this happened, Bert felt the resulting erection with distaste, as if it were a sin, which he felt it was.

Once, one of the girls had thanked him when he had helped her with a work-pan and he had found himself in a sexual encounter. He had not forgotten it. She had looked up at him with big, round brown eyes.

'Thank you, Mr Albert. Thank you very much. I'll give you a kiss at Christmas for that, Mr Albert or, if you don't want to wait, I'll give it you now.'

Her overall had dropped open as she lifted herself onto her toes and placed her hands each side of his cheeks and pulled her body against him, kissing him full on the lips. He could not ignore the feeling it gave him and he had grasped her waist tightly, feeling the double pleasure of the soft breasts and abdomen in close contact with his body. His body response became of control then and his hands slid down to hold her buttocks. She had pulled away, but the moment had imprinted itself on his memory, never to be forgotten.

'Oh! Mr Bert! Well I never! I never would have thought it! I never would have thought you was as big as that. You can do that any time you like, Mr Albert. You are a big man, aren't you?' She moved close to him again, her smile seeming to be just for him. 'Shall we do that again, Mr Albert? I liked that, did you?'

He didn't know how to reply. It was all too much for him. He was close to orgasm, just standing there. He reached for her and pulled her into the doorway, crushing her stomach against his rearing member, aching to enter her and, what? He had no experience, just his body responses to tell him what to do. He was silent, not knowing what to say.

She spoke into his ear. 'Mr Albert, if you like me that much, don't do anything now. Save it for later. See me after work. We can go for a walk, if you know what I mean.'

He knew what she meant, but he also remembered what his mother and father had told him about mixing with the factory girls. 'They are just trying to get your money out of you, Bert. You just keep away from them.'

It was all right for Mother to say keep away from them but she never said anything to Stanley, and he was talking to them all the time.

The day passed slowly, his thoughts interrupted by his

sexual desire for the young girl, Thelma. He could easily see her shape in his imagination, and his body responded to the slightest mental stimulus. He let the hands go two minutes early, much to their surprise. He didn't usually allow the slightest infringement of the timekeeping code. He went to turn into the office when he felt a tug at his sleeve. It was Thelma.

'Hello, Mr Bert.' He was a little surprised. He had no expectation that she would want to speak to him after the kiss, earlier in the day. 'Were you going to come for a walk? You never did say.' Thelma looked at him, her lips turned up into a smile. 'I've been waiting for you but I suppose you've got too much to do, what with guarding the gate. Do you still want to come with me, Mister Albert?'

She looked up at him as if the thought of a refusal would be too much.

'I, I can't, not tonight. I've got to work overtime, Thelma. I'd love to go for a walk with you. I've been thinking about it all afternoon. No, don't go, please.' She had started to turn when he, desperate for her goodwill, clutched at her hand. 'Will you come for a walk with me, tomorrow night, please?'

She stood looking at him, her shape in sharp silhouette arousing him in a special way. He knew subliminally that she was aware of the effect her body was having on him, but he didn't care. The shape of even the edge of a breast was enough to make him feel physically stronger and it was as much as he could do to restrict his body from just grabbing. He knew he had to conform to social rules but the knowledge didn't make him feel any better. His body wanted the possession of hers; that was all there was to it.

The shape of the women silhouetted in corset advertisements was enough to arouse his body but the sight of Thelma swinging the handle of the large hand press that she worked, the smell of her body odour, and the expression in her eye as she swung and looked at him at the same time made him feel almost delirious.

His look spoke of his desperation and at last she nodded briefly to him before she turned and was swallowed up by the crowds passing by. He was suddenly elated. He had received a 'yes.' It was the first positive response he had ever had and he determined that he would take every advantage of it. The thought of Thelma obsessed his mind to the exclusion of all else.

Life had suddenly become more exciting. All that evening, while ostensibly reading a book, his mind raced over Thelma's body and what he was going to do, in his imagination. He would do this and then he would do that. He couldn't say the words; the magic camera in his mind was the only mechanism capable of bringing his thoughts from the hidden depths of his mind to anything near the possibility of reality. He suddenly felt like a man, powerful and able to accomplish things that he hadn't been able to, before.

It would be some time before he would allow the hands to go early. They could go to hell, first. Any running off before the exact time and they would find themselves in the office, in front of his father!

How would he get what he wanted from Thelma? A way would be found, he felt sure. Perhaps she would solve the problem for him. She had seemed keen; perhaps she was keen enough to do something for him! Perhaps she wanted him as much as he wanted her!

15. Elsie and Stephen.

Stephen Stone wanted to start it all up again! Elsie Barr stared down at her hands. She had no doubt in her own mind. She needed the money; that was as true now as it had always been, but it wasn't just money that drove Stephen Stone. He had always wanted her. While Dan had been away with the Staffies, Stone had been round to see her, asking her to work a few hours, 'Just to help with the war effort', making locks for anything that had value, and had to be kept out of unauthorised hands. He had, she knew, a need in him for her that nothing she said or did to him would assuage. In a way she felt sorry for him because she had the same need herself.

She tried to keep to the sort of behaviour that was acceptable to the Black Country people she was living among, but every so often she had to break out and give full rein to her emotional needs. She could, with little effort, feel his eyes and hands upon her and the smell of his hard body. Sometimes it was as if they were magnets, repelling one day and attracting another. No logic could be used to resolve the way they felt.

It was useful, in a way, to do a few hours occasionally to show people that she needed the money. She didn't need it at all. She was one of the wealthiest women in the Black Country but liked to keep her wealth a secret, even from her own husband.

Stephen was married to Mabel, who always seemed to fit in with what was needed to successfully run the fashionwear part of their business; always tastefully dressed, courteous and attentive. Quite sickening!

No, she thought. I am just being bitchy because I am jealous. The woman was clean, yes, tidy; no, she wasn't all that tidy, the way she had those old clothes piled in the corner. She did the managing of the haberdashery well apart from that, though; and kept her daughters in line. That must take a bit of doing, what with them both being in their young blood, and all those young men just over the yard from the shop. Why does Stephen want to start it up again, now?

Suddenly she realised what it was. It was because Tom was away at the hop picking; Tom's absence must have made him think of her and reawakened the quiescent emotional need in him. He had seen Tom's absence as an opportunity to rekindle their relationship. Sometimes Elsie and Stephen Stone went for months without even seeing each other, then they just had to have a glimpse of the other one and it all started all over again.

She looked across the table at Dan, her mind made up. She had no choice, really.

'Yes; alright. I don't mind putting in a few hours to help them out while Tom is away. I'll go round and see him tomorrow morning.'

It would give her chance to get the sort of job she would rather do. She didn't particularly want to work alongside Mrs Stone, having to put on airs and graces, and feeling guilty because Stone fancied her above his own wife! She had a moment of recollection of the last time she had been in the shop; while Stepphen had been talking normally to his wife, his hand had been caressing the back of Elsie's thighs. She reddened at the thought then replied to Dan.

'When does he want me to start, Dan? Do you know? What does he want me to do?'

She couldn't help having a little giggle to herself. As if she didn't know! Dan was lifting his head from his dinner. How could he be so naïve? He was always so trusting! She wouldn't trust her, if she were he! He was so annoying in his trust; always trusting her when a fool wouldn't. She had stayed late, 'getting an order out', and her high tapping heels had drummed out her guilt on the pavement on the late walk home, but he hadn't even given it a thought.

'Another few bob you've earned, love. 'That was all he'd had to say when she had walked in. He was talking again, now. He always wanted to put in his two penny worth to show his approval, although he knew he had no control over the money she earned.

'I think he wants you on the packing. The girl who was doing that has dropped on to the job that Tom was doing. I'm only guessing, mind. He'll tell you himself. Monday morning, he wants you, if that's all right. He said to say your rate has gone up a penny an hour, so you should be able to earn a decent bit if it suits you. Mind you, it's only till Tom gets home, so you won't have time to earn a fortune.'

Packing; she had done that before. The locks had to be sent out all over the Empire, all over the world in fact. She had often wondered, as she wrapped the locks in greaseproof paper, what they would be used to guard. The size of the locks that Stones' made varied from less than an inch, to over six inches; massive padlocks with long arms, with keys to match, that fitted onto hasps on enormous doors; protecting great warehouses in India, Singapore and Malaya.

The room, known as 'Goods Out' where she would be working, was quiet compared with the rest of the factory, except when the cardboard boxes containing the locks were placed into wooden crates, then one of the men would nail up the crates, and swing them down onto one of the great drays that called for them each, periodically. She would be packing on her own from Monday until Thursday night. She would have to be careful if Stephen came to see her; she might be tempted. She hoped so; she needed him. Her answer was bright and breezy, belying her feelings of hidden excitement.

'Yes, all right Dan, I'll go in and see him on Monday morning. There's no hurry to see him before then. In the meantime, I'd better go and get a bit of food to put on the table. I haven't had my housekeeping yet, you know.'

She stood there, not holding out her hand but obviously awaiting her housekeeping money. Just lately she'd had to ask for it. If Dan knew how much she had saved, she wouldn't get any housekeeping. She stood, still except that her hands were wringing the towel she had in her hand.

Dan Barr reddened, as he usually did when the subject of money was broached. He couldn't help it. He always tried to avoid the handing over of money. He handed the few coins over to her with ill grace. It wasn't that he was mean; he just wanted to hang onto it as long as possible. He had earned it and it was his, he felt. Every time he handed some of it over to someone else, he was left with less of it in his pocket until, towards the end of the week; there was none of it left. It didn't seem fair; there should be some left, to start next week with, at least. He often had to borrow some from Elsie. That didn't seem fair, either. How could you borrow the money you had earned yourself? How could Elsie last out better than he could, himself? He couldn't escape the notion that he must be giving her too much housekeeping. He had raised the subject once, in temper. She had not argued with him. She had just given him all of it back.

'Do the shopping and paying of the bills yourself then, if you can do it any better.'

He had tried, putting the same amount of money that he gave to Elsie on one side, but had still run out of money on Wednesday, and had had to ask her for the loan of some money. She had put two half-crowns in his hand without a word. On Friday he given her the usual amount of housekeeping, and never brought up the subject again. He had never asked her where she got the five shillings from, either. He had decided that that wasn't his business. As long as she kept the food on the table and paid the bills he would be happy. He accepted the idea that he was skilled at his trade and Elsie was skilled at hers.

He never asked her what she did with the money she got from the occasional part time jobs she took on, either. Once he had seen a bankbook in her drawer; he had not looked in it, and he never saw it again. He had once decided to ask her about it, but changed his mind. Some things were better not known, as when he made a small household tool as a 'foreigner', an unofficial job for someone. He never thought of offering her some part of what he earned in that way. They now had an understanding about such things. It was part of their loving but familiar relationship that allowed the other the courtesy of small privacies.

It had been difficult when he had returned from the war. He had been much more assertive at first. He had fought his way through the ranks as he had fought his way through France. He was head-down and charge; no matter what he did. It had worked along, with a lot of luck, to get him through, but was not appropriate in trying to work at a loving relationship. He had no finesse, no delicacy. It was all there, inside him, but he had not been taught to use it. Strange really; he was quite good at guiding young men.

He had only had his own determination to get him from where he was, to where he wanted to be. This had sustained him until now, but he was becoming aware of it, and felt the lack. He knew that he was not what he called a 'good catch' for Elsie. If he had not returned from the war, she would have found a better catch than him, regardless of the shortage of men, he felt sure. Their relationship had deteriorated since the first joy of returning. He was impotent now, and achieved occasional orgasm only by masturbation. He was still excited by the young girls who worked in the factory, but familiarity had taken the excitement out of his marriage.

Sometimes he looked at Elsie and felt that wanting need, but she didn't encourage him to express it. Perhaps if she did, he would be all right again. He was not promiscuous in outlook, just aware of his own need. He knew he could not make the first move, but would respond if she did. What if she felt the same way? What if someone else made the first move before he did? What if someone made the first move, to him? How would she react to that? He gave up trying to work it out; you never knew, with women, what was the right thing to do. Did they have the same thoughts going around their head?

He pushed his plate away, his dinner eaten, whether he had wanted it or not. He had never had the luxury of being able to waste a meal and he knew Elsie did the best she could with the housekeeping he gave her. It was hard enough, earning the money to get it to the table, without being so fussy that you could afford to throw it away.

'I'm going to the Deer's Leap on Friday.' He hesitated, 'Do

you want to come? There's a darts match on; we might get a bit of snap for supper.'

He was referring to the local custom of laying on food for a visiting team. Team members often had to start playing without having had the time to go home from work before turning up to play their match. Elsie thought about it. It would be a change. He didn't often ask her to accompany him to the public house. There might be some female company for her and, if not, there might be some of the other kind! Anyway, it would be a chance to eat a meal that someone else had cooked, and she wouldn't have to account for the money she saved.

'Yes, all right Dan. It would be nice to get out from these four walls. Who are they playing?'

'The Red Lion, from Aston, so it should be a good match. It was a draw, last time, but the Fowlers have put on another player. I don't know where they get their talent. It seems to run in the family.'

She took extra care over her hair that Friday night, and put on one of her better blouses. She had not been out for weeks and felt like a butterfly in a cocoon, so she was going to look the part! Dan was ready almost immediately after his cup of tea. 'He's starving.' She thought, 'I should have put a little something in front of him.'

'Do you want a bite of something before we go, Dan?'

She shouted down the stairs. No one was going to blame her if he went out on an empty stomach! She heard his refusal with relief, and trotted down the stairs, knowing the effect she would have on him. He did not often make a pass at her, but when she dressed in her best, she knew she could still make him want her. She wondered how she would react if he wanted her. Would she accede, or would she try to pass off his pass (she smiled at her own pun) as just a passing notion! She knew that when he had drunk a few pints he would be in a more amorous mood. Maybe she would, too.

She linked herself into his arm and they stepped out smartly.

He still walked as if he were in the Army. She could keep up with his pace, though, and rather enjoyed the liveliness of the fast walk; it made her feel more alive, as if she had a purpose, somewhere important to go. It was as if they were announcing to the neighbourhood that they had an important but pleasurable activity to go to.

They turned up the next street and in a few minutes were at the small public house; the venue for tonight's game of darts. Two small children were standing outside, waiting for their parents to come out to them. There was a good crowd inside; with only one two seats remaining. Elsie sat down next to a large, middle-aged woman who seemed to have been there some time. She was a supporter of the visiting team. Her husband was at the board. He was obviously one of the better players. He had a very masculine style, leaning forward, not obviously aggressive, but as if he were ready to face anyone. That was the way Elsie saw it, anyway. It gave her a secret thrill, to watch men competing, and she tried to guess who was going to be best at the competition, whatever it was. Dan was signalling her, asking what she would like to drink: he knew what she liked, a milk stout, but always offered her the opportunity to select something different.

'A babby in every bottle.' It was the large woman, sitting next to her who spoke. 'I bet he tries, an' all, don't he?'

She nodded in the direction of Dan. Elsie smiled back at her. 'They always want more than they can get, don't they?'

'Well my chap always wants more, anyway. He's a nuisance, sometimes, especially when he's had a drink. He'll want his oats tonight if I'm any judge.'

The conversation went rambling on, describing the shortcomings of men in general. Elsie let her mind wander. She had had this kind of chat before; it was not serious; just noises in the air to pass the time. The woman's husband, if that was what he was, was at the board again. A treble top followed by a nineteen, and then a double six. He'd won again. Elsie joined in the short burst of clapping, and the player, Reg, came and sat by his wife.

'Lucky again, love. Lucky at darts, unlucky in love.' His twinkling eyes belied his words. 'What are you having? Would you like one of these babby mekkers, same as this young lady, next to you?'

His question was directed as much at Elsie as to his wife? Both women nodded assent and he moved over to the bar.

'He's always like this, buying drinks, when he's had a win. He 'as a bet on the side when he plays, so if he wins, it means he's got a few bob to come from someone, usually the one he's playing. The bet seems to frighten some players, seems to unnerve them, if you know what I mean. And he has a better chance of winning then. It makes Reg feel more of a man as well. I shall know about it tonight, when we get home.'

He came back, bringing drinks for all of them, against Dan's slightly false protests. The sandwiches and pickles were being passed round, now. The match was over and everyone seemed to relax. It had not been an important game, just a chance to try to get a few points in the league table. The large man, Reg, sat down between his wife and Elsie, and almost immediately she could feel his thigh pressing against hers. He was loud and full of himself she decided and moved away, as far as she could. Dan had caught sight of what was happening and was showing signs of getting angry although the player was ignoring him. She knew what Dan was capable of, so as soon as they had finished the sandwich in front of them, she turned to the woman next to her and spoke.

'I think we'll have to go now. We've left the children on their own, and we told them we wouldn't be long.'

Dan looked at her questioningly, but Elsie just said her 'goodnights', so he went along with her.

'What was all that about? I knew he was coming on a bit strong, but I could have put him down if he became a nuisance.'

'Yes, Dan I know you could have put him down. Now you don't need to, do you see?' She knew he was getting irate and interrupted what he was going to say. 'I have seen you in action before, Dan, and know what you are capable of, but you will only get yourself in trouble, one of these days.

'You're not in the war now; killing people is not allowed, just because a drunk has made a bit of a pass at your wife. He didn't mean any harm; just felt good. Don't you feel good, sometimes Dan? I saw you make eyes at one or two of the married women in there, even if you aren't the world's best lover. Sometimes a man, or a woman, just wants to break all the rules. It might do you a bit of good if you broke a rule or two, occasionally, Dan; why don't you try it? I wouldn't mind, you know; it might make you more, you know, virile.'

Dan pulled her into an entry they were passing and pulled her body against his.

'Listen, I don't want anyone but you. If I can't have you, I don't want anyone else to.'

He put his hand inside her coat, grabbing her breast with such force that he hurt her. With the hurt came the feeling that she had missed; the need for fulfilment of her bodily desires. She responded, giving herself to him, touching and holding him as he was holding her. She knew, now, also, that she could not turn her back on this side of her nature and that she would have to say yes to any suggestion that Stephen Stone might make. She had decided to live for the moment, every moment, and take the consequences, whatever they might be. This was another moment in her life that she did not wish to pass by!

She put her hand down the front of Dan's trousers and took hold of him. He was ready. She stroked him, gently at first, then with increasing vigour. It was always with a change, with fresh stimuli that he became like this, more animal-like and able to function as a lover. It was obvious that he was ready; she pulled him away from the entry wall and inserted herself in his place. Her dress moved up her legs until she took hold of her underclothes and drew them down.

'Come on, Dan, give it to me. I want you!'

She whispered loudly. She could imagine Stephen and enjoy

Dan, all at the same time. It was incredible, but she didn't want to dwell on it. She just wanted to get the most intense pleasure that she could out of the encounter. He had his lips on her breast, she noticed, and her emotions flew higher again, taking her to higher levels of sexual experience. Orgasm came after orgasm and her legs became weak, but she could not fall. He was holding her up, forcing himself into her body, almost rape-like in his desperation.

At last he reached his own ultimate climax, convulsing his body in great movements and relaxed against the wall; like Elsie he was almost too weak to hold himself up. After a few minutes he smiled at her.

'I've never felt like that, before. You're, I don't know, wonderful.' He was silent for a moment and Elsie started to tidy her clothes. He took her back in his arms, more tenderly than he had. 'You're my everything, you know. I really don't know what I would do without you. If I thought I was going to lose you, I would kill myself, but not before I killed you! I know you've not always been true to me; it's not in your nature to deny yourself what you want and I sometimes imagine I can see the eyes of one of your lovers looking at me out of Tom's or Ted's eyes, and it makes me wonder. Then I decide not to wonder, and just enjoy what I have with you, so there!'

He paused for breath and time, to put his feelings and thoughts into some sort of coherent order and Elsie stared at him, shocked that he might have got at the truth about their children's parentage. He didn't give her time to react but just went on.

'Do you think I am that much of a fool that I would just allow myself to be cuckolded by Stephen Stone, without getting wind of it? I knew the day I came back from France. You were too much of a woman to be able to restrain your feelings; well it's got to stop. There is nothing the matter with me that a faithful woman can't put right; it's up to you. If you don't want the job, just say and I'll look for someone else.'

Did he mean it? Had he got what it took to carry out his threat? Could he deny his love for her, just because of a principle?

Did he really know, or was he just guessing; bluffing? She was shocked to the core by the strength of his passion. If he could guarantee that, she would never want anyone else, or would she? His resolve, though strong at the moment, might weaken, anyway. All she could do was to survive each day as it came, living her life in the best way she could, lying as necessary. She determined to put her life in an order of sorts and tell him so.

'Dan, I've always loved you more than anyone else. All I've ever wanted was the strength of your arms round me. You must believe me.' She stepped back into the shadow of the entry again. Her smile seemed to reach across the darkness and connected with his eyes.

She pulled him towards her. 'You don't think I would ever want more than you have given me, tonight, do you?'

She saw the answer in his trusting eyes; she took hold of his hand, and they stepped out into the gaslight and walked slowly towards their home. He put his arm around her shoulders as they walked, and she felt that he had taken her at face value. She would face the temptation of Stephen Stone as it presented itself. She had to see him tomorrow, to start work in the inspection room. She would probably be telling Dan lies again, tomorrow night.

16. Unpacking and Packing.

Stephen Stone was angry with his Uncle Bert. The order had been made up incorrectly again, Bert was responsible, and the men on the shop floor knew. The foreman had been wrong not to check his work, but still, an experienced man like Bert, the son of the gaffer, should not have put German locks with Indian locks. They were so different in requirements that a child would know. That was how Stephen saw it. Overtime rates had been paid to put the mistake right. Not a lot, it was true, but it was another mistake that Bert had made that had lowered his status with the men, and the firm's profitability.

There was a knock at the door, and then it was pushed open. Stephen Stone was about to shout at the intrusion then saw that it was Elsie Barr. He smiled a welcome. They had been lovers in the past and, he felt, would be again. He gave her a swift, inspecting look. She was just as smart and proud as ever, slim, upright and svelte, standing out from a crowd. His look betrayed his feelings, he felt.

'Come on in, Elsie. You are just the one I wanted to see.' He hesitated, but only for a second. 'Will you be able to give me a few hours a week, until your Tom gets back from the picking? I hope so 'cos I've just had Germans locks mixed with Indians, and I need somebody who knows what they are doing, to repack them.'

He moved back from the door and sat down, looking at her. God, she was a lovely woman! He could not help but want her. He had always felt like that about her. Whatever she saw in that Dan, he couldn't see. What a face, what a body!

'Come and sit down, Elsie. You don't have to stand on ceremony here. You know that. How are you keeping?'

She was feeling similar emotions. The emotions had been hiding, awaiting the opportunity to air. Stephen and Elsie looked at each other, and joined. There was no other word for it. It was not a physical thing, although the feeling had physical attributes. They just seemed to come together; there was no sense to it and neither did it require sense. Each of them was part of a pair, like bookends she thought. She sat in the wooden chair, crossed her legs and looked him in the eye. For this fleeting, brave moment, she would maintain her principles. It mattered not that she had sworn her faithfulness to Dan.

'Steve, I will not risk my marriage, or yours. I don't want to get caught with your hand up my skirt. It was bad enough last time, with your wife standing next to us! I thought I would die. I won't stand for anything like that again.'

She attempted to sound irate but it did not seem to come out right. It was as if she was at a crossroads and having to take the wrong road, whether she wanted to or not. Stephen laughed, and his laugh was infectious. The memory of them standing there, his hand caressing her bottom, while his wife smiled engagingly at a customer was too much to bear, and he just burst out guffawing, and she, seeing the same mental picture as he, could not help but join in.

'Oh, Steve, you are the bloody limit. I've never known anyone like you. How do you keep your face straight? You are always making me laugh. I can't help it.'

She took out a handkerchief and wiped a tear from the corner of her eye. He was too much. She opened her eyes and saw that he wasn't there. Then she felt his arms enclose her from behind, his hands on her breasts and his lips on her neck. The same old thrill enveloped her and she remembered the promise she had made to herself, and she pulled at him, ironically, frantically.

'All right, then! Go on! Lock the door!'

She stood up, lifted her skirt up and pulled her underclothes down, kicking them under the desk, the deep pink making a bloodlike splash on the dark oak floor; the black shoes contrasting, but also harmonising with the pink. It reminded her of the front room; it was ridiculous. Black, to her, was always shiny. She looked at him once more.

'Is this what you want, Stephen? Am I just your bit on the side? Is that what I am to you? Well, let me tell you, I am more than that to Dan, despise him as you may. He loves me, needs me and wants me. He has got more to offer than you, Stephen Stone.' She was silent for a moment or two, feeling, thinking; trying to work things out, to make sense. She felt helpless in the face of her own emotions. 'Hold me, Steve. Hold me, Steve.'

What she was saying was more like shouting; it made no sense and yet he knew what she was trying to say to him. He stepped back at her seemingly violent change in conduct. She grabbed hold of him by the sleeves of his jacket, pulling it off his shoulders. It dropped on the floor on top of her clothes. It seemed appropriate to him. He stepped back until he had the wall behind him. She advanced further and taking hold of his braces slid them off his shoulders and pulled his trousers down to his ankles. Elsie was red in the face; red as a turkey cock's arse, he always said. He grinned again and wished he could stop grinning. What was happening was too serious to be laughing about. She started speaking violently, her words hitting him like physical things.

'Now you are in the same boat as me, aren't you? How do you like being unpacked?'

She looked at him; his face had gone red. He was laughing again! She had never met a man who laughed so much.

'Oh, Elsie, if you could only see yourself now.'

He stepped forward and lifted her skirt, then pulled her onto his body, his reaching for hers, and finding it. She gasped at the audacity of it, realised she was ready for it, and then decided to just enjoy it. She started to move convulsively, holding onto him with both hands. Her legs came up, as if they had a life of their own, and her weight pulled him forward and down, onto the slippery wooden floor of the office. He pushed away from the wall to give himself more leverage then they both struggled around the slippery floor, trying to get a grip on anything. Somehow they managed to move onto a mat and, still laughing and giggling, started to move in unison.

They stopped giggling and started to feel the moment, their bodies searching for ways to extend and increase the amount of tactile sensation they could find. Slowly, their bodies found what they wanted and gradually entered into each other, becoming more and more a single entity, until they could tolerate the sinuous slowness of the movements no longer, and started to accelerate their actions, causing them both to pant and gasp with the sheer physical effort.

When it came, the sudden climax surprised them both with the height of passion they had reached in such a short time and they lay still, slowly recovering from the exertion. The lying together was just as necessary and valuable to them as the violent passion they had been enjoying. It was a post-climactic fulfilment of feelings, not an anti-climax, not love, not passion but something else, a confirmation of a lifelong bond that they fully expected never to end, regardless of outside complications. It was like a marriage without rules or certificates, a relationship that they redefined each time they met, and created according to the circumstances existing.

The sound of a press thumping through a sheet of steel gradually encroached onto their senses. It seemed to be thumping in time with their hearts, as if it were trying to encourage them to resume. Stephen tried to move with it but found that he had not the energy. He smiled to himself, and at himself, knowing it might well be Dan Barr who was doing the pressing. Elsie saw him and whispered in his ear.

'Laughing again? What's so funny, now?'

He tried, lying, to explain that he was smiling at his own temporary inability and her mood seemed to slide in with his, and she started to smile, too. She took the opportunity of being superior to him and slid around, to look him in the eyes.

'So, this is how you spend your time, is it? Who is it you've been laying down with while I have not been here? Do you have it off with your wife, in the office, in between handing out pay-packets; do you touch her up like you touched me up, in front of the carriage trade customers? Or do you conduct job

174

interviews on this line? Mind you, you are a pretty good packer, even though I say it myself, who shouldn't.'

Stephen seemed to move away from her, in a shrinking sort of movement, but still trying to hold on to the feeling that she had roused in him. His reply was surprising.

'Would you believe I very rarely have sex nowadays? It's just you that makes me feel like this. It's just you and your body, but not just your body that makes my body come alive. It's your whole personality and being that seems to match and want me, as much as I, and my body, want you, and yours.'

His whole attitude was that of seriousness, the smile gone from his face, as he spoke. She knew exactly how he felt, because she felt the same way, her emotional responses matching his. She could never deny him, but could never leave Dan. It was impossible. She wanted both men absolutely and firmly to the exclusion of everyone and everything else. It did not, and never had, made sense. She forced herself to return to normality, dressing herself, looking herself up and down as best she could. Stephen was doing the same. She sat on the chair next to the desk.

'Well, do I get the job? Did I pass the trade test? When do I start?'

She brushed her hand through her hair and smiled at him. It was sad, really, the way things were. Life would be so much simpler if his wife died. She could just move in then, and marry Steve - if Dan was not around. It was all just a dream, but an attractive dream. He was staring at her, as if, in some way, he was sharing her thoughts. His words showed his depth of thought and emotion.

'Life plays some funny, dirty tricks, don't it? All you want to do is the right thing, and then your body, or your mind, finds something, someone else that seems more attractive than the moon at harvest time, and all of a sudden you think the right thing is somehow different to what the right thing was, yesterday. How do you make sense of it, Elsie? How do you? I don't want to do the dirty on Mabel; I just want to be good, honest I do. I bet you don't believe me, do you?'

Elsie was staring at him; he had the feeling she was sharing his every thought. They had always had this gift, of sharing points of view that others did not seem to understand. She spoke quietly so that her reply was soft, gentle, almost whispered.

'Steve, I've always shared my feelings for you, with you. I've always known you wanted me, and still want me, like I want you. It's a bloody nuisance at times, but I wouldn't change it. The only problem is; how can I, or you, justify it?' She pulled at her stocking, straightening the seam. 'What excuse is there to offer? What's the use of making vows, and all that nonsense, if you know you can't keep to them? Sometimes I think we are like magnets. If we are placed a certain way, we attract each other; if we are turned round; we push away. Do you know what I mean?'

Her face creased with the effort of trying not to cry. He put his arm round her shoulder and pulled her gently to him, turning her face up to be kissed.

'Well, don't you get worrying. I'm not going to upset Danny Barr's apple cart. I know it would break your heart to upset him, same as I don't want to upset Mabel. She's been a good wife to me; she don't deserve to have the dirty done on her.'

The impossibility of the situation seemed to cause their conversation to come to a natural end and they started discussing Elsie's rate of pay, and the work that she would have to do. He told her how the mistake had been found. That Bert!

She owed him a lot of pay, the way he made mistakes and the way she had to come in and rectify them. She ought to buy him a Christmas present. Perhaps he would be better employed on the shop floor, learning the trade from the bottom up. Her son Ted could then do his work. Ted had been quite ill, as a child. They never did have a proper diagnosis, but the symptoms were that of consumption. He had lost weight, and they had thought that they might lose him. Then he had started to recover in a gradual way, and had never looked back since. He had always been interested in learning more about everything. English, mathematics; history, he had been like blotting paper, soaking it all up; he was like an adding machine the way he dealt with things in such a logical way. Because he was not, at first, able to play the usual boyhood games in the street, he had never had a normal relationship with Tom.

Tom had been sorry for him, looked after him, defended him, but had never really played with him. They had grown up together, but apart. Elsie's thought returned to the present. Perhaps she could do something to arrange the lives of Ted and Bert! Now would not be a good time though! Steve was looking at her again, trying to mine her thoughts. She redirected the conversation.

'When do you want me to start, Mr Stone? I'm free, now, if you like.'

She spoke slightly coquettishly, to make sure he couldn't realise what her thoughts were.

'All right, Elsie. You can start by re-packing those export orders that were mixed up. You know how they should be packed. Put the Germans with Germans, regardless of the size or type. Just make sure they all get to Germany! Germany has to pay for them with other goods. The German Mark is worthless at the moment but we still have to try to trade with them. And make sure the Indians all get to India! When you have finished with them, let young Ted know. He has to send an invoice for them and send a delivery note with each batch. It's a good job he noticed the mistake, though Bert wasn't at all pleased, and denied it.'

She hadn't been told that it was her son that had noticed the packing mistake. She had a funny feeling about it, but couldn't put her finger on what it was. After all, there was no way that Ted could have repacked them, in the wrong way. He would not do that, anyway; it was not his style. Or was it? What would it profit Ted to do something like that? Who else could have done it? It must have been Bert; he was always doing something daft. He hadn't even been allowed to start at the bottom. Then he was blamed for doing something wrong when he had never been taught how to do it in the first place. Mabel was status conscious; none of her family would wish to mix with the working class! The woman had done her son a disservice, Elsie thought. He could have been a useful member of the family firm if he had been taught properly. She knew Dan felt the same way about Bert. Dan had always been patient with him.

'Look what he had to contend with, in growing up,' he had said to her once. She had known that he was talking about Stephen's attitude to his uncle's lack of training. Sometimes she wondered if he had always known about her and Stephen. He had always been sympathetic to the things she did that she thought, maybe, his understanding extended to her as well. It gave her a funny feeling, to think that he was making loving allowances for her! She found it difficult to think that he could accept what she couldn't. If she had found him out in a similar situation, she would have hurt him. She couldn't have accepted the humiliation of being second in his, or anyone else's affections. Her thoughts returned to the cause of her being there.

Although Bert Stone wasn't her son, Elsie had always felt sorry for him. She felt that if she had been able to guide him, he would have turned out to be a better person. It wasn't strictly true; she only had to look at Tom and Ted to see that they were entirely different to each other, although she had tried to give each of her children all of her attention. Tom was more open-minded and straight-forward than Ted, who was often oblique in his approach to life. She turned her mind back to the job in hand. It was no good trying to figure out the differences between one child and another. Maybe it was what was in them when they were born. It certainly wasn't in the way they had been brought up.

The rest of the day went quickly; she did not really like having breaks. She just had the need to work as efficiently as possible, and to get praised and paid for it. She was paid by the piece, 'piece-work', if she achieved a minimal number. After that she was paid an amount for each one that she packed. Her hands became a blur as she moved into a practiced rhythm of movement, sorting one type of lock from another and repacking them. Her mind moved away from the work; she could sort and pack without having to think about it.

She mentally added her earnings to her fund of savings and spent the other half. Spend half and save half! She still had the house to clean when she got home. It was about time she had some new curtains. She liked the look of those in the shop in the Willenhall market square. If they hadn't got what she wanted she could always have a look round the market. Some times there were bargains to be had there. She made up her mind to go there on Saturday. She liked the market at Willenhall. Often she met neighbours and had an enjoyable hour passing the time of day and gossiping about things in general.

It was at the market that she had first met Stephen. She had been looking at the beefsteak, trying to decide whether to wait until later in the day, when the meat would have its price reduced to get rid of it, or whether to buy it now, freeing her day to do with as she wished. She had heard his voice for the first time.

'Gi'e us a pound o' that steak, my mon, afore it walks away on its own.' The butcher had laughed along with Stephen. It was obvious that they were old friends. 'This pretty lady'd like a pound an' all, Sam. You can see the way she is eyeing it up; she's wondering whether she could catch it, if it got away to a flying start.'

Stephen had looked at her then, and their first 'joining' had happened. They had gone walking through the market as if there were no one else there. That had been over ten years ago, before the war. After walking through the market, he had led her to his trap; the recollection made her laugh now as it had then. They had driven into the country, talking about nothing in particular but both anxious for the intimacy of being alone somewhere.

They had stopped by a well-known beauty spot, to admire the view. Their lovemaking had been instant, intense, and bonding in result. She had looked for him, by the clock, every Saturday after that, for months. They had made no plans. Later, it would have been unacceptable to leave a husband who was risking his life for King and Country, almost an act of treason.

She still loved Dan. She realized that, even in the middle of a violent coupling. He was similar to Stephen in many ways, but

Stephen was a little taller where Dan had a thickness of chest and neck, like a Staffie dog, she thought. Both men were quiet in their ways, unlike many of the men who had been left behind by the draft because of ill-health or the demands of the work they did.

There were lots of men like Dan, who had learned to kill swiftly, in order to save their own lives; now they had discarded those skills and taken up where they had left off before the war, but things were different now. Men wanted a dignity that the landed gentry had never accorded them, and they meant to have it. It was 1923 and there was talk of social change, even whispers of a revolution like that in Russia. The death of the Monarchy was unthinkable but men and women had earned a better level of respect. There would be an election soon and that could bring change.

Baldwin had taken the premiership somehow. No one seemed to know how. It was all to do with Bonar Law having to resign after he had incurable cancer of the throat. It was still to be seen what benefits there would be to the nation.

Dan liked to talk about the political scene but Tom was bored by it. He felt that the country would work things out in its own time. Revolution was not part of his ethos but he could sympathise with the Germans whose Mark had suffered badly. A loaf of bread cost 200,000,000,000 Marks, an impossible price.

A new man, an Adolf Hitler was making inroads into the German elective population. Was it possible that that was what was needed here? Would England, the United Kingdom even, be better off if it had a strong leader? He wondered what sort of man it would have to be to kill the Royal Family. Even though he was angry with the Government, he knew he could never bring himself to support anyone who would kill the King and Queen.

His father had not long returned from the war to end all wars and Germany, even though it had lost the war, was making progress. They had always been good organisers

How could they even consider starting another war?

He had a feeling that there were changes to come.

17. Ted, Germans and Indians.

Mom was here, again. He wasn't surprised that she had turned up this morning. He had heard them talking about it, last night. Dad was always willing for Mom to go out and earn a few shillings, even at Stones'. If he only knew what went on there he would go mad. In a way, he thought, it was down to me that she had been able to start at a moment's notice.

That idiot Bert hadn't known how the Germans had come to be mixed with the Indians. It had been easy to go into the packing shop when no one was looking, and change a few of the locks that were about to be put into the wooden crates, ready for the carrier to pick up. Then he had steered Bill Morgan, the foreman, towards them, and pointed out the mixed order by asking if they were now sending Germans to India. Bill had cast an eye over them casually, almost by accident; it was second nature to him to check any work done, and had seen the pile of German locks, half packed into the same crates as the Indian locks.

If they had been allowed to go, the German locks would have simply disappeared, and the first that would have happened following their transit would have been an enquiry from Berlin, requesting delivery. Probably, Stone would have been suspicious and considered that a fraud was being carried out.

Morgan had gone straight to Stone and told him what he had found. Stone had gone to the packing room immediately, seen what the situation was and had almost hit Bert, who was responsible for packing them. Bert, of course, was too stupid to understand how the mix up could have happened. He had just stood there, saying how sorry he was and denying it at the same time. That would serve him right for what he had done to me, Ted thought. Stone had sent for him, to re-sort the packs into separate piles ready for whoever was going to re pack them. It was ironic that Mom had been offered the job while Tom was away, picking hops, like a country yokel.

It was about all he was good for. Oh yes, he had seen him and that Selina, holding onto each other like a couple of in-season dogs. I just wish I had half an hour with her, he thought. I would give her just as good a time as Tom. He brought his mind back to the Invoice Book.

People thought that this was his life, leaning over a desk all day, adding and taking away. Only he knew the world that lived inside his head. His mind dwelt on the potential adding and taking away he would like to do. The adventures he had! He'd had a good teacher in Mom. He had caught her engaged in her other activities with Stephen Stone. She had never found out that he knew, and he had never let on. There was no point. Once you opened up about a secret, its value had gone.

One day, perhaps, he would let Mom or Stone know what he knew. It was not a good move at the moment. He neatly filled in the details of the order that was ready for the carrier. There was nothing else for him to do for the present. The Invoice was what mattered. As he closed the Invoice Book, Stephen Stone walked through the office.

'If you've nothing else to do, go and see if Mrs Stone needs any help with her books.'

He spoke testily, as if he was recovering from some physical exercise. Perhaps he was! Ted liked being in the shop with the Stones' girls. He often felt that they were talking about him behind his back, much to his satisfaction. There must be nothing worse than having no one talk about you, he mused. You would be a nothing, then!

It was only a few yards across the shiny, blue-brick laid area between the lock-making area and the haberdashery shop that Mabel Stone and her two daughters ran between them. Jean, the youngest, watched him enter the shop through the back door and sniffed to show what she thought of him. If he noticed, he simply wiped his feet, as he entered. He did not alter his face in response.

'Why are you always like that with him? What has he done to you? You are not like that with his brother, when he comes in.' Laura, the eldest of the daughters spoke, admonishingly. 'What would you say if he was like that, with you?'

'Well, sometimes he just stands there, with a face like a bosted boot!' Jean replied, and then realised that she had talked herself into a trap. It wouldn't be right, would it, if she was to act in a way that she claimed to disapprove of? 'He just gets me mad. If he was like that with me I would tell him to go and get another job, the miserable wretch!'

She faltered as she spoke; trying to cover up her mistake, but it was no good; Laura, smiling, had seen through her attempt to show herself in a good light. Laura always did. She was too clever for her own good!

Jean turned from the unpacking of a box of liberty bodices.

'You are for ever fighting over men, if you can call them that. That Bert is about as gain as a pig with a pitch-fork, even if he is our own uncle!'

Her voice contained venom that you could almost feel, Laura thought. Bert's not so bad, really. At least, he's the sort of chap a woman could keep under control; that's more than you could say for some of them key-smiths in the factory. I bet that Tom will come back from the hop fields thinking he's God's gift to women!

'What's he done, now, any way? He's always making some mistake,' Jean, sniffing again to show how above it all she was, spoke up. 'He's like a spare spinster at a wedding, sometimes!' Jean spoke, disapprovingly, like she always does, thought Laura. 'He's bloody well gone and mixed them German locks up with the Indian locks. Dad's had to get Elsie Barr in to help to re pack them. She'll love that; putting right something what the Gaffer's son has done wrong.'

From the back of the shop there came a sort of sigh, and Mabel Stone turned and intervened in the discussion.

'If you girls don't mind, there is a lot of work to be done, here. If you could all work as quick and good as you can talk, we would all be millionaires. Well, we're not, so in the meantime, I would be grateful if you could do something towards earning your keep.'

She spoke as seriously as she could. She always let them give out the meat of the gossip before she shut them up. She spoke quietly but the girls knew she was getting serious with them, and turned back to what they were doing. They all had to start work at seven o'clock in the morning. The shop opened at eight. They closed up at six o'clock and left the shop how it was, to be cleaned the following morning. Jean, the youngest, made tea, as it was required. They all got on well most of the time, working with a will to please the many customers who came in to buy wool, threads, silks, clothes, buttons and all the seemingly endless variety of items that made up a haberdashery.

Mabel was their Manageress, Mentor, Mother and any other role she deemed necessary, as well as sometimes, the older sister. She watched each male who entered the shop like a protective falcon, her longish nose and close hairstyle adding to the illusion. She did not look well pleased with herself today, Laura thought. I wonder if it is because Ted has just come into the shop. What was he doing here, anyway? She looked at him in her, pretending to be serious, way.

'What are you doing here, in the shop, Teddy? You don't usually work here. Have you been promoted?'

'Mr Stone sent me to see Mrs Stone, to ask if there is anything I can do.'

He answered her question, defiantly.

'Well, ask her then! Don't just stand there like a stuffed dummy.' She turned to the figure bending over a large basket in the doorway of the next room. 'Mother, Teddy Barr wants to know if you can find him some work!'

They all laughed out loud at the nickname, and he turned a gentle shade of pink, but held his ground.

'You always have a laugh at my expense. I suppose you think it's clever. You may not always think like that.'

Mabel Spire appeared in the doorway, listening as she always was.

'Are you threatening my daughters, young Ted Barr?'

She deliberately let her tongue linger on the sound of his name. He was sure she was going to call him Teddy. When he replied, his voice had a slight catch in it.

'No, no, Ma-Mrs Stone.' He had returned the compliment by nearly calling her Mabel, but not quite. 'Do you have anything you would like me to do?' He had a way of offering, as if he were giving his body and soul. 'If your books need bringing up to date, I could do that for you, or anything else.'

He liked Mabel Stone, in spite of her sometimes-biting tongue, and it showed. He made her smile too, with his seemingly innocent double entendres, and that, itself, was something worth doing, thought Mabel. She didn't smile as often as she would like to.

'Come through into the office Ted. You can enter the sales for last week. They have not been put in, yet. I don't like not having that figure to hand, and no one else has thought to do it.'

She put the book in front of him, moving close. He was suddenly aware of her perfume, and looked up at her face. She was looking down at him, her face silhouetted between her breasts; caught in the act, she blushed and quickly turned to a slip of paper.

'These are the wholesale figures. Most of the purchasers have paid by cheques, so I would like you to reconcile the figures with the bank's.' When you have done that, add the figures to last week's cash sales; that way we know what the proper Sales Figure is, to be entered in the book.'

She was still blushing slightly, Ted noticed. I wonder if she likes me. He reached out to take the slip of paper, and took her hand, by mistake. He felt himself redden and she noticed, but she did not withdraw her hand, but slid her fingers into his palm. Her finger-ends caught at his reflexes and his body responded unwillingly and he stood up, breathing a little heavier, their hands still touching. She spoke, quietly.

'Are you making a pass at me, Teddy Bear? I hope you know your place.'

Her fingers were still moving on his palm, accidentally?

'I know what my place will be, Mrs Stone, one day,' he whispered. 'Very close, to you!' She snatched her hand away from his. 'Just get on with what you are paid to do, please. You know what has to be done.'

He turned and followed her eyes. Jean was standing in the doorway. She hadn't heard any of the exchange, he felt sure. He had thought Jean had a crush on him. She was always in a doorway when he wanted to go through it; making him struggle to get past her. Mabel had passed into the shop, now. Surely she was just having a bit of fun at his expense, the same as Laura and Jean. What a trick it would be, to have Mother and daughter!

He moved to pass Jean and lifted his hand as if to avoid her, letting it pass over in a parallel curve to, but not quite touching, her breast. She gasped and moved slightly back, and then he changed his mind and passed her again, and let his breath touch her neck. The effect was instantaneous. Her breath was drawn in as if she were a horse, out of breath. She didn't move, though. Well, he thought; there's a thing! I might be in with a chance, there. He moved back to the desk as if the incident had not occurred.

He glanced at the clock. A quarter to six; it was nearly time to go home. His mother would not have the evening meal ready tonight. She would probably just be finishing off what she was doing with those Germans and Indians. They would have yesterday's 'warm-ups', a hash made from the leftovers of yesterday's meal. She always cooked too much on Sundays. It was deliberate, to provide a cheap and easily prepared meal for Mondays. They all enjoyed the meal, lashed with sauce, and bread to dip in to soak up the rich gravy. A hand touched his shoulder. It was Jean.

'Day-dreaming again, Teddy Barr? It's time to go, unless you want to stay on for a bit.'

Was it deliberately a double meaning, or was it said in innocence? He took a chance.

'I wouldn't mind staying on if you will keep me company. I am sure we could find something to do that takes two people. If you could feed me the figures for this week, as well as last week's, I could enter and add them up as we went along.'

He was known for his ability to add a column of figures as they were read out to him. She agreed at once. She would get the gratitude of her father for getting the books straight.

'Mother, I'm going to stay with Mr Barr to get the Sales figures right up to date if that's alright with you. It should take about three quarters of an hour.'

It was a query, a request for permission to stay over. Mabels' attitude to men was well known. However, the advantage gained by the possible work that could be done overcame her usual resistance. She acceded; her daughter knew better than to allow any funny stuff to go on. She hadn't thought he had it in him, anyway, until their close encounter this evening; now she wasn't so sure.

'All right, Jean, but don't be all night. Your dinner will be on the table at ten past seven o'clock. Come along girls; it's six o'clock; time to go.'

They all put on their coats, Laura giggling as the thought of Teddy Barr staying with Jean occurred to her.

'Defend your virginity with all your might,' she whispered in Jean's ear. 'I'll stand by you if you become a fallen woman.'

'Get on with you, you cheeky madam. Sometimes I think you wouldn't mind being a fallen woman! The very thought of anything like that had never struck me. It's just that Father seems as if he's got the cares of the world on his shoulders, lately, and I think he should have the best from us that we are capable of, don't you?'

The answer was so unexpected that it shut any sort of accusation. Laura stared at her, wondering if it was a sincere reply, then giggled.

Her mother appeared. 'Aren't we the dutiful daughter, then? Just make sure you are in to wait on your beloved father, then. The keys are hanging on the hook under the counter. Good night Ted.'

Mabel left the door to swing to automatically, as she left the shop to catch up with Jean. Ted had listened to the exchanges between Mabel and her daughter, and was a little puzzled by the discourse.

'She is very understanding with you girls, isn't she? My mother or father wouldn't allow talk like that. Dad is so puritan, sometimes. I think he would be better off in a monastery, sometimes.' He sat down at the desk. 'If you come and sit by me and tell me the figures of the cheques, I will add them up and we'll soon get this job done.' He moved the small stool closer to him, and she sat down, almost touching him.

'What is the first figure then, Jean?' He leaned across her to point out the column that he wished her to read out, 'Seven pounds, six and four pence, right? That's the first one. Next?'

'Wait a minute Ted; I want to lock the shop. I don't feel safe this time of night with the door open. Anyone could come walking in. Goodness knows what they might find!' She stood up. 'Where did Laura say the keys were, under the counter?'

She walked towards the door and slid the bolt across that was fitted to add to the strength of the Stones' Lock.

'They are not here, Ted. Do you know where they are?'

Ted moved over to the counter, to stand behind her and as he did so, her buttocks pressed back until they touched him as she bent to look under the counter. He stumbled and as he did so caught at her hips, pulling her to him to steady himself; the contact was a stimulus to further contact. He straightened her body, still pressed against his, and slid his hands up, until they were almost cupping her breasts. She leaned back, looking over her shoulder.

'Are you sure you are looking for the keys, Ted? It seems to me, you are searching for something else!' She put her hands on his and slid them onto her breasts. 'There, that's what you were looking for isn't it?'

She turned in his arms and placed her hands each side of his face, then pressing herself against him she kissed him, full on the lips. Then she moved away and whispered in his ear.

'We'd better find the keys, hadn't we?'

We certainly had, Ted thought. If anyone sees us like this, there will be trouble. He bent and knelt on the floor, peering under into the darkness of the shadows under the counter.

'Can you see them?'

He looked up. Jean had undone her blouse and her shift underneath barely concealed her body.

'Let me help you find them.'

He reached for her, his body frightened but responding at the same time, pulling her down to the floor. His lips just touched the edge of the curve of her breast and she lowered herself to him, enabling him to give a firmer kiss, on the slightly tilted brown auricle that encircled her nipple. She unexpectedly pulled at him, with all her might, it seemed. Her blouse seemed to fall away, and the sight of her was almost too overwhelming for his senses. He had never seen naked breasts, before.

'Hold me tight, Ted! Tighter!'

He squeezed her as tightly as he could, feeling the passion that was surging through her, sensing the movement of her body against his, surprised that she could tolerate his pinching and biting into her breast. Suddenly she went limp in his arms, her eyes closed. Ted panicked and stroked her face, not knowing what to do. He buttoned up her blouse, gently stroking her face, straightening her skirt, but feeling her smooth silkiness at the same time, peering in the gloom to see if he could trace any sign of life. She stirred and spoke his name.

'Ted, oh Ted. What did you do to me? I have never felt like that, before. What happened to me?'

He replied as best he could.

'I don't know. We were kissing when, all of a sudden, you fainted. I have never known that to happen before. All I can think of is that it was your feelings at the time. What do you think, Jean?'

He fell silent awaiting her reply.

'Feelings? Feelings? I've never felt that way, before. It was as if we were together, if you know what I mean, really together, all the way. I wonder if that's what it feels like.' She pulled his hand back to her breast, again. 'Have you ever, you know, been all the way?'

She leaned against him intimately, making him feel that they had a permanent relationship. What should he do? Her breast felt just wonderful. He was aroused again.

'I think you are - I don't know what, Jean; you are just wonderful. No, I have never been all the way. I don't know how I held myself back, then. I just think it wouldn't be fair to go all the way, when you were, you know. Anyway, it's not right; I know you want to save yourself for when you are married. '

If only he knew! If he had known how much passion there was inside her, waiting to come out, he wouldn't have been so damned chivalrous! She replied to him in terms that he would understand.

'I think it was quite chivalrous of you, not to take advantage of me when I was out, so to speak, or didn't I have that much effect on you, Teddy? Perhaps there is something the matter with you. Would you rather it was my older sister, Laura that was with you? I think she likes you, the way she was mocking me, earlier on.'

The phrases she used were designed to make him deny, in protest, what she was saying, and cement their affiliation even more than it was. However, she was also planting thoughts and ideas in his mind that he had not considered before. He was having a mind-stirring time, tonight! Mabel had shown that she was attracted to him, so had Laura and now the idea was being put into his head that the youngest and prettiest of the Stones' girls was also paying attention to him! How could he make use of this information? He spoke to her unspoken fears.

'Jean, I have told you; I think you are wonderful. I have told you; I would not take advantage of you. I think too much of you, even if we are only just getting to know each other. You want to keep yourself pure, and I want to keep you that way, as well.'

How boring he could be. All that rubbish, when all she had wanted was to feel a man close, as close as a man could be, any man! She blushed at her own thoughts, and then decided that she didn't want to enlarge the importance of this evening's events.

'Come on then, Ted. We had better get these Sales figures done, quickly.'

She looked at the large clock on the wall. Twenty past six! She moved past him to the desk and picked up the next piece of paper. He moved beside her and started to add the figures as she read them out to him. He was feeling the warmth of her thigh next to his, and the frustration of un-fulfilment. Tonight had been an adventure, and other possibilities were opening up. He wanted to get home, now. His warm ups were waiting.

Jean was still feeling the effect of the short, dramatic episode they had just enjoyed together. She wanted to resume what they had been doing. It was her first orgasm and she wanted another one but, in a way similar to Ted, she didn't want to face the possibility of being found out. Her mind was racing between sexual thoughts and the anxiety of getting the figures completed in a reasonable time. She knew that if she arrived home later than a quarter to seven, her sister would punish her with sarcastic remarks, even though it might reveal her own feelings for Ted. Better not be late!

18. The Home going.

The next morning, Sunday, saw the first rain in Herefordshire for a fortnight. The last week had been full of hazy morning starts followed by day-long blue-skied periods that drew the energy from their bodies, sapping them, making it harder to carry out even routine tasks. It was pleasantly cooler now, and some mornings contained a nip of frost. Yesterday, there had been a hoar frost, covering the hedges and trees in delicate silvery whites. They had stared at it, gasping with its beauty; some of the frost was half an inch thick on the branches. Weather and its changes became more and more a matter for discussion.

'Do you remember the weather, when we first came down?'

Selina spoke wistfully, thinking back to the day when they had arrived, and the wonderful weather that had prevailed at that time. So much had happened since then! She recalled the night they had all made passes at each other. That had been Kate's doing! What feelings Kate had invoked in her that night. Jim had gone along with it, but wasn't as open-minded as Tom, nor Kate and herself, for that matter. Perhaps it was as well; if he was as loose as the two women, no work would ever get done!

Other opportunities for creating passionate moments had been engineered by Kate, she was sure. Selina had felt guilty about the whole thing at first but then decided to get as much pleasure as she could out of each occasion. Sexual pleasure was important to her now, and she accepted the fact. Sometimes it seemed that it didn't matter who supplied the stimulus so long as the feeling was produced. The only one she felt she could not find pleasure with was Harry. He had served his purpose but she felt that she had matured since him! He had not actually forced himself on her, but he had been an adult whereas she had been an innocent girl. If her family had ever found out, she would have been disgraced but Harry would have been crippled for life, if he had been allowed to live. She forced her thoughts to return to the present, listening to what Tom was saying.

'Yes, what a marvellous time we've had. The friends we have made; the experiences we have been through.' He smiled at her as he said it, the memories of their first night being evoked. 'The lessons we have learned. Now, it's time to go home!'

Tom spoke, agreeing with her sentiments.

'Now is the time.' Selina mimicked him. 'You should put that up as your coat of arms! You are always saying that. It must get stuck in your throat, I should think!'

They all smiled; it was true that the phrase seemed to come easily to Tom. The four of them were sitting under the overhang of the barn, round the devil, waiting for the water to boil for the tea. They had all become expert at cooking in this way, since their arrival a few weeks ago. They had just eaten eggs and bacon on fried bread, which was still the most popular, with a touch of brown sauce. Occasionally they melted cheese into a freshly picked mushroom as big as a plate and simmered it in an inch of milk.

Jim often brought them back with him early in the morning, gathered in the fire-bucket. There was a sliver of wood in the bucket with the heating water. It was almost tradition to put the splinter in; it was supposed to take away the taste of the smoke in the tea. The bucketful of water had been put on at eight-thirty. It was almost nine o'clock, now. The water was just beginning to bubble. There was no hurry. They had hours, yet.

'You know, Sel,' Tom said, 'you might be onto a good idea there. If I ever get a coat-of-arms, I shall use that as a motto. Now is the time! The most important time is always now.'

He sat back, leaning on a bail of hay, musing on the thought. Three of them were catching the train at lunchtime. Jim would be seeing them off at the farm, not wanting to extend the moment of parting. He was the matter-of -fact countryman now. He was staying on, to work a few hours more, finishing at about mid-day. Kate would be going with Tom and Selina as far as Dudley. Tom was getting very serious, they had noticed. He said the state of the country was enough to make anyone serious. There were ten million people out of work and they could easily join them, if things didn't improve. He seemed to drop into silence, as if he knew things they didn't.

Kate knew that when she got home, she had to convince her mother that her relationship with Jim would be a permanent one. That wouldn't be easy. Her mother was so mean-minded. After the explanations, and her denial of the inevitable accusation of pregnancy, her mother would want to come down to meet him, to weigh him up, to see if he could take whatever she would throw at him in the way of Black Country insults, to have a look at the little cottage where he and Kate planned to be living. She would want to see that there was a spare room, not just for their children but for herself if she wanted a holiday at their expense, and to see Jim, and decide whether she approved. Things always had to work out so that mother got a benefit from whatever was decided.

No doubt she would disapprove of the sanitary arrangements! All Jim had was a little dry privy at the end of his kitchen garden. Jim had wanted to go with Kate, but there was too much clearing up to do at the farm. Hope Farm was a mixed farm and there was the dairy herd to be milked, twice a day, and ploughing to be prepared for. Albert Walker was starting to grow his own food for the cattle.

If things went as Jim hoped, Kate would be returning next week, with or without her widowed mother. Their life together, then, would be shaped by the countryside, into a rural pattern that would follow the demands of the seasons, customs and traditions of the Herefordshire farming culture. With luck they would have children to follow the same pattern. There was a never-ending repetitive re-generation, creating and supporting a circle of activities that ensured the survival of the human species in this part of the country. It was a pattern that created a feeling of security in those who conformed. It would cement Jim's relationship with Albert, too; make him the farmer's life-long servant. He wouldn't be able to leave and go to other employment now; neither would he want to.

Jim had become part of the country and anticipated that his

young bride would take on the customs and lifestyle of country folk in the same way that he had. He had quite rigid expectations of Kate, expectations that came from the time he had spent in the country. Kate was more open-minded about the future, determined to be as flexible as was necessary to maintain a working relationship with Jim without surrendering her right to have an informed opinion of her own. She felt that she would always be receptive to new ideas, as they presented themselves. Jim might be in for a few shocks!

Tom and Selina had no illusions about the wedding ceremony they had been through together. They had a less secure future together to think about. It had, after all, just started out as a sort of response to a dare! Selina tried to express this feeling of insecurity to Tom.

'We've had had a good time. Now is the time to get back to reality,' she said, smiling at her use of Tom's motto, 'I am really looking forward to seeing that old gaffer at Stones' Locks. He won't know me with this suntan, and it's nearly all over me, too. You can bet he will be trying to see as much of it as he can. I shall have to see if I can get a transfer into Dan's department.'

She leaned forward, stretching her back and legs, lazily.

'Well, I can see most of it from here,' said Tom, suggestively. 'Could you bend a bit more forward so I can see all of it?'

'Don't be nosy, Tommy Barr. You have already seen as much as you are going to see. There can't be much more.'

She smiled in a mischievous way.

'I shan't miss Willenhall, at all,' said Kate, interrupting. 'I've spent too many years working in smelly factories. I just want the smell of the country.'

She was trying to tell them how she felt about her future. Tom answered.

'Yes, Kate, I wondered what that smell was. Is that what you call it, the smell of the country?' He laughed, and Selina joined in, then Tom continued. 'Well I rather like the smell of suds oil. You can't beat a good whiff of suds oil.'

The thought reminded him of Stones' and the smells of the factory and he found himself mentally re-experiencing the feel and smell of the work, the locks and keys, the Stones' girls and the other factory women. Selina interrupted his thoughts.

'It doesn't smell like the country to me. It's more like cow-muck. I bet I'll really miss it when I get back to the Black Country.'

She wrinkled up her nose in dramatic disgust and as she did so, a cow lowed loudly, making them all laugh with the timing.

They were all in a smiling frame of mind now, trying to take away the poignancy of the moment of their impending separation. What Tom had said was true. It was the end of a period in their lives that no one could take from them; that they would never forget. They were graduating from this particular class, ready to start another. Tom thought back to what Selina had said about his phrase, 'now is the time.' She was right; it could be his motto. He certainly acted upon it. Maybe it could.

He started to doodle on the earth with a stick. He drew a shield and put a bar diagonally across it; what did they call it? A bar sinister? A sinister Barr! Funny, how your mind wandered. He carefully drew a scroll above the top of the shield and inserted the words 'Now is the time.' into it. He thought again. 'The Time is now.' It looked good but seemed to take up a lot of room and, if he drew it smaller, was too small to be read. What would it be in Latin? He wiped the scroll clean and replaced the motto with the single word, 'now'. He added an exclamation mark. 'Now!' That was better.

He knew what it meant, even if others didn't. The single word seemed to exemplify all that he felt about life, now. That's it! That'll do! He tried to think of other things that might have a place in the imagined coat of arms, a clock, a key, a hammer, an anvil; something to represent the Black Country. He felt he hadn't done enough with his life to find anything significant to add to the design. The addition of keys, to add his involvement with the lock trade, seemed a bit ostentatious. He would draw it out again and keep it, to be ready for the next idea when it came out. He might never be well-off enough to consider having a coat-of-arms. He relaxed; it was nearly time to go. His eyes became heavy and he started to doze.

'Look, the sun is starting to come out! What time is it, Tom?'

Jim spoke loudly, bringing Tom out of his reverie; Jim was trying to put off and avoid facing the moment of parting, the separation that he and Kate would have to endure. Too many things could go wrong with the plans that they had made. He was making sure no one else was able to relax, if he couldn't.

Tom yawned and looked at his watch; it was almost time to go. They had been sitting, talking and reminiscing for nearly three hours! Kate was watching him. Tom had noticed her surreptitious observation of him, before. Sometimes he had felt himself grow hot, remembering the night they had shared with the others. Was she having regrets about her decision to pair up with Jim? He did know that she aroused sexual desire in him, but almost any woman could do that. He was a full-blooded man, easily aroused. It embarrassed him at times. Even old Mrs Walker had been able to make him stand up! And she was forty if she was a day! He wondered idly what she would be like in a haystack. A murmur caught his ears. It was Kate, musing out loud.

'I shall hold a memory of Herefordshire, like this, sun after rain, 'til I get back, next week.' Kate was cogitating, partly to herself. 'The day seems like a painting, with the weather filling in the emotional parts of the canvas. Sometimes, the huge clouds seem as if they are trying to show how they feel, the hugeness and fullness of things, if you know what I mean.'

She looked over at Tom provocatively. There was a cough. What was she trying to say or suggest? The cough came again.

'A week is all you will have,' said Jim, 'Any longer and I shall come and throw you over my shoulder!'

He was talking to Kate. He laughed, and they all joined in, to disguise their emotions. The rain had gone, now and the day was a sad, shiny, dark beautiful thing. They would never again make friends like they had at the hop picking.

As if to a conductor's wave of a baton the four friends stood. Outside the barn, people were moving. The great hay-wagon was filling up with hop pickers, some reluctant; some eager to be back with the loved ones they had been obliged by circumstances to leave behind. Jim moved over to the wagon, giving a hand with the great shire-horses, who seemed in no hurry to start. Tom and Selina were immersed in their own thoughts, torn between their love for each other and the potential of the future. They passed their hop-boxes up to the driver who loaded them all at the front end, climbed up onto the wagon and sat silent alongside Kate as the drover started the pair of shire-horses down the dirt-track that led to the road. As they sat, their feet dangling from the tailboard, they could see Emily waving: to whom? They all waved back anyway. She looked a little sad, as if she was missing the hop-pickers already. She was; the only romance she had been involved with was the young gypsy youth. He had been thrilling but there was no future in that relationship.

Their last sight of Jim was his arm, waving from the upstairs level of the barn where Tom and Selina had lived, learned and loved for the past month. Passing into the shadow of a great oak abruptly cut off their view of him, and Kate wept silently, her tears sympathetically ignored by Tom and Selina, her feelings so mixed that this was the only way she could express them. Soon however, she dried her tears and the journey become boring. They had all travelled the road before.

The ride to the station, the transfer of their goods to the train and the subsequent journey on the train passed with nothing noticeable about it, although they did travel, by coincidence, with the young woman and her two children that they had travelled down with.

They looked much healthier now, browned by the sun, than they had on the journey down. They had seen the children, from time to time, dashing about, 'like something let loose.' That was the way they had heard Albert Walker describe them as if he were annoyed. He wasn't really. Tom had noticed the secret smile on his face when he made these apparently deprecating remarks. He knew that Albert had never had grandchildren and tried to make up for the lack by treating everyone else's children as if they were his own.

The young woman seemed much healthier too. He had not seen her with a young man, though. Perhaps he had been a fiction. Perhaps she was on her own. Perhaps all sorts of things, he thought. You could imagine all sorts of history to the people you saw; like Selina, only she seemed to do it well, as if she had a gift for it.

The train was on time and it was soon scurrying through the midland landscape, belching steam, cinders and whistles. The sky was not as friendly now. Dark and almost ominous; it was like a portent of bad news. The weather seemed to deteriorate even more as they climbed past the Lickey Hills, adding to the depression that they felt. Tom had noticed that phenomenon before and wondered why it was so.

They passed near Birmingham and tried to make sense of what they saw; there were so many modes of transport in such a small area. There were roads and canals, railways and rivers. There were buildings everywhere, churches and chapels, factories, halls, cinemas, theatres and shops, large houses and small slum back to back houses and everywhere the smells of industry. They both wondered what sort of people lived there; it seemed to be a rough sort of city, although they knew that far-seeing industrialists had built villages in Birmingham to create better lives for their employees. Tom's imagination wondered again.

'Have you ever wondered what it would be like to live in a big city, like Birmingham, Selina?'

He asked the question casually. He had wondered before, about the differences between Black Country life and life in Leeds, Manchester, London or Birmingham. It might be simpler, in a way. Take finding your way around. Everything in Birmingham would be placed round a centre, the city. In the Black Country, the small towns seemed as if they had been dropped there at random, like pebbles from a giant hand, with no way to easily find a route from one small town to another. There were winding cobbled streets that seemed as if there were no proper design whereas in Birmingham there were straight arterial roads that led out, to other cities; Lichfield, London. Wolverhampton, Worcester. There were even main roads to Bristol via Cheltenham, and Gloucester and on, to the West Country. The train whistled again, as if to inform the passengers of the closeness of their destination. The sky darkened more, and a steady drizzle took the pleasure from the journey.

'Look, Tom. There's Dudley Castle.' Selina pointed forward and upward. The old castle stood silhouetted in black against the pale grey sky. It wouldn't be long, now. She turned and clung to him. 'I do love you, Tom.' Her words seemed to contain a hint of the desperation she was feeling. 'I have never had such a wonderful time as I have the last month. I don't really want it to end, ever. I am frightened of what is in store for us. What are our parents going to say to us? My step-father can be very difficult, and both of us know he don't like you, your folks or hop pickers in general.'

Tom thought about it. He did not visualise any serious difficulties. Both of his parents were open-minded; he would be able to talk things over with either or both of them. He could not see why Selina's parents should make life hard for them. If they did, well, so be it. He knew that Selina was the girl for him. He would find a way for Selina and himself to live their lives. Perhaps she wouldn't want him! Now was the time to find out. Now was the time! Now! The train, rattling over the points, added a rhythm to the words, placing the emotions of the day firmly into his heart and mind.

He found his mind recollecting the few short years since he had started work. He had been full of mischief then. He had hung from the main-shaft by curling his feet round it, having a conversation with his mates washing their hands in the bucket. Nothing seemed to have any real importance or seriousness.

He had chatted to most of the girls before he was sixteen, including the Stones' girls. He could still imagine himself flirting with them, regardless of the way he felt about Selina. There was no sort of sense to the man-woman thing. He had read stories of chivalrous knights, with lifelong loves, and their women who had been loyal all their lives. Romantic stories all found a sense to the relationships of their characters but life wasn't like that. You had, and loved a girl, then one day another girl made you feel so horny that you couldn't stand it.

Kate stood in response to the deceleration of the train and Tom felt the same desire for her that he had known over the weeks. Selina was also aware of the parting from Kate. She stood and put her arms round her, feeling the loss already. The three of them stood and embraced each other in turn, silently; there was nothing that could be expressed in words.

The train whistled impersonally, not caring about the feelings of its passengers. Kate trotted down the steps onto the platform and a few minutes later she was gone, swallowed up in the crowd, the train whistled and they were off again on the last leg of their journey to Blower's Green. It only took a few minutes and then they too said goodbye to each other, wondering what the Black Country was going to offer them. Tom finally waved to Selina as she turned the corner, her shoes clip-clopping on the dark setts of the footpath. Tom stood there listening then 'Now!' came into his mind and he strode out, ready to meet whatever challenge came to face him.

Selina found herself feeling frightened of the immediate future. Harry was sure to be awkward; he always had been. It was as if he wanted his cake and the eating of it. Still, she had told him how she felt; he had to get on with his life, as she had to get on with hers. What had happened? What had her mother been told? Had they cemented their relationship to the point that what Selina thought had no relevance? Perhaps they were already married. Her mind wandered over the possibilities as she walked. She didn't really think that Harry was good enough for her mother, but it wasn't her choice; it was her mothers

At least she had a few pounds to her name. She had been able to save twenty pounds, a fortune to her. She strode forward again, a new confidence in her step. She had taken the first steps towards adult independence.

She suddenly felt modern; as if she was full of new thoughts; not just an old-fashioned woman but an experienced person, with new knowledge of improved ways to live. Even her mother would probably seem old in her ways. The year was one of modernity, in many ways, and she had no intention of being left out of the benefits, including her relationship with Kate, which if she had her way, would last a lifetime. There were wonderful times in front of her!

19. Tom.

He walked down the street, whistling. It seemed like a year since he had walked away from home, a few weeks ago. He had over twenty pounds in his pocket, four big white fivers and a few odd shillings; the most money he had ever possessed! Today he was going to spend no more than the few odd shillings; about fifteen in fact. His mother had been right. It had been a good idea to spend some and save some. Just what he was going to do with it, he didn't know. He would tuck it away until a good idea came into his head. Maybe he could buy something and sell it, to make a profit. He realised that that was what a businessman might do. The thought came to him and he wondered if it was possible to do anything about it.

He had said goodbye to Selina at the station. She had seemed strange with him, a little distant somehow, almost as if they wouldn't meet again. They had decided that they would talk to their respective families about their relationship, the day after they got home. He knew that their relationship would last him all his life, but he wasn't always sure about her feelings for him; you could never be sure of someone else's feelings, he thought.

Kate had been even more emotional than Selina, kissing him goodbye and clinging onto him as if they were lovers. He had wondered if she still had affection for him. Now he knew! Now she was revealed as a sentimental as well as a passionate woman. You could never understand women. Kate was like an onion; as fast as one layer was removed and understood, there was an entirely different one underneath.

Oh well, that was women, always having a mood of one sort or another. It was what made women more interesting than men. So far, women had been one surprise after another. Perhaps he was a surprise to them, too! He had never tried to see himself from the perspective of a woman but it might be interesting to try it, just for fun. The thought, like others, was put to the back of his mind to be called upon when needed. He turned the corner into his own street, still whistling.

The house was in sight, now; it was no different from hundreds of others and yet he could recognise it immediately. The front step was shining bright red, as were the bricks next to the doorway, making it stand out from the rest, as if it were just a little better. The door was slightly ajar: it usually was. It opened from the street; there was no front garden or anything that separated the door from the black-bricked footway, just the step and that was what Elsie kept polished with Cardinal Red polish to show passers-by the invisible boundary between what was public and what was private.

Not that anyone would infringe the unwritten law of property, and intrude. There was a real sense of being unwilling to act without the courtesy of manners. Manners were what separated people from animals, who just wandered anywhere, taking what they wanted. People took the attitude that there was nothing to steal, and if someone did steal, they would soon be found out by the presence of what they stole in their own house. No one would receive stolen items so obviously from one of their own class. There was a certain honour among thieves, especially poor ones.

Most homes were open to whoever walked in, usually giving a little cough out of courtesy and hesitancy, to warn those inside of the imminent intrusion. He stepped in, and saw that his mother was in what they called the kitchen, washing up.

It was really the landing on top of the cellar steps, having a small crock sink with a single cold-water tap. There was a smell of coal from below the cellar steps. The kitchen was quite a modern innovation. Until two years ago they had been obliged to walk down the entry to the pump in the middle of the yard to fetch water. The wastewater had been flung in the gutter that ran along the street. Now there was a tap that you could turn, to get water and a proper sewer to take away the waste from the houses.

In the single room that they all lived in, a low fire was banked up in the black-leaded grate, keeping the small oven at the side of the fire warm and also warming the room. There was a smell of tea in the air; there always was. Tea was always available from the teapot on top of the oven. It was another family tradition of hospitality. Anyone who entered was immediately offered tea. The October day was cooler than when he had gone away but the banked up fire kept the small room at an acceptable temperature. He laughed to himself. He would surprise her.

'Hello, Nagger. How about a cup o' tay, then?'

His mother whirled round, and threw her arms around him, her face lighting up in surprise.

'Oh, Tom, love! How are you? I have missed you. When did you get in? We didn't know which week you were coming home. Why didn't you write and let we know?'

The Wednesbury phrase again, he thought. Now I know I'm home!

'Blimey! Give us a chance to get in! If I'd known it was going to be like this, I'd have come home every week!'

He separated himself from her arms, pretending a lack of feeling, but really enjoying the moment and observing her. She looked better than he remembered her. As if her life had improved in some way. He spoke again.

'We thought you'd know we were coming home, this week. How're things? You look all right, anyway. In fact you look ten years younger than when I went away. What's the secret, eh? What have you been up to? What's for dinner, today?'

His mother smiled, blushing; trying to think of how to hide how she felt. It was one part of her life that she could not discuss with him.

'Trust you to think of your belly before anything else. We've got a leg of lamb, for a change. I've been working at Stones' for a few weeks, taking your place, so to speak, so I've got a few extra shillings in my pocket, now.'

'Well, I hope you've been saving half on it, like you always told me to.'

Elsie laughed. He had changed his tune!

'Yes, I have as a matter of fact.' She was glad of the change of subject. 'You never know when you might need it, but you might as well enjoy it as well, mightn't you? I hope you've been taking that advice as well, Thomas?'

He didn't often get called that, nowadays; it was his childhood name, and made him feel foolishly childlike. Without waiting for an answer to her query, his mother continued.

'I suppose everything you've got needs washing, don't it? Did you see much of that Selina, who works at Stones' with you?'

She always got to the point straightaway, he thought. Was now the time to talk about it? He could at least make a start on it.

'Yes, Mom, We saw a lot of each other as a matter of fact. I'll talk to you about that, later. How're Dad and Ted? Is there plenty of work, still, at Stones'? I suppose there must be, or you wouldn't be working there. Yes, everything I've got does need washing. I'll put it all in the brew'ouse, ready for tomorrow.'

He had neatly evaded the question he thought. Elsie had noticed though, and had mentally filed it away for returning to the subject, later. She turned her back to him, continuing with the washing up she had been doing when he had walked in, and carried on talking. She had plenty to talk over with him.

'I'll have to do your washing later on, today. Monday washing is a thing o' the past now I'm working. I have to get things done when I can. No, there's not plenty of work at Stones'. I've done quite well, really. It all started when Bert Stones' mixed up the German locks with the Indians. Mr Stephen asked me to do him a few hours, to repack them, and then he kept me on, just until you got back from the hop yards.

I have not yet been told that I am finishing, so I don't know how long I shall be there. I'm in the packing room, most of the time. I like it. It's quieter than the rest of the factory. Your work is piled up at the side of your bench for you. There's plenty of it. How were Albert and Jenny Walker? I hope you remembered me to them. I had some happy memories down in Herefordshire. We used to have some fun, then.

'Your father and Ted have gone to the whippet racing. Your dad's had a good tip, he says. He always has a good tip! They should be back, soon. It's the first time Dan has taken Ted with him. I hope he doesn't make him walk too far.'

She looked worried. Tom smiled to himself. Mom always worried about Ted. He could walk and do anything, as well as anyone else, but she had always been extra cautious with him, ever since he had been ill when he was a child. Ted had always taken advantage of the fact as well. Still, he worn't a bad kid. A bit crafty in the way he did things, sometimes, but he'd met plenty worse. Tom had occasionally felt a bit jealous about the extra attention that Ted had derived from his past illness.

There was a scuffling outside the front door and Tom could see that it was his father and brother. Their faces lit up when they saw him. It was apparent they had been drinking. Dan was the first to speak.

'How do, son? You all right? Ya look as if ya bin in the sun. All right for some, I say. Hope ya got enough money left to buy ya dad a pint.'

Dan smiled. He was glad to see him. Tom responded in the same vein. He was enjoying playing a more adult role. He would show them that he was a man, now. This was his chance to buy them a pint, as a man.

'Yes, I've got a few bob left, enough to buy both on ya a pint, and Mom! Do you want to go now? Come on. Let's go and celebrate, eh? They'll let us have a drink in the back room?'

He draped his arms around his father and brother. He felt wonderful, in a ridiculous sort of way, to be falling back into old idioms and patterns of speech, as if it were part of his return home. ''Bout time we had a drink, together, eh, our kid? Good job I've got a few bob left!'

They all moved through the front door, except for Elsie who hung back. Tom looked at her, askance.

'I've just got to put the lamb on;' she explained, 'It has to go on a low shelf in the oven or it'll burn. The fire is banked up enough, I think.'

Tom waited outside the house for her, letting his father and brother walk in front, nodding at the neighbours who happened to catch his eye. Children were playing in the street. He kicked the ball that happened to come his way as a sort of homecoming greeting from one of the children, showing that he was recognised as 'one of us' He kicked it back, trying to do it in a grown up way. Not childlike, as he would have done, a few weeks ago.

They were all friends, sharing the environment and the life of lock and key makers. In a few more years they would join him at the bench or machine, playing their part in the evolution of Willenhall as a leading lock-making town. He was proud of the part he was playing in the story. The air was clean, a sure sign that it was Sunday. He remembered how he had been made to go to Sunday school and he'd had to learn a new verse from the Holy Bible each week. He had received a book of prayers as a prize for doing well at the memorising exercise. It was all part of life.

Elsie came out a few minutes later and they strolled off swiftly, her arm linked with his. They soon caught up with Dan and Ted who were ambling along. Elsie turned to face Tom as she walked.

'This is nice, Tom. I've really missed you. I would like to have come down with you, but I promised your father I would never go anywhere without him. I don't know why. I think he feels a bit lost, without me. He's always been a bit of a loner, you know. His heart's in the right place, but he can't always say what he wants to say. I suppose it comes from being in the Army, in the War. He's always been responsible for people, so he never let himself get close to them, in case they got killed the next day. It was the only way he could protect himself from all that pain, and the thought that it might have been his fault. He still has nightmares about it, you know.'

Tom was silent for a minute or two. Then he spoke, expressing what he felt about the revelation he had just been given.

'There's more to our Dad than meets the eye, ain't there, our

Mom? You go on, day by day; thinking you know somebody, and then, all of a sudden, you see him or her in an entirely different way. When I was down on the hops, I was talking to one o' the blokes who works there, Harry, I don't know if you knew him when you were there, and he said it was like going to University; but you do your own research, and then you come to your own conclusions, but you don't have tutors to put you right if you go wrong; you just have to see your own mistakes, and put them right yourself. And you don't graduate; you spend all your life, learning, and living by what you learn, whether anybody else likes it or not.'

His mother looked up at him, surprised at his unexpected and erudite eloquence. How had he managed to increase the breadth of his vocabulary so much, in just a few short weeks? He stood in front of her, knowing what she was thinking.

'You have certainly grown up, down at the hops. You're taller in the body and older in the head. I hope you'll be able to settle down at Stones'. It'll seem a bit narrow, if you know what I mean.'

Her reasoning got through to Tom.

'Yes, I do know what you mean, Mom. I'll just have to get used to it, won't I? I suppose I was lucky, really, to have a job where I could take a few weeks off, to spend the time in the country. The gaffer did tell me I wouldn't get permission to do that again. I suppose I'll just have to buckle down and get on with things. You never know, though. A chance to get on might come up, and if I ain't ready for it, I shan't be able to take it.'

Tom didn't have any business plans ready so he fell silent again, and Elsie picked up his thread, changing the subject slightly.

'Things have been a bit slack at work, the last few weeks. Stones' 'as lost a couple of big orders. He'll get them back, I know, 'cos no other firm could make them as good, and as cheap as we. Steve is going to see the agent about it on Tuesday. If the agent can't pull the work back for we, he'd better get himself another firm to look after. He's had good commission, to get us these orders. We don't want to lose them, now!'

211

Tom looked at his mother, his eyebrows lifting in surprise. 'Steve'? 'Us?' Who was this 'we' that didn't want to lose the orders? What was going on? He hadn't known that his mother was that interested in business! Seeing the way he was staring, Elsie offered an explanation.

'I have known Stephen Stone since he was in his teen years, Tom. He often talks things over with me. His wife is always too busy in the shop, and his daughters are not really interested. He's quite nice, when you get to know him. Your father doesn't get on with him all that well, but then, your father doesn't get on all that well with anybody.'

Tom listened, interestedly. He wondered if she realised just what she was admitting. He seemed to have picked up Selina's way of listening, now, and seeing what he heard! She seemed to have realised how she sounded for, as he looked at her, she suddenly blushed. Tom had never seen his mother blush, before; it was a revelation. He turned his face to the direction they were going and carried on walking as if he had not noticed. His mother was a woman as well as a mother! It suited her as well!

The racing tip his father had been given paid off for once, and they all had their fair share of drinks before walking home with a slight stagger. Elsie and Dan went upstairs immediately. They would stay there until they had slept off the effects of the drink. Ted stayed with Tom, asking him questions about the hop fields. He had been there himself, the previous year, and had a lot of memories to ask about. He surprised Tom by saying that he had 'fallen' for young Emily, the girl who had served Tom and Selina the first day they had been there. Emily hadn't said anything about knowing Ted, who had a similar appearance to Tom so perhaps that was the reason she had been so friendly.

Tom asked him about the state of trade and was surprised at his brother's inside knowledge. Ted had learned a lot since he had been keeping the main books for the firm. Working in the office next to the shop had given him insights, too, into the way that Stephen Stone thought about the trade. Stones' was always looking for new ways to increase productivity; buying in more modern machines, using girls to do, what were traditionally men's jobs, and offering bonuses to complete contracts early.

Ted seemed eager to share his newly acquired knowledge with Tom, and Tom let him. He was surprised at the easy-going relationship that Ted seemed to have with Mabel Stones' and her daughters, and hoped that Ted was using his status to his best advantage. Ted's ability to add long columns of figures in his head was a very useful asset, and would stand him in good stead in the office of whatever firm he decided to stay with. He just had to learn to use the figures, now, to see them as well as adding them. The afternoon sped swiftly, as they passed the time, sharing information. During their conversation, Ted turned to Tom.

'How's Selina, Tom? Are you still going with her? You're a lucky bloke, getting a girl like her. She's lovely.'

He was expressing what most of their acquaintances felt. He had always been attracted to her, himself, but had never moved in the same circle of friends.

'Yes, we're still together, Ted. We're hoping to get engaged, soon, when we've spoken to our Moms and Dads. Yes, I agree with you; I am a lucky bloke.'

He didn't want to tell Ted everything about the intimacy of their relationship. Ted was only a kid. He wondered how Ted felt about girls.

'Have you started going out with anybody, Ted? I should have thought that you would be a hit with some of the girls in the factory.'

Ted smiled; Tom had no idea what it was like, working in the office! His salary was less than the wage of the lads who worked in the manufacturing side of the business. It was barely enough to pay his housekeeping to his mother, let alone take girls out. Still he seemed to have his fair share of fun in the office. Perhaps he would try to make up a foursome with Tom, and two of the daughters. He thought again. No, he wouldn't. He was onto too much of a good thing to share it – even with Tom! He had a good thing going with Jean and didn't want to lose his advantage to

Tom. Tom might take over!

'No, Tom. I don't have time for wenches. Old girl Stone is too sharp to let one of 'er girls get involved with a worker. It's all work; nothing else, there.

He stretched himself out on the old settee under the window. Tom had gone upstairs to lie on the bed for a while, to recover from the journey. It was nice to relax, with the sunlight of the late afternoon picking out shiny black objects in the room, enhancing their sparkle. He dropped off into a reverie, thinking of Jean and Mabel, both at the same time. Visions of pale buttocks and breasts, legs and long limbs filled his mind and warmed his imagination and filled him with unfulfilled desires. In his imagination he was in the shop, back at work, holding erotically shaped body parts until he could stand the lack of fulfilment no longer and he finally succumbed to his needs. He slipped into a quiet, sexually induced sleep, exhausted by the activities of the afternoon; the collage of the mental images leading to the self-induced climax.

The sun shone in beams, into the little house with the dark black shiny things. The dust and cigarette smoke rose gently into the air, delineating the parallel rays of sunlight. There was no sign of the passion and love and jealousy that existed and fermented within the sleeping frames. The occupants all lay sleeping, each with a head full of imaginings. Dan and Elsie lay in each other's arms, he asleep, Elsie drowsy, her body completely relaxed, listened to the snoring of her husband. Her thoughts were elsewhere with Stephen Stone among the hops of years ago but the thoughts were her own, not to be shared with anyone.

Tom lay on the little bed, half awake and half asleep. He had had a busy week-end and needed to recuperate. His thoughts were absent for a change; he had lain down and thought 'now is the time', but his body had needed the sleep.

20. Selina.

What a day to be coming home. She walked briskly along the black-bricked pavement. The rain that was making the setts shine was wetting her hair. At least I've got some money tucked away. She passed her hand through the straggling ends of her hair. Perhaps I'll need it. She was apprehensive about the return home. All the time she had been laughing and joking on the train with Kate and Tom, she had been worrying about the reception she would receive.

How would Harry be with her? Had he told her mother about their relationship? Would her mother want the savings she had in her little bag? No chance! A dozen other questions seemed to impinge onto her mind, making her apprehensive as she turned the corner. It was the third house along. She paused outside, nervously. Here goes! She pushed the door and walked in. The house looked no different. Her mother was upstairs; she could hear her moving around the bedroom. A discrete cough made her turn. Harry was sitting on the settee, reading the Daily Herald. He looked up at her. He had really settled in!

'Hello, how are you, Selina? How was the trip? Come and sit down.'

He moved along to make room for her, and she recalled the last time she had sat by him, on this very settee. She felt disgusted by her own memory. Instead of sitting down, she went to the stairs and shouted.

'Mom! I'm home!'

She waited but there was no reply. She mounted the stairs, wondering what the matter was; why her mother hadn't come down the stairs to welcome her home. As she reached the top, her mother's face appeared. She was red in the face and obviously angry. Her harsh Black Country voice boomed down at Selina.

'What're you doing here, ya little slut? I don't know how you've got the bleedin' gall to show your face here!'

She raised her hand, as if to strike Selina, who retreated down the stairs, looking to her mother for an explanation.

'What on earth is the matter with you, Mom? What have I done?'

She knew immediately what she had done. Her stomach seemed to heave with the anxiety of what her mother was shouting at her. What had Harry told her? Edie continued shouting; the speed of her words seeming to accelerate and the tone lifting to accentuate the meaning of the hate behind them.

'You know what you've done, you little mare! Harry has told me all about you; making up to him while I was at work, slaving away for you, trying to earn a few shillings in the shop to buy you a few things. Then you go and do the dirty on me; in my own house as well! Well, you can get out now. I don't want to see you again, ever. Your father would have killed you. He would turn in his grave if he knew the things you have been getting up to! Get out! Piss off! Piss off! Piss off!'

Her face went even redder and she appeared to lose control of herself, as if she were going to faint from the sheer force of her temper. Her personality seemed to change as she spoke.

Harry had moved to the foot of the stairs, listening. He had never seen her in such a bad temper before. He poked his face into the stairwell, looking up the stairs, obviously wanting to try to bring the conflict to an end. His voice was nervous as he spoke.

'Now Edie, I did tell you; she's only a young girl; they often get ideas about older men. It's all a part of growing up. You shouldn't take on so much. It'll only upset you. Weren't you young, once?'

He was stuttering the words out. He waited a moment, trying to gauge her response. He didn't want to seem too defensive or it might seem that he was in league with Selina, and that wouldn't suit his purpose at all. He had told Edie, in a moment of weakness, a little of the relationship that he and Selina had developed. He had regretted it since. On one hand, he didn't want to distance himself from Selina; he had memories of their times together, times which he might want to repeat in the future. On the other, he didn't want the episode to come between himself and Edie, although she was displaying a side of her character that he hadn't seen before. The potential for the future was far too attractive for him to let it go easily.

'You know you'd miss her if you didn't see any more, and she'd miss you, as well. Why don't you see if you can find a way round it all?'

Edie seemed to be considering, gradually calming; she didn't want to throw Selina out, really; the neighbours would want to know why and she didn't want to expose herself to local gossip, especially of that sort.

She didn't want to lose Harry, either. He hadn't told her how far the relationship with Selina had gone so she was wondering if what he said in defence of her was true. Most of all, she didn't want competition for Harry from anywhere, least of all from within her own four walls, and Selina was obviously sexually attractive. Edie was relaxing a little now, and a way out suddenly occurred to her. She looked at Selina, her thoughts and feelings plainly visible in the changing expressions on her face. When she spoke, her voice still contained some of the venom of her mood.

'Well, I suppose you think you are quite grown up now you've 'ad a bit of experience with Harry, but think on a bit more. This is my house, and I can't have two grown women in one house, with one man, whatever you say. It's not right.' She turned to Harry, 'She can't stay here, that's for sure. The only thing I can think of is that she'll have to live and work in my little shop. You can help to clear a room out there for her. There's a little gas stove at the back of the shop where she can do her bit o' cooking, and she can sleep upstairs. She'll have to take her bed and put it up in the little bedroom over the shop.' She turned back to Selina, 'As for you, young lady, all I will ask is that you don't bring your young man, Tom Barr, or whoever he is, back there, right?'

She looked to Selina for immediate acceptance. Selina thought fast; she had no choice, really. She would still be able to see her mother when she wanted to, and it was unlikely that Harry would try anything on at the shop and if he did, she could handle it.

'All right, Mom. If that's the way you feel about it. I'm sorry if I've upset you. You are more important to me than any man.'

She glanced at Harry, attempting to show unity with her mother. The telltale bastard! She spoke again.

'At least, we shan't get under each other's feet, now. Let's have a cup of tea. I am as dry as a bone. I wasn't expecting this, as soon as I walked in the door.'

She smiled at her mother, letting her know that she didn't hold a grudge. Her mother often seemed to lose her temper. Selina had wondered if it was somehow connected to her period times.

The three of them were relieved that a sensible solution had been arrived at that would suit each of them. Edie would have Harry all to herself, and Selina would be out of the way, running the shop. She wouldn't earn much from it, but Selina didn't have to be paid a lot, especially as she would be having her board as part of her wage.

Harry would have Edie when and where he wanted her, and he could reduce his outgoings by giving up the house where he lived at the moment or, Edie could move in with him when or if they got married, and there was just a possibility that he would be able to fix something up with Selina. At least, the two women would be apart. Selina had enjoyed their lovemaking before, and she might again.

Selina was glad to have her independence, and a place that she could invite Tom back to, whatever her mother said. She had always fancied the idea of a shop of her own, and this would give her the experience to do it. She had ideas of her own about running the shop. She had helped her mother to run the shop, before, so she was no stranger to the work. She wouldn't see Tom as often as before, because she would have to give up her job at

Stones', but that would be offset by the more private life they would be able to live.

The three of them spent the next few hours clearing a living space in the two small rooms at the little general store that Selina would run for her mother. They were full of old stock that was no good for selling because they were faulty or dirty or simply out of date. Edie never wanted to sell anything; it might come in handy; it all piled up on top of each other. Selina made up her mind as they put it all in the small outhouse in the back yard, that she would get it all down to Willenhall market as 'second hand'. She would get a few bob out of it to buy her own stock with. Her mother might never even hear of it.

Selina's bed and few clothes were put onto a flat cart, and Harry pushed it round to the little shop, wobbling and rattling along the cobbled street. Selina felt the eyes of the neighbours on her as she helped Harry to carry her small bed in, through the door. As they put the bed down in the tiny bedroom, Harry made a move to take her in his arms but she had made up her mind that she would tolerate no advances from him. She just pushed him away, viciously.

'Keep your 'ands to yourself. Never touch me again. I always knew you'd be a nuisance. You really looked after me, dain't ya? Go an' be the man of the house in your own house. This is my place and you'll never touch me here, or I'll tell my Uncle Jim.'

She was getting in a temper, like her mother. He backed off, now conscious of the fact that Selina only tolerated him for her mother's sake, and went off, rattling the cart up the street in a pretended temper of his own. Bleeding women! At least, Selina was no longer a problem!

Later, Edie called round to talk over the arrangements for the work that Selina would be doing. She showed Selina how to order the stock that she would be likely to need, and how to bank the surplus cash into a current account. This would be needed to pay the representative who came to see them every month to collect their order for hardware and ironmonger's items for stock.

'I'll sign you the cheque and when he comes, you can fill in the amount. That'll do for the time being. Later on, you can open your own account at the bank.'

The shop was a 'general store' so there were hairnets and saucepans, lipstick and yard brooms, stockings and potatoes. It was a strange, mixed up kind of shop; Edie had bought it some years ago and some of the original stock was still on the shelves. Selina already knew how to fill the small shelves and serve the customers. She had helped her mother before. When they had finished, Edie outlined the other aspect of her plan to Selina.

'I'll go and let Mr Stone know what the situation is, to save you having to tell him. It will give me the chance to ask him for your job. You're lucky I'm giving you this chance. Many a mother would have just chucked you out!'

Selina pretended to be surprised and grateful.

'Thanks, Mom. Thank you for this chance to help you.'

She could get up and go downstairs to start work! It would save her the walk she had to make every morning, at the moment. She couldn't have believed such an advantageous arrangement had come her way. Perhaps she would be able to introduce some innovations into the shop that might make her a few shillings that her mother need not know about. She had already seen a few possibilities that might work. Some of the old stock would have to go, too. There was no point, to her mind, in giving valuable space to something that was not selling.

They sat down together for a cup of tea at the end of the evening. Everything had been moved, not that Selina had many possessions, but they were all neatly put away. Selina told her mother all about the times she had had on the Walker's farm, leaving out her sexual adventures with Tom, Jim and Kate. Edie had never been hop picking so it was like telling a story of foreign lands. The idea of sleeping over a barn horrified her.

They said goodnight and Selina settled down into the small bed, dreaming of her coming career as a shopkeeper. Her mother seemed to have got over her bad temper of earlier on, she thought. Strange, how she got these moods just before she had her monthlies. Perhaps there was a connection. Selina suddenly realised that she could influence her mother to give her the little shop while she was in the mood. She could show her that the neighbours might find out about her precious Harry! She took the idea to herself; that would be the best way forward. She didn't see why she should be thrown out, just to suit Harry's plans. She had plans of her own!

Edie went to Stones' the next morning, to complete the next part of her plan; Harry had already left for his job in Dudley. She dressed herself smartly and walked into the shop.

'Good morning, Mrs Stone, Could I have a word with Mr Stone please, about our Selina's job?'

She acted the part of a troubled Mother well, her face reflecting concern. Mrs Stone read her face and demeanour and assumed that something serious had occurred.

'Yes, if he is there, of course, Mrs Brown. Mr Barr,' She beckoned to Ted. 'Go and ask Mr Stephen if he could spare a few minutes with Miss Brown's mother, please.'

It pleased her to be over-courteous and formal with the staff, to show that she could afford to. Ted returned a few minutes later with a message that Edie was to go over to the Works Office; Ted was to escort her there. Stephen Stone ushered her into his office, wondering what she was going to tell him.

'Hello, Mrs Brown. I don't often have the pleasure of seeing you. Is everything all right? How is that daughter of yours? She should be starting back, today.'

His eyes seemed to look through her. He always had that effect on her. She had thought long on how she could put this proposition to him.

'Mr Stone, I'm sorry to have to tell you that Selina will not be coming back to work for you. I have talked it over with her and we don't think it is a good idea. She is seeing far too much of that young Tom Barr and I am frightened that he will get her into trouble. I don't say he is a bad person; just very, oh, I don't know what I mean, but I do feel that he would be a bad influence on her.'

She looked down at her hands in her lap, unable to face Stone. When she did look up he was smiling as if he had an amusing secret. Edie spoke up again.

'There is a way that I could sort of compensate you for the loss of her work, if you know what I mean.' She took a deep breath. 'I could take her place!' It might have felt dramatic to Edie, but Stone had heard it all before, and just nodded as she went on, 'I have done this sort of work before. At Chubbs' Locks I did all sorts of jobs before I saved up enough money to open my little shop – that's where Selina is going to be working, at my shop I mean, not Chubbs'. I'm sorry; I'm getting confused. I know I could be useful here. Selina has told me about the jobs she has done, here, and I know I could do them.'

She fell silent, wondering what Stone would say. The tiniest of tears fell from her eye and, instantly Stone offered his handkerchief, putting his arm round her shoulder. He had already come to a decision; she would probably be a much more useful worker than her daughter would ever have been. Pretty too, although he couldn't see her causing the same amount of trouble that Selina would.

'I couldn't have had a better idea, myself, Mrs Brown, or shall I call you Edie? I call all my girls by their Christian names. When would you be ready to start?' He sat, looking at her, 'Could you start tomorrow? Yes? Good. If you come into the works office at eight o'clock, tomorrow morning then, I'll have someone ready to show you the jobs I want you to do. There is only one thing; Work is not all that plentiful in the trade, at the moment, so I can't guarantee a long employment. Obviously, the better workers will have the best chance of keeping their jobs.'

He stood up and she felt obliged to do the same. She was ushered out of the office and into the street before she knew where she was. He hadn't really wanted to get rid of her that quickly; it was just that he had other things to do. He could see Edie as much as he liked after she started work for him. She was a nice looking woman, he thought. Although not in the same class as Elsie, she had the same sort of sexual appeal as her daughter. He turned back to the other problem he was wrestling with; how get back the work they had lost to that Walsall firm, for which his agent had been paid. Maybe they could offer a discount for a reasonable quantity. That might do it. In the meantime he would recover the commission they had paid to Perkins, the agent. That wouldn't please him but he couldn't expect to get paid for work they hadn't got, cheeky bleeder!

Edie had her own thoughts, too. She started walking along the High Street, her stride getting faster and faster. She had done it! She had a good job, now. She would probably be earning more than she had in her own shop. She had the profit from the shop as well, and a nice few bob from Harry to boot! This was a nice day. Good for me!

She couldn't wait to get home, to tell Selina of her success with Stone. She had a suspicion that Selina would be pleased, too. Well that was up to her, as long as she didn't bring that Tommy Barr back to the shop too blatantly. She didn't like him. He was rough and uncouth, not like his father, Dan, who had always struck her as a nice, mellow sort of man, who wouldn't be bad mannered to a lady. He might even be sweet to a girl who was the same to him! She was daydreaming as she strode out towards home. Perhaps she would have a good time at Stones' factory, after all!

Selina washed her face under the single tap and rubbed it dry on the old towel that her mother had let her have. Eight-thirty; time to open up. She had started work at six-thirty, clattering down the narrow wooden treads, determined that her shop, her shop, would be the cleanest, tidiest shop in Willenhall. She was conscious that other shops had been established longer and were larger and better stocked than hers but that could all be changed in time. Her bowl of cleaning water had been changed for fresh six times already, but she was ready now, to face the world.

One of the odd things that Edie had taken over when she had purchased the shop had been an agency for Hobbies, a firm that specialised in supplying tools for the hobbyist; Fret-saws, Archimedes drills, small planes and hammers. There were free plans inserted in the magazine of small models, usually of ornate design, and household items in the two-penny weekly magazine. These were designed to stimulate the reader's interest. A fretsaw could be bought for four and sixpence, and that was the basic tool required. Others could follow, as they were needed. A full kit could be purchased for sixteen shillings and sixpence. People still came in for a packet of saw-blades and Selina had often wondered why Edie didn't make more of the moneymaking opportunities the agency offered. Selina had cleared off the two shelves devoted to the hobby and scrubbed them white before replacing the selection of small items into a semblance of order. Everything was now tidy on the two shelves; she had regarded the two shelves as a separate department, with its own stock. Now it had to earn its keep. Everything in that department had its own price ticket clearly placed on the item. Now she had to find out what her minimum stock of fretwork items should be.

She would make a list later of the items to buy to fill the out- of-stock items. What she wanted to do was to create a shop where hobbyists could come; confident that the item they wanted was going to be in stock. She hung a sheet of paper on the end of the top shelf for writing down her shortages.

The shop was slowly changing its appearance; it was becoming Selina's shop. She looked round to find the next department she would create. Vegetables would be first, and then hardware. She paused, her pencil touching her lips.

21. Back to Work.

'Come on, son!'

The last time Elsie had called Tom up in the morning had been the day he had travelled to Bromyard, six weeks ago. So much had happened since. She had never been happier. Every facet of her life seemed more fulfilling, more exciting. She had been working at Stones' Locks for over a month, and was dreading the day when Stephen, or his foreman, Morgan, told her that, because Tom was back from the hop picking, she was no longer required. Dan too, seemed happier; she couldn't really work out why. It was just that he was more sociable, more ready to please. Even young Ted seemed full of life. She had a suspicion that it was since he had been spending more time in the shop.

She glanced at the clock. It was six thirty. She had washed and prepared the Billy-cans for Dan, Ted and Tom. She didn't have to bother for herself. She had a cup of tea whenever she wanted it, in the Packing Shop. Sometimes, Stephen found an excuse to join her, and they found a hundred things to talk about. He had seemed to accept the idea that she was never going to leave Dan; he was probably relieved, too. She certainly was. It saved so much heart-rending pain. Neither of them wanted to accelerate their affair to the point that there was no alternative but to separate from their partners.

There was the sound of feet on the stairs, and the three men came down, ill tempered as usual. It was Tuesday, and none of them seemed to like it. Yesterday had been worse, starting back after the week end, and starting back after a six-week break for Tom. It was a cold, dirty morning. They sat down, crowded round the little table, like the three bears, all eating their porridge. She had eaten hers. She put on her coat. It was raining hard.

'I've got to go in early, today.' She explained. 'There's an urgent order to be packed. I'll see you all, later.'

'You are always going in early, Mom.' Ted spoke, between

mouthfuls of breakfast. 'I don't know what you do to earn your wages. Nothing seems any different when I get to work.'

'What's it got to do with you, eh? Mind your own business, Teddy Barr!'

She had heard the Stones' girls call him that and he hadn't seemed to mind.

'I can't help my name, can I Mom? After all, you gave it me!'

He smiled, letting her know that he wasn't annoyed. He had noticed the change of subject that his mother had engineered, though. They all started getting ready as Elsie walked out of the door. She didn't want to walk with them; they would have men's things to talk over. In the mean time, she had her own things to do.

There was a new woman starting today and Stephen had asked Elsie to look after her for a few days, until she found her feet. She had worked in the trade before, it seemed, so she should be all right in a day or two. Elsie had been surprised that there was room for another girl. Somehow, it made her position seem that bit more secure.

Five minutes later, she turned into the works. She lifted her disc from its hook on the board and moved it to the other board. She was now officially at work and would get paid for it.

'Good morning, girls!'

The greeting was obligatory to the Stones' girls she nodded to as she passed them, walking up the alley that passed the side entrance to the haberdashery and led to the lock-making part of the premises, and turned into the works. Jean Stone always had a smile for her, not like Laura, who always seemed as if she couldn't face her. Elsie had an idea that there was something going on between her and one of the factory boys. She walked into the works and was surprised to find Edie Brown sitting on a chair outside the office. She had known Edie, in passing, for some years, now. Elsie had always thought Edie was a, 'bit on the sly side.' Elsie had bought groceries at the little shop in the past. What was she doing here? What was going on? She decided to act from strength.

'Hello, Edie. I didn't know it was you, starting today. Mr Stone just told me a new girl was starting. He never said who.'

She looked at Edie questioningly. Edie didn't look at all discomforted, sitting as if this was her shop.

'Hello Elsie. Yes, I'm taking our Selina's place. She's going to run the shop for me. It doesn't seem right to have two women round the house, not now me and Harry are going to get married, if you see what I mean.'

She said as little as possible, just enough to explain her presence there. Why should she tell all her family business to every nosy cow? Elsie could see how Edie felt about telling her, so asked her questions along a different line.

'Tom's going to have a shock when he finds out, ain't he? He never said anything to me about it. Does he know? I would have thought she would have had the courtesy to tell Tom.'

Elsie was surprised at the news. Still, there were plenty of other girls around looking for a nice young chap like her Tom. He wouldn't be left on his own for long. Still, he might be able to keep the relationship with Selina going, if he wanted to. Time would tell. She returned to the present without waiting for an answer to her question. What Edie and her daughter did was their own affair, so long as it didn't interfere with her family! She was in charge of Edie at the moment, and that was how she would keep it.

'Well, never mind the young folk; they can look after themselves, can't they?' She spoke briskly, determined to keep their respective ranking how she wanted it. 'You can hang your coat up by your machine for now; come on, I'll show you where you'll be working, today. I think what Mister Stephen wants, is to move you around a bit, sort of see where your abilities are; then he'll probably put you on a permanent job. You'll stay there unless there is a change in the orders, or somebody doesn't turn up. That's when you'll show him what you are worth. I expect you can do shop and office work, can't you?'

She knew the answer before it came. Edie couldn't run a shop without knowing a bit, could she? She wondered when Edie had been in to get the job. Stephen played his cards close to his chest, didn't he? Then she realised that there was no reason why he should be aware that they even knew each other. They were in the machine shop, now, and Elsie turned to the following woman. At least he would have no real reason to get rid of her, now. He would have refused Edie a job before he would have taken on excess workers.

'Here you are Edie. Put your coat on that hook, there. You can run this hand press. Let me show you what you have to do.' She didn't give Edie a chance to think about it. Why should she? 'Come over here so you can see properly. You pick up this length of strip off the rack and push it into this slot, until it comes against the stop, see? That's the stop. It stops the strip going too far into the tool.' She stepped back. 'Then you swing this arm, as hard as you can, at first. You'll soon learn how hard you have to pull it; then you push it out of the way and push the piece of strip in further. If you can do that a hundred times an hour, you will earn yourself a nice fat pay packet at the end of the week. What do you think about that? If you get in trouble, my Dan will put you right. He knows all the jobs in here. Just as long as it is only work you see him about!'

She smiled; Stephen had told her to give Edie the more difficult jobs at first; to test her mettle he had said. Edie pulled a face then rolled up her sleeves.

'Well, I asked for it. I can't complain when it's give to me, can I? Here we go!'

Edie was bending to pick up the first strip, ready to start. Her hands were oily already. Elsie relented slightly. The woman hadn't done her any harm, had she?

'Has anyone told you how to move your disc on the board, yet? I'll make sure you are signed in for today. Have you got a number, yet? Come and have a cup o' tea, first. The Works don't open 'til eight o' clock. It's only ten to. Have you brought the makings with you?'

She watched as Edie poured a few of the tea leaves she had wrapped in a twist of newspaper into her enamelled mug. She seemed to know what she was doing. She poured hot water from the large kettle onto them and added a little milk.

Other workers were starting to drift into the workshop, now, talking to each other volubly. As she raised her head, Elsie saw Tom walk in with his father and brother. He looked over to his mother, saw Edie standing there, and made his way between the machines to them.

'G'morning, Mrs Brown. Didn't know you had started worked here. How long you bin here?' He was looking round, for Selina, obviously. 'Where's Selina? Is she bad? I wondered why she wasn't at work, yesterday.'

Edie Brown cast him a long look. She was glad she was the one to give him the news.

'She's had enough o' working here. She's got high falluting ideas now an' she wants a better class o' work, with a better class o' people. I've had to let her work in my little shop to give her what she wants. She said the people here are not worth mixing with. They are good enough for 'er Mom, I suppose. Well, I'd better get on with me work. Nobody's going to do it for me, are they?' She was putting her double-breasted overall on as she spoke. 'No offence, but it'd be a good idea if you kept away from our Selina. She's got enough on 'er mind at the moment.'

She turned her back and picked up the length of strip metal. She inserted it into the press and swung the arm round with as much strength as she could bring to bear, then repeated the movement falling into a rhythm and letting the other two know that she had finished speaking to them.

Tom was surprised, but said nothing. He had wondered if Selina was regretting the closeness of the relationship they had formed. Oh, well, he thought, if that's the way she wants it, she can have it. It leaves a lump in your chest, but I suppose it's a part of life. Another lesson learned! He moved away from Edie; he had never liked her very much. He had the feeling she wasn't all that honest; not that he knew anything; it was just a feeling you got sometimes. She could do her own work; he would do his. There was plenty of work for him to do, and plenty of other girls.

The rest of the day went quickly for all of them. Elsie in the Packing Room,, Ted in the shop, working on the accounts and the girls, Dan filing lock parts and showing Edie some of the different jobs she might have to work on. Tom worked in the same department, but kept away from her. If Dad wants to show her, it's up to him, he thought, but I don't want anything to do with her. Over the following weeks, the pain of separation from Selina eased and Tom looked around for other diversions. He was not particularly anxious to take up another girl, but his hormones were normal. He started spending more time with his brother, Ted, mixing with the girls from the factory shop. He was getting used to being surprised by Ted. The girls in the office were so obviously attracted by him that Tom had to look at him with new eyes.

Jean was always in Ted's way, Tom thought; it was as if the office reshaped itself to bring them together. They were always touching each other, almost accidentally, as they passed by a machine or through a door. They had slid past each other as they passed Ted earlier and Jean had been blushingly sandwiched by their two bodies. It had been an experience. He wouldn't mind another! He thought about it all afternoon then decided he would just have to take his chance when it occurred. Jean came into the manufacturing part of the premises occasionally, to carry messages from her mother to Stephen Stones'.

That might be his opportunity to make a pass. He was working at his bench, later that day when his ears caught the sound of a swishing skirt behind him. He straightened up and swirled round, as if accidentally, and his arms went round the figure trying to pass by him. It was Laura, the eldest of the two sisters! He blushed, feeling like a fool. Laura was the tallest and most striking of the Stone girls and he hadn't been sufficiently ambitious to make an attempt to attract her attention. She turned to face him, not moving away from his arms.

'Well, the country boy returns. You seem to be holding me. Do you like what you are holding, Mr Barr? You don't seem to want to let me go.'

She still didn't move. He could feel her breasts moving against him as she breathed. The feel made him immediately erect, a fact that was not lost on Laura. She made to move away then changed her mind. He didn't want to let her go, either. She was right! This was his chance, but it was with Laura, not Jean! They moved, almost as if they were dancing, into a small alcove leading to the packing room. He pushed her through the door, still with his arms around her. Neither of them attempted to break the hold they had on each other.

'You are right,' Tom said. 'I don't want to let you go. I could hold you all day and not want to let go.'

He lowered his face closer to hers and slid his hand round to the back of her head, pulling her closer, until their lips met. The kiss was soft, teasing, touching and moving away, and asked for more of the same – and got it. He could sense that she wanted more, too. The magic moment seemed to hang in the air alongside their body scents. Then there was a noise outside and they parted, breathlessly. She slid her hand down the side of her skirt, smoothing it. She didn't wear an overall, like the other girls and her movement made her shape seem even more visible and accessible. She turned from him and started to move out of the small room into the alcove again.

'Wait.' He whispered in her ear. 'I'll see you later, if you like.'

He passed his hands caressingly around her waist. She looked back at him and gave an almost imperceptible nod. His heart jumped, and then he followed her, looking around to see if they had been noticed. He turned, and made his way back to his bench. He had a feeling that he might be holding Laura again, before the day was over, and he wanted his hands to be clean when he did. He moved to the bucket, looking over in the direction of the office as he gently rubbing his hands to remove the oil.

No sign of her. He moved over by the gate. Bert was standing there, doing his sentry duty! Tom went and stood by him.

'How are you doing, Tom? Don't get dodging off early. The old man is on the warpath.'

Bert spoke quietly. He never knew how to relate to the lock and key smiths. Although he was the brother of the owner of the firm, he always felt inferior. He didn't have the skills that they had and knew that they all knew it. He sometimes tried to make up for it by impressing his authority on someone; at other times he tried to act in a friendly way. Tom replied.

'I'm all right, how are you, Bert? When has that French order got to be finished by? Any chance of any overtime?'

Tom tried to keep the small conversation on safe ground. Work was a linking subject for both of them. Bert looked up. The clock was showing two minutes to the hour.

'Away you all go!'

He wanted to be seen as generous, so he let them all out of the gate two minutes early.

Tom hung back, waiting. You never knew your luck. The door to the office opened and a figure slipped put. He moved silently to her side and took her hand. She held onto it. They walked swiftly along the dark street, towards the town centre. As they passed an entry between two of the small houses, he pushed her in. She was breathless. He turned her so that she was facing him. His arms went round her. He was more expert in the move than he had been six weeks ago!

'What do you think you are doing to me, Tom?'

She started; then he put his lips on her neck sucking gently. She gave a little cry and tried to move, protesting. He held her more firmly and slid his lips along her neck, across her cheek and onto her lips. She moved, as if she were attempting to get away then yielded, moulding her body against his. He took his hand from her waist and moved it up, onto her breast. Another cry escaped her mouth, but she did not move. He slid his hand, insinuating it into her blouse, finding her breast. He took hold of the nipple and squeezed gently. Her hand moved onto his, pressing it tighter against her. He squeezed harder and she moved tighter against him. Suddenly she seemed to collapse in his arms and he had to support her to prevent her falling.

'What's the matter?'

He looked at Laura and she was shaking, her knees too weak to hold her weight. He took a good hold of her, afraid that she would fall. She did not reply, just looked at him, her eyes rolling. A minute passed then she spoke.

'What have you done to me, Tom? I've never felt like that before.' She seemed to be recovering now. She placed her arms round his neck. 'I've never had a feeling like that, before.'

He replaced his arm round her body, gently kissing her lips, touching and removing. She struggled against the teasing movement then pulled him to her, lifting his hand and placing it onto her breast. Tom moved her blouse to one side and touched her nipple with his lips, feeling the deep breath that came from her. She moved as if she did not know what to do next. His hand moved down from her breast to her thigh, stroking along the inner flesh as he lifted her short skirt.

'Oh no! It's wrong! We can't do that!'

She pushed against him with her hands. She had never been stimulated in that way before. It was against all her upbringing. How dare he do such dirty things to her? The feeling she was having now was completely alien to Laura, as if she were being violated. She stood, shaking; she had always been in control, having nice, pleasant feelings from a kiss and a cuddle, nothing like the passionate desire that was engulfing her now. She could not tolerate it!

Tom waited as she slowly calmed down, his eyes taking in the symptoms of her passion, then he gently put his arm round her shoulder.

'I am sorry; I don't know what came over me. You give me feelings I have never had before, for any girl.' He was identifying with her, making out that he was just as much a victim of passion as she was. 'How did you feel?'

This time he remained silent, awaiting an answer. When none

came he lifted her chin with his hand and kissed her on the lips, no teasing, no passion this time, just a sincere, boy loves girl type of kiss that was nice. She found herself responding to this way of cuddling and was able to continue holding him close to her; it was so comfortable! How could she find a way to make this feeling last for ever?

Her arms tightened around his neck, holding onto him as the time passed.

22. The Department Store.

The next days were the busiest of Selina's life. She rose at six-thirty each morning, had breakfast, and started work. Each small part of the shop was re-organised in turn. She regarded the shop as her own department store, each part playing its own role. She had a Grocery Department consisting of four shelves and a share of the floor space. There was a Hardware and Ironmongery Department with a few shelves of brackets and some crates containing boxes of mixed nails and screws. She also had a Greengrocery Department, with all of its stock put outside on the pavement each day. Each item of stock was tidied, and clearly priced according to her pricing policy. After a week she was satisfied that the shop was in the best order she could achieve.

The shop, although small, was on a main road approach to Willenhall town centre and she felt that the position was good. Many people passed the door on the way to the town or to the market. She liked to go into the town, a few hundred yards away, to examine each shop in order to evaluate its display. The area round the clock in the centre of the town was her favourite place. There was already a hardware shop close by, and she was fascinated by all the small drawers, with a list of the items held that seemed to go all the way up each wall of the shop. The owner knew her and also knew what she was doing there.

'Come on, our wench.' He said, 'Come and have a look. You'll never be able to beat me from your little shop. I've got too much stock for you to compete, and I've got the better position as well!'

She knew he was right but still went in, just to see what she could learn. The time would come when she would pick her own position!

In her own shop, she had moved the stock around until she felt that there was a balance between the different types of items that she had to offer for sale. There were items that she had not the space, the credit facility, or the working capital to buy and sell, but she made mental note of these items against the day that she had more room. A lot of her business was carried on in her head, in a sort of daydreaming environment, with decisions being made with reference to no one but her own imagination. The foundations were laid, in those few early days, for her complete obsession with business.

Her mother came to inspect often, to make sure she had no unwanted visitors and to check that the shop was being looked after properly. Edie was amazed to see the growing difference in the appearance of the shop, and in the sales figures. She did not get to see all of the figures; Selina had another set of figures for herself. However, Edie was impressed by what she did see, so did not carp at the new shelves, the paint on the walls and the improved appearance of the little shop. After a month, the stock of hobby equipment had doubled. There were full kits for sale alongside planes, drills, sandpaper and fret-saws, saw-blades and small hammers and tacks, all neatly arranged and priced.

Similarly, the Hardware and Ironmongery Department had increased the number of items for sale on its shelves, with wood-screws vying for space with nails, cup hooks and cleaning fluids such as bleach, washing blue, carbolic soap and polishes.

When Edith arrived, at seven o'clock one Monday morning, the fresh produce, brought from the market by a neighbour, collecting items for himself, was already outside on the pavement, set out in boxes, with artistic flair. Each item had a chalk-written price; King Edwards, two pounds for three-pence, cabbages tuppence each.

Selina was making a cup of tea for herself and when she saw her mother she placed another cup ready. Edie was silent at first, finding it difficult to bring herself to praise her daughter, having arrived with the idea of chastising her for something, she didn't know what. Eventually she spoke.

The shop looks nice.' She sniffed, as if wanting to take the words back. 'And so it should, after all, I have given you your first chance, and it was me that taught you all you know about shop-work.'

Selina turned on her, her eyes sparkling.

'Yes, you're right our Mom. It was you who taught me all about shop-work. You taught me to get up at six o'clock in the morning and go without my breakfast so the shop-work would get done before I went to school. It was you who taught me to pick up the spuds, bags as big as meself, and put them ready for you to sell them to the all-important customers. Yes, I've got a lot to be grateful for, especially the shop-work, and I'm paying you back as soon as I can!'

She stopped, realising that she was shouting, letting out all the detestation that she felt at that moment for her mother. Her mother looked at her in amazement. Her daughter had never spoken her to like that.

'Why, what's the matter with you, Selina? Do you think you are the only one who has ever got up at six o'clock in the morning? I had to learn the lessons as well, you know. I've done me share!'

The two women stood facing each other, willing the other to back down, two women, fighting for survival in the harsh conditions of the Black Country, neither of them willing to give way. Then they found they could not hold their serious countenances any longer and started to giggle. They reached out to each other, glad to rid themselves of the bitterness that had tainted their relationship over the last few weeks. Selina spoke first, her voice trembling slightly in time with her hands.

'I'm sorry, Mom. It's just that I have worked so hard, lately, that I get cranky. I never seem to knock off. I like what I'm doing in the shop and I know you like what I am doing. I just seem to be doing the same thing, day after day. I never get a break.'

She broke off, her voice tailing into silence, and then she turned and took hold of a broom and started sweeping the pavement outside the shop. Edie watched her for a moment, and then spoke softly.

'You need a bit o' time off, Selina. You should take yourself to the pictures. There's a good one on at the cinema, a talking picture, in colour, *The Jazz Singer*. It's Al Jolson. Harry took me the other night. It's a really good film; takes you out of yourself.'

Edie peered over her glasses at her daughter. Something was wrong with Selina. She was looking peaky. She was too hard on herself. It wouldn't do to let her make herself ill; the shop wouldn't run any better for having someone ill in charge.

'You knock off at six, on Saturday, my girl. That'll give you time to have a bite to eat and still have time to get to the pictures. I'll pay for you, and for an ice-cream. Call it a bonus for looking after the shop so well. I'll come and run the shop till closing time, when you go.'

She smiled as she made the offer, knowing that Selina had been given no time to call her own for a month. Both realised that Edie was being generous; she had to finish her work at Stones' Locks before she had chance to take over from Selina.

It was the first time that Selina could remember getting a word of praise from her mother and she determined to make the most of the time off that she was being offered. She caught the bus to Wolverhampton and saw the latest film, *The Jazz Singer*, her mother had recommended. As she walked past the shops in the large town, she observed how their windows were decorated, and the goods displayed, filing away the memory for use in her own shop. What she wanted was a shop with a big window so that she could dress it with her ideas!

She was developing an area of expertise that had come entirely from her own observations. Each new idea was tested by its results and by asking her customers.

The evening seemed to go by quickly and she felt, as her mother had told her, taken out of herself, by the plot of the new talking picture. She found herself crying half way through the film, then realised that the action set out on the film was designed exactly for that purpose; nevertheless she enjoyed the release of emotion that the film provided. Next morning, Sunday, she was able to relax a little, but on Monday it was back to normal, her naturally enthusiastic nature enjoying the sales side of her activity.

'What do you think of the new kits?'

She asked many of her customers, referring to the new Hobbies kits. Sometimes the answer was not favourable, but she would stick to her idea if she felt that her customers were prejudiced against a particular way of displaying an item. She paid a skilled hobbyist to sit outside the shop, on the pavement, the following Saturday, making items for which plans were on sale. Her sales of plans went up, as did her sales of saw-blades and other consumable items. She was beginning to carry larger sizes of plywood too, from which many of the items were made.

Gradually her sales figures rose and she kept ten percent of the turnover for herself in a bank account she opened for the purpose. She never told her mother about this 'ten per cent fund'. It was her business alone. Her mother was feeling the benefit of her work and the increased profitability of the shop. Selina felt that she was in business for herself, with her mother as a sleeping partner. The sleeping partner was getting a fair share of the profits; Selina's share was in the 'ten per cent fund'. Her social life was suffering, though; she did not accept as many of the invitations from young men that she could have. There was something missing from her life. She did not notice at first. It just seemed easier, when she was tired out, to lock up the shop and go upstairs and throw herself on the bed.

Tom had not been to see her since she left Stones' and she had missed the loving that she had got from him. Other young men were coming through the door of the shop every day, either as customers or as representatives of the local wholesalers, but none of them gave her the sort of thrill and lift as when she had been with Tom. Often she was invited out to the cinema or theatre but it was rarely that she accepted, making it clear that she did not wish to commence a serious relationship.

Her mother was more understanding of the hours that she was putting in at the little shop, giving her the occasional Saturday night off. Harry came round once, in the hope of restarting the good times he had had with Selina, but she quickly repulsed him.

'Go and sow your good times with Edie. She's more your barrer!'

She told him. She was so angry that he realised that he had no chance in the future, and did not try again. That was the end of an era for Selina. She was completely shut of him! She could not recall how she had ever found him attractive. When he had gone, she sat down and put her head in her hands and cried.

'What a bloody world!'

The words came pouring out of her. Everything seemed to have gone wrong. Her mother was just using her to make money to keep herself and her fancy man in high style! Harry was trying to use her as well as her mother.

She was working her fingers to the bone to keep herself. What was the matter with her? A few weeks ago she had enjoyed the feeling of independence that managing the shop had given her. She was getting more tired now, and she knew that she was late with her period. She sat down and tried to work out was happening with her body and the realisation slowly came to her that she was pregnant. She was two weeks late! Whose baby was it? Was it Tom's or Jim's? It couldn't be Harry's; too much time had passed. It had to be Tom's. It had to be. Anything else was too terrible to contemplate. What should she do?

The feeling came to her that she must tell Tom. Perhaps he would deny his responsibility, perhaps not, but he must be told, to make his mind up. If he wasn't told, he couldn't make up his mind one way or the other. She started crying again, the emotion releasing her from the stress of the last few days. She would tell him!

Once she had made her mind up, she decided to tell him at the first opportunity. She would see him on the way to work next Monday. Once she had made her mind up, the pressure seemed to recede from her. She had six days to work out how she was going to go about the explaining, and she knew she could do that. In the meantime she had things to do.

Her plans for improvements went on in the same way in the

shop, the Department Store as she had got used to calling it. The black-bricked back yard was cleaned as it had never been cleaned before. The shed in the back yard, that she used to store stock, was emptied and places found in the shop for everything with the result that the shop looked crowded now, and the turnover reflected the higher stock levels. Tuesday, usually a quiet day was busier than she could remember, and the cashbox was heavy when she had finished counting the takings. This was the life!

She had found her niche in life and was already obsessed by the business of business. The local people had accepted her in the short time she had been running the shop and she felt it was, in part, due to her enthusiasm. Wednesday was busier still, a surprise as many of the local people were hard up by this time of the week. Fred, the local hobbyist, who she had paid to sit outside the shop, creating items from the magazine, was feeling an upturn in his income, too. He sat outside three days per week, now, and didn't ask for pay to do it. He was picking up commissions from those people who liked what he produced but didn't have the skill or time to make them for themselves. These commissions were often works of art; not produced from the free plans, but designed by Fred himself.

On Fridays she took her addition to her 'ten percent fund' to the bank. The staff knew her now; she was respected, as a person is who is making regular deposits.

'Good morning, Miss Brown, nice to see you again.'

It was Paul Blackham, the under-manager. That was what she called him. He was tall, dark haired and always courteous to her. She knew he took the trouble to conduct her small transactions, himself. She checked her paying in slip, which showed the takings from the shop and checked her savings account balance.

'Yes, good morning, Mr Blackham. Everything seems to be in order. I wonder if I could have five minutes of your time, some time this week?'

She looked at him questioningly.

'Of course, Miss Brown. I will just check my appointments for this week.' He was back in two minutes. 'Yes, that will be fine. Would you like to come in now?'

She thought swiftly. She had to get someone to cover the shop while she was away at the bank. The bank was only two hundred yards away from the shop but it might as well be two miles. How on earth was she going to manage it? Seeing her hesitation Blackham spoke gently.

'If it would be of any help, I some times walk down to the little tea-shop, near your shop. I could pop in to see you during my lunch hour, about one o'clock today. Would that be of any help?'

'Thank you, Mr Blackham. That would be very helpful.'

She breathed a sigh. Everything seemed to be working itself out. She walked briskly out of the bank, knowing that she made an impressive figure as she did so. The next few hours were busy, serving customers, cleaning, preparing her sheets of paper. At last, one o'clock came, and with it, Paul Blackham. He had a small leather folio case with him, which he placed beside himself on the small table where she sat him, with a cup of tea. He looked down at her.

'Now, how can I be of service, Miss Brown? I must confess, we do not have many young women seeking financial advice from the bank. In fact, many bankers do not approve of the idea, at all.'

Selina hesitated at first and then gulped and started to try to explain her ideas.

'I don't have anything specific in mind at the present; what I want to know is, how do I go about giving a bank the sort of plan that I might have, to start a business of my own?'

She hesitated again, looked at him and realised that he was not about to mock her, as she had been half expecting.

'Well, you see, I am sort of educating myself in business as I go along, watching what other businesses do and deciding whether I would do it the same way, for instance, you know the hardware shop on the Cross?'

Blackham nodded but did not interrupt. Her enthusiasm was manifest in the light in her eyes as she spoke with maturity about her subject. Selina went on.

'Well, he has all these little shelves with his brackets and screws and things in. He knows where they all are so it looks impressive when a customer asks for something and he goes straight to it. The trouble is, he is hiding his stock, which, to me is the same as not having the stock. No doubt a lot of people will go to him for years, seeing him as an expert on his trade, but I would rather put all my stock on display, not hide it.'

She caught her breath. She hadn't told anyone of her aspirations, before. Blackham smiled at her, encouraging her to go on. She put her thoughts in order and resumed.

'I have other ideas, as well. The shop by the clock closes at one o'clock on Thursdays. I shall not close at all, so anyone who wants an item of hardware will have to come to me, if they are in a hurry for it. I can always employ someone, just for a few hours, to keep the door open, so to speak. There are plenty of people out of work. I keep having ideas but for some of them I need more capital to put them into practice. Is there any chance that the bank would help me; if not, where can I go to get the sort of help that I need?'

Selina looked appealingly at Paul Blackham and he paused to look round the shop, taking in the differences she had made to the small premises. It was obvious that the lay-out had been carefully designed. He could see that there was a degree of flexibility to the design, so that she could alter it to take account of varying demand for the products that she had displayed. He turned his attention back to Selina and made up his mind that if he could help her, he would.

'Look, Miss Brown, the shop belongs to your mother, Mrs Brown. I have to admit that the ideas that you have told me about are all good ideas, but really, they will never benefit you. You are in the same position as any employee. If you have an idea for the business that is good for the business, the business benefits, not the employee! It is not likely that your mother will transfer the business into your name, so you are working for her, not yourself. You may acquire the business if she dies, of course, but there is no other way that I can see that you will ever get control of it. The only advice that I can give to you is to keep making your small deposits to your savings account and when you think you have enough savings to stock a shop, look for premises. I am sorry I cannot be of any help to you.

If you ever decide to branch out on your own I would look favourably at any plan you might put forward, and consider helping you financially. I am very impressed with what you have done, but you must realise that your mother is the beneficiary!' He stood up and replaced his hat. 'I wish you good day, young lady.'

Selina found herself looking at the space he had occupied. Fat lot of good he had been! She found herself getting angry. Could no one help her? His words came back to her, 'your mother is the beneficiary.' He was right! She had to make the business work for her, not for her mother. How could she do that? It was a problem. In the meantime she had to see Tom, to find out what his intentions towards her might be! She would know by this time next week. By this time next year, her life would have changed completely. The idea was frightening and she laid her head in her hands and silently wept, praying for help with her difficulties. How was she going to cope? Her life had changed so many times in the last few months that she could barely contemplate them. Harry, then Tom, then the move to Bromyard and then the move to the little shop. After that she had found she was pregnant. The only little hope in her was the faith that Tom would look after her in some way. Just how she could not work out but she would have to see him and plead for his help and the sooner she did that the sooner she would know her fate.

23. Bad News.

'G'morning, Tom. How are you, love? I haven't seen you around, for a while.'

Tom looked round, hearing the sound of Selina's voice. He was on his way to work and was totally immersed in his thoughts. Tom hadn't known how to meet up with Selina since her mother had told him that Selina no longer wished to see him.

He had thought the problem over, many times. He knew that he still cared for her but if she did not want to see him, who was he, to presume on her love? He had looked elsewhere to fill the void of her absence but had not succeeded completely. The pain of her absence had become a sorrowful void in his life. He had heard that she was running the little shop for her mother and didn't want to see him any more. He was considering whether to call at the shop to talk to her, but didn't like the possibility of rejection.

Tom was a normal healthy young man, with a body that was capable of being sexually aroused by almost any attractive young woman but he was conscious that more than sexual desire was needed to fulfil his life, and he felt Selina's absence acutely. They had parted since their return from Herefordshire, no longer seeing each other. Now Selina wanted to see him. Was that good? Something was wrong. It was obvious, really. She did not usually seek him out at this time of the morning. He had a feeling in his stomach about it, too.

The coolness of the late October morning, combined with the industrial fog of Willenhall, was making the weather seem more like that of November. It was all so different from Herefordshire. A layer of ice lay on the small puddles of the gutter that lay along the road. His mind seemed to replicate both the sharpness of the temperature and the fogginess of the surroundings. What was Selina doing in this neighbourhood, when her shop was a mile away?

'I'm fine, Selina. It's nice to see you. How are you?' He leaned forward and kissed her on the lips, shyly. 'I have missed you, you know; but your mother told me that you wanted me to keep away from you. Is something wrong? You look worried.'

He had to get that off his mind, tell her how he felt about her. It was the only way he could think and feel towards her and it had to be told. Her face was serious as she replied.

She pulled him to the side of the road, allowing the pedestrians on the way to work, to pass by them. Her face seemed to crease up as she blurted out the secret that she had been keeping to herself. For her, too, this was a serious meeting and she wanted to let him know.

'Tom, I never wanted you to keep away from me. That was Mom's idea. She is jealous of any man I ever look at, even if it's just to ask what time it is. That's why she made me move out of the house, to keep her chap, Harry, from looking at me. He always fancied me, you see, and she couldn't abide that, so she moved me out, into the little shop, so she would have him all to herself. Not that I ever wanted him; I think he is a child-lover, if you know what I mean.'

He realised what she meant and found he was getting angry and protective at the same time.

Selina paused, trying to put her thoughts and feelings into some sort of order, then went on, speaking as if a dam had burst.

'Tom, I've got bad news. I, er, we, are going to have a baby. I am about four weeks late, you know.' She pulled him by the sleeve. 'What am I going to do?'

She started crying, in a choking sort of way. She also, illogically, looked more desirable than Tom had seen her before, and his heart melted at the sight. He thought about it. There was, to his mind, only one honourable thing he could do. Discounting the possibility that the father's baby could be Jim's, there was only one thing he could do. Face up to it.

He was going to be a father! Although the news was a shock to him, he felt suddenly proud that he had done something that marked him down as adult. He was going to have a child! His fatherly feelings, newly acquired, expressed themselves in his responses. He lifted Selina's chin, and kissed her. He was a man and was content to play the part of a man. He spoke gently, comfortingly and with authority.

'You are not to worry any more, Selina, my darling. We'll face this together - if that's what you want us to do. We'll go to see your mother and make a clean breast of things. I will tell her that we want to get married, if that's what you want?' He looked at her, questioningly and saw the response in her eyes. 'Don't you get worrying; your Mom seems a nice, understanding sort of woman. Surely she will help us.'

He didn't agree with his spoken assessment of Edie, nor did he feel the authority he was trying to express to Selina, but he felt Selina's need for consolation and support. Once again his sense of responsibility was taking him where he wasn't sure he really wanted to go. Selina's response to his words was joyful, loving and enthusiastic.

'Oh, Tom, you're wonderful. I do love you. I have loved you since we jumped the pole together. I should have known you would stand by me. With you by my side, nothing can go wrong!'

Selina, sustained by Tom's courage and sense of responsibility, agreed to go with him. Tom, fortified by her fighting spirit was willing to tackle any difficulty. First of all, to avoid being caught out by circumstances, she took Tom back to her little shop and collected the small amount of money she had been able to put on one side. She knew that if the worst came to pass, she might need every penny. Tom had never been inside the little shop since Edie had handed it over to Selina and he was enthralled by the innovations she had put in. He had never thought about the way a shop could be improved and he was only just learning about Selina's ways of doing things. The shelves with the fret-working items on it took his eye. He had been a hobbyist since he was a lad and anything to do with his hobby was of interest. When she came down the stairs, her clothes in her small case, he brought up the subject.

'What made you start selling fret-working things, Selina?'

'Oh, there were a few fret-saws lying around, and some blades, so I decided to make them tidier, and it just went on from there.'

He changed the subject back to their immediate problems, 'Have you got what you came back for?'

He didn't like to say anything about her money. It was nothing to do with him. He still felt the total responsibility for Selina and her unborn child. He pondered the situation again. Tom didn't want to involve his own parents. He felt that the problem was his, and he must see it through. He was under the impression that they would completely disown him and Selina. His father had always been a stickler for keeping to the rules of society. They were getting closer to Edie's house as he was thinking and it was with a start that he realised that they were there. The house seemed to have a forbidding air that made him recall Harry waving his stick at him, cheeky bastard! Especially as he had just been told of the man's proclivity!

Selina led the way in. Edie was surprised to see them both as she had reckoned that Tom was a thing of the past. Tom tried to be as courteous as he could, thinking that he was likely to be their, or at least, Edie's son-in-law. To his surprise, Edie and Harry listened carefully to what Tom said, as he explained the situation, without apology but as he talked he noticed that a disapproving atmosphere gradually pervaded the discussion. Harry was the first one to respond. This was his chance to clear the obstacles to his ambition with Edie. He took the moral high ground straight away, speaking from a height of proper indignation.

'How on earth could you think of coming to us, for help?' He turned from Tom, to whom he had been listening, and faced Selina. 'You little slut! I always thought you were too good to be true. The way you tried to lead me on when your mother was out!' He turned back to them. 'She has always been like that, even when she was fourteen!'

He suddenly shut up, realising the trap he was leading himself into. Selina could not believe her ears. After the way he

248

had seduced her, at the age of fourteen! She was tempted to expose him, but felt that she could not, because of the way it would affect her mother's life. Then it was her mother's turn to deliver judgement. She was just as condemning in her attitude, and the jealous anger showed itself in her eyes.

'I quite agree with Harry. You are just a little mare! I don't know why I thought you might change your ways. You can't come here, to live and there is not enough room over my little shop for the three of you. What would the neighbours think? Whatever possessed you to behave in such a way? You have made your bed, now you'll have to lie on it! Get your things packed and get out of my house! I suppose I'll have to run the shop myself. Don't expect any help from me! I never want to see you, again!'

She bent her head into her hands and poured out her sobs of anger, shame and despair. She had thought she had got their lives tidied up!

Harry Bentley sat silent while Edie poured forth her tirade of abuse. Then he added his own final words.

'God will punish you for the way you have behaved. You should pray for forgiveness. You are nothing but a young trollop. Now get out quickly, before I put you out.'

Tom stepped forward, ready to hit him but Selina pulled him back.

'Don't bother, Tom. He's not worth it.'

Tom stepped back but a hatred for the child-molester filled him, and stayed with him and he knew that if he ever had the chance to do him a bad turn, he would take it. They left the house not knowing what to do. They had nowhere to go, and only a few pounds between them. Each of them had an aversion to asking Dan Barr for help. They called on Selina's married sister, Joyce, but she told them she could only help them secretly, with a few pounds she had in the bank, and that would not be available until the following day. Thanking her, they left and took a room for the night at a commercial hotel near the railway station, looking forward with mixed feelings to the future. To their surprise, no one at the hotel expressed any disapproval as they booked in for the night.

They spread their few clothes on a chair in their room to give some appearance that they were not entirely penniless and they quickly climbed in to comfort each other, feeling the benefit of each other's arms. After a restless night, Selina woke up, realised where she was and woke Tom. The feeling of panic she'd had the day before had returned to her.

'Tom! Are you awake, Tom? What are we going to do? What are people going to say? I have no wedding ring, and every one will know we are not married.'

She was frightened of moving into the world of adults who, until then, had seemed all powerful. Tom climbed up on the bed, awkwardly, balancing himself between the movements of the mattress and took a ring from the curtain. Turning, he fell down on the bed laughing, then, still red in the face, took her hand and slipped the curtain ring onto her third finger. Although he was still smiling, the sincerity was obvious in his face.

'There you are my lovely. It's a bit loose, but I'll get you a gold one that fits, as soon as I can afford it. I'm asking you again, Selina. Will you be my bride?'

The answer was evident in her eyes as she answered with her lips and they felt that the bond that had led them to the hop pole was still pulling, pulling them closer together. Somehow, things would come right for them.

In spite of the bond, they were both still apprehensive at the way things were working out. Tom tried again to reassure Selina and they went down to breakfast and, to their surprise, no one seemed to think they were socially unacceptable. They sat in the fashionable lounge of the Station Hotel, before going into breakfast, and agreed to await the offer of help from Selina's sister, Joyce.

'I don't know why I didn't ask my own mother and father to help.' He thought about it, considering. 'They would have been easier to talk to than them pair.'

The idea came to him that they must ask his parents for help. He could not expect help from her parents and not expect the same from his.

'We'll go and ask my Mom for help, Selina. They can't be any worse to talk to than your Mom, can they?'

He looked at her questioningly and she answered with despair showing in her eyes. 'Oh, Tom, do you think it will do any good? No one seems to be of any use to us. Not even my own mother.'

She started to cry again and he put his arms around her, seeking to console her. 'Don't be so downhearted, Selina. You're making difficulties before we even ask for help. Let's cross our bridges when we come to them, eh? You'll feel better after we have had breakfast, so put on a smile and pretend that everything's lovely.'

Despite the encouragement that Tom was giving Selina, they were both slightly intimidated by the strange looks they thought they had received from other guests and members of staff yesterday. They talked the problem over again and agreed to wait until noon and then leave the hotel if they had heard nothing.

At five past twelve Selina's sister, Joyce, walked into the hotel with a letter from Selina's mother saying that Selina's potential stepfather was still just as unforgiving and never wished to see her again. Joyce had put five pounds in the envelope along with the address of their cousin in Birmingham who might help them with a roof over their heads for a few nights and possibly help with finding employment for Tom. They said goodbye to her, promised to write and started out towards the railway station. Tom explained his thoughts about his mother and father to Selina, along with the idea of seeing if they would help. Selina was nervous about the idea.

'It won't take us long to pop in to see my Mom. We should at least give them a chance to help.' Tom said, reassuringly. 'If they don't want to help, it won't take them long to throw us out, either.'

They walked the short distance to the Barr's tiny family home, and explained their dilemma to Elsie. She was sympathetic but unable to offer any helpful advice. It was obvious that the news was a shock to her. She tried to explain that she was bound by the traditional respect for the views of the man of the house, and she knew how he would feel about their situation.

'What do you expect of me?' She questioned them. 'I was worried to death when you didn't come home last night. You should have trusted me! I cannot help you, at least not directly. Your father would not allow it. The only thing I can possibly do to help you is to give you some money to tide you over. If you allow time to pass before we see you again, get married and have your baby, then you could visit and your father would welcome you, and maybe his grandchild as well. I know I would! In the meantime, just know that I love you, son; and I wish both of you nothing but good.

'Maybe times will change and the arrival of a baby outside marriage will not bring disgrace. The best advice I can give you is to take Joyce's help; go to Birmingham and start a new life with the few pounds that we can give you. Your father just could not face the neighbours with a bastard in the family.'

Her face crumbled with emotion. Her favourite son was going away! She might never see him again, and all because of this little trollop. She knew that she would regret whatever harsh words she felt like saying now, so kept her thoughts to herself.

Her words sounded so final and condemning that they could not bring themselves to try to change her mind. She had wished them a good life, with the door left open to resume their relationships. As she watched them go up the cobbled street, Elsie was reminded of the last time she had said goodbye to her son. She had been right; a boy had gone away and a man had returned. She was proud of him, facing his responsibilities, as a man should. She had given Tom fifteen pounds from her savings. It was up to him and Selina, now.

She was left to face Dan and Ted with the news. It was later in the evening that Dan Barr came home from a drinking session at the Deer's Leap. He was morose and had drunk more than was good for him. He was angry, even as he entered the house.

'That gaffer at the Deer's Leap has decided to stop the darts team giving suppers to visiting teams; just because the team from Tipton had a few too many for their own good. That bloke's too miserable to be born! Never known anybody like him. And what's the matter with you, Else'? You've got a face like a bosted boot! Come here; gi'e us a kiss. Yo' ain' gi'e us a kiss for a fortnit! What a life! Misery, Misery! Misery everywhere! Come 'ere, wench.'

He reached for Elsie, trying to put his arms round her. She couldn't let him. She had to let him know what was going on. She grasped him firmly by the arms.

'Stop it, Dan! Listen to me! Sit down an' shut up! I've got things to tell you. Important things, an' I want you sober when I tell you.'

He looked at the expression on Elsie's face and his demeanour changed instantly. He sat down, contrite; slightly comic in the way he sat straight-backed in the corner of the table that was always his, like a pupil at school.

'What's up wench? What's up love? Come on! You know you can tell me anything. Spill the beans, then. Is it Ted? Or is it Tom? I've had a feeling something's the matter with one o' them.'

He lapsed into silence, looking at her, knowing that Elsie would tell him the problem in her own good time, as she always did. They sat in silence for a minute then Elsie told him the story, just as she had been told.

'It's our Tom, Dan; Tom and that Selina. She's pregnant, poor sod. Now don't start mouthing off. I've sorted it out. They've gone to Brummagem to find somewhere to live. It seems that Selina's got an aunt there who might put them up for a few nights, and they might be able to help them with finding a job. That's what they told me, anyway.'

'I know you would have lost your temper with them, and

regretted it later on so it's a good job you weren't here when they came. You'll have nothing to regret, now. When you do see them they'll probably be married, with a baby, your first grandchild, so think on before you start on them.'

Dan was silent for a moment, adding up the facts he had been given. Nothing would make him forgive Tom and that dirty little bitch that had led his eldest son off the rails. Still, it would be nice if, one day, they should happen to bring him his first grandson to see and, maybe, bounce on his knee. His imagination led him on, and then he came back to earth.

'I suppose you didn't see them off without a penny, did you, missus?' As she shook her head, he went to shout and then thought better of it. 'Eh, that's a good job, then. I wouldn't have forgive ya if you'd sent 'em off without a penny.'

He smiled at her and she thought, 'That's the Dan that made me fall in love with him.'

The thought brought back memories of their courting days and how she had been impressed at the qualities in Dan, his attitude to life, and how he coped with changing circumstances. Even now, in spite of the fact that he had been half drunk when he had been given the news, he had been kind and understanding about the situation, even asking if she had been able to help the young people with a bit of cash. He did not have what some people called, financial acumen, but he did have a heart. She had often wondered; which were the most important characteristics? She'd had had experience of men with both attributes. As long as she lived, she would never know which way she was, herself. There was more than one kind of survival, and both were needed. Perhaps what it was, she thought, was good judgement in the application of heart or head.

How would Stephen Stones' have answered the problem? That would have been a good one! That would have let the cat among the pigeons, wouldn't it? She had a good mind to tell him, just to see his reaction. She had to see Edie in the morning as well! How should she react to her? She wouldn't let out any more information to that old bag. If she wanted to know anything she could ask 'til she was red in the face. She would probably leave Stones' now there was nobody to look after her little shop for her. There was always her chap, wasn't there? Now Edie would see how he might help with her problems. If the woman had been a bit helpful to the young couple, a better outcome might have emerged.

Now it was down to the Gods of Birmingham what luck they might have. She blamed herself on one hand but knew that any young couple might have been snared by love. In a way, what was happening to them was a more open and direct story than the one that she and Stephen had written for themselves, over the years. God only knows what her mother would have thought about her life and the antics and tricks she and Stephen had pulled to get a few minutes together. She prayed for the young couple as she prepared for bed and then tried for a long time to sleep.

24. Off to Birmingham.

Selina and Tom made their way towards Blower's Green railway station, each full of similar, disturbing thoughts. Would they ever see their family again? Would they ever come back to the scenes they had grown familiar with whilst growing up? Would they ever see their friends again? What lay in store for them in the great city of Birmingham? Birmingham was only a few miles away but it might as well have been on a different continent. Most people still only travelled less than ten miles from the home of their birth during a lifetime.

The weather seemed to emulate their feelings, cool weather soon being replaced by hard, driving rain, then the sun appearing round the edge of a black cloud. Twice they had to shelter from the rain that seemed to envelope them on their walk towards the station. Mirroring their emotions they were first wet and miserable, feeling low and negative then dry and steaming, feeling as if they were in an oppressive situation and then, when the sun shone, almost smouldering in the heat, the warmth sapping their energy.

They had some money to sustain them. Tom had fifteen pounds that he considered to be a debt to his mother, and eleven pounds, the sum left from his hop picking and last week's wages. Selina had five pounds that her sister had lent her, and she had eight pounds, fifteen shillings in her bank account, as well as five pounds four shillings in her purse. A total of forty-four pounds, nineteen shillings, though neither of them knew the full total of what they had, being unwilling to tell the other of their full assets.

They knew nothing about the great city. What opportunities would it offer? What problems? Would they fit in? What sort of person was this aunt of Selina's to whom they were going for help? The journey would be beset with worry and doubt, and yet, there was the possibility of freedom and excitement and the possibility of a new life.

Neither of them really knew a lot about the other, just what they had learned during their time together in Bromyard. Selina was wondering what sort of person Tom really was. Would he really support her, practically and emotionally, as he had promised? Would he be faithful? They had only had a 'Hop Pole Wedding'; would he ever want a church wedding? She recalled the event and knew she would never regret it. She felt that, in spite of her previous sexual experiences, she had been quite as innocent as he on the night of their wedding, and their first naive attempts at consummating their relationship had almost been disastrous. We learned though, didn't we, she thought. She looked up at him as they strode along together, admiring the way he carried both their small cases as if they had nothing in them. She felt that he would willingly take on any task that would help them to survive.

He looked down at her and smiled. She gave him a protective feeling.

'It's not far now Selina. Then we're on our way to making our own way, with nobody to tell me or you that I can't kiss you, as often as I like.'

'And nobody to say I can't kiss you as often as I like either!' she reposted.

They turned into the entrance to the railway station and he turned to her as they came to a bench on the first platform.

'You sit here my lovely,' he said, 'while I go and get the tickets.'

He strode off, disappearing through the billowing steam - a train had just stopped at their platform - and she felt a sense of loss immediately; it was like a conjuring trick. One moment he was there, the next he had gone. She looked round the station. A poster took her eye; it depicted a young woman wearing a striped skirt, advising the reader to drink Barbers' tea. I wouldn't mind a cup of that, right now.

The steam had cleared now, momentarily, and she looked along the length of the platform. There was a busy atmosphere;

porters were carrying cases, pushing sack-trucks full of luggage, doors were thudding shut along the train, steam was pouring out of the chimney of the engine at the front of the train, filling the platform again. There was a loud whistle, people were waving goodbyes; it was moving, slowly at first, then faster, clattering past her, people waving through the windows; illogically she. waved back at a pretty little girl, then the train was disappearing into the short tunnel round a bend in the track. Suddenly it was silent and she wondered if there was something wrong with her ears until she heard Tom speak,

'Here you are my love. I've brought you a cup of tea. The next train to Birmingham is in half an hours' time, on this platform, so there's no hurry. You can sit there and drink it up nice and easy.'

He had a lilt to his voice that was oddly discordant with most Blackcountry men.

She looked up at him, saw the loving concern written on his face and suddenly knew everything was going to be all right. Young, he might be, but he was made of the right stuff, and would win through, despite the odds. They always seemed to be journeying together, she thought, always travelling towards a future together. She relaxed, the warm tea bringing a sense of contentment, hardly noticing the passage of time.

Twenty minutes later she heard the next train coming towards them. That's ours she thought. Then it was arriving at the platform adding acceleration to the time that they were part of. Then they were off again, once again finding a compartment to themselves. No one entered the compartment and they were able to watch the countryside fly past without hearing comments about them.

This time, the journey they undertook was over in less than an hour. Everything seemed squashed in time; events seemed to take in less time than they should have. The speed of the journey seemed be squeezing time, with the clickety-clack, clickety-clack, of the wheels seeming to assist in speeding up time itself. It was easy to tell when they were getting near to the great city. People were getting up as if they were in a hurry to get there. Not like us, she thought. Suddenly she was delighted as if her life had just taken a wonderful turn for the good side of life. She turned to Tom and it was as if he, too, was feeling the same enthusiasm.

Life was going to be beautiful. The second city was about to embrace them and share its treasures. She was no longer impatient to get there. That would happen to the beat of the city, not to her desires. She looked out of the window again and as they passed a black wall, it reflected Tom's features.

Emotions were chasing across his face, reflecting in his expressions his feelings. Then it seemed to happen to him, too. A smile lit his face and he turned to her, speaking his thoughts.

'Selina, I think we are going to have all sorts of difficulties and hard times but I don't care. We shall overcome them and live life as we find it. In a few months we shall have our own little Brummy, born here in this great city. I don't know whether it will be a boy or a girl but I do know we shall love the child as no child has been loved before, like I love you. We are very lucky though not everybody would agree with me. Not one in a thousand starts a life in a great place like this. If we do well, we may find the chance to buy somewhere nice to bring up our family. We could never have done that as well in the Black Country.'

The train was slowing now; people were filling the narrow corridor. It stopped and the passengers started to jump down, bustling towards their next task, whatever it might be. It seemed to Selina and Tom that the speed of life here was greater then they were used to. This city, this Birmingham, was a fast moving place and therefore must be the same as regards money. It was not possible that a city like this could be idle. It must be fast moving to create fortunes like Joseph Lucas and George Cadbury had built in their time.

Tom sighed, relieving all the feelings that were coursing through him and Selina clung to him, full of hope for the first time. She had wanted Tom; now she had got him! She recalled the dreams she had had, how she had planned to have him totally to herself. Now those dreams had come true. They were just entering a new world and there was nothing they could not overcome. In a way they had come home. They had come home to Birmingham.

Tom picked up their luggage and motioned towards the door. The train had stopped but they had to go on. She moved slowly towards the door to the carriage. Tom was in front, waiting for her to put her foot on the step, waiting to save if she stumbled.

Daintily she stepped down onto Snow Hill Station and into another world. It had been raining but now, although the platform was shining, it was drying quickly and the sun was warming them. It was time, she knew, to hurry but she didn't want to. This place was there to be looked at and she didn't want to hurry her introduction. It was too much of a thrill!

25. Birmingham.

Disembarking from the train at Snow Hill, finding their way to the bus stop outside the station, where they were to catch the bus to Hockley Brook, all seemed to be activities in a portion of time that was compressed. There was a selection of buses they could catch, going to West Bromwich, Wolverhampton, Handsworth and Sutton Coldfield. The rain had started pouring again and they got wet while they were waiting.

There seemed to be a lot of dirty buildings in Birmingham with millions of pigeons and starlings fighting for places to perch on the window-sills of the tall buildings. They had noticed dirt too, when they had travelled before, to other places in the Black Country but here there seemed to be bits of metal everywhere, washers and brass rivets in the gutters alongside nuts and bolts. You'd never be short of a screw or a rivet, Selina thought. There was an old man shouting "Despatch an' Mail! Get yer Mail!' Tom bought one and she wondered why; it was probably to see if there were any jobs going.

They caught a bus and were at Farm Street in a few minutes after travelling along famous roads, Snow Hill, Constitution Hill, Great Hampton Street, Hockley Hill and then they were there, Hockley Brook. Five minutes walk brought them to Uncle Pete and Aunt Florrie's home in Ventnor Road, a side road off Farm Street, just past Saint Saviour's Church. The road seemed to be straight, as if the whole scene had been drawn by a draughtsman, as an exercise in perspective, the furthest end of the street just slightly smaller than the near end. This seemed to in contrast to Wellesley Street, a street that they had just passed, where the street curved gently with the houses disappearing from view as they hid behind each other. All the houses appeared, at first, to be the same, but she soon noticed the differences in the curtains and the quality of the polish used to colour the steps and the bricks round the doors. The paving was of very hard, black bricks, with a small, diamond-shaped pattern set into them. They shone black in the after rain wetness of the afternoon, reminding Tom of home. The shiny blackness brought a poignant memory of his mother, black-leading the fire-grate.

They stopped at number forty-two after approaching it slowly and cautiously, seeking from within themselves the courage to face the next hurdle in this difficult period in their young lives. The house didn't seem much different to the others in the street but the step shone red with Cardinal polish and the net curtains hiding the inside of the parlour from view were pure white, showing a pride in the home. Selina looked at Tom and nodded, like a signal to the executioner. Tom knocked the door and they waited as they heard footsteps approach the door. There was a short wait and then a tall woman answered the door.

'Yes, can I help you? Oh! It's Edie's young 'un, Selina. Come on in my love! Don't stand outside as if you were strangers. Who's this; your young man? He's handsome, ain't he?' She pulled them through the long narrow hall into the back room; a sitting room cum living room first, then changed her mind. 'Go and sit in the front parlour while I go and make you a cup of tea. I expect you're thirsty after your journey?' She waited, briefly for a nod of assent from them both, and then called out. 'Pete! Come and look what the cat's dragged in! It's our Selina with a young man. Come on, come and meet them. I bet they've got a story to tell.'

A spare looking man appeared from the backyard, his hands dirty from coal breaking; the preparation for tomorrow's fire.

'Hello, Selina; nice to see you again.'

He didn't say anything further, being unwilling to shake hands with coal all over his own, just allowed himself to be introduced to Tom and then relapsed into a silence, obviously expecting Florrie to take the lead in any discussions that might take place. Tom and Selina didn't know that Florrie and Pete already knew their predicament.

The telegram had arrived the night before.

'Selina and chap arriving yours tomorrow. Expecting. Help. Edie.'

It was a cryptic message with little enough in the way of clues as to what to expect. Fortunately Florrie could read between the lines so she was able to work out the substance of what the few words meant. Florrie and Peter had had given themselves chance to talk things over and had already decided what help they were willing to offer.

Tom looked at the warm, glowing fire in the cast-iron grate. He could see the half burned remains of the telegram disappearing into the flames. Florrie caught his glance, but ignored it. She had known they were coming! That was good news because she had invited them in, in a welcoming way, even knowing something of their circumstances. He decided to keep the knowledge to himself. If he knew Selina, she had already worked it out for herself!

Florrie didn't even pretend to be at all surprised to see them; just ushered the young couple into the parlour, at the front of the house, where they waited, sitting separately, Selina on the settee and Tom on a high-backed chair, hemmed in by a sideboard on one side and the pianoforte on the other. Florrie went striding off into the regions at the back of the house. In a few minutes she returned, smiling, with a shining tray, full of tea things. It was clear that she was enjoying the display of hospitality that she was being called upon to provide. Every movement of her long fingered hands as she poured tea and handed out slices of cake showed her pleasure at being able to put her parlour on display to her visitors.

She made no mention of the reason they were there, just acting as if their presence was the most natural event in her day. After asking about the health of Edie, and enquiring about Tom's family, the conversation lapsed, Florrie allowing it to happen to give Selina the opportunity to state her reason for visiting.

Eventually, Selina, blushing, handed over the letter that her mother had given her. Florrie took the letter and opened it with a little flourish, as if she were a queen, held it up to the light, read it and then summed up the problem.

'Well, my girl, you seem to have put the cat among the

pigeons. I am surprised at Edie; I would have thought she would have been able to cope with this.'

She leaned back, sipping the first, warm drops from her cup of tea, her little finger crooked at exactly the correct angle. She appeared very astute, thought Selina. Florrie went on.

'I wonder why she turned you out – not that I am condoning what you two have been up to, but your mother has never seemed to me to be particularly frightened or concerned about what the neighbours might think. I think there is more to it than you have told me, my young girl? Tell me about this chap, Harry. What is he like? How long have your mother and him been courting?'

She looked sharply and questioningly at Selina.

'No', Selina replied. 'There is no secret, Aunt Florrie. I got pregnant while I was in Herefordshire, with Tom, hop-picking. That's all there is to it.'

She fell silent. The questions were getting too close for comfort. Her aunt was much too shrewd!

'And what have you to say for yourself, young man? This is a nice pickle you have got this young girl into, isn't it?'

She looked over her spectacles at Tom. This was his opportunity to tell her where he stood. Collecting his thoughts he outlined how he felt about the situation.

'Now look here Auntie Florrie, I don't know what else to call you. What we have done has been done by hundreds of young couples. I am not trying to make myself white as snow. I know we did wrong in most people's eyes. I have already seen Selina thrown out of her home by a nasty piece of work, for making a mistake that thousands of young girls have made. My own parents have disowned us, and we have had to move away, to try to make a new life for ourselves. Both our parents have chastised us. That is enough! If you don't want us here, that's all right. We will have to manage on our own, but I tell you this. I intend to look after Selina and marry her. I am going to look after our baby, too.'

He stood up, looking defiantly at Florrie. He was taking no more!

'Sit down, son.' Florrie smiled at him unexpectedly. 'No one is going to chastise you. You've had enough of that, I expect. I just wanted to be sure in my own mind that you are going to do the right thing by Selina. I am satisfied now, and I know that Pete and I will help you all we can.'

Uncle Pete, opportunely, came into the room, looked at the young couple, and read the letter that Florrie handed to him. He made no comment on the contents, just asked about the journey and the weather, filling the small gap in the conversation. Selina could not decide whether it was deliberate, or whether he just jumped in. Then he continued his questions, this time to more purpose. Then he informed them of what he and Auntie Florrie had obviously already talked over.

'Well, we are going to help you as much as we can. What we are going to do is this: you are going to stay with us for a few days while we try to get something sorted out, between us. What sort of work do you do, Tom? Are you a qualified journeyman at any trade? If I am to help you get a job, I need to know what you can do.' He held his cup out to Auntie Florrie, 'Can I have a refill please, love? All this talking makes me thirsty.' He winked at Tom behind the back of Florrie, 'Men have to get rid of the women sometimes or we would never be able to discus anything. Go and give your aunt a hand, Selina, would you please? And tell her not to hurry. Now, where were we? You were going to tell me what you can do.'

He paused, waiting for Tom to speak. Eventually Tom replied, stating how he felt about the situation.

'I'm a locksmith, Pete. I've been qualified for about a year, now, although I am not yet twenty-one, but I am picking up the full rate. There aren't many of my age who can say that. I don't know how much goes on in my trade, in Birmingham. If I can't find work in my own trade, I will try anything that offers the chance to improve myself. I know I can learn because I have already learned a lot, so I know I can learn more. I know it's my job to provide a home for Selina and the babby and myself. I'll do it as well. I just need a chance. There must be a place for a man with the skills of a locksmith, and I don't mean breaking into safes!'

He sat looking at Peter, his eyes open and frank. It was obvious from his demeanour that he wasn't frightened of anything the world could throw at him. Peter made up his mind that he was going to do everything he could to help this young couple.

'Well, son, if you can use a file as good as a locksmith, there should be a place for you, somewhere in Birmingham. I'll have a word with my manager in the morning and see what he says. With a bit o' luck, you should get a start, even if it's on production work. They've been taking blokes on who dain't know one end of a file from the other.'

'What sort of things do they make at your place then, Pete?'

Tom was curious all of a sudden. Was he really going to get a chance this quick?

'We make car parts and bike parts. None of it is what you would call skilled, you know. They have introduced a system where everybody works on a production line, each adding a bit until the last one finishes it off. Sometimes it's bike bits; they make good money on that but they don't half have to go. The sweat rolls off you. There is not much pride in it but it pays the rent. You know what I mean?' He stopped, looking at Tom. 'You are not too proud to do a bit o' piecework, are you? Rolls-Royces are made in Coventry, not Birmingham. In Birmingham we make things for the people who can't afford Rolls-Royces and there's plenty o' them. We make a good living at it as well, if you just keep your nose clean, turn up and do your job properly.'

Florrie came back into the room, a tray in her hands again.

'I suppose you're starving, if I know anything about young men. Just take your cases up the stairs. Selina is tidying the back bedroom up for you. There is no point in trying to keep you two apart, so you can share the bedroom. While you are sorting yourselves out I'm going to lay out the dinner. I suppose you're ready for it?'

Tom smiled back at Florrie. He hadn't thought anyone existed who would have taken the news they had brought, as coolly.

'Yes, thank you Florrie. I am a bit peckish. I'll go and help Selina.'

They seemed to have landed on their feet! He felt distinctly lighter as he made his way up the dark stairs. As he entered the room, Selina put her arms round his neck.

'Tommy Barr, aren't we lucky?' We couldn't have dropped into a better spot, no matter how we tried to work things. Come here, let's celebrate!'

He gasped as her hands started to explore his body and he felt the familiar thrill of excitement take over his body. His hands reached out to Selina in an animal-like instinctive movement. He turned her round so that she was facing away from him then his hands started to caress her body. His lips came, as if in a reflex movement, to her neck, caressing her back and shoulders at the same time that his hands were stroking her breasts, smoothing small circles round her nipples. He tugged at her blouse, suggestively and she pulled it over her shoulders, throwing it on the floor in sheer abandon. The sight of her body excited him even more, as did the feel of her buttocks against his body. He was scarcely able to control himself, his organ reaching for her centre.

'Wait, Tom, please. What's the hurry? Just calm down and we can make it last, please.'

He took hold of himself, to prevent any further loss of control, then came back to the moment, realising that there was plenty of time; they did not have to hurry. He smiled to himself and he could not help but think of Kate. She had been the first, the one who had given him his first lesson. Now it was Selina. He had control of his body, now, and decided that he should do a little teaching. His hands went back to her breasts, resuming their circular strokes. Then he moved his hands down her body, lingering at her navel, feeling her reflex movement as he inserted his finger into the tiny crevice. Then his hand resumed its journey, over her small pubic mound, then finding her centre of pleasure.

She squealed as he rubbed the tiny organ, rearing back to get the fullest contact between them, her buttocks, moving back and forth and playing havoc with his self-control. He pushed her forward, bending her body, and this time would not be denied. He entered her swiftly, the way already lubricated by her passion. He felt a sudden increase in the wetness then, he too was moving in and out, not giving any thought to the world outside the one they were familiar with. An almighty surge, forward from Tom, backward from Selina completed the union and they collapsed onto the bed, their tensions released.

Selina lay back and relaxed; her body full of the feel of him. How lucky can you get? He was laying at the side of her his chest moving slowly up and down. She smiled as she watched him, wondering how long he would sleep for. She swung her legs round, gently, being careful not to disturb him. There were things to be done. Within five minutes she had unpacked their cases, sliding them under the bed. There was a ewer full of water on the little wash-stand, with a bowl to wash their selves in. It was cold but she didn't mind. She had got used to washing in cold water in Herefordshire.

Swiftly she washed herself down and towelled herself dry. Her Aunt would be calling her in a few minutes. She opened the door and went down the stairs. Florrie was waiting.

'I wondered where you had got to, Selina. I wondered about the hop picking. I've heard about it, of course, but I don't know the first thing about it. What does it entail?'

She settled back into her chair and poured the tea. There was plenty of time to find out more about her.

26. A Bit of Cash.

The screech disturbed him, as he lay, half asleep, half awake. He was remembering his mother's words to him before he had started out for the hop fields. Selina was not in the bed. They had been staying at Florrie and Pete's house for a fortnight, now. Nothing seemed to be working out. He tried to recollect what had disturbed him; the screech in the night. He lay and listened to the noises of the morning. The screech was not repeated. His mother's words came into his mind again.

'Save half of the money you earn and do something useful with it when you get home, in October.'

If only he had taken her advice more seriously! He would have been able to buy something pretty for Selina, and a toy for his little Brummy. As it was, he had three-ha'pence in his pocket, no job and no prospects of a job, unless Selina's Uncle Fred could find him a job. There was their borrowing of course, from their parents, but Selina had been given the responsibility of looking after that. She had hinted that there might be a job going at the factory where her Uncle Pete worked. He had handed over the money he had saved, to Selina so that she would feel secure. Now, he didn't. It was Monday morning. He had no cigarettes and he didn't want to scrounge the money to buy some. His head ached from the drink the night before. He was in a foul mood.

Downstairs he could hear Selina polishing the grate with black lead. She was always up to something, now. Reaching out, trying to be better at whatever she was doing. 'I suppose that's what we all do, all the time.' he thought. 'I suppose I've got to get better at trying to get a job. I should be able to get a job, really. I know I can do any job in a lock factory, and it ain't any different here, just because it's a big city.

They just don't like Black Country people here. They think you're going to pinch their jobs. I suppose I would as well, if I got the chance. They say a Black Countryman will work for a penny an hour less than a Brummy, so they do their best to make sure you don't get the job in the first place. How can I get a job if nobody will give me a chance, in the first place? He had tried a few places but they seemed to be against him because of his Black Country accent. He sat himself up on the bed, pondering on the problem.

Selina had surprised him by the way she had been able to survive in a strange city, with few friends. She seemed to see things in a different way to him; as if he could see only the surface and she could see underneath to know what made people do things in the way they did. They had fallen in lucky too, having such a friendly and supportive aunt to let them live in with them, until they could find somewhere for themselves. Her husband Pete was all right too; hopefully his gaffer would offer him a job soon and then he would have the chance to show what he could do.

Pete always seemed to be very interested in politics; he was always commenting on something the Government had done, or was going to do. He reckoned there was going to be another election, soon. It looks as if I am going to get another tutor in the University of Life, he thought. First you have your mother and father, then you have a teacher, then you have other teachers and you have to decide for yourself whether they are the teacher for you. There have been people who had tried to force their opinions on me, but I have been lucky, so far, in having mostly sensible people giving me their opinions.

Tom dressed, made his way down the stairs into the kitchen and warmed his hands by the coal fire. There was a black kettle with water bubbling in it. He poured himself a cup of tea and lit a cigarette. He nodded grumpily at Selina; she was polishing the furniture now; she was always doing something.

He supposed he should be doing his share of the household jobs. Stepping through the back kitchen into the yard at the rear of the house he saw some wood, and a small chopper lying against the wall of the yard. He picked up the chopper, looked at the edge and started to slice the small logs into kindling. It was something to do to pass the time. He remembered seeing a man in Dudley, with a cart, full of similar pieces of wood, tied in small bundles, walking the streets, shouting, selling it. The thought held him.

'He must have been hard up. Same as me. I suppose I could do that. I bet I could get three-halfpence pence a bundle for that wood. I wonder how much of it I could sell today.'

He started chopping, faster and faster, until he had a large pile of kindling. He was getting out of breath now, so he stopped and leaned on the wall, smoking a cigarette from his packet of five. He was looking round for something to tie the wood together with.

There was a shed in the yard and he stepped over to it to look through the window. There was a bench with a vice and a few small tools. Lying on the floor, amongst the sawdust, was an old leather apron. He opened the door to the shed and stepped in. He picked up the apron and reaching for a pair of scissors from a hook on the wall he cut up the apron into narrow thongs. In an hour he had made a neat pile of about fifty bundles of kindling. The next thing he needed was something to carry it around with. He looked round the back yard; there was nothing there.

He stood on a pile of bricks and looked over the three-foot wall into the next-door yard. He stayed and looked a little longer, then realised that he was being nosy. He stepped down, slightly shamefaced, and looked into the yard at the other side of the house. There was an old pram in the corner of the yard. It looked as if it had not been used for years, but the wheels appeared to be in reasonable shape; that is, they were round. There was no one around that he could see, or hear, at home in the next house.

'Hey! Is anybody there?'

He shouted. He waited patiently. There was a screeching of the door. That was what the screech had been! A head came into view. It was an elderly woman.

'What do you want, son? What are you shouting at? I'm trying to get a bit of shut-eye here. There's never any peace round here. What do you think you are you doing?'

Her voice tailed off as she started coughing. She stalked into the middle of the yard, still with a questioning look on her face.

'Well? What do you want? Eh?'

Tom looked at her. He had never seen anyone like her. She wore a filthy old black skirt and a jumper that looked as if it had been found in the gutter. Her shoes were as old as he had ever seen a pair of shoes, with the sole hanging from them and her dirty foot showing through. How could he explain to her that she had become part of his ambition?

'Me and my missus, Selina, are staying with Auntie Flo and Uncle Pete for a few days.' He explained. 'I just wondered if I could borrow your pram.'

He could see her trying to add up the information he had just given to her. He spoke again, more persuasively, letting her in on his ambition.

'I'd only want it for a couple of hours, just to hawk this wood round, so I can get a few coppers to buy a packet of woodbines.'

Her face lit up, understanding and sympathy to a small measure showing there. She coughed, and then spoke, offering him a packet of cigarettes

'Help yourself, son, and while you're at it, I'll have a bundle or two. If you forget to bring the pram back, it don't matter.'

She turned and retreated into the house. Tom smiled to himself, lit the cigarette and climbed over the wall. He picked up the pram, and then noticed a pile of wood leaning against the wall. He threw it over the wall, then picked up the pram and lifted it over the wall, and then climbed back over himself. He took a hard broom and swept the yard and the inside of the shed. The pram seemed to be all right. He loaded it with about thirty of the firewood bundles, opened the back gate into the entry and manoeuvred the pram, down the step, into the entry. He pushed the pram down the entry and turned into the street. He looked round. There were just a few folk, going about their business. Now is the time. His motto came to his rescue as he was almost deciding to give up and take the firewood back to the house. He cleared his throat.

'Firewood! Get yer firewood!'

His voice sounded pathetic. He tried again. A man turned round, looked at him and continued on his way.

'Firewood! Get yer firewood! Best firewood!'

He shouted again, louder this time. The man turned round and looked at the wood.

'Ow much, our kid?'

Tom looked at him, and then looked at the size of the bundles he had strung together.

'Three halfpence a bundle, mate, or five for a tanner.'

'Gi'e us a couple o' bob's worth then, our kid.'

Tom was surprised. He had not expected to sell as much, so soon. That was the last, as well as the first, that he sold for over an hour. He lost track of time as he pushed the rickety pram. His throat was getting hoarse from the shouting. He looked round; he was by a small shop, not far from where he had started. The last hour had seen him go almost around the block. He looked into the window of the shop.

It was no different to the house where he and Selina were staying, except that a trestle had been put into the front, bay window. A second-hand table served as a counter. They were both littered with small items for sale. Candles, a few cigarettes, England's Glory matches, small Union Jacks, gas mantles and tins of polish. The table had a large round bottle on it with a sign: Large pop, 1d, small pop, ½d. There were also two bundles of firewood, two pence a bundle, smaller than the bundles on the pram. He went in. There was a small, tidy looking woman leaning on a pair of steps behind the counter.

'What can I get yer, son?'

She asked the question as if she really wanted an answer.

'A packet o' Woodbines an' a box o' matches, please.' He waited silently while she got them for him. 'Could I 'ave a cup o' water, please? Me throat's fell out wi' me backbone.'

She smiled at him, her smile taking over her whole face. Her reply was quick. 'I'm not a bit surprised, the way you were shouting. Have you done any good with the firewood, then? I suppose you realise you're taking the bread out of my mouth? How much do you want for the rest of your firewood then? I'll give you a penny a bundle for the lot, all right? That way we can both make a bit.'

She seemed to fire the questions at him like machine gun bullets, with barely a pause between each one. He looked in the pram. There were twenty-two bundles.

'Throw the fags in and you've struck a bargain.'

He answered her quickly and waited for her answer. She was going to make a penny a bundle out of his work! He was only getting a penny and he had had to chop it! Another thought came to him. He hadn't had to pay for the raw materials!

'Five fags I'll give you. I can't afford any more. I'm only dealing with you to stop you taking all my customers off me.'

He relaxed and reached for the packet of cigarettes, tipping it to take one and put it into his mouth and lit it, luxuriating in the feel of the tobacco entering his system. He sipped the carbonated, fruit-flavoured drink that she had brought him. It was wonderful! He stood there for a few minutes enjoying the combined tastes of the drink and the cigarette.

'Thanks very much.'

He went outside and brought in the twenty-two bundles of kindling, lighting another cigarette. The woman dipped her hand into the pocket of her voluminous pinafore apron and reached across the table. The shilling and small pieces of silver and copper shone in the sunlight that lit up her hand at that moment, winking into Tom's eye. She spoke again

'Can you bring me another two dozen bundles, the day after tomorrow?'

He did not hesitate, 'Twenty-four bundles on Wednesday? Yes

that will be alright'

He turned to go, feeling elated with his first business deal.

'What's your name, son?'

'Tom', he replied, 'Tom Barr.' 'What's yours?'

She smiled at him like a ray of sunshine. Her hair was in a mobcap, with curls showing from the edges. Her full-length, almost black pinafore apron was soiled. It was obvious she had been working hard. She was the first customer of his new business.

'Mrs Briggs to you, son; Myrtle Briggs and I'll see you Wednesday morning. First thing if you don't mind. It's no good having firewood in to light fires in the afternoon. It's too late then. Tara, then.'

'Tara.'

He turned, to see her watching him. She liked him.

Tom felt in his pocket. One and ten pence! And a packet of fags and a box of matches! He made up his mind then, to save half of the money, and share the other half with Selina. His mind seemed to be working more quickly. There were other small shops who would like to get their firewood supplies for a penny a bundle and a good bundle at that. He could make a full-time job out of it, no, not a job, a business! All he had to do was to shout his wares near a small shop instead of walking round all day. Of course, he had to acquire some more wood first.

He wondered where he could get some more wood, and his mind seemed to take the problem on board for it was only a few minutes later that he passed a yard with lots of wood standing, leaning and lying around. A smart looking man, coat hung on a nail in the fence, was bending down, and obviously trying to tidy the wood up. He was not looking at all pleased. Tom walked over to the gate of the small establishment and leaned on it, just looking at the man's efforts. After a few minutes he turned, noticed Tom, and spoke,

'What do you want, mate? I ain't open today. I've got to get this lot tidied up. I've got a big order for chairs to do, and the wood for them is coming in, first thing in the morning, and I don't know where I am going to put it all. My labourer has had a day off, just to be awkward.'

'It was as if he had been waiting for me to turn up.'

That was the way that Tom described the event later. He offered to tidy the whole yard for ten shillings, and to get rid of the scrap wood to provide room for the incoming raw materials. The man, Bill Smith, had jumped at the offer, even offering Tom a part-time job on the spot, telling him he would teach him how to use the woodworking machinery, the next time he came in. Here was his raw material, free of charge.

He stood back, the sweat running from his face. He had been home with the pram full of scrap wood three times now and the wood-yard was looking a lot tidier. Bill Smith, the proprietor, beckoned him from the doorway of the machine shop. Tom walked over, curious.

'You've done a good job there, mate. Here's your money. Keep the change. When can you come again? I shan't need you tomorrow, but if you can come in Wednesday afternoon I think I'll have some more scrap wood by then. What on earth are you going to do with it?'

He had no idea what its intended use was. It wouldn't have occurred to him to do the same thing himself. It wouldn't have been economic.

'Yes, Mister Smith; that will suit me fine. I'll see you about one o'clock Wednesday. Thanks for the work.'

He didn't answer the man's question. Curiously he looked through the doorway. There were a number of men working on various machines. By each machine there was a pile of chair parts, seats, legs, back-spindles or back hoops.

A boy was moving the finished parts to a room where a man was assembling them. Another man was dipping the finished chairs into a large container of evil coloured wood-stain then hanging them up to dry. The finished chairs were all a dark-oak colour. About fifty of them were being stacked onto the back of a large, horse-drawn wagon. A dozen tabletops were lying on the back of the wagon with their legs alongside. The aging horse was eating out of a leather feed-bucket hanging from its neck. The whole system was simple, with wood coming in to the factory at one end, and chairs and tables going out of the other.

One of the men shouted out to him.

'Oy! What do you want? Piss off and do your scrounging somewhere else.'

Tom put two fingers up to the man, feeling satisfied, and then he walked off whistling. What a day! He had twenty five shillings and eight pence! He also had a packet of cigarettes, an order for firewood and the chance of earning more on Wednesday! He slowed his walk to a stroll, thinking things out. Had he been lucky, or had he been looking for the opportunity that came along? Which was the cause and which the effect? It seemed puzzling.

He walked back along Farm Street, went into the small shop that he had been into earlier, and bought a Birmingham Mail. Uncle Pete would be pleased with that! He turned the pram up the entry to the backyard of the small house. He placed the wood against the garden wall, leaving it waiting to be chopped. He leaned against the wall and smoked another of the Woodbines. Things were looking up. He had all day tomorrow to chop the wood if he wanted to take his time. No, now is the time. He picked up the small chopper, put it into the vice and started to sharpen the edge with a flat file. He could not afford to work with poor tools. He had to be ready for more business in his business. Barr's Wood, Limited! He chuckled to himself.

The next two hours went quickly sped, the second-counting strokes of the small chopper keeping time. He ran out of thongs for wrapping of the bundles and had to buy some string. His first business expense! It was getting dark as he finished stacking the wood inside the shed. The shed was full. He now knew how he was spending tomorrow. He would be canvassing the local shops. His business would be his business. He didn't have to tell anyone.

'What have you been doing all day?' It was Selina's voice. It was obvious she had heard him chopping. 'You've done a good job, there. There's enough firewood to last Florrie and Pete all winter, I should think. Thank you, Tom, but you should really be looking for work. Tomorrow you will have to see if you can find a job. It'll suit you better than messing around, chopping wood all day.'

She didn't come out; just flounced; he imagined her flouncing, back into the house. He smiled to himself. He knew what he was doing, it didn't matter that no one else did. He stood, thinking things out, how he was going to get new customers for his firewood business, how to save the money he hoped to get from Bill Smith, how to put to the family the idea that he didn't want a job. He would face the family with his ideas when he was ready.

The evening went swiftly. He was aching, and felt he was out of favour with everyone, so he went to bed early, pleading an aching back. He lay back in the bed luxuriating in recalling the luck he'd had, earlier. He was in business for himself, a business he had started with three ha'pence in his pocket, which he hadn't had to use. He now had one regular customer, maybe the first of many. He had a job, of sorts, and a promise of future supplies of raw materials, at a cost of nothing! The ten shillings would feed him and Selina for the week, ten bundles of wood would pay for their rent, and the rest would build up for the business to expand; he didn't know how, but it would, he felt sure.

He dropped off to sleep, thinking more optimistic thoughts than he had had for some time. What would tomorrow bring? Later, Selina came to bed and placed her body next to his. They were still in love! He went to sleep happy.

27. A Bit More Cash.

'I know I said I would speak for him at work, to see if I could get him a start, but it isn't my fault if there isn't a place for him, just when he wants it.'

As he approached the house, from the entry at the back, where all the dustbins were kept, Tom could hear the sound of raised voices. He recognised the rough, Brummy growl of Pete, Selina's uncle.

'Perhaps it would help if he could offer to pay a bit towards your keep. I know you've been paying out of that money your mother gave you, but that won't last forever, and what will you do then? You don't owe us a penny at the moment; it's just that we worry about your future – and Tom's. He's a nice young man, but you will have a baby to keep soon, and they don't come cheap'

He stopped, catching sight of Tom in the backyard, looking in the window; his hands still on the handle of the old pram. Tom had been out selling his firewood and had done well. He now had five wholesale customers, small shops who were willing to give him a chance to supply them with kindling wood. He had also kept his appointment with Bill Smith, to tidy the yard and his pocket was getting fuller now. He was feeling quite pleased with himself. In the last few weeks he had changed his occupation from locksmith to hop picker, from hop-picker to firewood chopper and now he was in business for himself. He was more thoughtful, now, trying to think out the next move he might make to improve himself. Selina and Aunt Florrie looked round, at the expression on Pete's face and saw him, too. Selina looked horrified.

'If you think my little one is going to be pushed around in that old thing, you can think again, Tom Barr! I don't know how you have got the nerve to even bring that thing into the yard. Wherever you got it, you can take it back, and be quick about it!'

Tom stepped back, surprised by the anger in her voice, and found he was getting angry, too. He hadn't asked for this, on his return home from working all day, had he? No one was going to talk to him like that! He did not speak but walked into the back-kitchen, poured himself a cup of tea from the ever-brewing teapot, walked back out to the end of the yard and sat down on a pile of bricks. He tried to relax by lighting a cigarette. Selina followed him out and stood; red-faced, arms akimbo, high-bellied; looking down at him.

'What have you got to say for yourself? Eh? Eh? I suppose you've been hanging around the street corner, waiting for me to call you in for something to eat which I've had to pay for, in my Uncle's house, which I have been paying the rent on. When are you going to pay something – anything? That's what I'd like to know.'

She started to lift her arm as if to hit him when he opened his hand, and she saw the money glint in his hand of the sovereign and the other money.

'Where did you get that that from? I hope you haven't been stealing, Tommy Barr. I don't want you getting in trouble, no matter how short we have to get. I'm sorry I shouted at you but it's not easy, trying to keep Auntie Florrie and Uncle Pete good-humoured, and trying to manage on the last few coppers that Mom sent to me.'

She started to cry and Tom did not know what to do. She did not often cry. He put his arm round her, tentatively, and she snuggled against him, contrite in another swift change of mood. She was unpredictable.

'I'm sorry, Tom,' she repeated, 'I know I shouldn't shout at you; I wouldn't blame you if you gave me a clout. I do go on, don't I? Where did you get the money from, anyway?'

She looked at him in a way that seemed to be a mixture of a glare and an expectant smile. He responded in a way that was more forceful than she had seen in him before.

'Right, you've had a go at me, now it's my turn! What about

the fifteen pounds that my Mom has lent us? What about the eleven pounds that I put in your hand on the day we moved in here? Twenty-six pounds altogether! That has to count for something! I suppose you'd forgotten about that! That was enough to keep us going for at least three months. What have you done with that? Did you think I would forget it? Don't say you've spent it already. At least my Mom didn't throw her own daughter out!'

He was raising his voice now, an unusual thing for him. He quietened down. She was looking more contrite, now, so he explained to her the series of events that had occurred from the time he had started out, that previous Monday morning and, unexpectedly, she listened to him without interruption. Then she wanted to know where the little shops were that he had sold the bundles of firewood to, and where Bill Smith's wood yard was. When he had finished she spoke.

'Can I help you to chop the firewood in the morning, Tom?'

'In your condition? I should think not,' he answered, almost savagely, 'You can bring me a cup of tea occasionally and make sure you look after my babby, my little Brummy. It seems as if we might make a go of it in this city after all, so our babby is going to be a Brummy, whether it's a boy or a girl, and we had better make sure that it has a decent place to live in, eh?'

He saw a change of focus come into her eye and turned. Florrie and Pete were standing there. They had obviously heard everything he had said. Pete started to speak, his face showing a serious demeanour, but Florrie interrupted.

'Well Tommy Barr, we're pleased to see that you have been out and made a start on your life. We've been waiting for something like this to happen so we could give you some more good news. No, Pete hasn't got you a job. He's done something better! He's had a word with the landlord, Mister Hickman, and there's a double-fronted house going for rent in Wellesley Street off Farm Street, just down the road. It's five and sixpence a week but it's worth it. It's got three bedrooms and a parlour with a bay window. You'll have to furnish it as best as you can, but it's a start ain't it? You can't say we ain't tried to help you. It's a big house, really for you two, but if I know you, you'll soon fill it up!'

Tom looked at her, then threw back his head and roared. His joy was obvious to all of them. This was a day! This was a day! Now was a time! This was a wonderful, marvellous day! Right from start to finish, he had never felt so good.

He looked down at Selina, still in his arms smiling at him, and at the pleased looks on the faces of Pete and Florrie.

'You knew didn't you? The two of you knew. You knew, and didn't say anything, you crafty pair, you! Well, you are not the only ones who can keep a secret! I've got things to tell you as well.'

He explained what he had been doing with his time during the last few days and then announced that he wanted to have a look at their new home, before they moved in.

'We'd better go round and see the landlord, first thing in the morning. There are things to do. I don't know how we're going to furnish it, but we'll find a way.'

They spent the rest of the evening looking for bargains to fill their new home. They wanted to be ready when the house was ready for them the following Monday. When they came to move their belongings the quarter of a mile from Uncle Pete and Aunt Florrie's house to their new home they realised just how little they were starting their new life with. The landlord had seemed quite dour in his interview with them, but had been pleased by the month's rent that they gave him, as deposit. They now had a rent book to record each Monday's payment of five and sixpence, and on the back of which was a list of rules and regulations and their responsibilities to look after the property. They had paid five and sixpence, a week's rent in advance, as well as the deposit, and had received a set of keys in return.

Tom had been up since five o'clock, chopping kindling wood for Mrs Briggs, which he had delivered at eight o'clock. He now had until one o'clock, about two hours, to move in, when he was expected at Bill Smith's wood yard to do whatever was required of him.

They had borrowed a flat truck and were now outside their new home. Selina had the front door key in her hand. They were looking through the window into the bay-windowed parlour; it was as if they were street urchins. It seemed too good to be true, that their fortunes should improve so much in such a short time. Selina was dancing from one foot to another, excitedly, pointing into the house.

'We could have a piano just there, on the back wall, just where everybody can see it when they look through the window. I could learn to play it for you and we could stand round it, singing with the children.' She broke off, blushing, as she realised what she had said. 'Let's try the key in the door; see if it fits.' She was changing the subject, quickly. 'Here you are, Tom; you do it. You're the man of the house. You should see us in.'

Tom took the key and inserted it in the lock. The door caught for a moment, then opened at his push, and they were in. Holding hands, they silently passed through the parlour, the kitchen and the 'back kitchen', more like a scullery. She handed him the other key, to the back door, and they stepped into the yard. At the end of the yard there was a gate that led into an entry, where the dustmen came to pick up the dustbin. There was no dustbin. They would have to get a dustbin. It was going to fill, quickly!

The yard needed sweeping. They would have to get a broom for the yard – and another for the house – and a brush and shovel for picking up the ashes from the grate. They would have to get some coal. It was getting cold in the evenings. They would have to get a hearth plate and a fender to stop the ashes falling on the wooden floor. They walked back through the house to their flat truck, half empty in the roadway.

Tom spoke, his voice trembling slightly at the thought that they now had a home of their own. There was so much to be done.

'Come on, let's get on with it. There's a little shop on the corner, at the top.' He put his hand in his pocket for one of the half-crowns he had received for the kindling. 'Get a broom. I'll be taking the furniture in. At least we can clean the place. I've got to be at work at one o'clock. I'll do what I can until half past twelve, have a cup of tea, and then I'll have to go. I'll be back about six. With a bit of luck there'll be a few shillings in my pocket and we shall have to see what we can do to fill the house up. Just be careful what you are doing. Just start sweeping the upstairs rooms first, and then work your way down.'

He picked up the cases with their clothes from the truck and strode into the house. There was a lot to do! The next two hours saw them both busy. Tom carried the bed, a piece at a time, from the truck; up the stairs to the front bedroom of their new home and then reassembled it. After making it up with sheets and blankets, he stood, relaxing with a cigarette, looking through the front window. How were they going to furnish the house? The idea of buying a piano, as Selina had suggested, seemed completely out of reach. He could hear her, sprinkling drops of water on the floor to lay the dust, and then sweeping the back bedroom, and went through to her to help pick up the dust, which seemed to cover all the floors of the house.

He touched her on the shoulder. 'I've got to go now, Selina.' His voice sounded apologetic, 'I'll be back as soon as I have finished tidying up the yard. I'll bring as much wood as I can get in the pram. There are a few bundles on the truck. At least you can have a bit of a fire, for a time. I notice we've only got three mantles in the whole house. I'll buy another three on the way home; that should do us.'

He kissed her bashfully, and made his way to where the old pram stood on the back of the truck, and then disappeared down the street, wheels squeaking in a gradually reducing volume.

Selina stood and stretched her back. She had swept all the upstairs rooms. She seemed to get back pain more frequently now. She reckoned her dates; she was about three months pregnant and should have registered at the local Welfare by now. She made up her mind to do it later that week. She would do it tomorrow, while Tom was at work. She started brushing the stairs, sprinkling each one with a little water to keep the dust down, brushing the accumulated dust and dirt into the small metal coal-shovel. When the shovel was full, she tipped the contents gently into a paper carrier bag and when that was full she carried it out into the yard and tipped it into the brick-built screen that was supposed to hide the dustbin, or miskin as the Brummys called it.

There was nothing in the house that they could use, not even a discarded old chair that she could sit on. They had a bed, a few pots, cups, a teapot and Tom's tools. She had bought some vegetables to make a stew for when Tom came home. She noticed, in passing, that he had not taken all the kindling wood to Mrs Briggs; he had left some of it in the front parlour, along with some of the wood awaiting the chopper. She dusted the windowsill and put as many of the bundles of kindling on it as she could find room for, so that she could sweep the floor. She stepped back and looked at them and as she did there was a knock at the door. She answered it, wondering who their first visitor could be. It was a small girl, dressed in a scruffy brown skirt and jumper. She stood on her little toes and spoke.

'Can I have two bundles of firewood please?'

Selina thought fast; she could have all of them if she wished! She reached two bundles from the windowsill, and then reached two more.

'How much money have you got with you? If you have four bundles you can have them for two pence each instead of three pence.'

The girl opened her hand and showed the shilling that she had brought with her, and Selina took it from her. The girl seemed quite bright, and excited to be given the task of giving a message to her mother. Selina gently told her what to say.

'Tell your mother what I am telling you. If she still only wants two bundles, she can send two back and I will give you four pence change. Tell her I said so, and tell her I would sooner sell them cheap than dear.'

Selina put the bundles of kindling, two under each of the girl's arms, and sent her out of the shop. Selina looked around. There was a square piece of wood leaning on the fireplace. She picked it up and took a pencil out of Tom's toolbox. Carefully she wrote upon it, 'Firewood, 3d a bundle or four for sixpence.' She placed the piece of wood on the top of the bundles, facing the street. She had a shop; and a tanner working capital!

Her back was aching again. She swept up the last of the dust, tipped it into the carrier bag and took it out to the miskin. When she got back, Tom was standing in the middle of the front room. He looked at her, inquisitively,

'What made you decide to do that, Selina?'

He asked her. He hadn't thought of it himself, but it seemed like a good idea. She answered him quickly.

'Well, we can't afford to furnish it yet, so I thought it makes more sense if we made use of it. What do you think, Tom? I just took a sixpence, and if we can get some more cash, perhaps we could buy some stock to put alongside the firewood.'

Tom walked across the room to where he had just brought the wood he had 'tidied' up from the yard. He picked up a piece of wood about four feet long and placed it across the bay window and marked it with a pencil, then sawed it to fit across the bay, resting on the window sill, making a wider display area in the bay.

'That was a brilliant idea, Selina. What I am going to do is to give you half of whatever I earn, to buy stock and build up the shop. The rest will have to feed us and everything else. We will have to get by until the shop starts to pay for itself. Here's ten bob for the shop and that leaves ten bob to feed us and buy whatever else we want. I shall have to try to earn some more, as soon as I can. I don't want to spend the money that Mom lent me, but we could use it to buy some stock, if you like.'

He saw by the look in her eyes that he had said the right thing.

'Oh, Tom; could we? We could sell all sorts of things, the same as I did in Willenhall.' She started verbally making lists of possible items for stock. 'Batteries, fret-saws, hammers, matches, cigarettes, potatoes, oh, all sorts of items.'

'Wait a minute, Selina. Don't get carried away! I've only just got started with my firewood business. I don't know how long Bill Smith is going to want me at his wood yard, and you are setting up shop in our new home before we have even finished moving in. Give me a chance to get my breath, will you?'

He laughed at Selina's excited face. Suddenly she was contrite again. He noticed again this aspect of her character, the ability to switch moods at a moment's notice.

'Sorry, Tom; you are quite right. We should walk before we try to run. It's just that today is such an exciting day that anything and everything seems possible. Let's explore our new home. We've never had a home of our own, before. Let's find out what we've got.'

The rest of the day saw them busy. They explored the house from attic to cellar, cleaning as they went. Selina was having more pain in her back now, and was beginning to feel as if her time must be near. She had not really tried to record the passing of time in her pregnancy but she knew that it must have started during their sojourn in the hop yards – unless it was Harry's baby! The thought had frightened her so much that she sat down and tried to work out the number of months she had 'missed'.

She could not come to a clear outcome in her mind, so that all she could do to make an accurate determination was to wait until the birth and work it out from then. Having arrived at that conclusion she felt a little more content, especially as only she knew, and none of the possible fathers were likely to argue with her arithmetic. There was the possibility that the father could be Jim. She decided to ignore the problem. The baby had one good father. That was enough for anyone!

Tom was down the cellar with a candle; looking to see if he could find anything useful. She could hear him moving round, cursing when he bumped into some object, making her smile to herself. She hoped the last occupants had left a little coal in case she needed some hot water. They had heated some water, for the cleaning, in the brew house, at the back of the house. Most of it was done, now, and although the house looked bare, at least it was clean. The thought pleased her, as her aunt and uncle had promised to call on them as soon as they could, to see if there was anything they could do, to help with the settling in.

Tom still had not found a job, but it hadn't mattered; he had brought more money home without a job than if he had found work, and she was wondering if this was the better option. His head appeared above the cellar steps,

'Look what there is down here.' He had a boxful of mushrooms in his hands. There are a lot of them down here. We could have them for tea, with an egg, and put the rest of them up for sale, in the shop. What do you think?'

His face was black and she felt like giggling at his appearance, but realised that he was being serious. It wasn't a bad idea, after all. That's another little step, she thought. They seemed to be moving into trade, little by little. They needed money though. As the thought came into her head, she saw a movement at the front window. It was her aunt and uncle. They each had bags in their hands. She opened the front door and Auntie Florrie walked in, taking in everything they had done.

'My goodness, girl; you have been busy! This place is sparkling.' She turned to Tom who was putting the mushrooms onto the window ledge, 'What a good idea, Tom. I didn't know you had it in you!' This is a perfect position for a general shop, being on the corner. It looks along two streets.

Uncle Pete followed her in; he always did. He was just as enthusiastic, wanting to do anything that would help them. He had his arms full of armchair as he entered.

'Here you are then young lady. This chair will be kind to your back when you need it to be. There is another one outside, Tom. They're not new but we thought they would do you until things picked up. It looks as if you are not waiting for things to pick up; you are picking them up, yourselves!'

How on earth have you gone into business already? You've only been in five minutes!'

He turned on his heel without waiting for an answer and marched outside while Tom and Selina watched him with puzzled eyes. He was back in seconds with a cot and mattress on his head as he walked through the narrow door.

Selina screamed with laughter at the sight of him, but she was really pleased. She had been thinking about her baby's needs but had not yet started to buy things for it. Somehow it seemed to be like bad luck to get too far advanced with preparations for it. Tom was pleased as well but really wished he had been able to contribute. When he got that feeling, he got a bit surly and Selina had to persuade him to be happy with his good luck. What was Pete going to bring in next? Every day seemed to be filled with new, exciting things to do and to happen. How long would it last? There had to be an end to it.

28. The Representative.

There was still plenty to do. The four of them had formed a single brain, it seemed, discussing different ways of proceeding with the formation of a small business. Aunt Florrie had given Tom the credit for thinking of it, especially as he had already started one small business.

It wasn't my idea, 'he had admitted, 'it was Selina's.' but he was quite pleased to have been given the compliment.

Uncle Pete, too, was looking round. He seemed quite impressed by the small changes they had made since yesterday.

Whatever made you decide to turn it into a shop?' He asked Selina. 'You will be the only one at the end of the street; and on the corner, so you can be seen from two roads.'

Selina hadn't thought of that. It did make sense to be where more people could see you. She started to explain but Aunt Floss interrupted her, telling her she wasn't responsible for it. It was just luck, really. Luck seemed to play an important part in life.

'Come on, Selina, put the kettle on. We can talk over a cup of tea. I've bought you a china tea set to mark the day you moved in.'

The set was a collection of cups, saucers and tea-plates, featuring a floral pattern of small pink roses and seemed to Selina to bring a cheerful prettiness to the table, when it was set out. Selina thanked her; she did not have a tea set of her own and the gift relieved her of showing the lack. Florrie was speaking again.

'What are you going to do for stock? Have you made any enquiries for credit, yet?'

Of course they hadn't. They had only just moved in! Selina looked hard at Florrie. Everything was moving so fast. Yesterday, it seemed, they had been barely surviving; today they had a home of their own, two embryo businesses to run and a baby on the way!

The kettle was boiling now and they all sat round the counter in the window bay. Uncle Pete told them how to go about seeking credit facilities from a local wholesaler, and suggested that they made enquiries about selling newspapers. There was not another newspaper shop near so they might be allowed to sell them. The local newspaper had strict rules about how close to each other their outlets were. He also suggested that they open a current account with the local bank.

He provided them with a reference, though they had not yet had time to even think about seeing the manager of the local branch. There was not much money to deposit, anyway; as fast as money came in, so did a need for it. There were so many things they could spend their tiny amount of working capital on. They could grow their own mushrooms; they could pay someone to chop the wood for them, freeing Tom to tout for new trade customers. They could get vegetables delivered. The day flew; doing and talking made the time seem to move more quickly. The day ended at nine o'clock, with the house tidy and lists prepared, of things to do, things to get and things to think about.

*

Selina was sitting down as she tried to ignore the pain in her back. She was black-leading the grate in the living room, and it seemed to make her back ache more than most other activities. Looking up, she turned round. She could hear someone in the shop. Tom was at work, delivering his firewood to his 'round' of small shops. Selina wished he were there with her. It seemed to make the day go better when you weren't on your own. The noise from the shop was repeated.

'Hallo, who's there?'

She called. She didn't want to get up from her knees. It was too much trouble. A moment later she saw a red face appear round the doorway that led from the kitchen to the shop. They had meant to put a curtain up as soon as they could afford it, to separate the two parts of the premises.

'Excuse me, young lady. I'm looking for the proprietor. Is that yourself?'

His gentle, Scots accent was pleasant compared to the local, Brummy way of speaking. He advanced a little into the living room and looked around. His eyes seemed to take in everything. He was a tall; spare looking young man of about twenty-five.

'Yes, I am the proprietor Mr ...'

She looked at him, enquiringly. Who could he be?

'I'm sorry. I should have said. I am James Cameron of Cameron and Sons. I am the 'Sons' bit. We are grocery wholesalers. We have warehouses at Manchester and Edinburgh, and we are in the process of opening a branch in Birmingham, on the Lichfield Road at Aston. I noticed last week that you and your husband were working on the premises, turning the front room into a shop, and I wondered if we could be of service to you.'

His last sentence sounded like a question and an invitation all at the same time, and it didn't take long for Selina to respond. She put down the black-leading brushes and moved towards him.

'Well Mr Cameron, I've been waiting for you, or someone like you, to answer a lot of questions. If you would like a cup of tea, and you have half an hour to spare, maybe we can do some business.' She wiped her hands and reached for the large black kettle and poured water from it into the teapot. 'Do you take sugar and milk with your tea, Mr Cameron?'

This was her opportunity to find out some of the things she didn't know. She prepared the teacups and poured the golden liquid into them, while Cameron sat back, enjoying the comfort of the chair. He had been making calls since eight o'clock and was feeling dehydrated and a little weary. This was a turn up for the book! He looked up. She was speaking to him again.

'Would you like a slice of fruit-cake with your cup of tea, Mr Cameron?'

She was holding a small plate out to him, with a large piece of cake in the middle of it.

'Well, thank you. I don't mind if I do, thank you er, Mrs...?'

Again, there was a question in his words. He seemed to have the attitude of a well-educated, well-mannered young man; she decided to take a chance on him; she had nothing to lose, anyway, and she could only learn from whatever they discussed. It was obvious that he was quite bright. He must have kept his eyes open, to notice them working on the front room. She looked up at him.

'Barr, Selina Barr, Mrs Selina Barr. We, that is, Mr Barr and I, have been wondering how we should go about it; going into business, and turning the front room of the house into a shop.'

She paused, deliberately, to see how he was taking her words. He sat quietly, encouraging her to go on. She explained how Tom had been out of work, the start with the wholesaling of the fire-wood, the idea of turning the front room into a shop, maybe a grocery shop, their lack of money to buy the groceries to put on the shelves; the fact of her labour and the way it might effect their plans the following spring. She also told him of the way she had gained experience from managing her mother's shop and the way the local bank manager had respected her.

Cameron listened in silence, absorbing the story of this young couple, fighting their environment, daring to move into business without working or, indeed, any other sort of capital. As he thought, he came to a decision that was to affect his life for years.

When Selina had run out of words, he explained that many people went into business using money belonging to other people and that maybe the bank would help them if they had at least part of the money they required, or if they could borrow part of what they needed from a friend or a relative. Eventually he came to the conclusion that if he was going to do business with them he was going to have to offer more than words.

'Look,' he said, thoughtfully, 'I can see you are in a bit of a bind, here. You have no real track record of being in business that a bank would lend on, so I'll tell you what I will do. I'll take a chance on you! You are obviously of the right stuff to open a business. I am going to take an almighty chance on you, and offer you a credit of a hundred pounds. If it works out, I shall have a good customer who is using the services of my firm. If it doesn't, I feel sure that it won't be because you haven't tried!'

Then, seeing the shocked look on her face, he explained that the hundred pounds would be ongoing for twelve months, by which time he would expect that they would be able to trade 'on their own two legs.' They would be charged a smaller rate of interest because the cash that was realised each week would be spent only with Cameron and Sons Ltd. She shook hands with him then, on impulse, threw her arms round his neck and kissed him.

'Whew,' he said, 'If that's all I have to do, I should be able to open up twenty new accounts every day.'

He tempered her enthusiasm for his proposal by explaining that his judgement was on the line with his father, who would have the final word.

'You got my offer of this arrangement because I was impressed with the amount of dedication you and your husband Tom have put into this enterprise. Please don't let me down, or my father will never trust my judgement again. I understand that this business will be in your name only, as your husband trades in his name only, for his fire-wood enterprise?'

'Yes, it is not a partnership anymore than Tom's firewood enterprise is,' she answered, 'I know that he will help me with the shop, as he knows that if there is anything I can do for him, I will. We are partners in our marriage but not in our business.'

Cameron was impressed again, this time by Selina's dedication to her concept of owning her own independent business. *Why can't I find a wife like that? She would be an asset to any man.*

He had been brought up in a rarefied business environment. His mother had died from cancer when he was five years of age, leaving his father the task of bringing him up, and trying to expand his newly formed business at the same time, by the expedient of using a succession of nannies and governesses. He was a stern but fair man, brought up on Kipling as second nature. He hadn't had the time to find another wife.

'My business is my marriage,' he was wont to say, whenever his friends raised the subject of a second wife. Cameron raised himself from the reverie that he had fallen into, as he heard the sound of Tom's boots coming into the shop.

The whole thing had to be explained to Tom after he was introduced to Cameron. After recovering from his initial surprise, he was all for the venture, offering to run the shop while Selina was recovering from her birth, as he said, enthusiastically,

'I can make up the bundles round the back, in the morning, and deliver them in the hour we shall be closed for lunch.'

More tea was made to celebrate the new business's commencement, and an initial order was made, using up most of the hundred pounds. No mention was made of the forty odd pounds that they now had in reserve. They didn't feel they had to tell Cameron everything. The order would be delivered in five day's time. In the meantime, Tom would finish off the painting and make a sign to go over the shop, and call on the landlord to get permission to run the business from the premises and find out if he would want any extra for rent. It was planned that the shop would be open from the following Monday morning. Cameron could not help but be amused by the enthusiasm of the young couple. He doubted whether the time scale they envisioned could be adhered to, but gave them his encouragement, and explained his attitude to Tom.

'If you work out for me, and with my father; who knows where things might lead to? I feel that if I help you now, you will help me in the future. That's what business is all about.'

'That's a good idea, 'said Tom, 'businesses helping each other instead of fighting to be top dog.' He had not thought of that before. It could be the start of another philosophy. There would always be the opposition however, and they would have to face them, or possibly buy them up! The thought filled him with excitement. Cameron did not have any opposition among Tom's competitors – only small businesses that he could either help, or not help. But he could help Tom and Selina to buy them up, one at a time. It would be beneficial to Cameron's, too. They would then have more reliable customers for their range of grocery items. Tom, too, could introduce his firewood into each of the shops. He realised that it probably seemed much simpler than it was in reality, but he could adjust his thinking as required by circumstances. There were plenty of possibilities to think of!

Getting the shop ready for the following Monday was not as easy as they had thought. The sign, 'S. Barr', over the shop took Tom longer than he had thought to make and paint; the wood had to be brought round from the wood yard after planning; the sign had to be primed, undercoated and top coated, and allowed to dry, before the name, ' S. Barr' could be carefully painted onto it in carefully measured spaces. After drying, the sign had to be lifted up into place and fastened by screws into position. Just on a whim, Selina covered the whole thing with a length of plain curtain material; it seemed to be tempting fate to show the board before they were ready for it.

Cameron's father came the following week to oversee the stock delivery, accompanied by an enormous driver, who unloaded the lorry under Cameron's supervision. Tom and Selina stood around, waiting to be delegated tasks by the experienced older man, putting up additional shelves, tying up cardboard and filling the wooden boxes, putting up on the outside wall, the metal adverts for 'Pear's Soap' and 'Will's Woodbines'.

As they watched, Tom and Selina found an unexpected sense of pride in what they had accomplished; it was as if they had moved up a notch in society. Instead of being at someone else's beck and call, with the constant fear of dismissal, they were now in charge of their own destiny. They tried to explain this shared feeling to the older Cameron, who soon brought them down to earth. He was dourer than his son but was full of useful advice.

'You both think that you are your own bosses, but you'll soon see; you'll have five hundred bosses within a fortnight, any one of whom can change their supplier at the drop of a hat. You have to keep their custom in spite of the other businesses around you, who may well regard you as deadly enemies who have arrived newly on the scene to take their livelihood away.' He looked at their fallen faces and smiled, 'Now, don't you get worrying. I can see you've got the stuff that business people are made of. I've seen it in your faces and the determination that you have shown in quite difficult circumstances. No money, four months pregnant, strangers to the area and no business links. Mister Barr is also trying to start another business out of thin air! You are impossible, really. I've a good mind to take all the stock back!' Again he smiled and this time they smiled with him. 'How is it going, Fergus?' He asked the driver.

'It's all going fine, sir. It's just a matter of keeping the place tidy so that I can get around this wee shop.' Tom immediately started to pick up the empty boxes; carrying them through the living room into the backyard, which was getting quite full, now. The dustmen would be calling on Monday and he would have to persuade them to take their trade waste away as well as the ashes from the fire.

There was always a new problem. It was like playing Snakes and Ladders; every time you threw a six on your die, you landed on a snake and had to go down the board. The thought amused him and he found himself tittering to himself. He started looking for other metaphors, like reaching in the dark for a sight of the business future, like tossing a coin for a decision of whether to stock this, or that, product.

He picked up a piece of paper and wrote them down before he forgot them. They seemed to be landing on ladders, lately. He suddenly realised that what he and Selina were doing was quite extraordinary, and that it would be an idea to keep a record of their progress, or lack of it, for the future, and also to keep a record of the ideas that they had, so that they could remind themselves of them.

He looked round, and saw that the shop was almost ready to start trading. All the stock was on the shelves, on the counter or on the floor, either in front of the counter or on the wheeled vegetable racks, ready to be rolled onto the pavement in front of the shop. How would they cope if they did well? What would he do while Selina was in hospital, having their baby? They would need some help in the shop! He reached out for a piece of clean cardboard and wrote upon it, 'Assistant required. Must have some experience and be willing. Hours to suit.'

He looked at Mr Cameron, 'Do you think that will do, Mr Cameron?' He reached across with the board, 'I don't think we shall be able to manage on our own, and it might be a good thing if we can get someone to help when we need them.'

The older man quickly assessed the small notice and commented, 'An excellent idea, Tom. You certainly won't manage on your own for some time after your good wife is home with the little one, and if you have someone in, part time, before, you will have time to train them in your ways, so to speak. Just one thing, willingness is often more important than experience, especially if the assistant lives handy. Just leave it to your instinct. You sometimes get a feeling that the right person has arrived. You don't know what the going rate is, for an assistant so just ask the applicants, if there is more than one. You'll soon get an idea of what is acceptable.'

There was a call from the front of the shop.

'Mr Cameron, sir. We are finished now. There isn't a thing to be done. Just one thing I would like to know; where are you going to keep the cash, sir?'

The question was addressed to Tom, who smiled wryly.

'I really don't know, Fergus. You have caught me out there, but I suppose I, or rather Selina, will keep it in her apron.'

He looked across the stock and boxes at Selina. She was standing, her slightly swollen belly taking up room in the shop, her hair curling round her ear. She returned his look with a smile.

'Indeed I will not Tommy. I want a proper till drawer put into the underneath of this counter until such time as I can afford one of these new tills, with the pounds, shilling and pence ringing up sweetly with each transaction.'

'She said 'transaction' as if she were rolling the money round her mouth as she spoke,' thought Tom. She certainly had a business attitude to everything they were doing. It must have rubbed off from her mother.

'Of course you can have a till drawer. I will make it straight after dinner.' He smiled at the young Cameron, 'She's the worst gaffer I've ever had. Never stops wanting something making, mending or building.'

'Well it could be worse, Tom. I bet you've seen worse gaffers.'

Tom looked across the shop and realised that Cameron, in spite of his better education and good start in life, was jealous of what they were doing. He had noticed the way he looked at Selina. Not that he could blame him! She was absolutely radiant, with fulfilment showing from her, in all directions. *She could do with somewhere to sit.* The thought pleased him and he determined that he would go out later and buy four chairs.

Cameron's admiration did not anger him; he just thought of it as her due. The more people that admired her, the better they would do! He had already moved his mind into another gear, thinking about the next move, the opening of further branches. If James Cameron and his father were willing to finance them, they would soon get them. He started to price the stock. He had to ask advice for that.

'How much are these going to be, James?' He picked up a tin of Ovaltine.

'They are one and six for the small tin, two and six for the medium size and four and six for the large. I don't expect you will sell many of the large size, so don't buy too many of them until you see how the land lies. The Bird's custard is one and six a tin, one and a penny, and sixpence halfpenny, for the boxes and three-halfpence for a packet. You'll soon get used to it, honestly. I have a list of current prices at the office; I'll bring it for you, in the morning.'

The four chairs and a table were bought second hand, from 'Myrtles Second Hand Shop', further up Ventnor Road, after a little haggling. He also bought a set of 'bangers', scales for weighing the vegetables, and a few items for the house. 'We have plenty of time to buy posh things, when we can afford them,' he told her. 'Let's get the basic things, first. Now, what's our next problem?'

29. A New Line.

The tiny brown sparrows were quarrelling over the handful of crumbs that he had just thrown them. They always seemed to be quarrelling among themselves. Like us, I suppose, he joked with himself. He was always joking with himself. It was a way of not taking life too seriously. It was a bright Sunday December morning. Unusually, there was little of the industrial fog that seemed to be forever present. Tom was sitting in the backyard; there was little to do at the moment; he was just enjoying the winter sun that, perversely, was shining into his eyes.

He finished chopping and tying the last of the firewood. He now had a small amount of time, half an hour perhaps, to do nothing, a rare luxury. He leaned back and allowed himself the indulgences of relaxing in the sunlight, letting his thoughts wander without restraint, and lighting a cigarette.

Selina had stayed late in bed, today. Her time was in May, next year, but sometimes it seemed that it was approaching fast. She had been acting strange lately, he thought. It must be something to do with her slowly approaching childbirth. Sometimes she was like a bright summer day; at other times she seemed full of thunder.

Yesterday had been extraordinarily busy, what with the shelf-filling, wheeling the flat truck to the second-hand shop to fetch the chairs and other items. They hadn't gone to bed until one o'clock. Both of the Camerons had stayed until eight o'clock, and then departed as if by a signal, just a shake of the hand and a nod from Mister Cameron senior, and then they had gone. There had still been a lot of clearing up to do, after they had gone.

There were wooden boxes, which he would use for firewood, and cardboard boxes that had contained the jam, Golden Syrup and tinned items that were already on the shelves. The boxes were all stacked high in the small backyard. He had got up at six o'clock and cooked eggs and bacon. Selina wouldn't have appreciated being awoken; she would have likely been sick at the sight and smell of a cooked breakfast.

Now he was sitting among the piles of assorted debris, wondering what he should do next. He would be delivering firewood, tomorrow, to three of the small shops that bought from him, while Selina opened the shop for the first 'official' time. The man who had promised them regular deliveries of fresh produce would be coming at six o'clock in the morning. The thought of sitting doing nothing still made him feel anxious and guilty. Still, it gave him time for new thoughts. There always seemed to be something new to think about, something to be concerned about, something he should be doing now.

There was a small, round, off-cut of wood in his hand, at which he kept staring, as if he were trying to make sense of it. It was circular in section, and about an inch and a half in diameter. It was about six inches long, and had been sawed from a long length of the material. He smoothed the rough edges and it seemed more finished, just from having the smoothing done.

As he looked, he realised that if he drew it from the side, the drawing would show an apparent rectangle, six inches by an inch and a half. It was only if viewed from the end that the circular nature of the piece was perceived. He viewed it again from the end; it was now a circle. Tom picked up another round piece of wood, about an inch in diameter. He put the wood into the vice that was bolted to the bench and carefully marking the centre of the circular end, he drilled a small hole, deeply into the wood. He was watchful to keep the drill bit parallel to the floor. Then he took up a saw and cut off a slice of the wood about half an inch long. He cut three more and knew he had made wheels for the larger piece, if he could find a way to join them together.

His back ached; yesterday he had been sweeping the wood yard for his new employer, Bill Smith. The broom was long, a yard broom, and heavy. After he had finished sweeping he had loaded his flat truck with off-cuts and wheeled it home. He had stopped for a cup of tea and then unloaded the truck and carried the wood into the back yard and chopped and tied most of it up. His back still ached, but something about the wood held his attention.

He picked up a rectangular off-cut, cut it to ten inches long, and nailed the round of wood to the side of it. He realised what he was doing and sawed off three more circles and nailed them, too, to the side of the rectangular piece. The cylinder of wood was then screwed to the flat off-cut with the wheels attached. He reached down and picked up a small staple and knocked it into the end of the wooden piece. It was now, in his imagination, a truck, ready for a length of string to pull it along. The holes in the wheels were loose enough for the wheels to spin easily on the nails. Tom picked it up and examined it. He liked it. It would make a nice toy, painted up, for his little Brummy to play with. There were a number of small off-cuts lying around, so he put three on the truck, as a load. Experimenting, he placed a larger piece on, in place of the three smaller pieces, and it reminded him of a railway engine.

Swiftly he cut two small, circular pieces and glued them onto the top of the engine. After trying a number of combinations of shapes, he had a model railway engine, with a coalbunker behind it, and three load-carrying trucks. Metal curtain hooks and eyes joined them, and a length of string could pull the whole thing along. The material had cost him nothing, and assembly time had taken about half an hour.

He had small amounts of red and black paint left from the shop name board so he took the wheels and funnels from the engine and the loads from the trucks and painted the engine and trucks red. The black paint left from the shop sign was used to paint the wheels, funnel and loads. He put them all on one side for reassembly after the paint had dried, and then relaxed. The toy engine and trucks would be his secret, just for now. He would save it for his little Brummy, when he or she was born. He had made his first gift! The thought pleased him. He lit a cigarette and relaxed.

The firewood orders were already put onto the flat truck, prepared for delivery early the following morning. He looked around the yard and noticed that there were still a number of round off-cuts and, on impulse scooped them into a sack. They might come in handy for something! What else could he make?

'Tom!'

He looked up. It was Selina calling him from the house. The mid-day meal was ready.

'Alright, love, I'm coming.'

He dropped his cigarette onto the tiny patch of soil that passed for a garden and ground it into the ground. It was time to eat; time to go in. Later that afternoon, he tried to bring up the subject of the toy train with Selina but for once she was not interested. She had kept herself to herself all day.

'I don't care about toys, Tom, especially toy trains. If we have a boy, he might like a train, when he is older, I suppose, but if it's a girl she won't want a train, will she? Don't you think I've got enough on my plate, with the shop opening up tomorrow morning? I haven't even got enough money for a float to start off with. Another thing, it is Christmas in three weeks and we have nothing in the shop to sell for gifts. I might have a word with James, next time he comes in.'

She seemed to melt away into her own thoughts, as if she was thinking at a different level to him. She didn't see things in quite the same way that he did. It was strange; Selina was usually quick to see and exploit the potential of a new idea. She had a business sense that always had an appreciation for fresh ideas. What was wrong with her? It was probably because she was getting nearer to her time. They finished their supper in silence, and then Selina spoke.

'I'm going to bed, Tom. I don't feel too good. My back's been aching all day, and I don't feel like sitting around. I'll probably feel better later on. I'll see you later, love.'

She moved to the door to the stairs, turned, and gave him a wan little smile, saying nothing. Once again he wondered what was wrong. It was four o'clock.

'Yes, see you later, Selina.'

He sat back on the armchair and settled down, gazing into the flames of the dying fire. The nights really drew in at this time of the year. He could see shapes in it. There was a fire engine, with a funnel, racing towards a glowing coal. It reminded him of the little toy train he had made. His thoughts returned to the potential of the pieces of scrap wood. What else could be made out of the small pieces of wood that he got for nothing? At the moment, he received the raw material free, for the firewood bundles that he wholesaled, but he could probably make a more profitable use of them. His mind flew to other small toys, a push-along truck, with painted bricks on the back, a tender for the engine he had made, wooden shapes that could be painted and used to build things. He imagined a tunnel for the little train to run through, but could not decide what material to use for it. Perhaps he should try to make something to put in the shop for Christmas.

Somehow, the shape of the little toy train reminded him of the train that had taken him and Selina to Bromyard. That started a train of thought, reminding him of the life in the country they has shared. What were Kate and Jim doing now? Kate would be in Jim's cottage, now, making the evening meal. Were they married yet? They had not been certain of the way Kate's mother would react to the news of her relationship with Jim. What a night they'd had! The memory excited him, but he hadn't the time now for such pleasures. He returned to the matter in hand.

There was no real hurry; he could just save any useful pieces of wood and put them on one side until he had the time and ideas to use them. He walked through the house into the front room that would be used as the shop, and picked up a notebook. Sitting down, he drew the shapes of the individual pieces of wood that he would need to make the railway engine. There were fourteen pieces; some of them, such as the wheels, were identical. He placed the pieces of paper together, slipped a paper clip on them and hung them on a hook. That was the first one. With a bit of luck there would be others.

Restlessly he went back into the living room and sat staring into the fire again. He started drawing again, this time the truck. Something was needed to make a handle to pull it, or should he make it so that it should be pushed? He looked into the fire again, the curling shapes of the flames stirring erotic thoughts. A curving blue flame reminded him of the girl next door as her hips swayed. He didn't know when he had noticed, but he had. Perhaps she would be interesting to get to know.

The feeling that the thought aroused in him was unwelcome and he decided to go for a walk. He liked to walk round the streets in large squares, sometimes turning left out of the house, sometimes right. He walked along Farm Street and then turned back up Wellesley Street. After a few turns he found himself on a busy shopping centre and noticed it was Lozells Road. The windows of the shops fascinated him, with their displays of the goods they sold. He sometimes admired them but often wished he could alter them in some way so that they would be more effective.

It was almost dark now, and the lamplighter was carrying his ladder from lamp to lamp. It got dark early at this time of year. The road came to an end when he reached the junction of another road. There was a cinema, the Orient, and he decided he would take Selina to see the latest film, when she was in a better mood. A smile crossed his face; his own mood was improving. A brisk walk often seemed to do the trick. It was a nuisance, this mood business. Why couldn't he feel in a good mood all the time, instead of relying on Selina for his moments of happiness? He had always been in a good mood, before they met.

When he returned home, Selina was up and seemed in a better frame of mind; he had the feeling she was trying and he couldn't make up his mind whether to be pleased about that, or not. He did some more work on his little toy train. It was looking quite finished now and he amused himself by attaching a length of string to the engine and pulling it along the yard. He felt like a small boy on his birthday. He looked up at the window, next door, and saw the girl who lived there, watching him, a faint smile on her face. He felt himself blush, but managed to smile back at her, when she seemed to blush, too. That pleased him, and he thought again that it might be nice to get to know her better.

He turned his mind to the shop; there was plenty of tidying up to be done before they opened up. He picked up the broom and started to sweep the back yard. He seemed to be spending a lot of time in the yard. The girl from next door was looking out of the window again. Was that why he was in the yard? He didn't even know her name, but he would; he knew he would. He caught her eye, and she smiled in a friendly sort of way, the sort of smile that made him think that she might not be annoyed if he made a friendly pass at her. Perhaps she was married, perhaps not. He somehow didn't think she was. He gave a wave to her and she waved back, just a small, meaningful movement of her hand. Suddenly he felt good and uncomfortable again. Perhaps there was hope yet!

It was time to go in. Although it was dark now, he still hadn't tidied up outside. Another hour saw the worst of the mess tidied up. The shop was clean, clean enough for opening in the morning. He cleaned the whitewash from the windows and put all the spare stock underneath the counter he had made. He was finished as far as he could see. The bacon-slicer was covered up and all he had to do was put his new overall on and start serving.

'Goodnight, Tom.'

Selina spoke from the doorway. Her mood had undergone another change. She seemed very quiet.

'Goodnight love. I'll be up as soon as everything is ship-shape in the shop.'

Upstairs, Selina wept; it was the first time they had gone to bed separately. She always seemed to be in a mood lately. It must be the baby. When was it going to come? There were still five months to wait. Why hadn't Tom come upstairs when she had?

Whose baby was it, anyway? The thought often came into her mind. She had tried to tell herself that it didn't really matter as long as it had a mother and father who loved it, but she couldn't help speculating about Jim. She wouldn't mind, too much if it were his; the only thing she couldn't stand was the thought that it might be Harry's. She had counted up the dates and knew that it could not be his, but even the thought of the possibility filled her with dread feelings.

Why hadn't Tom come to bed to comfort her? Didn't he love her any more? She felt deprived, lonely and forlorn, as the hours of the night seemed to pass by remorselessly. The night went by in small sleeps and small awakenings. The first light of dawn found her with her eyes closed but still vaguely restless. Both of them dropped off into a fatigue-laden sleep. Tom had crept into their bed at three o'clock and lain there thinking for a short time and then dropped off.

The morning saw them both in better humour and Tom again raised the subject of the toy train.

'Selina, I know you weren't interested last night, but I think I might be onto something; perhaps a new line for the shop. You used to sell models at Willenhall in your mother's shop. Perhaps we could sell them in your new shop. Let me show you what I mean.'

He went out to the shed and assembled the little train. He felt silly carrying it in, as if he were a small boy, showing off. The time outside seemed to do him good.

'Here it is.'

He put the train in front of her, on the table. The look on Selina's face told him how she felt. She looked up from her breakfast.

'I'm sorry, Tom. I can't feel how you want me to feel. I would have done at one time, I know, but nothing seems to interest me now. Anyway, I've got a lot of things to think about this morning, before I'm ready to open up tomorrow.'

She turned her back on him and moved into the kitchen to wash up the two cups and saucers. A weight seemed to come onto his mind and his mood plummeted. Why did he rely on Selina for a good mood? He looked in at the shop and unlocked the door. It was time to open up. He knew he should be smiling and he stretched his facial muscles to help him to smile at whoever came in the door first. He reached for the piece of card he had written on. '**Assistant required. Must have some** experience and be willing. Hours to suit.'

He reached for the apron he had decided to wear in the shop. It was brand new, making him feel self-conscious. He lifted the swing door-bell and screwed it to the door, and the little catch to the wall, so that the bell would ring when the door was opened. Everything was ready. *Now is the time!* Reaching in his pocket he counted out a handful of small change and put it in the till. The amount was written on a slip, of paper. That was the float, and it had to be deducted from the cash amount in the till when the shop was closed and the takings reckoned.

All they needed now was customers. They would have a job weaning them from other small shops. Uncle Pete and Aunt Florrie had wished them well. Pete had been on about politics again. There had been a General Election this week. He and Selina had not been eligible, only recently having arrived in Birmingham. The result had been a surprise; Stanley Baldwin, an outsider, had won. Most people had thought that Lord Curzon would have won. That was one of the delightful facets of British politics, Pete had said. Baldwin was for protecting the home economy, protecting British jobs and businesses against foreign infiltration. Now it was a matter of how long Baldwin could stay the course. A lot of people had been turned off politics by the machinations of Lloyd George, and Baldwin was a real contrast.

Uncle Pete said that unemployment was the big problem that politicians had got to face, and that would affect small businesses too. Some small businesses gave credit to their customers but Selina had been quite adamant; she would not give credit. If she did, she said, it would deprive them of working capital to make purchases. Anyway, it wasn't their money to lend out. They owed it to the Camerons to use their borrowed working capital wisely, to re-invest in stock and expand the range of goods that they had to offer.

There was more to this working capital than met the eye, thought Tom, it is as if money is just a tool, to be used to make things happen in business, and there were different ways of using the tool, some of them better than others, according to the circumstances. They had the advantage of credit for working capital, but it also restricted them. If the working capital had been theirs, they might have been tempted to give credit unwisely, and that could bring dire results.

The door opened and a young woman came in. It was the young woman from next door who he had noticed earlier.

'Hello, Mr Barr. I am Jean Summer, from next door. I saw the sign in the window and wondered if I could apply for the job?'

She paused, looking at him. She seemed personable enough. He didn't quite know what to say. He knew who she was, he had already fantasised about her. He stopped his mind from wandering.

'Excuse me Jean, I'll get my wife. It's her shop, you see, and she's the one you should really be speaking to.'

He saw her smile and felt that he was not occupying a man's position, having to call his wife in. He walked through the curtain, into the living room.

'Selina, there is a young lady in the shop; she is looking for a part-time job. Will you have a word with her, please? I have told her that it is your shop, so you are the one to deal with job enquiries.'

It must have been the right thing to say because Selina gave him a wide smile and brushed past him to see the young woman.

'Yes? Can I help you? Mr Barr tells me you are looking for part-time employment? Have you had any experience?'

Tom, listening from the other room, smiled to himself. Selina was coming out of her mood. Things might improve now. Perhaps Jean would be a friend as well as an assistant. He hoped so.

30. Great Days.

'Yes, Mrs Barr, I am Jean Summer; I live next door and I saw Mr Barr put the notice in the window. I would be grateful for any work you would be willing to give me. I have worked behind the counter before, in a newsagent's shop, but it closed down and I was given notice.'

Her breath seemed to give out, as if she had not quite got her lines right. Selina thought about the slim girl; she seemed young, but willing. What was it that Mr Cameron had said? *Enthusiasm is more important than experience*, because you can teach them your ways. *If they live close, you get more use from them.* The girl seems clean enough, and looks as if she might have a head on her shoulders. After all, Selina thought, I was younger than her when I started behind the counter, for my Mom.

'Alright, Jean Summer, We'll talk it over, Mr Barr and me. We will let you know shortly. Thank you for offering.'

Jean looked at her and realised that she was being dismissed. What a funny woman! She turned on her heel and walked out of the shop, back to her own house. Perhaps Mrs Barr had been obliged to get her husband's agreement, whatever he had said about it being her shop. She felt that he would take her on, anyway. She had seen the look in his eye. He had lovely arms. What would it feel like? She dismissed the thought and picked up a duster and started polishing the table. If they wanted her, they would be in touch soon enough. Mrs Barr looks as if she might be pregnant. If she is, she will want help soon. There was a knock at the front door. It was Tom.

'Miss Summer, Mrs Barr would like a word with you, if you please.'

The formal words made both of them smile.

'Yes, of course.'

She slipped the pinafore over her head and closed the door

behind her as she moved towards the little shop. Was her life about to change again? It was all so important. Her life had gone downhill since she had been obliged to leave the newsagent's. She barely managed to get through the week on the small amount of money she allowed herself, out of the savings she had. They would run out soon and she would have nothing. She could hardly believe she might get a job this quickly. It wasn't certain but she had a feeling. As she walked into the little shop, Jean noticed that Selina was beginning to show her pregnancy in earnest.

'Come on in, Jean. I've decided to offer you the position. I hope we shall be able to get on; it will be very important to both of us; to me because I know that I shall soon need help badly; to you because the position could offer you more than just a part-time assistant's position. Mr Barr and I have no intention of just being a small corner shop. We hope to expand, and you can be part of that expansion.' She stopped talking and sat down, slightly out of breath. In a short time she looked up at Jean. 'Do you see what I mean, Jean? I am already getting out of breath. You can see what I am going to be like in a couple of months. What do you think, Jean? Is what we are offering, attractive to you? If you don't want it, I expect it would not be too difficult to find an ambitious young woman.'

The threat was implicit in the way she spoke but Jean did not feel threatened. She had learned to disregard most threats. Her own mother was a hard taskmaster, as were many mothers after the war.

'I would like the position very much, Mrs Barr, Mr Barr. It sounds like the sort of opportunity that would suit me very much. Just say the word and I will be ready to start work!'

Jean smiled, her demeanour making it obvious that she did not feel threatened.

'Well, that's settled, then, Jean. You can start in the morning. Eight o'clock sharp. That is when we are opening the shop so if you could get here a little earlier, that might be useful to both of us. You will be on your own a lot of the time. Mr Barr has other things to do with his time, and I shall be spending less and less time in the shop, so I need someone here who I can trust. Now, would you put the kettle on for a pot o' tea? You might as well know where the teapot is.'

Selina led the way, brushing the curtain out of the way, into the back room. She had only just noticed the curtain. Tom must have put it up while she was in bed. She felt good. She had been more nervous than the young girl she had just taken on, but she had done it! It was the first time she had ever employed anyone and all of a sudden she felt the responsibility and the authority.

'Tom will show you where everything is, Jean. Just for now, I want to have a sit down.'

She half-sat, half-fell into the armchair they had purchased yesterday, second-hand. The thought somehow made her feel like laughing.

Tom steered Jean round the stairwell to the tiny space at the top of the cellar stairs.

'Come on, Jean. I'll show you where we keep the food, not that we've got much. We've only just moved in, but we can always buy some tea from the shop, as long as we put the money in the till for it. Selina is a stickler for things like that. She has strict rules, how about you?'

He laughed as he showed her the food-store at the top of the cellar steps. If she only knew how little food of their own they had!

'I keep to a set of rules as long as they work for me, Mr Barr. If not, I change them.'

Tom had learned now, to listen. What was she saying? Was she offering herself, in some sort of symbolic way? Or was it symbolic? That was the question. That was always the question. What was being offered? It was always interesting to speculate on the answer. People played games. Sometimes women seemed to offer more than they were prepared to give, but if their 'offer' was taken up, they would scream in protest. It was a delicately balanced game. For all he knew, she might be wishing him to make the first move.

It was like politics, with Labour, Liberal and Conservative all offering something, like whores, with a price to pay for the benefits of alliance for one side, and the price of different legislation as the benefit to the other party. Baldwin had got off cheap. He had been so open in manner, so different from Lloyd George that the voters had flocked to his flag. How long would he last?

He turned his thoughts back to the pot of tea that Jean was making. She was just pouring it out. She picked up a cup and handed it round the corner, to Selina.

'Ta, love. I needed that.' She sipped at the cup. 'You've made a cup of tea before, I can see that.'

She put the cup down on the table and dropped off to sleep. Tom and Jean looked at each other, each seeing the woman asleep, with different eyes. Tom put his hand on Jean's as she was picking up the cup. She didn't move. He slowly picked up her hand and lifted it towards his mouth. She took a sharp breath but didn't protest. His lips caressed the back of her hand in silence, and then he turned her hand over and brushed her palm with his fingers. Her response was more violent this time. She pulled him round so that their bodies were facing each other and put her hands on his cheeks, pulling him towards her. Their lips met, hard and passionate. Jean spoke.

'I thought you'd never get round to it.'

She kissed him again, pulling him closer, her hands pulling his close to her breasts. A sigh left Selina's lips, startling both of them, reminding them of the risk they were taking. She was still dozing but the moment was over for now. There was a thrill in taking chances but the consequences were so unthinkable that Tom determined, for now, to behave, as he should. He released the soft fingers, feeling the loss as he did so. Another thought hit him. He had to make Selina an honest woman. There was a wedding to arrange. There was also a shop to open up in the morning! He led Jean back into the shop, still holding her hand as if it were the most natural thing in the world.

'These are the vegetables, Jean.' He felt silly saying the words. 'In the morning I shall take them outside onto the pavement. You will have to keep an eye on them or they'll disappear before your eyes. We thought we would give this way of displaying them a try. Inside, we've divided the stock, as far as we could, into dry goods, groceries and hardware. Hardware has a good margin of profit on it; that is why we have chosen to sell it. We'll have to see how it works out.' He suddenly noticed that he was still holding her hand and she had made no effort to remove it from his grasp. 'It seems all right, up till now, what do you think, Jean?'

'Well, yes, everything seems satisfactory, Mr Barr. I am sure I shall be satisfied, here. Everything seems easy enough. Will you want me later on today, or shall I just come round in the morning?'

She stood there looking as if butter wouldn't melt in her mouth, Tom thought, and she had flirted as outrageously with him as he had with her! He reached for her hand again and held it for a moment.

'If I can find something for you to do later, I shall come round for you. Otherwise, come round at eight o'clock in the morning.' There was a long pause as they stood with their bodies touching softly, their faces an inch apart. 'I should be back in the shop by then, and if you want anything, I shall more than likely be in the back yard.'

'Yes, I have noticed that you spend a lot of time in the back yard, Mr Barr. I can't think what you find to do, there.' She moved her hand away from his and smoothed it down the front of her dress. 'I'll see you later then, perhaps, or in the morning. Thank you for everything, the job I mean. I will do my best for you, Mr Barr.'

They both smiled at her formal use of his name, and she opened the door to the shop and disappeared. He started missing her immediately. There was a potential for excitement in this relationship! It was stupid, and would, if discovered, bring him pain, but he could not deny the feeling that she gave him. Life was always like that to him. Did all men feel that way whenever another desirable woman crossed their sights?

He looked round the little shop. It had a different quality now; it was the place where he and Jean had held hands! He took a broom and started sweeping the floor. He would be better occupied being busy than mooning around. Selina would want everything to be just so. He picked up the small amount of dust on a coal shovel and threw it out into the gutter. It was time for a little lunch.

Selina woke from her nap and looked around. She never felt like this. She was always full of energy, never dozing off in the afternoon. Where was Tom? She stood up, stretching herself as she did so. There was a brushing sound from the front of the house. Of course; that's where he is, she thought. She reached for the teapot; it was full. She poured two cups, her hand wobbling a little with the effort of lifting. It was a heavy pot.

'Tea, Tom!' She looked into the shop and saw him throwing the shovel-full of dust into the street. 'Tom, you know you shouldn't do that.' She bit her lip. It had only been a tiny amount; she shouldn't be finding fault with him. 'I'm sorry, Tom. Come and have a cup of tea; I've just poured it. There's some cake in the cupboard as well, old-fashioned fruit cake; you like that, don't you, love?'

She was feeling better, now; the sleep must have done her good.

'Thanks, Selina. That will be nice.' He put his arm round her. 'How are you feeling now? I didn't want to wake you up; you looked so peaceful. Jean's gone. She said she would come round if you need her later; otherwise she will be round at eight o'clock tomorrow morning.

Jean! His use of the girl's name reminded Selina that she had dropped off to sleep. How long ago had that been? Oh, well, she must have needed it.

'I don't think we shall need her today, Tom. Miss Jean Summer can start as soon as you go to work, in the morning. I'm sorry I dropped off. Fancy leaving you alone with a young woman while I sleep! Whatever will she think of me? Not that it matters what she thinks, does it, Tom?'

Selina smiled at the guilty look in his eyes. He would look guilty if he even thought about another woman! He was guileless. There were still a few tidying jobs to be done but within an hour the shop was looking ready to commence business. They were both excited at the prospect. It would be their second way of earning a living, a way that had seemed impossible a few weeks ago. They had fifteen-shilling float to put in the till, so they hoped that their first customer didn't tender a pound note for a shilling's worth of purchases. Bed seemed a pleasant prospect, in all sorts of ways, so, almost by mutual consent; they climbed the steep stairs and fell into bed.

*

There was a strange ringing noise in her ears. It was the new alarm clock! Bloody row! Tom was missing when she felt for him. She picked the clock up and peered into the dawn light. Six o'clock! Tom was already up and eating his breakfast, she knew. He had to take his deliveries of firewood before he would be any use to her. She felt sick. She swivelled round in the bed and put her feet onto the floorboards. This was no time to be feeling sorry for herself. She had things to do. She felt her way down the dark stairs, dimly lit by the gas mantle in the living room. There was a cup of tea waiting for her. She sat down heavily. Suddenly she felt a revival of her old, energetic self. She had been through a bad patch, but now she was feeling better. Perhaps today would fulfil its promise of being a great day!

'Morning, love. Lovely morning. Just the sort of day for opening a new business.'

Tom smiled at her. He was usually pretty good in the morning, she thought.

'Good morning, Tom. There is nothing to do here, so you can get on with your deliveries as soon as you like.'

She knew that he already knew that, but it was just a matter of being conversational, showing willing to the day, so to speak.

He was already putting his coat on. He wanted to get his firewood delivered early so that he would be early back to give a hand in the shop, if it was necessary. The two women should find it fairly easy. After all, hardly anyone knew they were opening, did they? There was another reason he wanted to be back early, but he didn't really want to face that.

To Selina and Jean, the first few hours were strange, with just a few people ringing the bell on the door. The first customer was a stranger on the way to work, buying a packet of cigarettes, with no comment on the shop, after all, he hadn't known them before so why should he comment? The next one was a customer who knew Jean.

'Hello, Jean. You didn't waste any time getting your feet under the table, did you? I saw the notice for staff yesterday, and I was going to apply myself. I worked on the Flat last year and got to like shop work.'

'Well I suppose I was just lucky; that's the way it goes sometimes.'

Jean replied.

'Just a minute, please.' It was Selina, breaking into their conversation. 'Would you mind leaving your name and address? You never know, we may open another shop, and then we shall want more staff.'

She passed over a writing pad to the woman. Jean watched, curiously. It was not very likely that the Barrs would be opening another shop, especially with Mrs Barr in her condition. Then she realised that Selina was covering a situation where Jean had to leave quickly for some reason, leaving the Barrs without staff.

The number of customers seemed to increase in the afternoon and helped the time to pass more quickly. At five o'clock, Tom returned, and the number of customers gradually dropped off.

'I think we can manage without you now, Jean. Will you come in at the same time in the morning please?'

It was as if the tone implied that if she didn't, there were others willing to fill the position, but the smile was just as real as ever.

'Yes, of course Mrs Barr. Thank you. I will see you at eight o'clock in the morning, then. Goodnight.'

She slipped the overall off and went. Selina reached for the drawer under the counter. There was still some time to go before they would close but she couldn't wait to add the takings!

The evening fled; they had added the takings, seventeen pounds. Not bad at all for their first day! It was a great feeling. It meant that they had made over two pounds profit. Perhaps it was just the novelty of having a new shop in the neighbourhood but it was a start, and that was more than they had been expecting when they had first arrived in Birmingham. They could begin looking to the future without so much fear in their minds. Selina looked at Tom across the fireplace. He was looking at her.

'What's up, Tom?' She could see there was something on his mind. 'What is it?'

She started back as Tom fell to his knees.

'Selina, will you marry me? I've wanted to ask you but there always seemed to be other things to do. We ought to get married as soon as possible. Please say you will. I love you and want to marry you, and look after you.'

He looked so sincere, kneeling on the floor in front of the fire, with the firelight twinkling from his eyes. Selina felt as if her heart would burst. She knew she found other men attractive but she would never love anyone in quite the same way that she felt for Tom. She reached out for him, her hands touching the sides of his face with exquisite tenderness.

'Of course I'll marry you, my dear Tom, of course I will. I never wanted anyone as much as I want you. I love you, too. I just want to always be able to look across the fireplace and see you. Let's get married as soon as we can. Birmingham is going to be good for us. We are going to be three Brummies, soon, so let's get it done with, as soon as we can. We don't have to wait for the banns to be read, if you don't want to.'

Tom sat silent for a moment, thinking things through. What

would be the right thing to do?

'No, we are not getting married like that! We are getting married in church, just as God intended.' He hadn't known he felt like that but the words just tumbled out of his mouth. 'Our little Brummy will get christened in church, so her parents will get married in church! Our parents will have the chance to come; it's up to them, but at least they will have been asked.'

Tom stood and stroked her hair, trying to put it the way he liked it. Selina could feel that he was sincere in the way he was holding her and could not help responding. Suddenly she felt proud of him and proud of herself that someone cared for her as much as Tom obviously did. She somehow felt a little taller.

'Yes, all right, Tom. We will do it just the way you want it. You will have to go to see the vicar as soon as you have finished delivering the firewood. We'll just have time to get married before Christmas!'

They immediately started discussing the arrangements for the wedding, who to invite and where to hold it. There was no money available for frivolous spending, no money for a reception, and no money for 'posh' wedding cars. They would walk to the church and walk back. Anyone who wanted to witness the ceremony would have to do the same. Selina would get married in a new dress and Tom would have a new collar-attached shirt. That would be the limit of their spending. They could not afford to dip into their takings; they were needed to buy fresh stocks in their attempts to expand.

Tom rose early next morning and after delivering his firewood he went to make arrangements with the vicar to marry them. He agreed to perform the ceremony on Saturday the twenty-second, three days before Christmas Day. The two women ran the shop successfully again; Jean was still there when he got in from work. She was proving invaluable to Selina who was resting in the back room of the shop.

'You are home early!' What have you missed out, then?'

Selina looked worried; she knew that Tom would not leave his work without a good reason. Why was he home this early? Suddenly she saw his face break into a smile; everything was all right. He had done something that he knew she would be pleased with. She wondered, was he like that with everyone or was it just with her? She reached for his face and pulled him to her.

'What have you been up to, Tom Barr?' She suddenly realised that Jean was still there. 'Never mind, you can tell me later. I've got something to tell you; we have taken twenty pounds, today, twenty pounds! This is a day, Tommy Barr. This is a day!'

She had heard Tom use the same phrase, and now he repeated it.

'This is a day, Selina; this is a day!' He picked her up, regardless of her condition and swung her round. 'This is a great day, a perfect day! We are going up!'

The realisation struck both of them at the same time. They really were going up; it was a reality, not just a wish. Tom was speaking again.

'The way up goes to the ones who do, not the ones who wish or hope but the ones who actually do whatever has to be done!'

They reached for each other again.

31. Early Days.

That Selina don't know she's born, Jean thought. If I had a man like that Tommy Barr, I would …then she realised that what she would do was precisely what Selina was doing. Jean stood looking at the young couple with a mixture of jealousy and affection on her face, wondering if she would ever get to that state of happiness. They were lucky, she thought. No, its' not luck; it's sheer up and go! No one else in their predicament would have achieved so much from such a poor beginning.

She suddenly realised that she was proud to know both of them. I would never do anything to hurt either of them, she thought. They were going to get on, and I am getting on with them! The thought excited her. She repeated the thought. I am going to get on! She had never thought of herself as ambitious but it was as if a new Jean was being born, a more vibrant, more doing sort of Jean. Some people got on by sheer drive, some people got on by pulling other people down, and some people got on by flying beneath the wings of others. That must be me, she surmised. Well, so what? It was as good a way as any, and better than some! And what was more, she thought, if I can't marry Tom, I will have whatever there is of him that becomes available to me!

'I suppose I'd better go now, Mrs Barr.' Jean spoke up, and even her voice sounded different. 'I think I've done everything that can be done, before morning, so I'll go now.'

She allowed her voice to retain the thought of a question in it. She was an independent woman, knowing her job, and equal to Selina. She was actually making a management decision, to go home. She had left the business poised for the moment when the first customer came through the door in the morning.

'Yes. Goodnight Jean. Thanks for everything you've done.'

It was Selina, expressing her friendship and gratitude. She was no longer Miss Summer, at least, not in the back room. The door closed quietly behind her. Selina turned, to see Tom staring at the door.

'What's the matter with you, Tom? Have you just realised what a wonder we have got, in Jean? She's going to be with us, all the way. I can see ambition in that girl, and loyalty as well. That must be a rare combination; what do you think, Tom?'

'What do I think? I think you may be right. She has seemed to alter just since this morning; she has become almost like one of the family. I think you are right, Selina. She is going to be an asset to you. If you play your cards right she may be your first manageress – for your second shop! Now, I've got something to tell you. We shall be getting married on Saturday the twenty-second, three days before Christmas!' He took hold of her and pulled her body to his. 'That's if you haven't changed your mind.'

A look of delight appeared.

'Not likely, Tom Barr. I know when I'm onto a good thing. I don't quite know how we are going to manage the shop and get married, in the middle of a Christmas rush, and get your firewood delivered; especially now you have got twelve shops taking wood from you. We'll have to sit down and try to plan it all out. I don't suppose anyone from our families will want to be invited, but we've got to give them the chance, I suppose.'

Tom hadn't thought about anyone wanting to come. All he wanted to do was to marry Selina and just get on with life; he was marrying her, not her family. They hadn't offered to help when their support had been needed; why should they be offered any consideration now? He tried to express how he felt, to Selina.

'Look here, love. We asked for help from your family and mine; we got nowhere; why should we ask them to the wedding? We can't afford a big do, anyway; let's just get married. Uncle Pete and Auntie Florrie have helped us; I don't know how we would have managed without them. They put us up for three weeks, and did it without asking for anything towards the rent. They are all we need in the way of witnesses. If you need someone to give you away, Uncle Pete would be the most obvious person, and I'll ask James to be my best man. Auntie Florrie can be your Matron of

Honour. Do you really want your Mom, and her chap Harry, to come?'

Tom had hit on a good point there, Selina thought. The last person she wanted to help her to celebrate was Harry touching her. She knew he would call on her if they invited him to their wedding. He would be likely to pop in on the pretence that he was in the area, and ask for a packet of Woodbines or something like that. He would want to give her a friendly kiss, and then try to seduce her, again. The thought filled her with revulsion.

However, it would be nice to see Mom. She recalled how they had collapsed in each other's arms after a quarrel. She felt her love for her mother well up inside her, and the idea of excluding her didn't feel right, whatever she had done. Selina thought back to the circumstances surrounding their departure, only a few weeks ago. Edie had been vulnerable to anything that could upset her newly found happiness with Harry. Recently widowed, her mother had felt, Selina thought, as if the end of her life was near. Harry had offered a new lease of life, only to find that she was threatened by the suggestion that her daughter had been making up to her man. Selina was beginning to understand her mother's motivation and response to the perceived threat from her daughter. For all she knew, they might be married, or have fallen out since they had moved to Birmingham. They had not been in contact at all.

'Let's sleep on it, Tom. We've got a couple of weeks yet. Let's make up our minds, next week end.'

She looked intently at him and he immediately agreed. She smiled to herself, recalling how she had thought that she would be able to wind him round her little finger. He seemed to fall in with any suggestion she made. It looks as if she might have been right!

'Look, Selina, I know how you feel. I would like my Mom and Dad to be there, to be part of our happiness. If there is some way that it can be managed, we ought to try. If they don't want to come it will be their fault, not ours. Let's do as you said, make our mind up next week. Have you still got the money that my

Mom lent us? That should be enough to pay the expenses of the wedding. She might like that.'

He wasn't so easy, she realised. He agreed at first and then tried to change her mind. Or was it that he was thinking out loud, persuading himself as well as her? Tom was learning faster than she had thought. That Harry down at the farm had taught him a thing or two; so had Kate. She hadn't thought of Kate and Jim for some time. Would they want to come to the wedding?

They both settled back in front of the fire. The slowly dying embers sometimes seemed to be an area in which ideas could float around inside his head, Tom thought. It was as if the future was trying to form itself in the small flames above the embers. What sort of a future was he trying to form? It seemed that luck had played a part in their increasing prosperity since they had arrived in Birmingham, but the ideas he had built on had also contributed; it looked as if luck was there, if you tried to figure things out and acted on them.

Selina drowsed, envisioning herself in white, next to Tom. She would write to Kate and Jim, tomorrow. Perhaps the gypsy Parson would come, too. She giggled to herself at the thought that he might interrupt the vicar, and take over the service. Perhaps Albert and Jenny Walker would come, if they were invited. The thoughts she had in front of the fire didn't seem to be, or need to be, practical; they just arrived uninvited. There was a movement; it caught her eye as she dozed. It was Tom. He touched her gently on the arm.

'Come on, love. It's time we were in bed.'

He helped her to get out of the chair and gently pushed her up the stairs. It was time for sleep.

*

The big alarm was sounding out. She sat up in bed. There was a cup of tea on the fruit box that she used as a bedside cabinet. It looked quite pretty with a small tablecloth draped over it to hide the bare wood. It was Sunday; the shop didn't open on Sundays. It was against the law. Their first week had sped by. If she was around, and she knew the person ringing the doorbell, she would serve them, business was business after all. She could hear Tom moving round, downstairs. She sprang out of bed. She was getting married in less than three weeks! How would they manage it?

The floorboards were cold to her feet; she sat and picked up the cup of tea. She had to take stock today, just a rough check, to find out what was needed to fill the shelves back to their opening stock levels, and then she had to have her list of purchase requirements ready for James Cameron, when he came. He might come today, she thought, and the thought brought a mental picture of him as he had looked the first time she had met him. Tall and dark, shy and young, that's what he had seemed to be. Perhaps he would want to come to the wedding. He would look nice as a Best Man. She trotted down the dark and narrow staircase and Tom growled at her; that was what she called his rare remarks of admonition, growling.

'Just you be careful with my baby, never mind rushing down, trying to break your neck.'

He turned and smiled at her; his love for her was so open and obvious. She returned the smile and held his arm, to regain her balance. She thought again of the tasks that were ahead of them for today.

'Do you think it would be worthwhile having Jean round for an hour or so, Tom, just to help with the ordering? This is the first time, so it might take longer, and I want to make sure the order is ready for Mr Cameron, whether he comes today or tomorrow.'

Tom was silent for a moment, thinking. He didn't really see how they could avoid it, if the girl was willing. Everything in the shop was new to both of them, and it would help if they had another pair of hands. Selina was feeling her pregnancy now. He hoped everything was going to be all right. The idea of Jean helping was a little disconcerting.

'Yes, that would be a good idea, Selina, for this time anyway. I wouldn't like to think that she would be in the shop all day, every Sunday. I want you to myself some of the time.' He put his arms round her. 'Do you want me to go and ask her? You could offer her a lunch, I suppose; on second thoughts, no. Just offer her three hours work. If she wants it, she will do it; if not, she won't. If we do well, you can cook lunch while the stock is counted.'

Selina didn't relish the idea of leaving Tom with the shop assistant all afternoon but she could see the practical benefits.

'All right, Tom, just go and give her a knock, see if she is interested.'

She turned and started counting the tins of beans on the shelf next to her as Tom went out of the front door. Tom knocked Jean's door, next door and there was a moment's silence, and then he heard a voice say, 'Come in.'

He gave the door a tentative push, and walked in. He strode through the adjoining vestibule into the back room. Jean was sitting in front of the fire with a cup of tea.

'Oh, I'm sorry Mister Barr. I didn't realise it was you!'

She started in confusion. She must have got up late, he thought. She looked, what was the word, not attractive or beautiful, just as if you would love to have her in your arms! She went to stand and he waved her back down into the chair. She looked surprised to see him.

'It's all right, Jean. Mrs Barr has asked me to enquire whether you would be willing to give her two or three hours this afternoon, to help with the stocktaking.'

Somehow he felt as if he was in a sexual situation and it made him act in a more formal way. He had felt like that the other day, when their hands had met and joined. The thought made him uncomfortable. He stood quietly, his hands tied to each other.

'Of course I will come, tell her. I would do anything for you, er, two.'

The hesitation in her voice made him realise what she had been about to say. He moved closer to her.

'We appreciate that, Jean, we really do. Will you come round about two o'clock, then?'

He stopped; the question on his tongue.

'Don't worry, Tom, Mr Barr. I shall be with you on the dot of two. It should be an interesting afternoon, don't you think?'

There it was again, the promise of 'something interesting'. He turned to the door and went to walk out when she gripped his sleeve.

'I hope you do make it interesting for me, Mr Barr.' She took his hand. 'I really do!'

He turned on his heel. It was too much, and too close to home!

The next three hours flew, and then it was two o'clock. The afternoon meal had been eaten when Jean had walked in and spoke,

'Come on Mister Barr, I'll wash and you can dry.'

They had all laughed, as they were meant to laugh. Selina had gone into the shop and started counting tins.

Jean had flicked little bits of suds into his face and he had reached out for her, to stop her. She had moved into his arms as if dance music had started, and started to move against him. His eyes were full of soapsuds but he had known where every part of her body was, in relation to his. Her breasts were against his hands as if they had jumped there on their own. He felt her buttocks against his hips, and felt the surging power of the passion that was upon him. Her skirt lifted and he pulled at her, drawing her closer to him.

'Jean! Jean!'

He could hear his voice whispering. She replied.

'Mister Barr, oh my Mister Barr, what have you got there, Mister Barr?'

Suddenly she pushed his hand away. There was a movement from the shop, Selina. No, he thought, not Selina. Jean pulled herself away from him, smoothing her skirt and picked up the tea towel as if she were putting it down. Tom gaped. How had she done that? You would have sworn she was putting it down, as if she were just finishing off the wiping up. Selina's head came round the doorway.

'Any chance of a cup tea, I'm dying of thirst. Will you make it, please Jean?'

She smiled, as an employer does, when asking a favour from a worker.

'Of course, Mrs Barr. It's two sugars isn't it?'

The moment passed, and Tom breathed a sigh of relief. It must never happen again! There was too much at stake. His breathing slowed, and he felt himself return to normality and safe. The three of them worked together, counting the stock, moving each item as it was counted. At the end of the count, they needed to replace fifty-five pounds worth of goods at wholesale prices. They had ninety-five pounds in cash, apart from the fruit and vegetable money, which they kept separate from the grocery money. Because it had never played a part in the loan from the Camerons, it was kept in a different till drawer. They had decided that the profit from it should pay their household expenses.

Jean made the occasional cup of tea, a relief to Tom; he didn't want to be left alone with her, again. The thrill and delight of her body's closeness was balanced by the feeling of guilt he had. The work went swiftly and they were finished at five o'clock. Selina smiled.

'Well, that's it Jean. That's the whole job done. Mr Barr and I are really grateful for the help you have given us, this afternoon.'

Selina always called her Miss Summer in the shop but Jean, afterwards. Jean smiled; her smile always seemed to give the impression that she was just being very friendly.

'Thank you very much, Mrs Barr. I will see you in the morning at eight o'clock, then. Is that right?'

As Selina nodded Jean moved towards the door, Tom following to lock it.

'Goodnight, Jean.'

There was a brief touch of hands.

'Goodnight Mr Barr, see you in the morning, then.' Then she

had gone.

They should have discussed the arrangements for their wedding but somehow all they wanted to do was to get to bed.

Over the next few days they spent much time trying to work what would be the best wedding guest list. They each changed their minds, sometimes wanting to invite everyone in the family, then deciding that they would get married with just two witnesses.

Tom decided to sound out the way by telephoning Ted, at work.

'Dan! Dan Barr! Your Ted is getting a telephone call, in the office.'

Dan could hear the voice calling him from the other end of the small factory. He looked up; it was Stanley, the Stones' younger son calling him. He waved to him, to let him know he had heard, put down his file and hung his apron over the vice on the workbench. Quickly he walked along the walkway, past the other locksmiths who were staring at him.

'Bloody snob!'

One of them muttered. He smiled to himself. There would be talk, just because he had received a telephone call. Who was it, anyway? It was true that a phone call was a rare thing. He would be told off for receiving private calls. He stepped into the office. Ted was talking on the phone. Mabel Stones' was watching inquisitively.

'Who is it Ted? Is it your mother? Could she be ill?'

He stepped forward and took the phone from him.

'Hello, Stones' Locks. What can I do for you?'

He felt nervous, just making a call. He had only made about three telephone calls in his life. He recognised the voice. It was Tom.

'Hello, Mrs Stone'. This is Tom Barr, here. I wonder if I could have a quick word with Ted, please. This is a bad line.'

He seemed to be in someone else's conversation.

'Hallo, Tom. What's the matter? Has something happened? Is Selina all right?'

Dan spoke urgently. Tom had tried to explain the reason he was calling but Ted seemed to have things mixed up.

'No, there's nothing the matter, Ted. Nothing has happened and Selina is all right. All I want to tell you is,' He paused for a brief moment, attempting to choose the best way to put it. He still hadn't realised who he was talking to. 'It's like this; we are getting married on the twenty-third, two days before Christmas. Do you think Mom and Dad will come to the wedding, if we ask them?'

He stood nervously, wondering how much credence he could put on his brother's appraisal of the situation.

'Are you there, Ted?' Tom spoke.

Dan spoke into the receiver, replying.

'This isn't Ted, it's your Dad, Tom. Why have you telephoned here? I thought we had heard the last of you.'

He slammed the phone down and, turning on his heel he stalked out of the office. Ted picked it up again and listened to make sure he was connected.

'Well, that should tell you how Dad thinks about the whole affair, Tom. I'm sorry Tom but he just took the phone out of my hand. I'll see you when I see you.'

He put the receiver back on the stand, and then he too just walked out of the office.

Tom thought; what was going on. There must be something he could do to get through to Dad. Then he lost his temper.

'The hell with them! We can manage on our own.'

He shouted into the empty telephone kiosk. The curses came to his mind and made him feel more than ever that he would be independent.

'The hell with them! That's the last time I reach out to them!'

Tom was explaining what had happened. Selina listened with tearful eyes. She could sympathise with Tom. What a terrible way to treat your eldest son! Still, that didn't mean that she couldn't invite her mother. She would have a word with Uncle Pete and Auntie Florrie about the situation. They might have an idea or two. She still hadn't made up her mind whether to ask her mother to the wedding. She recalled how they had laughed at each other when they had quarrelled about the work in her little shop. Perhaps she could write to her and drop a hint that she would be more welcome than Harry. She would love to see her – she was her mother for God's sake!

32. Relatives.

Elsie sat thinking. Why was Dan so quiet? It wasn't like him. He'd usually got something to say, even if it was only about the International Situation. He sat chewing his meat as if it was horsemeat instead of good English topside. She had heard of women who had served up horsemeat to their husbands and got away with it. The thought made her giggle and she had to lower her head to disguise the expression on her face.

He had finished now, placing his knife and fork in parallel, exactly in the centre of his plate. He turned to the fire to warm his hands and lit a cigarette. Something was troubling him, she knew, and it would be placed before her shortly. It always had to come out. He was probably in debt. He had as much money to spend as any man she knew and yet it seemed to disappear quicker than most. He had often borrowed money from her to pay a debt and they had both known that he would not be repaying it to her.

She had to try to appear hard up or he would be onto her all the time. They had never bought a cruet set. He would have asked her where she got the money from. She had a small eggcup that she half filled with salt and Dan was quite content to put the tip of it into the salt and gently tap it to shake a little salt onto his vegetables.

She had plenty of money but she was very nervous about telling her husband how much she had. She didn't really know how much she had now. She had been saving and dealing in property for over twenty years now and the contents of her portfolio made her one of the richest women in Wednesbury. Her mentor, Mary Bowyer had taught her the value of money since she had first arrived in the Black Country as a teenager. Now Mary was gone and she answered to no one but herself on financial matters. She glanced again and Dan was still sitting there in a quiet, morose way. This would have to be brought to a head.

'What's the matter with you, Dan? You've got a face as long as Livery Street.' She'd brought that saying with her from Birmingham, years ago. 'Come on, tell me. The worst thing that could happen is that I'll cut your throat.'

She tried to make a smile out of her expression and he responded.

'All right then, 'he said, 'I've opened my mouth when I shouldn't and I don't know what to do about it.' He paused for a moment and then let his problem come out of his mouth. 'Our Ted had a telephone call today, from Tom; him and Selina are getting married in a couple of week's time. Ted passed the phone to me and I let meself down if you know what I mean.'

Elsie sighed with exasperation. She had known something had happened and he had been the cause of it. What had he said?

'What did you say then? In what way could you let yourself down? Did he insult you or shout at you or ask you for money?'

She became silent to allow him time to think before he answered. After a moment he turned to look at her.

'It's just that I was mad at him, the way he got that young Selina in trouble. We had to let him go, so to speak, after that, didn't we?'

It was true, Elsie thought. Dan couldn't be flexible as they called it. He was as rigid as a casting, not a thought of how their eldest son might be suffering. She had thought of the young couple often and wondered how they were getting on. Life must have been hard for them. Was it possible that they were asking for help? She waited silently for the answer to come from her husband. She was getting angrier as she waited.

He decided to get it off his chest. 'I told him not to get in touch again. We had disowned him for what he had done and hadn't changed our minds. I wish I hadn't spoke to him like that, Elsie. I am a fool sometimes. What shall I do? You usually have an answer. What shall I do?'

His face had crumpled. Elsie reached out to him sympathetically and put her hand on his. There was always a way, she thought and let her hands fall into her lap. There was a sound from outside and then Ted walked in. He too had a strange, angry look on his face. He looked at Dan; the angry look got worse and he made his feelings become apparent.

'Mom, our Tom's invited us to his wedding and Dad's disowned him! I don't care. I'm going to the wedding. I never did think him and Selina were bad people, whatever you think!' His voice carried in the small room. 'We don't even know their address but I tell you I'm going to their wedding.'

He stopped, saw the expression on his father's face and realised that his father was regretting his outburst on the phone. Perhaps he shouldn't cause another! He sat down on the settee under the window. Perhaps he would be better off listening than mouthing off! He reached for the teapot. Perhaps he would see some sort of miracle and everything would work out all right. The tea was nice, Strong, sweet and hot. He drank it in silence waiting for some sort of response to what he had.

'I'm proud of you, son.' Dan spoke, 'I hope you do go. I expect your mother will go as well. I don't know exactly how I shall be able to go after my stupid ranting and raving but I'd like to go. Either of you got any ideas?'

He couldn't be any more open than that, could he? Both Ted and Elsie looked at him and then looked at each other. It was not often that they had seen Dan in this abject state. Perhaps he was learning as well as them!

Elsie coughed to get their attention and the men turned to her as they had often done. What was she going to say? She stood and faced the men in turn.

'Now listen to me, both on ya. I'll tell you this just once. Tom is my son, my eldest son and I love him very much. I had to let him go because I knew his father was too rigid in his way o' thinking. He has to be right, whatever the consequences. Tom wouldn't have had a chance living here. He is too much like his dad and they would have fought before long.

'Now, the way I look at it, my husband is the one I owe my loyalty to, before anybody else, certainly before my children and never mind who's right and who's wrong. That doesn't mean I have to think he's right in everything he pronounces – and he ain't! I've known your dad a long time now and I've seen him wrong more times than I've had hot dinners.

'So, what I think is this: I think I am going to see my eldest son married. You two are men in your own right so, if you want to go or if you want to stay away, that's your choice: I've made mine. After the wedding I expect to come home and carry on living in the same way as before. If you,' she pointed at Dan,' think you can throw Ted out because he has a different opinion to yours, you can think again. I ask you not to press it because it will not be easy for any of us.'

Dan stood then, as if he were at a public meeting. 'I've heard what you have to say, Elsie, and I agree with you. If I can find a way to make the peace with the young couple, I will, and come with you to the ceremony. I will not say a word against either of them, or either of you!'

He sat down and Ted stood, looking uncomfortable. 'Thank you both,' he said. 'You know how I feel. I shall go to the wedding. That said, I think that's enough for all of us to keep the peace in the family.'

He sat down and Elsie got up. 'This is the first time we have had a family meeting about anything as important as this and it has worked out well. Shall we have our dinner now?'

Elsie sat down, knowing what the others didn't, that she was the owner of the house and would have won anyway in any attempt to oust her from her own property. Just exactly what had influenced her husband and her son she did not know and she was pleased that she did not have to use her most powerful weapon.

*

Stephen Stone listened; it wasn't often that the Barrs had a phone call. He couldn't remember the last time. Teddy Barr came out of the office, his face red. He didn't even look in his direction, just strode out in the direction of the gate as if he had somewhere important to go. Stephen smiled; he had heard most of the call and guessed the rest.

Danny Boy had made a mess of things again. It was to be hoped that Elsie would be able to repair things. Young Tom had decided to do the decent thing by Selina Brown. They were going to get married. Now, Dan had disowned the lad again even though he had more skill in one of his fingers than Dan had in the whole of his body. Whatever would Dan say if he knew that his gaffer was the father of the one he disapproved of?

Stephen sat down, seeing for the first time how the wedding invitation could affect him. There had been no invitation yet but there would be one, he knew. Mabel would see it before him. All letters went to her first and she decided who would handle any problems that came with them. He would go, though, whatever she thought. It was possible that she might come with him, just out of curiosity, you could never tell which way Mabel would jump. Let them all think what they liked; he was going.

Stanley would want to go; he had got on well with Tom. He had noticed that they had gone drinking together on the night that Tom had been given his journeyman's rate of pay. They were half-brothers; did they know? They had both got on well with the girls in the factory side of the business. That meant that Bert might want to go. He had been jealous of Tom's success in the trade but he had probably forgotten that by now. He had liked Selina but so had half the lads in the factory and he couldn't blame them.

*

Kate opened the packet of oats and poured them into a cup to measure how much she would have. She always used the same measure for both of them. Jim liked his porridge first thing in the morning. She put it on the low fire, always using the same saucepan. She knew that if she simmered it for too long, it would burn.

Jim had gone earlier. There was a lot for him to do. Albert

343

Walker was not as fit as he used to be and Jim covered a lot of his work as well as his own. It seemed that whatever Jim had owed Albert from the war, he was repaying it now.

There was a rattle of the letterbox that Jim had made when they had first moved in. The porridge was about done now. She poured it into a bowl and put it in front of the place where she always sat at their table. It would cool there. She poured a cup of tea and then remembered the rattle. She opened the door and opened the box. There was a letter in it. She recognised Selina's writing and sat at the table for her breakfast, teasing herself with the thought of the letter waiting to be read.

She slowly drank her tea and then snatched the envelope and tore it open unable to wait any longer to discover the contents. It was too unusual to be unimportant and left 'til another time to be read.

Selina and Tom were marrying just before Christmas. She was invited, if she could make it. Nothing would keep her away, or Jim if she knew him! Jenny would have to do something to help Albert with his work – unless they were going too! Jenny had helped to organise their previous wedding so she couldn't see Jenny forgoing the chance to be at the second! It would be interesting if they did. They had all been at the hop pole wedding so they might want to be at this one as well. In a way it would be like a confirmation of the vows they had made at that time.

Maybe Jim would know something when he came home from the farm. Jenny might have had an invitation and if so, she would guess that she would want to be kept abreast of things in that direction and would at least drop a hint to Jim. Three days before Christmas! It didn't leave them much time to get ready. There was no time to consult Selina about the choice of a Wedding cum Christmas gift.

She went upstairs and took out her little savings tin, a souvenir from a visit to Weston-Super-Mare, in Somerset. She had three pounds in it. That would be enough to buy the happy couple a nice present. What would she get for them? How much should she leave in the tin for emergencies? She had time to think about it but her mind went towards some Worcester china. Maybe. She didn't know what they had already got and she didn't want to buy them something they didn't want or need.

*

Harry was browned off. Perhaps it was because he was now linked with a Brown. He hadn't minded when he had been friends with Selina Brown but her mother, Edith Brown, was boring. He much preferred younger women, always had and always would. He might find some excuse to get rid of her and go back to his other little lair. He liked to call it his lair because he tried to trap young women into it. It was rarely he seemed to succeed recently but he had trapped himself at the Brown's house so it was not surprising.

He went into the back yard and, as quietly as he could, lifted the bicycle up the small step into the house. He dropped it and wheeled it silently along the long hall to the front door. He was off into the fresh air for the day. Edith could stay in bed as long as she liked. He liked Saturdays. There was always the chance of meeting someone young and fresh.

He undid the lock on the front door and closed it behind him. There was a really fresh feel to the air.

'Good morning. Looks like being a nice day.'

It was the woman from next door; Brenda. She liked him; he knew. She was younger than Edith.

'Yes, I might get a few miles under my saddle before lunch.' He smiled at her and she pulled a letter from her apron pocket.

'A letter came to me yesterday, by mistake. I've just remembered. It's for Mrs Brown. How is she?'

He didn't know what to say; she was alright. He had to give some sort of answer.

'She's alright. She's having a bit of a lie in, today. Women do, occasionally, don't they, Brenda?'

He went to put the letter in his pocket but she stopped him. 'If you like, I'll give it her, Harry. Save you carrying it around all day

345

and maybe losing it.'

He thought for a moment and then gave it back to her. He didn't need her stupid letter, did he?

He grinned at her. 'I'll see you later then. I'd better make tracks.'

He pushed the bicycle down the path and onto the road that was waiting for him. As he gathered speed he looked back and saw Edith on the doorstep. She must have heard him talking to the neighbour. He waved and turned his head back to the direction he was pedalling.

Edith turned her head to the lady next door. 'Hello, Brenda. He's off early ain't he? I don't know where he's off to and I really couldn't care less. I bet he's hoping to pick up some innocent young thing. I think he's that way inclined.'

Brenda looked shocked for a moment then remembered the letter. 'I've got a letter for you; it came yesterday but I forgot it. I was going to give it to Harry but I thought if it was meant for him, it would have his name on it, but it ain't. It's got your name on it.'

She handed over the letter and Edith peered at it over her glasses. She knew who it was from immediately. 'It's from our Selina,' she said. 'I wonder what's the matter with her.'

A moment later she knew; Selina and Tom were getting married for Christmas and she was invited. The letter did not mention Harry but she knew she could take him with her if she wanted to. She did not want to take him but she did want to go herself. She would not reply; she would just turn up.

*

It was quiet in the barn; the cattle had been turned out to pasture and the Shire horses had been taken to collect some fresh hay. Albert was in bed with the flu or something like it. It was very quiet. Jenny had done her washing and hung it out. There was work to be done, getting rid of the bines. It should have been done last month but Albert didn't seem to have any enthusiasm just lately.

She decided to have a cup of tea and then change into her field-working clothes. If she didn't start doing the job soon, it wouldn't get done at all. Jim was driving the horses; they didn't have far to go and it wasn't usually his job but the usual driver was also ill with the flu. The trouble was that all these jobs had to be done by a smaller number of people. She made her way to the farm kitchen and put the kettle on. Her foot scraped on an envelope on the floor under the letterbox. It was a letter addressed to both of them. It was not a business letter; you could see that from the style of the writing. She picked it up, closer to her eyes. It was Selina's writing. What was this about? She picked up a slim knife and sliced the letter open.

That was a surprise for certain. Fancy inviting them to her wedding! They had been to one – and provided the clothes for her and Kate! The memory made her weep a little. She read on. The wedding was on Saturday the twenty-second of December. They still had a couple of weeks to get organised and she had no intention of missing it. It was about time they had something a bit different in their life. Probably Jim and Kate would be invited too so at least there would be someone there they knew. Jim wouldn't spoil things. He would be on his best behaviour for the event. He always was a stickler for doing things the right way.

They could travel together now Albert had bought the car. For once he was a little bit up to date but he had justified the purchase by saying they would pay less because of it and they might as well get some advantage out of it. I suppose I'll have to sit in the back with Kate while Jim sits in the front with the owner. She smiled at her own old-fashioned way of expressing herself. Kate was good company anyway.

They would have to get them something, something that reminded the couple of Hope Farm and the way they had got married there before they got married in Birmingham! Perhaps a cheque would be the easiest. It wouldn't have to be shopped for, would it?

She would have to check that Albert's suit was clean; he would wear it to clean the car in, if it was left to him. She would have to get a new hat if she didn't get anything else! They had

347

been paid for the hops so they should be flush with money so she was going to have her share of it!

The tea was sweet and she took a cup of it up to Albert. He was still looking pale but not coughing as much.

'Thanks love; I was wondering when you were going to get round to it.' He smiled. 'How's your day going? Has the hay come yet? Jim doesn't seem to rush himself since I got this dose o' lurgy.'

'Jim has been at it since seven o'clock this morning; that's more than I could say for you, Albert Walker, and he's not too well either. You are not the only one with the lurgy, you know. Now, I've got a bit o' news for you. You remember Tom and Selina don't you?' She watched as he nodded. 'Well they are getting married again, in Birmingham, at Saint Georges Church, Hockley. It will be a couple of days before Christmas and they have invited us. I shall have to have a new hat I suppose. I might even have a new costume. I've got nothing to wear for a Birmingham wedding.'

'What do you mean; a Birmingham wedding?' her husband said. Why should a Birmingham wedding be any better then a Bromyard wedding? I can recall a double wedding we had on our farm and nobody said anything about Birmingham being better at that time, did they?'

He smiled as if he had caught her out in some sneaky activity. She had to defend her view so she picked up the pillow to attack him and he laughed, the first laugh she had heard from him for weeks.

'That's better. Now I know you are going to get better. I thought you were actually going to die. All I hoped was that if I had to get a new hat it wouldn't have to be a black one!' She smiled at him and it was as if the sun had come out. 'What do you think we should get them? Something that looks fancy? Something useful, or something posh; what do you think?'

'I think I'll just let you run around spending. You are better at it than me.'

'Alright then,' she said, but don't blame me if I spend too much.'

*

Harry stopped pedalling and allowed the bicycle to coast down the hill towards their home. He lifted his leg over the crossbar and steered the bike through the gate, right up to the front door. A push and it was open and Edith was standing facing him.

'What are you doing home this early? I wasn't expecting you till about five o'clock at the earliest.'

Harry stood and confronted her. 'I didn't know I had to account for every pedal of my feet. Sometimes the ride seems good and sometimes it don't. This time it don't. Now, any more questions?'

'Yes, as a matter of fact I do have a question. What do you think I or we should buy our Selina for a wedding present?'

She stood silent, waiting to see what she would have to say. They both knew that there was at least a possibility that the baby that Selina was carrying could be his and the thought frightened each of them. It was unlikely though. Selina had confessed to her mother that she had slept with Tom and that she thought the child was his. That settled that. They both had a feeling of relief and turned their minds back to the question that Edith had asked of him.

Harry realised immediately that the letter that Brenda given him had been from Selina, with news of a wedding. He tried to hide the fact that he knew of the letter.

What do you mean; a wedding present? Is she getting married? When is it?'

He tried to keep his tone sharp but she would not stand for it.

'You know she is. Brenda told me she gave you the letter from Selina this morning. We have been invited. It is on the twenty-second of December. She will expect me to give her something. That is what Moms do. They give their daughters a wedding present. That is what I did for my older daughter – who has given me no trouble at all. Selina is a different kettle of fish but I still feel bound to contribute to her wedding day. I was just trying to talk it over with you but if you don't want to, that's alright by me. I'll decide for myself what I am going to give my youngest daughter and you needn't have any part in it.'

'Alright, alright, you might know I would want to give her something. What do you think she would like from us? I'm talking it over with you now. Why don't you get her something of really good quality but is quite small, so it doesn't seem as if you are showing off?' He hesitated for a moment as if thinking. 'You er, or we, could get her a top quality cruet set. I saw one the other day that was over a pound! Perhaps we could get her one that was even dearer than that. Do you see what I mean?'

Edith thought; he might be right for a change. She didn't want to be seen to be throwing her money around, nor did she want to be seen as cheap.

'You might be right then, keep your eyes open for something that fits the bill and tell me when you find it.'

They were both fed up of discussing the subject now so they went on to other things, what were they going to wear? Where were they going to get them from? Eventually they went to bed, each with their own ideas jostling their brains for answers. Loving each other seemed old-fashioned to them now; they had to arrive at better ideas than they had already thought up.

*

'Do you remember that tea set that we bought for Tom and Selina when they first moved into their house, as it was then?'

Peter nodded. Of course he remembered; he had paid for it.

'Well, I think if we bought them a dinner service in the same pattern, they might be pleased with it. What do you think?'

Florrie was crossing her fingers behind her back. It was a pretty penny but it fitted the situation. Peter nodded, 'Whatever you like, Flo.'

They were in bed. It was cold and Peter was tired. It had been a long day. He leaned across and kissed her. 'Good night, my lovely. See you in the morning.'

'Goodnight, Pete, God bless.'

33. The Wedding.

It was Saturday the twenty-second of December, 1923. When she looked back over the short period in which they had been in Birmingham, Selina could not believe they had achieved so much. The shop had gone from strength to more strength; their policy of cash on the nail had paid off, as had their late closing.

Strangers had become customers; customers had become friends; some had taken offence when they had been refused credit, but it had been explained that the only reason they were able to offer reasonable retail prices was because they paid for all their goods by cash as they were delivered, whereas other small establishments who paid at the end of the month were unable to get discounts for dealing in cash.

Jean was to run the shop, today. She was golden, Selina thought. It was obvious that she liked Tom, but that was an advantage in the same way that it was to their benefit that James Cameron liked her. She smiled to herself. She liked him too. You never knew which way life would take you so it was best not to make any more enemies than you had to.

The girl from the house at the other side of Jean, Joyce, had offered to help out if Jean needed her, so that was nice, helped to keep the pressure off. James was acting as Tom's best man. He had been delighted to be asked. It was obvious that he would do anything for Selina. He would be in, later, to *make sure everything is all right!* He had offered, jokingly, to take Tom's place in church.

There was a bang from the back yard. She looked up, puzzled, then realised that it was Tom bringing his empty pram up the back entry; it was the only thing that he could bring up and down the entry. She shouted.

'Tom, is that you?'

He would want another cup of tea. She looked at the clock. It was eight o'clock. All his deliveries were done. *Now.* He still kept to the same motto. She recalled how he had discussed it, down on the farm. She poured the tea.

'You all right, love? I've finished now, just a few bob still owing. I'll get that in on Monday. Thanks.' He picked up the enamel mug that he seemed to like drinking from. 'I suppose Jean will be in, in a minute or two?'

'She's in the shop. She's been here half an hour. We managed to put the vegetables outside, between us; it was no trouble. All we've got to do is get ready, and we've got two hours to do that. Come and sit by me. There's no hurry; everything is how it should be.'

Her face lit up as he sat down. She had thought he might be finding things to do, right up to the ceremony. They sat back, enjoying the gentle heat from the fire. There was a sprinkle of snow on the ground. If it got any worse, Jean would have to cover the vegetables. The ceremony at eleven o'clock would give James time to take a photograph or two. She didn't really relish the idea of having her picture taken with this lump at the front of her dress. She had had a large bouquet made, to cover her lump as best as she could.

They would be back in the shop by two o'clock. They couldn't afford to take the day off. There was too much to be done. She allowed her head to relax onto Tom's shoulder. He too, was relaxing. They could vaguely hear small sounds from the shop, people getting served. The till ringing, a nice sound, seemed to quieten her thoughts. This was a rare time; usually their time was being used to extract the maximum value from it.

The curtain between house and shop swished; it was Jean, waving a five-pound note. Seeing Tom's head lolling back against the couch, she whispered,

'Got any change, Mrs Barr?'

The formal tone brought Selina back. She reached into her apron pocket and pulled out a small, paper bank bag. She gently unfolded five notes out of it.

'Here you are, Jean. Have you had a look at the fiver?'

Jean nodded and, putting the five-pound note on the arm of the couch, moved silently back into the shop. Tom was still lying, still asleep. He had been up since three o'clock. Selina decided she would let him have another ten minutes. She allowed her own head to relax upon his shoulder again.

'What time are you going to get ready, Selina?'

It was Jean. She swivelled her head to the clock. Nine o'clock.

'Thanks, Jean.'

There were two cups of tea on the table. Jean had made them.

'Come on, Tom. Do you want to get married, today?'

She gave him a shake and he stirred into movement, glanced at the clock and stretched himself.

'God, look at the time, Sel. Is everything all right?'

He had an anxious look on his face, as if he was guilty of something. She moved her body against him.

'Yes, everything seems to be all right. Don't you think so?'

She moved again, allowing his arm to fall across her breast. His hand moved, cupping her.

'Yes, everything seems wonderful.' He stretched again, and then stood. 'Come on then, lazybones. You shouldn't be tempting me, before we are married. I might make a bad woman of you! What would your mother say, then?'

He bit his tongue. He had intended to make a joke, but it seemed to have gone astray. Selina didn't speak for a moment, then,

'She would probably blame you, knowing what you kay-mekkers get up to, always looking for something to get your kay into!'

It was an old joke, but it stopped her being upset at the reference to her mother. Tom thought back. It was only a few months since he had been a locksmith; now he was a businessman. When he was a locksmith, life had been fun; he had known what he was and what he would be doing each day into the future. Since then, he had been away to the hop-yards, to be educated, and he had been educating himself ever since. Nothing now seemed certain; each coming day seemed to carry risks, even if it was only the loss of a customer for a weekly dozen bundles of wood.

There was a thrill to life as it was lived, now, though. He had been lucky, gambling with his life, and winning most of the time. Oh well, no time for hanging around brooding; there was too much to be done. First thing was; did they have enough hot water? He reached for the kettle that was standing on the hob. It was full, and hot. He strode into the kitchen. He lifted the kettle on the small gas stove; it was empty. He filled it and lit the gas. He strode into the garden for the bath, hanging on the wall. He slipped on the snow and fell against the wall. She heard him cry out an obscenity.

'What's the matter, Tom?' She looked through the window; he was on the ground, slipping on the snow, laughing. She felt a sense of relief. 'Are you just trying to get out of marrying me, making me an honest woman?'

He sat, his shirt covered with snow.

'It would take more than a broken leg to stop me making an honest woman out of you, I've been trying for months, but you still keep cheating me!'

He laughed again as he slipped round the yard on his seat. Eventually he got up and staggered into the house with the metal bath, placing it in front of the fire.

'Now I know it's a special day; you are having a bath!'

'Well, I suppose you want to go first, you being the cleanest?'

She watched him fill the bath with hot water, topping it up with cold water from the tap in the kitchen. They were lucky, she thought; some families still had to go down to the back yard, to the pump.

Half past nine. She had never bathed so quickly. She pulled up her stockings. Tom would be wearing a tie today, and a waistcoat. They were going by taxi. They wouldn't have time to walk it, anyway. Uncle Pete had arranged that as part of their wedding present. It was coming at half past ten. That should get them there at a quarter to, plenty of time. They should be home at half past twelve and serving at one.

'Come on Tom; move your arse.' She had been looking at his back. 'You've never spent so much time in the bath. What do you think this is, a public holiday?'

She watched as he stood still, letting the water run down his body.

'You can laugh but it's the first time I've had more than five hours off at once! I'm celebrating.' He turned to face her. 'Would you like to join me, in a celebration?'

His meaning was obvious, as was his physical condition. She turned away, in apparent disgust, looking down her nose.

Swish; the curtains again; Jean. Her face became red

'Have you got change, Mrs Barr?'

Redder still. Swish; Jean disappeared.

'Sorry, Mrs Barr.'

There was a quiet giggle in the shop.

'Let's see if I can find enough change in the till. Here you are; do you mind having a few florins? Good morning, Mrs Rawlings.'

The bell on the door rang as Mrs Rawlings departed. Selina smiled to herself. That would keep Jean Summer awake tonight! Tom was frantically putting on his trousers, having dried himself in double quick time.

'What's the rush, Tom? I thought you were enjoying your holiday!'

'All right. All right! I suppose you think that's funny'

He hadn't forgotten the quiet giggle in the shop.

Selina burst out laughing; the look of discomposure on his face following his exposure made her think of a rhyme to do with disclosure. She brought herself under control. It was a serious thing, for the staff to see the employer naked and in such a condition! She must make sure it doesn't happen again; Jean might get ideas above her station!

The next hour went quickly, both of them dressing in a few minutes. Uncle Pete and Auntie Florrie were taking a taxi, along with Selina. There was no one else to go and Tom was going in James' car. Both cars arrived on time

'Morning, Tom. Are you ready? Has Selina gone?' James stalked into the shop, barely glancing at Jean. 'Farm Street is very slippery with the snow; I want to give myself plenty of time.'

Selina walked through the curtains. She felt beautiful; she was beautiful, she knew. Both men stared at her, as if seeing someone royal. Tom turned away, feeling he might bring bad luck if he looked at her before the ceremony. James had no such inhibitions, gently taking her in his arms, being careful not to crease the dress.

'You look wonderful, Selina. Now off you go. Your car is outside. Take your time. I believe it is customary for the groom to be kept waiting. I shall do my best to make sure we arrive before you.'

He opened the front door and followed Selina out. Tom was left alone with Jean.

'You look beautiful as well, Tom. You really do.' She moved forward and put her arms round his neck. 'If you want to change your mind, I'm not going away. 'She stopped and blushed. 'Right, Mr Barr, just one little kiss and then you're gone forever.' Her lips met his, reviving the memory of earlier, gently at first, then harder, more passionately, pulling at his body. She gave a deep breath then pushed him away. 'I'll look after things while you are gone, Mr Barr.' She brushed her hands down the front of her dress. 'Good luck!'

There was no hurry. The journey would have been an easy stroll but Florrie had insisted on the taxi, thank goodness. She didn't feel like walking today. The snow had mostly turned to slush, dirty half-melted snow, not pleasant, especially where horses had left their mess. They moved along New John Street West quite smoothly and in a few minutes were outside the church. They were not expecting anyone but there were a few people inside the church, sitting on the left, her side.

Edie and Harry were there, sitting by Auntie Florrie, who had scurried down the aisle to be sure of her seat in the front pew. Selina smiled back at her mother. Harry kept his head down but managed to give her a smile, as if to signal a new period of peace. There were a few others on the left of the aisle; she couldn't make them out at first; Mr and Mrs Walker, from the farm; Jim and Kate! She felt a pleasant wash of delighted surprise as Kate made a kiss with her mouth. They were still betrothed! There were still some good things in life.

Tom and James were both looking over their shoulders at her from the front pew on the other side of the aisle. She felt good, knowing she was looking her best. Tom's mother had come, with young Ted. That was a nice surprise. It was to be hoped that no one was expecting a 'do' when they got back; she didn't owe any of them a thing.

'We are gathered together...'the vicar started the ceremony, and she felt immediately transported back to the day in September when she and Tom had jumped the hop pole. What a time they'd had. For all its 'official' status, the ceremony seemed to pass quickly and without anything particularly memorable about it.

James had a camera with him and took some photographs of the wedding group, and was introduced to Elsie and Edie, and charmed both of them with his quiet Scots brogue. Albert and Jenny Walker were round, making a fuss of her. They knew Tom's mother, Elsie, of course, from earlier years at the hop picking.

When the ceremony was over, Mr Walker suggested that they all go for a little drink, on him of course, and no one said no, so they did, and it was three o'clock before they got back to the shop. Both of the moms had to be shown round the little house, and

Edie looked round with her knowledgeable eye, taking in the breadth of stock they had; Selina didn't see why she should tell her how they had managed to get the money for the stock, so she said nothing. Harry didn't have chance to say much to her; she made sure of that, and she felt that Tom was keeping an eye on that situation as well.

The shop had been busy; Jean and Joyce had each taken a tea break for ten minutes then got back to work. Joyce made them all a cup of tea, and then it was time for them all to go. At six o'clock, Jean closed up and they were left on their own.

They both fell quiet; it had been a long day. For Tom it had been since three o'clock in the night, when he had got up to deliver his firewood, and for Selina it had been hectic, with no time to relax between surprises. James had been one of the last to leave. Joyce seemed very interested in him. Perhaps something would come of that. James had shaken hands with Tom at the end, when he had said goodbye. She knew he had done that to give him an excuse to kiss her goodbye. Men! They think you don't notice these things. Jean had said goodnight in a very quiet sort of way, to both of them, Mr and Mrs Barr. Perhaps she realised she would have to look elsewhere, now. Tom was not available!

'What a day!'

Tom repeated the phrase. Selina glanced over at him, realising that her thoughts had been spent in recalling the day. She hadn't heard him speak, the first time.

'I'm sorry, Tom. My mind was somewhere else. Yes, you are right. It's been a day and a half. Who would have thought Mom would turn up – and with Harry, of all people. I am just sorry your Dad couldn't make it. I spoke to Elsie, and she said he's not at all well, keeps having bad turns.'

'Yes, she told me,' Tom replied, 'He's had to have time off from work with it. I suppose I should go and see him sometime. The trouble is, I don't know when, there is always something to do. Ted seems to be growing up all of a sudden, don't he?' He paused and let the question sink in. 'You don't seem to notice time passing, do you?'

'The reason you don't notice, Tom, is that you are always trying to get the most out of each moment. What did you say your motto is, *'Now'*, wasn't it? Do you remember, down at the hopyard, drawing it in the soil? I've never forgotten that.'

Tom grinned.

'Yes, I do remember. I remember thinking I would like to put it in my coat of arms, if I ever had one.'

They started tidying the room; it was a natural thing for them to do; they never went to bed without leaving the house tidy. For Tom, it was that any untidiness would add pressure to him, in the morning, and he had enough of that. It was part of his philosophy, his 'do it now' way of living; who knows what problems would arise tomorrow; why add to them?

They had a few wedding presents and decided to open them now, to avoid a mess in the morning. A dinner set from Auntie Florrie and Uncle Pete, to match the tea set they had bought for them, a few months ago, when they had moved in. A tablecloth from Jean, a three-piece cruet set from Selina's mother, a set of knives and forks from Tom's family.

'At least we can eat respectable, now.' Selina commented

'More things to wash up.' He had countered.

'Let's go to bed. I bet we shall be the first into bed, out of all those at the wedding. At least we can have a bit of a lie-in, in the morning. There's nothing to be done that an extra hour in bed will hurt. Fancy, nothing to do! I can't believe it! Still, I expect you will think of something, won't you, Mr Barr?' She smiled in her coquettish way. 'Do you think you can remember how?'

Tom blushed.

'Yes, I think I can remember, Mrs Barr. Come on, up the wooden hill, and I'll remind you!'

She squealed as he caught her bottom and pushed her towards the stairs.

'Oh! You bully! Look at you, not married a day, and pushing

me round already!' She moved quickly up the stairs, removed her wedding dress as soon as she went into the bedroom and stood in the light of the street lamp, outside. Tom stood still, capturing the picture of her in his mind and holding onto it, enraptured.

'Come here, you little hop picker. Let's get into the straw!'

He spoke, reminding her of their first time. Selina relaxed; it had been a long day, and it might be a long night, yet!

They each had their thoughts and memories of their day and the thoughts flitted in and out of their minds as they made love in the gaslight, their bodies moving under the cold sheets to a rhythm that was made of gypsy airs interwoven with the organ music of the church. The number of people who had attended had been a surprise, over twenty, Selina thought; her breast rising in passion as Tom caressed her. She let her hand wander over his body; she would show him! Her hand moved between his thighs and she heard his breathing become more excited. She moved her legs apart to accommodate him, and the thought of James came into her head, exciting her more. She loved Tom to the exclusion of anyone else, in her heart and mind, but her body had unasked for thoughts and needs of its own.

James would be so wonderful, her body thought and felt for the moment. It had been lovely to see Kate, her secretly betrothed. They had managed to steal a moment when their hands had touched in that special way, renewing their bond. Life was complicated. Her body began to writhe against the bed, no longer cold; hot now, and she felt the rise of orgasm begin, again.

Tom felt it, too, and his body responded. That Kate had made love to him with her eyes, as soon as she had spotted him, in the church. He had never forgotten that she had been his first love, on the way home after their separate betrothals. He entered Selina, feeling the soft and damp heat that came from her, the heat mingling with her body odour, as if they were two senses joined by passion. It was almost too much for him; he tried desperately to think of something that would lower his own body heat; that Harry had had his eyes on Selina. He didn't want to see him around any more! That's better! It was nice to see young Ted again.

The thought of Jean re-entered his mind, the memory of her body against his, in the tiny kitchen. He imagined himself pressing her against the sink, as he had earlier. No! Wait a minute; Selina was moving faster now; it didn't matter who he thought of. He felt Jean's buttocks against his body, Selina's breasts against his lips and Kate's hands on his body as he finally gave in to the wonderful, most wonderful images, and succumbed to the pleasure of the moment, and then the post-climax of sleep.

Next door, Jean was coming to terms with the needs of her body in front of the fire. She had imaginings that were not allowed for but still arrived in her mind and body. Her hands traced her needs automatically and she slowly dropped off to pleasurable sleep.

The other guests were all asleep. The day had been the end of an exciting period in their lives. They seemed to be on the edge of a new, even more exciting time. Fate would play its part but if they were lucky life would be theirs to be enjoyed; enjoyed now and lived living!